"You'd be hard pressed to ever forget *The Memory Tree* once it takes root. This wicked tendril of folk horror reaches down deep, rummaging through the reader, making a home for itself that will last for years to come, perhaps a novel to outlive us all."

CLAY McLEOD CHAPMAN, author of *Devil Inside*

"A warp and weft of folklore, fear and the power of remembrance, Davey's latest is striking. Old things have memories too and not all are good. *The Memory Tree* is brilliantly Gothic, thoroughly haunting and a damn fine read."

ANGELA "A.G." SLATTER, multi-award-winning author of *A Forest, Darkly*

"A dark and crooked journey down a shadowy country lane, *The Memory Tree* is a haunting, atmospheric exploration of how tragedy echoes though the ages and seeps into the twisted roots of the heart."

DELILAH S. DAWSON, Bram Stoker Award®-winner and author of *Monstera*

"Tense and compelling, this is a Gothic thriller to chill every reader's heart."

RHIANNON WARD, author of *The Quickening*

"A Gothic gem dripping with atmosphere… Dark and dread-soaked, *The Memory Tree* is a truly chilling novel that never flinches away from the question: how well do we really know those closest to us?"

AMY JANE STEWART, author of *Hex House*

"A wonderful reimagining of Gothic tropes, weaving together two time periods to tell the story of a haunting stretching across centuries."

A.C. WISE, author of *Wendy, Darling* and *Ballad of the Bone Road*

"A lyrical interweaving of past and
how deep-rooted memories can

ALISON LITTLEWOOD, autho

Also by Heather Davey
and available from Titan Books

The Ghosts of Merry Hall

The MEMORY TREE

HEATHER DAVEY

TITAN BOOKS

The Memory Tree
Print edition ISBN: 9781835414392
E-book edition ISBN: 9781835414408

Published by Titan Books
A division of Titan Publishing Group Ltd
144 Southwark Street, London SE1 0UP
www.titanbooks.com

First edition: September 2026
10 9 8 7 6 5 4 3 2 1

A CIP catalogue record for this title is available from the British Library.

EU RP (for authorities only)
eucomply OÜ, Pärnu mnt. 139b-14, 11317 Tallinn, Estonia
hello@eucompliancepartner.com, +3375690241

Designed and typeset in Warnock Pro by Richard Mason.

Printed and bound by CPI Group (UK) Ltd, Croydon, CR0 4YY.

For my family

If the Yew be set in a place subject to poisonous vapours, the very branches will draw and imbibe them, hence it is conceived that the judicious in former times planted it in churchyards on the West side, because those places, being fuller of putrefaction and gross oleaginous vapours exhaled out of the graves by the setting sun and sometimes drawn by those meteors called 'Ignes fatui', divers have been frightened, supposing some dead bodies to walk, not that it is able to drive away Devils as some superstitious monks have imagined.

ROBERT TURNER – *BOTANOLOGIA*, 1664

Beneath those rugged elms, that yew-tree's shade,
Where heaves the turf in many a mould'ring heap,
Each in his narrow cell for ever laid,
The rude forefathers of the hamlet sleep.

THOMAS GRAY – 'ELEGY WRITTEN IN A COUNTRY CHURCHYARD', 1751

On the eve of May
To keep Barrow Man at bay,
We dance and we sing,
And to the yew tree we bring,
Garlands so bright and so gay.

LOCAL FOLKSONG – HOPE-UNDER-BARROW, DORSET

The Beginning

They laid him in the earth and placed a bell-shaped beaker beside him. Next to it, they set his gold lozenge traced with a fine zig-zag pattern, then a mace, a spear, and three large bronze daggers. These were the goods he would need in the next world. For beauty, they gave him his pipes.

The air was frigid, the winter bitter, and sealing the mound with the unyielding sod was hard, necessary work. The men's fingers were chapped, their backs bent stiff as the punishing labour tore at their sinews and birthed a bone-weary pain that would last for days.

No one spoke as a cold mist fled down from the hills and hung low over the grave. It clutched at the men's scalps, shivered beneath their skin, and chilled the blood in their veins. But it did not hinder them. They must finish this work. For the chief must have his burial place.

In later times, druids came to the mound. It was soft then with moss, and the sun grazed the dome with lemon light. There they planted a branch which they had brought with them from afar. A yew. It grew, strong and certain; a bold tree, a wise tree that held deep intelligence within its branches and sucked secrets through its roots.

When the nearby church was built, the yew was already one thousand years old.

1

KATE

Cheshire 2026

I buckle Noah into his car seat, wiping a smear of chocolate spread from his cheek and brushing the mousy curls out of his eyes. He wriggles and pushes his toy crocodile into my face as a weapon. 'Mummy,' he protests. 'No, Mummy. Croccy don't like it.'

'Doesn't. Croccy *doesn't* like it.'

Noah's face creases and he sticks a thumb in his mouth.

I laugh and kiss the top of his head before shutting the car door with a neat click. Heading for the passenger side, I pause, fingers brushing the handle. Ben's driving. He's already strapped up in front, tapping his hands on the steering wheel, key in the ignition. He wants to get going, that much is clear, and I get it – it's a long drive. But I want to feel. For the last time. I need it. I need to feel what it is to be here, to feel the life I've always known.

I inhale deeply, taking in the familiar tang of the petrochemical manufacturing plant as it pumps out streams of white. Out of habit, I curl my nose, even though some days, I don't even notice the stink anymore. The fumes are reflected in the rippling surface of the River Weaver as it snakes past in the distance, mirrored together with tall, narrow, chimneys. Everyone calls it *The Cabbage Monster*, on account of the stench of rotten cabbages that forever permeates the area.

I turn to the tight row of Victorian workers' houses crammed in two dark, dismal lines on Patten Road. Homes to some of the poorest people in Hillsby and conversion fodder for Ben and his boss. His *former* boss. The houses are tiny two-up, two-downs, but large families crossing the generations live in them and everyone knows everyone. The road is noisy and it's always in the local rag. But not in a good way. Our house – our old house – is tagged right on the end, slightly bigger than the others and near the footpath to the river. And from it, there's a perfect view of where *she* used to live. Looking down on us all in her house from another world.

I turn my attention back to the factory. Not a pretty sight, but one that is as familiar to me as my own hand. Because it's the landscape of home. Long before I met Ben.

'Kate!' Ben opens the passenger window. 'We should go. We've given the removal van more than a head start.'

'Just…' I glance once more at the factory, then down the grim lines of Patten Road. '…just saying goodbye.'

'Putting those ghosts of the past to rest, eh?' he says, with a grin.

'Something like that.' I shrug. More accurate than I'd care to admit. 'I'll miss this place, in a way.'

He says nothing, and I'm not sure he really understands. Why should he? It's been tough for him here. A rigorous placement to finish his training.

So, we're off to the countryside. Ben's familiar territory. *Always been a bit of a country bumpkin,* he jokes time and time again. And it's true. He's lived in the middle of nowhere for most of his life. Apart from a stint at university, then theological college. And, of course, a curacy here in the industrial north which he refers to as *a lively experience*, but which I can tell by the tone of his voice is something he'd like to put firmly behind him. *Besides*, he keeps telling me whenever we discuss our move to Dorset, *it's where God's calling me. I simply have to go.*

That I can't argue with. It's a dead-end sort of discussion. One I can't counter without hurting Ben's feelings or annoying some Higher Power. But what about me? I always want to ask. Am *I* being called too? To a life of fields and farms and a tiny community, miles from anywhere?

I get into the car.

Behind me Noah coughs, and a wheeze whines from his small lungs. Petrochemicals. I jam the seat belt into the socket. This place is no good for his asthma. Noah needs fresh air. He needs a wholesome place to breathe, a place to grow up safe, rather than learning about life in the needle-strewn, graffitied park behind Patten Road.

And me? Well, I need to be where Ben is.

Ever since I met him – it sounds a cliché – we've been inseparable. I found him quite by accident. At the time, I was doing a mindless admin job at a solicitor's across town, and I used to pop into the adjacent church – St Michael's – on my lunch breaks, just to get some headspace, away from the office politics and the tedium of it all. I used to stare at a stained-glass window depicting Michael the Archangel slaying the serpent, marvelling at the brilliant reds, greens and blues that were backlit on sunny days. And on dull days, when the colours were muted, I loved knowing that the window was hiding a glorious secret. I'd wish, whenever I looked at it, that I had the same power as St Michael to crush my own monsters. It made me cry sometimes.

Then, one day, a young man slid into the pew next to me. We sat in a strangely comfortable silence, before he spoke. 'He's the leader of the celestial army, you know.'

'What?' I turned to look at him.

'St Michael.' He nodded at the window. 'Defeater of evil, protector against dark forces, guide in times of trouble. Wouldn't you like him to be on your side?'

I laughed, not really knowing how to respond, though I desperately wanted all of those things. 'Is he real?' I found myself asking.

The man smiled. 'Of course he's real! Why else would someone have taken the trouble to make such a beautiful window?'

We got talking. He felt familiar, as if I'd always known him or had met him before. The tilt of his jaw and the way he pushed back his hair when he talked seemed as if it had been written into my story long ago. He was a student at the local theological college, he told me. Both his parents were dead, though he didn't really like to talk about his family. It was too painful. But it was a painful past that made him want to be a priest and he was in the process of looking for a training post. I didn't really understand any of it, but with Ben, everything was so different and new that I rode the adventure with him, making plans and dreaming up a future. By the time he'd secured his curacy, we were married, and Noah was on the way.

I've always needed Ben in a furious, vital sense and, even though I have my doubts about this move, there's no way I'm going to hold him back. As long as I have my art, I'm sure I can make it work. And now I'll be able to paint nature, instead of cityscapes, channel my creative energy into living, breathing, green things. Nourishing things.

Noah coughs again.

I sigh and sit back, closing my eyes as Ben starts the car.

I need to see this move as a positive, necessary thing for the family, for us, for Noah.

Mostly though, I need to forget about *her*.

I need to forget about Julie Moon.

2

OCTAVIA

Dorsetshire 1866

Father is in a terrific temper. Since morning church, he has been lumbering around the vicarage like a wounded bear, thrashing at things that happen to be in his way. He shouted at poor Cook for the quality of the mutton we've been served up for Sunday luncheon and told dear old Nanny Butterworth that she must keep me out of his way for the rest of the day.

'Such an abomination. Pure insult! I cannot eat this wretched meat,' he complains, after dismissing Cook from the room. He prods at the pink lump of flesh on his plate. 'And the potatoes. They are still hard. Are yours hard, Octavia?'

I slice into a greying potato, sitting in a puddle of gravy marbled with blood. 'Just a little, Father.'

'Hopeless!' He puts his knife down with a clatter. Fatty gravy splashes on the white cloth.

It is a strange thing. Father is such a respected gentleman about the village. The vicar, the great preacher and tender of the sick. The listener and the orator. Yet, here at the vicarage, hidden away from the parishioners, his demeanour is quite in conflict with the clever exterior he presents. There is nothing religious or pious about him at all and there is always something amiss that makes him annoyed or upset. Only the staff ever witness his real persona but they would never gossip. They revere him too much. Or fear him, most likely.

His complaint today is that there is water pouring through the chancel roof at St Hilda's, after the spring rains we have had. That, and the non-conformists who, he frets, would have us all dissent or would, at least, steal our congregations while the water is threatening the structural integrity of the church building.

'The place will go to wrack and ruin before long,' he declares, pushing the offending mutton to one side of his plate. 'It is a certain calamity.'

I am not sure whether he is talking about St Hilda's or the non-conformists.

'The roof will fall in unless something is done,' he concludes, clarifying the focus of the conversation. 'It must be attended to immediately.' He bangs a hand on the table. 'The funds must be found.' Last Sunday, he had stated that he was ashamed of St Hilda's. He wanted to raise money to modernise the building, to remove the deeply unfashionable box pews and to dismantle the three-decker pulpit. And now this.

Spending large amounts on a building did not seem entirely worthwhile to me.

'What if we were to hold church services out of doors?' I counter. 'If the building really does collapse, that is.'

Father looks at me, as if he is surprised to find that I have something to say on the matter. I suspect he was rather enjoying his monologue. He narrows his eyes as Cook takes away the plates, mutton uneaten, hard potatoes split open and discarded. 'Octavia, you know nothing of such things.' Not thinking to use his napkin, he brushes his whiskery moustache. A bead of gravy clings there, and his fingers miss it. 'Ritual is the path to understanding God and you cannot perform rituals out of doors. Really, you know nothing at all.'

I think of the great yew tree in the graveyard, of how marvellous it would be to attend a service beneath its cool, green canopy. To smell the sweet air, to hear the birds, to be so near to—

'You spend too much time out of doors. It does not do to have you roaming the countryside like one of the village children. This afternoon, you must stay indoors and read your Bible. It is a Sunday, after all.'

I twist my hands in my lap, bite down on my lip. I seldom roam far, not daring to go any great distance from the vicarage. I lift my eyes. 'Might I visit Mother's grave… if only to place flowers there?'

Father's face distorts, the bulbous vein on his forehead pulses. He brings a hand to the table again, hard. 'No, Octavia. You may not. Not today. We will go together another time. Dwelling on the past day after day does not do anything to enliven the present. Which is where we live, after all. Besides, I have other things to attend to this afternoon.'

My stomach falls. His excuses mask a refusal to accept Mother's death. It is denial that twists at his core, and which eats at him from the inside. He hides it well, with anger and apparent disinterest, but I know it's there. I can feel it. I stare at the gravy globule on his moustache, which glistens in the sunlight that spills through the dining room window. I do not want to visit the grave with him. I want to go on my own, to whisper secrets into the earth, to conjure up the magic of Mother's soul as it shimmers around me, as I listen to the rush of the elm branches near her resting place. To savour the space, as I dream and lose myself in the memories I have of her. At times, when Father is not around to spoil things, I almost fancy that she is really there.

'You may go to your room now, Octavia.'

I hesitate. We have not yet had dessert.

But Father pushes back his chair, scraping it loudly on the wooden floor. The sound is deliberate, final. 'I have work to do. A sermon to refine for this afternoon. Please leave.'

I ball my napkin as Cook bustles into the room. Carrot pudding. Steaming, adorned with candied lemon. Saliva pools in my mouth; my stomach growls. The mutton really had been a disaster.

I finger the handle of my spoon, edge the napkin back towards me, watching as the pudding is placed in the centre of the table.

'Your room, Octavia. Go. This instant.'

I do not go to my room. Of course I do not. The weather is far too glorious, and despite Father's orders, I know that Nanny Butterworth will not keep me confined to the house. The vicarage is old and uncared for; it rattles in the winter and is dark and gloomy in the brighter seasons. I think Nanny Butterworth hates it almost as much as I do. She and I have a quiet understanding, built over the years, and she allows me my freedom. That is, if I do not disappoint her or provide her with reason to mistrust me. Rarely does she scold, and rarely do I give her occasion to wish she had kept a firmer hand on me.

At fifteen, I feel far too old for a nanny, but without a mother to take care of me, I do not really mind, and it saves me the bother of the everyday practicalities: deciding what to wear, when to bathe, how to arrange my hair and the like. Besides, I like Nanny Butterworth and, in truth, cannot imagine life without her.

I find my bonnet on the peg by the back door and tie the frayed ribbon securely under my chin. The sun is warm for early spring, and I do not waste time in fetching a coat or shawl, but slip quietly into the garden, going the long way around the house so that I do not have to pass by Father's study window. Then I race across the lawn scattered with daffodils nodding in the breeze, and through the little iron gate into the churchyard. It's the quickest way from the vicarage to the church and Father and I use this gate all the time. It opens onto a narrow path shaded by trees and weaves its way past rows of graves to the vestry door. Some of the graves are quite old and just simple headstones, but some of the modern ones are large, like pieces of sculpture – angels, obelisks, highly decorated urns with carved drapery mounted on platforms, even the Virgin Mary, arms outstretched, a look of pity in her sad, stony eyes. Growing alongside the path are clusters of golden primroses and I snip a few and carry them with me.

Mother's grave is small and neat, just off the path, near to the church. The afternoon sun casts a thin ray of light over the stone, and I smile. Angel light, I think. Shining especially for Mother. I stand in front of the grave for a moment, reading the epitaph, although I have read it a hundred times or more. I let the words scuttle across my lips in a whisper.

Here lies

ANN KIBBLE

Beloved wife of PHINEAS KIBBLE, *priest*

An affectionate mother and fond friend

Born Apr. 20th 1830

Died Nov. 6th 1865

Remember me.

Tears prickle my eyelids. 'It is me, Mother,' I say, crouching. I place the primroses on the grass in front of the headstone and make them into a circular pattern. They look like the sun or, perhaps, a golden star. 'It is me, Octavia.'

Overhead, a crow makes a throaty *caw, caw.* There's a battering of wings and rustling of leaves as two velvety birds rise from the nearby elm tree, staining the perfect blue sky with ink. I watch as they circle, bluey-black feathers gleaming in the sunlight. They come to land on the large yew tree at the other side of the graveyard and croak, one to the other. Then, one spreads its wings and wheels through the air, flying low over the graves and coming to land on Mother's headstone. There it perches, its black bead-like eye glinting. It moves in odd jerky steps, clasping the stone with its claws, at one point threatening to topple.

I cannot bring my gaze away from it. Mother loved all living things. She loved the countryside, she had often told me, from the moment Father had found a patron here and they had moved from his curacy in Saffron Hill, when I was a small child. Often, I had watched her feed birds from the kitchen windowsill, especially in the winter. I had seen her nurse a baby rabbit with a broken foot, an abandoned starling chick with grey, ragged feathers, and once, even, a fox cub that had a shot wound in its leg. Nature has meaning and purpose, she had told me solemnly, and every living thing in our world is imbued with deep wisdom that we can hear if we listen hard enough. *It is in the green folds of the hills, Octavia,* she would say, *in the trees and the streams, and in each one of God's perfectly made creatures. Listen for the songs of glory they sing and look for miracles, every day. If you pay attention, my sweet one, I promise you will grow far richer than any man!*

The crow jumps with a loud *caw*, bringing me back to the present. It lands in my ring of primroses and picks at one with its beak.

'Stop that,' I cry. 'Please, stop.' I make a shooing motion. 'Those are Mother's.'

The bird disregards me and flaps, the flower still in its black beak. It opens its wings, rises and, carrying Mother's primrose, flies back to the yew tree. Then, there's a dot of yellow and I see the flower falling from its beak, tumbling in a fast-rotating helix towards the ground.

I scramble to my feet and, ignoring the large green stain on my skirt, run through the long grass, skipping over smaller, broken headstones, skirting around tombs. The air is dizzy with the smell of cow parsley, a bee buzzes, small flies rise as I disturb the grass.

The yew tree is situated upon a mound in a much-neglected part of the graveyard where no one goes. Here the grass is long, there are nettles, and I feel stings bloom beneath my stockings. But I reach the tree and delight upon the primrose, surprised to see that not one petal has been lost. Carefully, I lift the delicate flower and hold it in my warm palm. I'm breathing hard, a trickle of sweat is running down the back of my neck. But I have Mother's primrose and that is what matters.

I turn to retrace my steps, more slowly this time. My head is aching, and I look up at the dark green branches above my head, at the bright sunlight flashing through the gaps. It must be hotter out here than I realised. I should not have run like that. It was foolish of me. A sudden unease grips me, and some inner sense tells me that I am not alone. I need to get out of the shade of this tree and back into the light.

I have just taken a step when I hear a voice close by.

A man.

My heart hammers and I look all around, gaze darting between the headstones, across at the church, over at the vicarage. I scan the nettles and brambles near the tree, but there is nothing.

Father?

It did not sound like him.

The sexton, Mr Jefferies?

There is no sign of him.

Pain needles the side of my head, and I hear the voice again. I cannot hear what he calls, but it is a single word. Urgent. Intense.

A squirrel scampers up the yew tree and the sudden movement makes me jump. It's then that I think I see a man, close by, standing by the reddish, peeling tree trunk, a bulky figure, solid, black, and exuding a terrific power.

I freeze and screw my eyes tight. My heartbeat thrashes in my ears, my head pounds. In my mind's eye, I see him. His eyes are dark, hollow holes and his long hair is matted and tangled like wild undergrowth.

I open my eyes, flicking my gaze to the shadows.

There is nothing. No man. But I feel something still. Something unnatural.

Dropping the primrose, I cover my mouth, my scream ripping through the graveyard as I run.

Extract from a sermon given
by the Reverend Phineas Kibble,
December 1865.

The text for today's homily is taken from the book of Job, chapter fourteen.

'Man that is born of a woman hath but a short time to live and is full of misery...'

... Brethren, whilst we live in the shadow of death, yet must we have hope. Hope of eternal life in Christ Jesus, our Lord.

Grief is a spectre that haunts many of us in this world and yet, learn that, if devoted, we follow in the ways of our Lord, we may once again be reunited with those we have lost, in that everlasting kingdom, which is Paradise.

Hold, steadfast, to this promise. Believe it with all your heart, my friends.

And, until that time of glorious felicity, we must pray for the souls of our dear departed brothers, giving thanks for those we have lost and mourned...

3

KATE

Dorset 2026

The car winds along narrow country lanes. It's taken us ages to get this far. Ben insisted that he didn't need to use satnav and has been navigating since we left Patten Road. *I know Dorset like the back of my hand,* he'd assured me. *I grew up a stone's throw from Hope-under-Barrow.* Possibly true, but it turns out that he didn't quite know how to actually get there from Cheshire. Several wrong turns means that the four-and-a-half-hour journey has taken us nearly six. Put that on top of having to stop a couple of times for Noah to do an emergency wee on the side of the road, then having to deal with the distress of him seeing a dead fox on the hard shoulder, it's fair to say I've had enough.

'Daddy, where are we going?'

'The new house, buddy.' Ben flashes a look at Noah in the rear-view mirror. 'We're going to live here, in the countryside. Look, over there – lambs!'

Noah presses Croccy's snout against the window so that he can see, and I too watch as the lambs skip and dance in the late afternoon sun. It would be idyllic if I didn't have a dragging sensation in my stomach. I wonder, not for the first time this journey, what exactly we're letting ourselves in for. How we'll cope, miles from anywhere. Or rather, how *I'll* cope. Ben will be fine. He has the countryside, a new job, new people to meet and organise. He has God. Once more, I mentally list the reasons why this is a good move, trying to convince myself all over again. Noah, Noah, Noah. Forgetting and rebuilding.

The car turns a sharp left and then we're climbing a thin track bordered by hedges so high that the view is obscured. I hope to God that we don't meet anyone coming the other way and I find myself holding my breath as the bends get tighter and tighter. But we reach the top without event, and the hedges fall away so that suddenly we can see for miles. Green fields and heathland dotted bright with yellow gorse stretch out for eternity, and chalky paths wiggle their way across the hills as if someone has drawn them in. There's something else too: lumpy mounds of earth peppering the landscape.

'All those little hills,' I say. 'Are they—'

'Burial mounds, yes,' says Ben. 'They're round barrows. Dorset's famous for them.' He begins a winding descent. 'Hope-under-Barrow is basically situated beneath a Bronze Age cemetery.'

Oh great. 'So—'

'Lots of history. They've done digs and stuff. Probably found some interesting things. We should check out the museum in Dorchester.'

'We should,' I say, distractedly. I'm concentrating on the tiny village nestled near the bottom of the hill. Is that it, I wonder? Is that Hope-under-Barrow? Our new home.

'Almost there, bud,' says Ben, before I have chance to ask the question. His gaze flits to the rear-view mirror again.

When there's no response, I peer over the headrest to see that Noah has fallen asleep, his small fingers curled around a drooping Croccy. I smile. Then look at Ben. He's biting his lower lip, concentrating on the spiral of the road. But there's something else too.

'It's going to be fine,' I say. 'I'm going to love it.'

Although I'd been invited by the churchwardens, I'd been unable to accompany Ben down to Dorset on the day of the interview. I'd been involved in an exhibition in Chester. So, he'd sent me photos on his ageing phone: the view from one of the vicarage windows across a large garden, the church, a snap of the village with its picturesque row of thatched cottages and an old red phone box turned lending library. A million miles from Patten Road, that's for sure. I push my hair back. 'And judging by the pictures, Noah will have oodles of space to play, and he can really learn about nature.'

'Thanks, Kate,' says Ben, evidently sensing the effort I'm making. He rubs my thigh, his sleeve edging up to uncover a honey-coloured birthmark on his forearm. It's shaped like a lopsided heart.

We reach the bottom of the hill and roll into the village. It's more of a hamlet, really. Aside from the stuff in the photos Ben had sent me, there isn't much else. A small school, an even smaller convenience store, a village hall, a rather dismal-looking pub – The Red Lion – and a tiny rec with a broken football goal.

'Oldy-worldy, isn't it?' says Ben.

'Uh-huh. Hey, did you see the name of that road we just passed?' I say, swinging my head back over my shoulder. But it's gone already. 'Coffin Lane. One of those eccentric English place names, I'm guessing. I wonder what the history is.'

'It's from the days when transport was limited,' says Ben. 'People who died from the farms up in the hills would be brought down that lane to the church for burial. Sometimes, in bad weather, it would take days.'

'I see.' I don't much like the idea, even if it does make sense.

I wonder how people nowadays can live on a road with that name. Especially if they know the history of it.

We pass by the church. A pleasant, squat building, Norman, I think, and rather overshadowed by trees.

'That's St Hilda's,' says Ben, 'and here's…' He pulls the car onto a large drive, overgrown with weeds, bright dandelion heads sprouting up all over the place. He cuts the engine. 'Here's our new home.'

I gape out of the window, unable, for a moment, to move. The place is huge. An L-shaped house with large windows and a front door so wide, I'm pretty certain you could walk in three abreast. A network of some climbing plant or other sprawls across the grey stone exterior. 'It's massive!' I say, opening the car door.

'Comes with the job.' Ben grins, gets out and heads to the back of the car to unstrap Noah.

'And you have the keys?'

'Mrs Butterworth's meeting us here. With a set for us.'

'Mrs Butterworth?'

'The previous vicar's housekeeper. Also, one of the churchwardens.'

I laugh. 'My God, this place is quaint. Housekeeper? I mean, who has a housekeeper these days?'

The front door edges open.

'Reverend Allen did for starters,' mutters Ben. 'But don't worry, she's not going to be ours.' He hitches Noah onto his hip. Noah immediately buries his head, together with Croccy, in the crook of Ben's neck.

I stare at the house and watch as a short, dumpy lady in an overall and baggy corduroys, shiny at the knees, steps onto the drive. She smiles, broadly. 'Reverend Thomas,' she says.

'Ben,' says Ben. 'Please, call me Ben.'

The woman's mouth twitches. 'You're not wearing…' she brushes her neck.

Ben frowns, then laughs. 'Oh, my dog collar?' He shrugs. 'Well, I'm not working today. I'm moving house.'

The woman purses her lips.

Ben smiles, undeterred. He's good like this, all part of the job; appeasing people, playing along, getting them on side. He gestures in my direction. 'So, this is my wife, Kate, and this little monkey...' he strokes Noah's arm, '... is our son. Noah.'

'Pleased to meet you,' says the lady, more as a matter of form. She turns straight away and heads into the dark interior of the house. 'I'm Mrs Butterworth,' she says over her shoulder. She offers no first name alternative.

Ben and I look at each other and follow her into a gloomy hall, narrow and dim, despite the magnolia walls. An old set of servants' bells hang to one side, a wooden coat rack to the other.

'The house has been thoroughly cleaned. From top to bottom.' Mrs Butterworth turns and looks at me. 'I hope you'll find it comfortable, Mrs—'

'Greenwood,' I say. 'My name's Kate Greenwood. Ms.'

Mrs Butterworth frowns.

'I didn't take Ben's name when we married. I was already working as Greenwood for one thing – I'm an artist – and for another—'

'These modern ways!' Mrs Butterworth shakes her head and runs a hand over the top of the hall radiator, looking at her fingers, as if inspecting for dust. She brushes her hand across her corduroys. 'Your removal firm arrived – and left – some time ago.' She glances at her watch. 'I was expecting you much earlier.'

'My fault,' says Ben with an apologetic smile. 'I should have phoned. We got slightly lost.'

Mrs Butterworth sniffs. 'Well, I hope you don't mind, but I told the removal men where to put all your things. I know which rooms Reverend Allen used for which purposes, you see.'

I think of our boxes carefully labelled in red sharpie: *kitchen, study, lounge, Kate & Ben, Noah.* Some rooms were obvious, but had she really decided where we were going to sleep? I bite back my reaction.

Mrs Butterworth leads us from the hall to a room at the back of the house. The kitchen, fitted, like our last house, with nineties units. Chunky, shiny, real oak. But also, pumpkin orange and scratched. Our folding-table stands in the middle of the room. Dark-wood and clashing. But the view from the window is great. There's a small terrace and a large lawn, recently mowed by the looks of things. Clumps of daffodils stand tall and proud, and there's a broken hammock, hanging from a cedar tree, which I'm sure we can repair. I wander across to the window and survey the scene, imagining Noah playing on the grass, or Ben and me sitting on the terrace with glasses of wine. I inhale the scent of cut grass from the open window before turning back to the kitchen.

Our boxes have been dumped next to the table and with annoyance, I notice that one has been prised open.

'I wanted to find mugs and a kettle,' says Mrs Butterworth, catching me looking. 'For tea.' She gestures to a small box of PG Tips. 'I also bought you some milk and a packet of chocolate Hobnobs.'

Immediately I feel guilty. 'Kind of you,' I say. 'Why don't we put the kettle on?'

Mrs Butterworth attends to it, the kitchen tap gurgling and sputtering as she fills it. Meanwhile, Ben slings teabags into the mugs Mrs Butterworth unearthed and finds the milk in a whirring old fridge. *'The fridge was left here by Reverend Allen,'* we're informed. And just as well, as we don't have our own and his cast-off will save us a few hundred.

Clutching our drinks, Mrs Butterworth leads us around the rest of the ground floor, Noah hanging onto my leg, sucking his chocolatey thumb, and holding Croccy close. He hasn't said a word since we arrived which is completely unlike him. Downstairs, aside from the kitchen, there's a study for Ben housing a horrible stack of plastic chairs and a great hulking photocopier, a dining room which I can't imagine us using, a spacious lounge which makes our tiny Ikea sofas look out of place, a loo – cold and spidery – and a small empty room which I think we could make into a playroom for Noah. That way, we won't have to tidy away all his toys every time Ben decides to hold a Bible study or something in the lounge. Despite the fact that our furniture has been moved in and there are boxes stacked in every room, the place echoes as we move about, and our voices spiral to the high ceilings. We head back to the hall where our footsteps resound on horrible brown linoleum.

'Plenty of space,' I say, taking a sip of tea. It tastes weird and I suspect there's been water sitting in the pipes for a while. 'How long has the house been empty, exactly?'

'Two years,' says Mrs Butterworth. 'Almost to the day.'

That probably explains the water.

'It's been a long interregnum,' she continues. 'There are a few retired priests in the area, and they've taken services and whatnot, kept us going, but it's not the same, is it?'

'No,' I say. 'It's not.' Though, really, I don't know.

'Well, we're very pleased to be here,' says Ben, fixing a broad smile at Mrs Butterworth. A shaft of light pushes through the multicoloured glass above the front door and he squints. Red, and yellow, and purple. 'Very pleased indeed. Aren't we, Kate?'

I nod and, desperate to escape for a moment, take the mugs to the kitchen, grabbing another Hobnob for Noah while I'm there. 'We're going to find your room, now, Noah,' I say, returning to the hall and handing over the biscuit. Noah takes a small bite before pressing the Hobnob into Croccy's snout. 'Snack time,' he whispers.

‘Four bedrooms, of course,’ says Mrs Butterworth, glancing at the biscuit crumbs on the linoleum, before mounting the stairs. We follow. I count out the steps for Noah, ‘…fourteen, fifteen, sixteen,’ I conclude as we reach the top.

Mrs Butterworth sighs with an impatience she doesn’t bother disguising. ‘I’ve put your little boy in the room next to you.’

I feel like I’m a guest, but I smile politely as she leads us across a gallery landing, carpeted in a faded green, and pushes at a solid wooden door. ‘This is one of the smaller bedrooms. You could use it if you have visitors.’ The door swings open to reveal what is actually a fairly substantial room. Sunlight is gushing through the window sending patterns of brilliant white light dancing over the walls. In the middle, against one of the walls, is an old-fashioned bed.

I frown. It doesn’t belong to us.

‘Oh,’ says Mrs Buttterworth. ‘The bed. Reverend Allen left that here. It didn’t belong to him, you see. It was made by a local carpenter, I gather. Years ago. Before my time, even.’

‘It’s a proper antique,’ I say, fingering the bedpost. It’s smooth, as if countless people have run their hands over the wood before me. ‘They don’t make them like this anymore.’ I glance up. ‘Ben, we should claim this room.’ I prod the mattress. It’s firm, deep, and I can imagine waking up on it in a room full of light. ‘Let’s sleep here,’ I say. Immediately, my words change something in the room, and I have the sense I’ve said something wrong.

Mrs Butterworth steps towards me. ‘Actually, I’ve put you in the front bedroom. It overlooks the church. It’s where Reverend Allen used to sleep.’

‘I see.’ I flash a look at Ben, but his expression is unreadable. We can sort this when she’s gone.

Mrs Butterworth turns. ‘Let me show you. You’ll be quite comfortable in there.’ She shuffles back out onto the landing. I glance once more at the bed, a slight shudder rippling across my shoulders as I look at the dark wood, with its swirls of yellow. There's something about it I can't place, a feeling, a sense of time maybe. But shaking my head, I leave the room, closing the door behind me.

Our assigned bedroom is huge, dwarfing the small double bed we brought with us from Cheshire. The floors are covered in the same shabby green carpet as the landing and there's a black grate on one side of the room filled with fake coal. I shiver. It's cold. And dark too because it's in the shadow of an enormous yew tree that stands in the graveyard. I head for the window to take a closer look. Thick branches stretch in a twisted network of reddish-brown bark, and green, glossy needles reach for the ground or gash the spring sky. It's like a great beast, waiting for its moment, rearing up, ready to attack.

I turn to Ben. 'Well, we need to see about getting that thing cut back. It's taking all the natural light.'

Ben joins me at the window, hands in pockets. He regards the tree. 'I dunno, Kate,' he says, after a moment. 'It's quite a monster but it's got to be pretty old. I'm no tree surgeon but I'd say it's probably valuable too, aesthetically.' He cocks his head to one side. 'I think it's rather impressive, actually.'

I look around the bedroom, at the walls mottled with the tree's shadow. 'But it's making this room really gloomy. I'm sure a bit of careful pruning...'

Behind us, Mrs Butterworth gives a neat cough. 'I'm afraid the Reverend's quite right,' she says. 'You can't have it cut back Mrs... er... Ms Greenwood. Not that tree. *That* tree is extremely special to us here in Hope-under-Barrow.'

4

OCTAVIA

Dorsetshire 1866

'What's the matter? Are you hurt?'

I feel a cool hand on my arm.

'Do speak to me. Should I fetch help?'

Grass is tickling my nose, my body throbs, and I see blood on my hand. Carefully, I lift my head. Everything spins. 'Where is he?' I breathe. I am still fearful, the terror running through my body, making the skin on my arms flare with tiny bumps.

'Who's *he*?'

I try to focus.

There's a girl kneeling at my side, long blonde curls cascading over her shoulders. Her face is smudged with dirt, and her dress is slightly too short in the arms. I recognise her. She lives on one of the farms, I think, and I've seen her in church sometimes.

'Are you hurt?' she says, again.

'No, I...' I move slightly, my head circling, the blood on my hand making me giddy. I wipe it on the grass. It's only grazed where I've scraped it on a grave, and already the bleeding has stopped. I breathe out. 'I'm well enough. I was running and I fell. But there was a man...

or at least I thought…' I look behind me. The yew tree stands dark and silent. A giant mounted upon an ancient barrow. Nothing moves. Even the crows have disappeared. 'Over there – by the tree.' Although now, I'm not so sure what it was that happened, but I recall the man's eyes, the intent with which he stared, his slow, lumbering steps towards me. 'He… it… he scared me.'

The girl glances at the yew tree. 'Was it Mr Jefferies?'

I look at her.

'You know, Mr Jefferies, the sexton. Lives in the cottage opposite.' She points across the low graveyard wall towards a row of small, neat cottages.

'I know who Mr Jefferies is.' I shake my head. 'But no, it wasn't him. This man was rough-looking, unkempt. Like…' I stop before I say, *like a farm labourer.*

The girl holds an arm out to me. 'Can you stand?'

'I… I think so.' I shuffle to a sitting position, straightening my bonnet. My dress is a mess and there's a tear up the front from where I fell. Father must not see me like this, and I will need to concoct a story for Nanny Butterworth too. If she thinks unsavoury men are lurking around Hope-under-Barrow, she may well stop me from going out alone.

'What did the man do?' says the girl. 'To scare you, I mean.'

I consider. 'He didn't do anything, exactly,' I confess. 'But it was the way he looked at me, as if he wanted to…' I trail off. *Harm me?* I am unsure. It is difficult now to say exactly what his intention might have been.

'Shall we take a look?' says the girl.

'What?'

'To see if he's still there.'

'I don't know… I…'

But she is already heading for the yew tree, skipping through the long grass, taking the same route I'd used earlier. I follow, more slowly. I'm bruised and tender and am not entirely sure I want to risk seeing the man again. But I do not want to look as if I have lost my nerve. I can imagine this girl telling all the other village children that Octavia Kibble is a coward.

'There's no one here,' calls the girl from up ahead. 'I can't even see footprints.' She's scuffing in the dust with a worn boot. 'Are you sure—'

And then I hear it. A soft *thud, thud, thud.* It is a sound that I cannot discern but it reminds me of the flowerbeds in our garden being dug over.

'Do you hear something?' I ask.

The girl strains. 'I'm not sure,' she says. 'There was a cuckoo earlier and I thought I heard a woodpecker.'

'No, not that,' I say. My head is aching again, and I fear that I will need to ask Nanny Butterworth for a remedy.

The girl cups a hand to her ear.

'It's nothing,' I say. The noise has stopped, and I begin to doubt my sanity. Perhaps I have imagined the whole peculiar episode; the man and the strange sound. 'I think I may be unwell.'

The girl frowns. 'Should you go home, then?'

I think of Father. Of the temper he is in. Of the dark, cool vicarage, my bedchamber, the endless search for something to occupy me.

'Not yet,' I say.

'I'm Alice,' says the girl, satisfied by my answer. 'Alice March. I live at March's farm, straight up the coffin lane, right near the top of Barrow Hill.'

I open my mouth, to exchange an introduction, but Alice gets there first. 'I know who you are. You're Octavia Kibble, the vicar's daughter.'

I nod.

'I read the axen in the hearth this morning,' says Alice. 'They said I would make a new friend today. So, that's you, isn't it?'

Extract from a sermon given
by the Reverend Phineas Kibble,
January 1866.

The text for today's homily is taken from the book of Genesis, chapter two.

'And the Lord God formed man of the dust of the ground, and breathed into his nostrils the breath of life; and man became a living soul...'

... Friends, we must always be mindful of our souls, framed for us by a rational Creator. When we go hence from this world and into the next, our bodies will rise in glory, but it is our souls that will receive the greatness that God has prepared for us in heaven.

Therefore, take good care, people of Hope-under-Barrow. Live good and holy lives so that, at the last, you may share in the heavenly banquet prepared for all godly men.

5

KATE

Dorset 2026

Eventually, we free ourselves of Mrs Butterworth and suddenly, the house feels vacuous. A silent space has opened up around us, and we have to fill it. We're back in the kitchen. Noah is making his way through another chocolate biscuit, spewing crumbs all over the floor and wiping his messy fingers on my jeans.

'Nice pad,' says Ben.

I can't quite agree but I can't bring myself to disagree either. 'It's a big house,' I say. 'And the light in the back bedroom is good. The one with the old-fashioned bed. Screw Mrs Butterworth. I want that to be our room.'

Ben shifts from foot to foot.

'What is it?'

'It's just that—'

I throw my hands into the air. 'Surely you're not going to let some random old lady dictate where we sleep? She won't even know. It's not as if—'

'It's not that.'

'Biccy,' says Noah, chubby arm reaching in the direction of the worksurface. 'Please,' he adds.

'Then, what is it, Ben?'

'Biccy, Mummy!'

I hand Noah a biscuit. Too much sugar for one day. He's on his fourth already. But it's also not the time for tantrums.

Ben runs a hand through his hair. He's struggling, I can tell. And I don't want us to argue on a day like this. Not that we ever really argue, but I can tell we're both frayed, and the drive has already been stressful enough.

'Don't worry,' I say. I push the packet of biscuits firmly to the back of the worksurface, out of Noah's sight. 'It doesn't really matter. I just liked that room, that's all, and I could use it as a studio, if we're not going to sleep in there. As I said, the light's good.'

'Sounds perfect,' says Ben. He rolls up his shirt sleeves and leans back against the worksurface, visibly relaxing.

'Though what do you think Mrs Butterworth meant about not cutting the big yew tree back?' I say, emptying the dregs of our tea into the sink. 'We need to let more light into the room.' Ben straightens, eyes me carefully. 'I know you think it's *impressive*' – I place air quotes around his word – 'but surely you can see the benefits of getting it trimmed, just a little. It kind of dominates, don't you think?'

'Well, Mrs B seemed pretty adamant about not touching it,' says Ben, evading my question. 'Maybe it's some kind of historic tree or something. She did say it was special.' He glances at me. 'Shall we go and take a look?'

I hesitate. There's unpacking to do, an evening meal to think about. Going to check out a tree in the graveyard doesn't seem high on the priority list.

'Besides,' continues Ben. 'I want to show you the church.'

He rummages in his pocket and separates a long bronze key from the bunch Mrs Butterworth gave us. He looks around the kitchen; the boxes clamouring for our attention, the open packet of Hobnobs, the sterile sense of disuse. 'This lot can wait,' he says. '*There's a time for everything*, as the great King Solomon said. And now is not the time for unpacking.' I laugh. Ben's frequently spouting this particular Bible quote to justify all sorts of things. He tucks an arm around my waist. 'And, after that, how about we find out where the nearest chippy is?'

There's a small path leading from the vicarage garden to the churchyard, but it's half-covered with weeds and the yew tree is so large that it overshadows it, making this part of the garden dark and dank. I shiver, despite the warm evening. Noah clings to my arm.

'Where are we going?' he says, his voice small, uncertain.

'To look at Daddy's church,' I say, making my own tone bright with expectation.

'Is it like our church in Hillsby?'

I think of St Martin's. A modern building with a large hall where the children did their own version of church under the enthusiastic direction of a bubbly lady called Jax who wore floral dungarees and purple eyeshadow. 'A little bit,' I say. 'Only this church is older.'

Ben is striding up ahead. 'Come on you two,' he calls. He struggles with a small iron gate all tangled up with ivy. 'I don't think this has been used in a long time,' he says, wrenching away long tendrils and wiping his hands on his jeans.

I pull Noah along to the gate. Here the ground is sludgy, last autumn's leaves a slurry of rotting, stinking ooze. I wrinkle my nose and lift Noah so that he doesn't slip. I can't cope with baths or washing machines today.

'Not bad for an office, eh?' Ben says once we've fought our way through the gate. He regards the church. Together we follow the path to take a closer look at its sandy orange stones, its slate roof, its unusual, rounded apse. The low sunlight warms the building, and I think about how it has happened that way for hundreds of years. Very different to St Martin's.

We stop by a headstone, the inscription stark in the last light. I squint at it. *Sacred to the memory of Revd. Phineas Kibble.* One of Ben's predecessors. Died 1866. Next to it is a smaller headstone, that of his wife, Ann Kibble. I scan the dates. They died within a year of one another and while they were still so young. By today's standards anyway.

I look at Ben. We're both young, healthy, with full lives ahead. And I morbidly wonder what would happen to Noah if we were suddenly snatched away.

A flutter of wings breaks me from my thoughts. A crow lands on Ann's headstone, its feathers almost purple in the light. It walks along the rim of the stone, tail wagging, before taking flight and wheeling towards the church tower with its warm, orange stones, the colour of gingerbread.

'It's pretty,' I concede. 'Very oldy-worldy English.'

'Well, looks can be deceptive.' Ben lowers his voice, even though there's no one around to hear us. 'It's a challenging parish, apparently. The bishop has warned me.'

I look at the tufts of white and yellow daffodils, at the old graves bright with lichen, some leaning at odd angles, one bearing a statue of the Virgin Mary. Her arm has broken off at the elbow, but she still manages to look serene in this forgotten place. Primroses spring at the base of her plinth. I breathe deeply as birds chirrup in the edges of evening, and a sleepy bell tolls the hour. 'It doesn't look very challenging,' I conclude. I think about where we've come from. Patten Road. The drugs, the noise, the crime. 'Besides, surely Hope-under-Barrow isn't even big enough to be challenging. Unless the bishop meant cows blocking the road or something.' I look back towards the village, though I can't really see it from here. Just woodsmoke weaving its way into the sky from the chimney on one of the thatched cottages. 'Everything's small and charming.' I laugh. 'Except for the offending tree, of course.'

Ben turns his attention to the yew tree. 'Look how wide the trunk is,' he says. 'And the branches are so thick. To give Mrs Butterworth her due, it probably would be hard to just lop a few off. It's hollow too. See!'

I clasp Noah's hand and step towards the tree. Ben's right. It's enormous. A red, gnarled confusion of thick bark, gaping in the middle where there's a dark hole. At some point, there have been iron railings around the tree, but they're now warped or fallen and choked by ivy. The tree also stands on top of one of those famous Dorset barrows, which partly explains why, with the extra height, it has the effect it does. Now that I'm here, I see it would be great to paint, whatever else I think about it.

Noah's eyes light up when he sees the hole. 'Can I go inside?' he says, letting go of my hand. He trails Croccy in the detritus.

'No,' Ben says at the same moment as I say, 'Of course, sweetheart.'

Noah looks from me to Ben, confused for a moment by the contradiction. Ben and I usually agree on pretty much everything, especially when it comes to anything Noah-related.

'I don't think…' Ben begins.

'It'll be okay,' I say, glad that Noah actually seems enthusiastic about something in our new environment. 'It's not as though he's climbing right up it or anything. He can't fall.' I hold out a hand to Noah. 'But I'll look after Croccy while you explore… and Daddy and I will be right here to watch you,' I add, to please Ben.

Ben tucks his hands in the pockets of his fleece and says nothing.

Noah hands over his toy and runs towards the trunk, as if afraid Ben will suddenly change his mind. I wrap my arms around my chest, Croccy dangling from one hand. It's cold under this tree and I have the strongest desire to step out into the sun. It will set soon, and I want to savour the last rays of warmth. But instead, I watch as Noah manoeuvres himself inside the hollow. Then, when he's obviously happily exploring, I idly scan the inscriptions of the two headstones set under the tree.

In memory of OCTAVIA KIBBLE
Daughter of REVD. PHINEAS KIBBLE
And his wife, ANN KIBBLE
Born 1851
Died 1941

I frown. Strange that she wasn't buried near her parents. I wonder what happened to her after they died, who took care of her. I tuck my hair over my ears, then trace the lettering with a finger. The stone is cold. Must have been some reason, her being buried here. A reason lost in time, I suspect. Still, she lived to a ripe old age. Ninety. Pretty unusual in those days, I'm guessing. I move to look at the other headstone. It's marked simply:

ALICE
Born July 1851
Died October 1866.

A short life, unlike Octavia's. I swallow hard. And, not for the first time, I think about how cruel, how asymmetrical, life can be.

'Do you know why you always find yew trees in churchyards?' says Ben, coming to stand next to me. He too peers at Alice's grave. I can smell his woody deodorant mixed with his black pepper shower gel. Safe, homely scents.

'Why's that then?' I ask.

He stops and stares at the tree. 'They used to believe that yew trees could absorb the nasty gases released from decomposing bodies.'

I screw up my face. 'Nice.'

'Yews are also deadly poisonous so, on top of that, they deter animals from trying to graze on holy land and upsetting burial places.'

'Right,' I say slowly. I'm not really engaging. Rather I'm wondering now why Noah has gone so quiet. 'Noah,' I call.

There's no answer but then there's a scuffling sound from the hollow.

'You alright in there, bud?' says Ben.

I take a step towards the tree. I have a headache coming on. My mind feels fuzzy. 'Noah?' I call again. My throat is blocked too, my voice thick and pasty.

Unbidden, I think of Julie Moon. Running. Twigs snapping. A tangle of branches. A shout.

I shake my head. 'Noah!' I call louder this time. Still no answer and a surge of panic rises in my chest. Why isn't he answering? He can't have disappeared. Surely not. It's impossible. He—

'I found something,' cries Noah. His voice is dampened, tiny from inside the tree. 'Mummy, I need you to make it better.'

Ben and I look at each other.

'Make what better?' I say. 'Noah?'

Silence.

A steady *thump, thump, thump* builds on one side of my head. Out of the corner of my eye, I see a flash of bronze. Like light catching on metal. Bright. Sudden. Gone. With it comes another dart of pain in my head and, for a moment, I think I'm going to be sick.

I blink, take a deep breath. A migraine?

'Bud, is everything okay in there?' Ben's voice is loud in the quiet churchyard.

No answer.

Then, there's a burst of something else. Voices. Flashing through my mind. High speed. A memory. Like a dream of something that happened a long time ago. Men's voices, calling to one another. Coarse, loud. And then I hear animals and a woman laughing. A child crying.

It's gone and the pain is there again. Dull this time. I brush my hair from my face, trying to grab at the memory, pull the strands into the present, remember where it came from. My childhood? But it's slipped away. As if it never was.

'Are you alright?' whispers Ben, snaking an arm around my waist, but keeping an eye on the tree.

'Fine,' I say. 'Just a bit of a headache. I suppose the move, sitting in the car all day...'

Ben kisses me lightly on the side of my neck. 'It's all going to be fine,' he says.

I let him nuzzle into me. 'Yes,' I say. 'Yes, I know.'

I turn my attention back to the tree. 'Noah?' I say again. 'What have you found in there? Come and show us.'

Noah emerges from the hollow and I scream, dropping Croccy.

His hands are covered in blood.

6

OCTAVIA

Dorsetshire 1866

Alice settles under the yew tree, emptying the contents of her skirt onto the ground. She has collected heaps of daisies from around the graveyard and, using her skirt as a bowl, has carried them to the tree.

'Since you're not that hurt and the man's gone, let's make a chain to go right around the trunk,' she says. She sits next to me, unconcerned that the ground is dirty and, while I look in dismay at the state of my own clothes, she simply arranges herself so that she is comfortable, disregarding the soil and dust that streak her skirts. I try to relax. The grass surrounding the tree is so long that when we sit at the base of the barrow, we are almost hidden; a private kingdom, a place where Father is unlikely to chance upon me.

'Do you often come to the churchyard?' Alice says.

'I like to visit my mother's grave,' I say. 'I try to come every day if I can. Father doesn't like me to, though.'

Alice scrunches her face. 'Why ever not? If it brings you comfort.' She has a mole under one of her dark eyes and when she looks at me, it's as if she has a third eye searching me out.

I scrabble for an answer. 'He says that I must simply pray for Mother's soul. That there is no need to visit her headstone so often.'

Alice is silent. We thread the daisies, one into another. Over and over again. 'He may be right,' she says, at last. She pushes her curls over her shoulder. 'Your father, I mean.'

I look up, a trail of daisies cascading from my fingers.

Alice sniffs. 'I have six brothers. Two of them are up at the farm right now, working. One – the younger one – is blundering around the heath, looking for snakes. The other three are out there.' She waves a hand beyond the graveyard.

'What do you mean?'

'In the hills, in the gorse, in the wind. They are wherever I choose to remember them.'

'But their bodies...' I begin, sensing her meaning.

'Buried. Yes. In unmarked graves on the other side of the church. Not that it matters. That part of them is no-but bones. But their spirits are elsewhere.' She shrugs. 'That's what I think, anyway. Probably not what your father would say, is it?'

And though after my skin worms destroy this body, yet in my flesh shall I see God. 'I... I don't know,' I falter. I look over my shoulder to where I can just make out Mother's grave beyond the unkempt grass. 'I just need to come here,' I say. I cannot think for too long about her body, under the ground, rotting. Worms, insects, dark earth.

'Shall we head to the heath, now?' says Alice, changing the conversation like a new wind. 'I think our daisy chain is quite long enough. I can show you some awful good places. I know where we can find bittercress, and water so sweet, we can drink it right from where it bubbles.' She describes the farm to me; the dog they own, the wall we can sit on and eat the new seedcake her Ma has baked, the huge natural boulders behind the farmhouse that we can climb upon and see for miles. 'Do come!' she says, her face alight.

I thread the last of my flowers onto the chain, desperately wanting to. 'I can't,' I say.

'Why not?' Alice takes the chain and trails it around the tree. 'Why can't you come?' she repeats, having made her circuit.

I gesture towards the church. 'Father will expect me at the afternoon service. It is a Sunday, after all.'

Alice screws her nose. 'Must you go to all of the services?'

I nod.

'Then I suppose I'll have to show you tomorrow,' she says, with a shrug. 'After I've finished my work up at the farm. We have lambs and I look after our bull, too. I have a way with him that the others don't.' She smooths over her skirt and smiles at me.

I smile back, curious about this girl who has shown such an unusual interest in me. There is something about her that makes me feel warm inside, that smooths the anxious discomfort I so often feel. I want to ask when and where we will meet but, before I can frame my questions, she is gone. I look beyond the graveyard, first towards the village, then towards the hills, where I see a slight figure running up the coffin lane, blonde hair streaking behind her.

A sudden gust of wind hustles through the branches above me.

I stand, scrub in vain at the mark upon my skirt.

It is dark under the yew tree, the area full of shadows, and there's a subtle change in the atmosphere that seizes me. Our daisy chain suddenly looks wretched, spindly, broken where my boot caught it.

A hint of a headache shoots across my temples and I'm clutched by a sudden shiver of cold. I have the sense that someone is close by, watching me.

7

KATE

Dorset 2026

'Noah!' I rush towards the tree and seize my son. His hands are red and sticky. 'Did you hurt yourself?

Tears blossom as he shakes his head.

'Then what—'

'Something hurt it,' Noah says, his little face crumpling. 'It needs help.'

'What's up, buddy?' says Ben. 'Who needs help?'

Ignoring his bloody hands, I let Noah tug me towards the hollow. Overhead, the tree hangs dark. 'The crow,' he says.

'Crow?'

'It's stuck inside the tree, and it's hurt. Badly.'

My stomach rolls. Birds, alive or dead, are not my thing. I actually think I have a mild phobia. 'Are you sure?' I try. Though the evidence – the blood – is telling.

'Let's see then,' says Ben, coming to my aid. He crouches by Noah's side. 'You show me, and we'll see what we can do.'

I wipe my blood-smeared hands on the grass while the two

head for the hollow, Ben squeezing inside, cursing as he snags his hair on the trunk.

I stand, arms folded. I want to get back to the vicarage, wash my hands properly, start unpacking a few things. Dealing with injured birds was not on my agenda for today.

But there are voices: Ben, quiet and serious; Noah, rising in pitch. Then seconds later, there's sobbing and they emerge, Ben carrying a large crow. It's clearly dead; its feathers are gluey with blood, its dark head lolls at an unnatural angle, one wing is snapped. Probably a cat got it or something.

'Daddy can't make it better,' cries Noah. His face is streaked with dirty tears, and he has blood on his hoodie. He runs to me and flings his arms around my waist. 'Why can't Daddy make it well again?'

'Because…' Ben sighs and, for a moment, I catch a flash of irritation dart across his face. 'Because it's too late for that,' he finishes.

'But Daddy—'

'I said it's too late,' snaps Ben. A vein on his forehead twitches. 'The crow's dead, okay?'

At this, Noah howls and tightens his clutch. I try to catch Ben's eye, warn him off his impatient tack. But he avoids my gaze and instead looks about him, apparently assessing the area.

'We're going to bury it,' says Ben stiffly, as Noah bawls. He lays the crow on the dirt and pokes around until he finds a loose bit of iron railing which he uses as a makeshift trowel. 'Do you want to help, bud?' he calls, flinging earth about haphazardly.

Noah shakes his head and buries himself in the soft folds of my oversized jumper. He's going to need a bath, after all, and then there's still the matter of sorting an evening meal, making up beds for the night.

The church clock tolls half past the hour. I shift from foot to foot. How much longer will this take?

But soon it's done. The crow is beneath the ground, there's a soft hump of earth marking the spot, and Ben is saying an impromptu prayer.

I raise an eyebrow.

'All God's creatures,' he says, and then he takes Noah to pick dandelion heads which they scatter over the new grave. Bright, like tiny suns.

That night, I wake to a sound. The bedroom is stuffy but I'm drenched in cold sweat. I've been dreaming – the crow, the yew tree, Julie. All mangled into something I can't quite pull apart. And why Julie? Why now?

I sit.

The room is black, cut by a shard of moonlight that arrows through a gap in the curtains. It slices the room in half and picks out the stack of boxes, the tangle of bloodied clothes on the floor from earlier, Ben's humped figure, cocooned in sleep. My mind hums with the dream as I remember the evening; Noah crying for ages, inconsolable, the bath filled with rusty coloured water, our pathetic supper of Hobnobs and out-of-date Cup-a-Soup we found in the back of one of the cupboards. The nearest chippy, we discovered, was over ten miles away and the local grocery shop was closed. My stomach gapes with hunger as I lie back down, trying to settle. I can't. The sheet on my side of the bed has come untucked and one of my pillows has fallen into the black. Apart from the sound of Ben breathing softly, everything is silent. A yawning silence that compels me to listen into it, to pick out what has woken me. And then I hear it. A tapping on the windowpane.

It's a sharp sound, irregular, piercing the quiet of the night.

Carefully, so as not to wake Ben, I slide out of bed. My pyjama top sticks to my back and my bottoms are damp with sweat. I shiver as I tiptoe towards the window, the tapping louder now, insistent.

I edge back one of the curtains and my heart leaps to my throat. There, on the window ledge, wings outstretched, beak wide, eyes shiny and staring, is a large owl. It hisses and trills, then with a scream, lifts into the night.

I stand, transfixed, my heart thrumming, trying to pick out its black shape as it flies away. But all I can see is the yew tree, matted in silhouette against the moon-streaked sky. Everything is still. Pulling the curtain back in place, tugging it so there's no longer a gap, I become aware of another noise.

I freeze, pressing my ear to the darkness.

Out on the landing, there's a creak and a shuffle of footsteps.

Noah?

I creep back across the room and ease our bedroom door open, peering out into the unfamiliar cavern of the house.

There's a whimper.

'Noah?' I whisper. 'Is that you, sweetheart?' My skin prickles.

'Mummy?' His voice is broken with tears.

'Noah!' From the silver glow shining through the un-curtained landing window, I see his small figure as he runs towards me in his too-big Spider-Man pyjamas. I enfold him in my arms and press my nose into his newly washed hair. 'What's the matter?' I say, my words weaving through his soft curls. 'Did you have a bad dream?'

A nod.

'Do you want to tell me about it?'

Noah shakes his head. But then, in a voice so quiet I almost miss it, he says, 'crow.'

'The crow?'

'It got hurt. By an owl.'

I tug Noah closer, my thoughts flashing to the owl at the window. If Ben was here, he'd say something about the crow being in heaven, but I can't quite bring myself to offer the platitude. 'Look,' I say. 'Why don't we go to your room and tuck you back in bed, nice and tight with Croccy. I'll sit with you for a bit if you like. Make sure the dream doesn't come back. How does that sound?'

Noah pulls away from me. His eyes are glassy, fresh tears bubbling.

'What is it?' And then I realise.

Oh God. Croccy.

I remember dropping Croccy by the yew tree during the crow incident. And then we were so preoccupied with Noah and the blood, and the burial, that we must have left him there. It's a small miracle that Noah hadn't realised earlier. But he'd been too upset, and, after a bath, we had just stuffed him with biscuits until he was too tired to stay awake any longer.

'Lucky Croccy, getting to camp out,' I try. 'He'll be able to tell you all about his adventures in the morning.'

Fat tears run down Noah's face and splash onto my hand.

'We'll fetch him first thing,' I say. 'I promise.'

Noah brushes at his cheeks. His jaw trembles. 'I'm going to get him now. The girl will help me find him if you don't want to come.'

'No!' Then, 'What girl?'

But he pushes past me and heads for the stairs, making a weird gulping noise. I think about waking Ben, getting him to deal with this, but after a six-hour drive, a bad night's rest is the last thing he needs. 'Noah. Back to bed!' I hiss. 'I'll fetch Croccy, okay?'

He falters, turns.

'You get in bed and start counting. See how far you can get. I bet I'll be back before you make it to one hundred.'

Noah sniffs and retraces his steps. The moon goes behind a cloud, and, for a moment, we're plunged into the black, but then it's back, the silver light shining across Noah's tear-stained face. I smile at him in what I hope is a reassuring way.

Of course, I need to fetch his cuddly toy.

I need to be a good mum.

'Start counting,' I whisper.

The graveyard is much darker than I expected. I've grabbed my phone and a sweater, then left the kitchen light on in the vicarage so that it illuminates the path across the garden. But once I unlatch the iron gate and step onto the path, I need to use the torch on my phone. At once, I almost regret it. Everything on the periphery of my vision suddenly seems much, much darker. Apart from the little pool of torchlight, it's black everywhere, in front and behind; the unknown surrounding me and pressing in so completely that I feel like I'm melting into nothing. The graves rise out of the ground, dense lumps of stone, and beyond them the church is a dark, solid mass. But the yew tree dominates everything, seeming a much larger monster than it looked in the daytime. I breathe slowly and deliberately. It's just a tree, I tell myself, as I draw closer. Just a tree. It can't hurt me.

My heart thumps, twigs crack beneath my feet.

For a moment, I consider turning back, but then I think of Noah, relying on me and I tell myself not to be so pathetic.

An owl trembles from somewhere near the church. I think of the owl at my bedroom window once more: its fixed stare, its terrific power. Possibly the same bird. Riding the night, hunting for smaller birds and mammals.

I take a shaky breath, my heart racing as I try to pull myself together. All I need to do is make it to the tree, find Croccy, and get away from this place. In less than five minutes, I'll be tucking Noah up in bed, pumping his pillows, Croccy snug beside him.

I dash for the tree before I can work myself up any more and shine the torch at it. I curse. There's no sign of Croccy. I swing the light around, trying to remember where exactly I was standing, sweeping it haphazardly across the ground.

He's nowhere.

My pulse quickens and the wind shivers through the branches above my head.

Where is he? Did I take him back to the vicarage after all? Could I have dumped him somewhere when we got in?

I draw a blank, my mind thick like cotton wool. I can't remember. I really can't remember. Ripples of pain run along the sides of my head.

Then, like before, I remember something.

I'm sitting beneath a tree, somewhere in the past, threading daisy stalks, making a chain. I pierce each stalk with my nail, feel it soften and give. The air smells of spring; floral and yellow.

She died, I say. *She left me.*

There's a voice. Familiar, but I can't quite remember who it is. *Perhaps she's still here*, says the voice. It's a soft voice, warm, a girl. *Perhaps she's watching you.*

And I want to believe it because my grief is so real and raw that it's eating me from the inside. A sorrow that won't go away.

She left me, I say again.

Who? I ask myself, now. Who left me?

I see Julie's face in my mind, and I push it away.

It wasn't her. I try to think. Try hard to remember.

But there's nothing. The memory fades and I can't grasp it.

The voice says no more and I'm just standing there, trembling with cold under the tree.

But I feel like I'm being watched. Eyes in the dark.

A crack sounds above my head, somewhere high in the branches. I want to run, but I can't because my feet are rooted to the ground, my heart galloping. A bird or squirrel, I tell myself. That's all it is.

I stumble backwards, my heel catching the trunk of the yew tree so suddenly that I cry out. I drop my phone and at once, scrabble around in the dirt, trying to find it.

She died. She left me.

The memory comes again, jumbled, cutting in and out. I pat the ground. My hands find something hard – my phone, thank God. I shake as I negotiate the torch function again, my fingers failing, once, twice, a third time as I try to draw the unlock pattern.

It was my fault. She died because of me.

I finally get into the phone, find the torch and shine it around frantically. I need to get away from this place.

I'm sorry. Forgive me.

The light catches something, and I whisk the phone back to that spot, training the beam on the ground.

There, by the entrance to the hollow, is Croccy.

It was me. My fault.

I snatch him and run.

8

OCTAVIA

Dorsetshire 1866

I return to the yew tree the very next morning, curious to see whether or not Alice March will be there. She is not. I am disappointed but then reason that we did not arrange a time to meet, nor a place. She had told me about the lambs at the farm, and the bull, but knowing nothing about keeping animals, I cannot guess how long her work will detain her.

I consider making my way to the coffin lane and walking up the heath to the hills. I might meet Alice there. But I am not certain that I will find my way to the March farm and what if I did, and Alice still had work to do? What then?

I decide on the safety of the graveyard.

The day is soft and warm, and a spring haze sits low on the horizon. I settle myself under the tree to wait. Bees hum on the air and a robin hops across the dusty ground. I lean against the trunk of the tree and rest my head on the peeling bark. I smell the sting of the tree's sharp needles and run my hands across the ground. A fine mist of pollen forms small clouds amongst the branches and I sneeze and rub my eyes hard.

My head pulses and I wish I had thought to have a drink before leaving the vicarage. But I do not want to risk leaving the tree and missing Alice. I shut my eyes and as my thoughts scamper, I remember an old melody. I try singing it out loud, pulling it from deep within, but when I try to voice it, it comes out wrong. I snatch at the tune, listen as it wraps itself around my mind. It's played on pipes, a lyrical spiral of a melody that takes me to a memory of something that once happened.

A man playing pipes.

An open fire leaping and crackling.

Laughter and joy.

And love so deep and full.

Love for neighbours. Love for every living thing. Love for the moment.

The music stops.

There is clapping and cheering. I remember a woman passing me a beaker of fresh, sweet milk. I cradle the rough, patterned pottery and drink.

Keep playing, I say, when I have had my fill. *Never stop.*

The pipe player smiles, his dark face crinkling, his black eyes shining. His fingers hover over the wooden pipes he made himself. He blows once more and a soft note drifts on the air before disappearing into nothing. I suddenly know what it is to be him, and, for a moment, we seem to exchange places, and I feel the familiarity of the pipes beneath my fingers as I stare into the faces of those listening.

The memory fades. I cannot remember where it should travel next. What happened after the tune.

I open my eyes. Pollen floats before them, then dissipates.

What was that memory? Where is it from? Is it something that happened to me as a small child? It is so vivid, I need to find out. Ask Father.

I get to my feet, a sudden unease throwing my temper off

balance. A gust of wind whisks pollen in my face and, when it clears, I think I see him again. The man from the previous day. The one with the hollow eyes and tangled hair.

Except this time, I recognise him.

He is the man from my memory. The pipe player.

'You!' I say, as he steps away from the tree trunk. 'Who are you?'

Before he can respond, there is a cry from behind me. Someone calling my name. I turn and see Alice running towards the graveyard. She climbs over the low stone wall, her cheeks flushed, her face bright with the fresh air and the run down from the farm.

I raise a hand in greeting, then turn back to where the man was standing.

But he has gone. As if he never was.

At midday, Father and I sit down to a luncheon of pie and asparagus. I am not hungry. I am also eager for the meal to conclude so that I might resume my adventures with Alice. She has promised to take me to the farm this afternoon.

'Father,' I say, when I have allowed him several large mouthfuls of pie and a spear or two of asparagus.

'What is it, Octavia?'

Father prefers not to have conversation at the table, unless he initiates it. He says it gives him indigestion. Secretly, I believe that the speed with which he eats his food is the more likely cause.

'May I ask a question?'

'If you must.'

I pull apart a piece of asparagus and push it around my plate, scuff my feet across the thinning rug beneath the table. 'I have a curious memory, and I wondered whether you might be able to place it for me?'

Father pauses. 'A memory? Of what?'

'Sitting by a fire with music playing. Singing and laughing.'

Father helps himself to another slice of pie. 'That could be a good number of Christmases,' he says. 'We have often sung carols around the fire in the parlour.' He smiles at the memory, and I know he is thinking of Mother. I remember those evenings too. Mother at the piano, Father and me seated on the settee, singing for all we were worth. Candlelight, decorations, gingerbread.

'I am not thinking of Christmas,' I say. 'For one thing, the fire was outside.'

Father chews a piece of asparagus thoughtfully. Behind him, the mantelpiece clock strikes the quarter hour. 'Might you be thinking of bonfire night? When we lived in Saffron Hill. It was always quite a riot. There was a peal of bells, fireworks, an effigy of Guy Fawkes. You were very young back then, but I suppose it is possible that you remember.'

'It wasn't bonfire night,' I say, with conviction. 'There was a man with long hair and dark eyes, and he could play pipes and make the most beautiful music with them.' I want to say that, in my memory, I *was* the man for a short while, but realise how this will sound. I nibble at a bit of pastry crust and keep the detail to myself.

Father frowns. 'Pipes? I think you must have been dreaming, Octavia. We have never known such a man.' He loads a forkful of pie into his mouth. 'Forget it, now,' he adds, through a spray of crumbs. 'It was simply a fancy.'

We fall silent. I eat very little. I think about the man and the memory I have. What is he doing now in Hope-under-Barrow? And the memory – it was all so vivid. It was not a dream. For one thing, I had not fallen asleep; of that I am certain.

In my mind's eye, I see him again, I hear his music, and I know, *I know*, that there has to be an explanation.

9

KATE

Dorset 2026

I reach the vicarage, panting after my sprint from the graveyard. There, I tuck Croccy in beside Noah and creep to my own bed where I doze and wake, my dreams twisted and dark. And then it's morning, and the doorbell is ringing. A sharp institutional-type drill that's impossible to ignore, even though I desperately want to. Ben rolls over and shoves his face into the pillow. 'Who on earth?' His voice is muffled.

I look at my phone. It's only just gone seven-thirty.

The bell lets up, then starts again. Someone is obviously just pressing the button and leaving their finger there. They're pretty insistent, whoever they are.

Maybe it's the post.

Noah appears in the bedroom doorway, Croccy tucked under his arm. He looks sleepy. 'Mummy, what's that noise? I don't like it.'

'Nor do I,' I say, grimly. 'It's our new doorbell.' I look at Ben. He hasn't moved. 'I guess I'll go then.' I swing my legs out of bed and pull on the sweater that's crumpled on the floor after my overnight excursion. 'I'm coming, I'm coming,' I mutter as I hurry down the stairs. The linoleum in the hall is cold on my bare feet and I curse. Whoever is at the door had better have a good reason.

I struggle with the lock – a complicated system of bolts and a key that has to be fitted just at the right angle – and pull the door towards me.

On the doorstep stands a tall, thin man with stringy, greying hair and glasses. He's wearing a hand-knitted jumper with a purple woollen tie. A battered green Toyota is parked on the drive. Not the post, then.

'Can I help you?'

The man looks me up and down as if he thinks, for a moment, that he may have come to the wrong house. But then he offers a hand. 'Moss,' he says. 'Gordon Moss.'

'Er, hi… I'm Kate.'

'Ms Greenwood, I hear,' he says, with a sniff, putting an unnecessary emphasis on the *Ms*.

I nod. So, news has obviously got around.

Gordon Moss clears his throat. 'Is the Reverend at home?'

Of course he's at home, I want to say. *It's only just past seven-thirty in the morning. He's in bed.* But instead, I muster up a smile. 'He is, but—'

'Good, good.' Gordon Moss straightens his tie, rolls his shoulders, as if limbering up.

I realise that he's expecting me to fetch Ben right there and then. 'Oh,' I say. 'Only, he's still… it was a long drive yesterday, and what with all the unpacking…' I think about the boxes we've barely touched.

Gordon Moss tries to peer past me into the hall. There's a light patter of footsteps and I turn to see Noah at the bottom of the stairs. 'Daddy says, is it someone important?'

My insides curl with embarrassment. I feel my face redden. 'Yes…' I falter. 'Yes… it's—'

'Gordon Moss. Churchwarden.' The man half-smiles, edging towards the door.

Suddenly, I'm aware of my unbrushed hair, my baggy sweater, and my pink pyjama bottoms patterned with black cats.

Gordon puts a hand on the door, as if he has some sort of right to the house, as if, by the fact that it belongs to the church, every parishioner part-owns the place.

Behind me, I hear Noah scarper back upstairs. 'It's a churchwarden,' he yells. He knows the word. He's used to it. 'You need to get dressed, Daddy.'

Gordon Moss smiles again. 'Perhaps, Ms Greenwood, we could get to know each other over a coffee,' he says. 'While... ahem... while the Reverend makes himself presentable.'

'Of course,' I say, standing back to let him through. 'But please call me Kate.'

'I'm afraid we only have tea. Of the builder's variety.' I hand Gordon a mug. 'The cafetiere is in there somewhere.' I wave a hand vaguely in the direction of the boxes.

Gordon sits awkwardly on the edge of one of the kitchen chairs. 'I'm sorry for the early call,' he says in a clipped tone. He doesn't sound in the least bit apologetic. 'But now that we have an incumbent, I thought it best that we get down to business straight away.'

I hoick the teabag out my mug and take a sip. It tastes awful. 'Is there some kind of emergency?' I can't help asking.

Gordon frowns. He looks genuinely confused. 'I came here to talk about Barrow Man Day,' he says.

'Barrow Man Day?' I put my tea on the worksurface and leave it there.

'Well, St Hilda's has always played an important role in the ritual. After all, it does take place on our patch, so to speak. And we're halfway into April, already.'

I rub my forehead.

'Barrow Man Day is at the end of the month, of course.'

I sit opposite Gordon and prop my elbows on the table. My eyes sting from tiredness and I'm hungry too. I sneak a look at the near-empty packet of Hobnobs. 'I'm afraid I don't follow,' I say.

'Did the Reverend not tell you? We did mention it at his interview. I'm rather surprised that he—'

'Ben didn't go into all the details,' I say, prickling with annoyance. 'He only mentioned the vital things.'

Gordon takes a sip of tea and grimaces. He puts his mug down. 'Barrow Man Day is vital to this community, as you will soon find out. Without it, we would have ceased to exist a long time ago.'

I shuffle in my chair. Above us, the toilet cistern gurgles noisily, pipes clank as if the whole system is about to burst. I wish Ben would hurry up.

'I take it you've noticed the large yew tree in the churchyard?'

'I could hardly miss it.'

'Well, quite.' Gordon purses his lips. 'It's a couple of thousand years old. In fact, it's one of the oldest yew trees in the country. It's had a tree preservation order on it since the sixties, which has saved it from being damaged on several occasions.' He sighs. 'These days, of course, we wouldn't dream of doing anything to it. We locals have learnt to respect our tree.'

I recall what Mrs Butterworth had said about not chopping it back. 'Well, that's great… I was thinking about painting it, actually. I'm an artist.'

'No, no, no…' Gordon Moss shakes his head. 'I wouldn't do that, if I were you… Kate,' he adds, stiffly.

'Excuse me?' I sit straight. I think of last night. Of the weird, unplaceable memory I had there, and the sense that someone was watching me, just out of sight.

Gordon clears his throat. 'It's just that…'

The kitchen door swings open and Ben saunters into the room, hair tousled, shirt creased. He smiles widely at Gordon, as if they have known each other for years and it's perfectly normal to find the churchwarden sitting at the kitchen table at breakfast time.

'Reverend,' says Gordon, getting to his feet.

'Ben,' says Ben. He flicks the kettle switch and rummages around for a teabag.

Gordon lowers himself once more and pulls his own drink towards him. 'Kate and I were just talking about the arrangements for Barrow Man Day.'

Ben gets some milk and slams the fridge door. He helps himself to the last two decent Hobnobs, leaving only a crushed one at the bottom of the packet. 'Arrangements?'

Gordon clicks his tongue. 'We talked about it at your interview, if you recall. Barrow Man Day is probably the most important annual event in Hope-under-Barrow. Apart from Christmas and Easter, obviously. So, the arrangements must be perfect. No room for error.'

'Absolutely,' says Ben, crunching on a biscuit. He shoots me a glance, scrabbling for help.

But I can't offer any further enlightenment. I give a subtle shrug.

'Mrs Butterworth will organise the posies, as usual.' Gordon looks at me. 'Perhaps you would like to help, Kate.'

Or perhaps I wouldn't. Why do people always presume that women want to get involved with anything to do with flowers? 'I'm allergic,' I say.

Ben smothers a laugh.

'Traditionally, the vicar says prayers at sunset and then we have the reception in the village hall. Iain and Lisa Hall have agreed to take that on this year. Nice to get some young blood involved.'

Ben sloshes boiling water into his mug.

'Just for my benefit,' I say, wincing as Ben bangs the kettle back on the stand. 'Could you explain what this Barrow Man Day is all about exactly?'

Gordon glares at me, two spots of colour blooming across his cheeks. 'Barrow Man Day is a ritual that has been performed in this village on the eve of May Day for many, many years – that's the thirtieth of April,' he adds, in case I'm in any doubt. Or maybe he just thinks I'm stupid. 'There's a procession, the vicar blesses the yew tree, and we lay flowers around it. After that, there's a party where the local Morris side dance. We usually put up a maypole too.'

'And what's it all in aid of?' I ask. I ditch my tea. 'Is it for charity? Or is it an old country custom or something?' I realise that sounds patronising, so add, 'Sounds like fun.' And then I'm unsure whether I'm actually making things worse.

'Fun?' Gordon narrows his eyes, his expression deadly serious. 'It's for protection,' he says.

I stare at him.

'The tree grows on the site of an ancient burial mound. If we do not honour its inhabitant, misfortune – some terrible evil – will befall someone in the village. The thirtieth of April is when we are at our most vulnerable, when the veil is at its thinnest and when disaster is most likely to strike.'

I lift an eyebrow. 'Terrible evil?' I fight the inappropriate urge to laugh.

'Exactly that,' says Gordon. 'Unless we take the proper precautions. The yew tree holds great power. Which is why you shouldn't paint it. Keep away from that tree and keep your son away too.' He heads for the kitchen door. 'It's always better to be safe than sorry, I'd say. Your husband's prayers will protect us, but we all have to do our bit as well.'

I make noises of assent while Ben promises to write the necessary prayers for this ritual. But inside, I feel a fluttering sensation. I know now that I am going to paint it. I don't believe in evil or supernatural powers or any of that nonsense. The strangeness last night was, I now decide, simply a case of being tired and unsettled after the move. In the full light of day, it's obvious and this odd conversation has just cemented the fact that giving into fanciful ideas leads to craziness. So, I will paint the tree and neither Gordon Moss nor a bunch of superstitions are going to stop me.

I turn the spare room into a studio. After sorting out Noah's bedroom and the playroom downstairs, it's the next thing I turn my attention to. The antique bed is in the way, really, and I tell Ben we should get rid of it on eBay or something if we're not actually going to use it. But he says we can't. It might be valuable and whoever it belongs to might want it back. He's right, I suppose, and it is a beautiful piece of furniture. Although having a bed right in the middle of my studio is less than ideal. Still, I have my large desk placed right by the window, overlooking the back of the garden. In the summer, there will be roses, if we cut the weeds back, and I can't see the church from here. Just the heath beyond. Somehow, it makes it feel more like my place. Not Ben's.

In my spare moments, which are few, I work. Just making ideas. Line drawings of the tree from my mind's eye. A few studies: needles, bark, branches. A distant view with the church in the background. Soon I will find my focus. Soon it will come, I assure myself. As it always does. There's no reason it won't. I will go and sit by the tree and draw properly at some point. When I have a decent amount of time.

Ben knows not to disturb me when I'm working and so I spend the time in my new studio alone. Sometimes though, it feels as if there is someone else with me, standing right behind. But there never is. When I look over my shoulder to check, there's just the big, old bed that I want so desperately to move.

10

OCTAVIA

Dorsetshire 1866

Sometimes, when I look at Father, I like to imagine that perhaps he loved Mother as much as I did. I fancy that I see it in the tilt of his brow as he fingers her Bible, with its covers so soft they might have been made from new shoots of moss, and its pages so thin they are like skeletal leaves left after a winter frost. At other times, I catch a depth in his gaze when he lays flowers at her grave and mutters prayers to the ground. For the most part though, he is cold and silent and, at times, even forbids me to talk about her. He certainly does not want to share his memories of her with me – such intimacy is not something that unites us as it might in another family. He mourns alone, and any lasting love he has for Mother is a private thing, something he locked away after she died. Even before that, for all his talk in the pulpit, his love was not something to be exhibited or demonstrated in kindness of word or gesture.

At the March farm, this is not so. Here, love is something that you can almost touch. It oozes from the thick whitewashed walls of the farmhouse and drips from the eaves. As soon as Alice leads me into the low-ceilinged kitchen with its blazing hearth and the chaos of cooking and mending and washing, I feel it. Spring sunshine bursts through the tiny windows, sending patterns of bright, white light across floor where three kittens skid across the flagstones trying to catch the rippling movement of the sun. It is as if I have just arrived home after walking on a cold winter's afternoon and, at last, know that I am safe from the elements. I am sure that if I lived here, I would be happy, always.

Mrs March is kneading dough at a rough wooden table, slapping the gloopy mixture onto the surface, stretching it, rounding it. She has a dusting of flour over one red cheek and greets Alice enthusiastically, nodding at me as if she half-expected me to step into her kitchen this blustery spring afternoon. Mr March – the farmer – is reclining by the fire. Above the flames hangs a blackened cooking pot with something bubbling fiercely within.

'He's not a man for talking,' Mrs March says as her husband simply inclines his head in my direction. 'And he'll not sit there for too long either,' she adds. 'Idle hands are the devil's workshop.' But she says it with a wide smile on her face and the look he returns is full of good things; of cream and new bread, of the soft fleece on the lamb that Alice's younger brother, Edgar, is nursing by the fire. At least, I presume the skinny, golden-haired boy crouched on the grey flagstones is the brother she's told me about. The one she dotes upon.

'Can't suckle,' says the boy when he sees me looking at the lamb. 'I have to feed her every two hours or so. The ewe drownsy in the stream above the farm. Got her head stuck between two rocks while taking a drink, daft animal. She rake something proper when Pa and I got her out from there.' He tangles his fingers through the lamb's fleece. 'We buried her up on the heath. What was left of her. Rather than let her be ripped apart by foxes or pecked to pieces by chattermags and ravens.'

I say nothing but watch as the boy dips his hand in a brown

ceramic bowl of milk and lets the lamb suck his fingers. 'Who are you, anyway?' he says, after a moment. 'You're not from any of the farms, are you? Not seen you before. I'm Edgar, by the way.'

Mrs March tuts before I have time to introduce myself. 'This is Octavia Kibble. Vicar's daughter from down the hill. You'll have seen her at the church, if you were paying attention. A proper young lady.' She winks at me.

'Then what's she doing here?' Edgar grins.

Mrs March makes a pretence of wafting a hand over her son's head. Flakes of flour float and spin in the sunlit air. 'Ask her yourself, Eddie.' She winks at me again. 'Don't mind the bantling, blethering on and on.'

'Well?' says Edgar.

I shuffle. 'I... well, I...'

'We're friends,' says Alice. 'New friends. I've been showing Octavia the heath and a thousand and one secret places.'

'Haven't you ever been on the heath before?' Edgar says, looking me up and down so intently that I wonder whether something is amiss with my appearance. I smooth over my skirt. 'If you only live down there in the village with the vicar, surely you know the heath as well as any of us do?'

'I'm not usually allowed up here,' I say, burning with the embarrassment of it. Mr March gives me an interested glance as he slips out of the door and into the yard. 'I have to stay indoors, mostly.' A flutter of panic runs through my stomach. I have no idea what the time is, only that I mustn't stay at the farm for too long. Father will surely have noted my absence by now and it's quite a long way back down the coffin lane.

'Well, stay and have some milk before you go,' says Mrs March, evidently sensing my disquiet. She gestures to a large jug at the other end of the table. Alice pours two mugs and hands one to me.

It is warm and sweet, like honey, and reminds me of milk I've drunk before. I remember the strange recollection I had at the tree while I was waiting for Alice to arrive earlier. Fresh milk in a pottery beaker. The pipes. The man.

I had wanted to tell Alice about the man. That I thought I'd seen him again. But, so far, I had not found the opportunity. Not with all the running about the heath, peering beneath gorse bushes to see badger setts, lifting stones to find earwigs, and watching shield bugs jumping across the scrub. Alice had chattered on and on, eager to tell me all about the joyous life she leads in parallel to my so very sober one.

I finish my drink.

'Good, isn't it?' says Mrs March. She lumps her dough into an earthenware bowl and dusts her hands together. 'Fresh as it comes, that milk.'

I nod and thank her, shooting a glance at the door.

'Come again,' she says. 'When you have the time.'

'But Octavia only just got here,' says Alice. She turns to me. 'Won't you stay longer?'

'I can't.' I say. 'Father, he... he worries.'

A look passes between Alice and her mother that I can't quite place.

'Well, mind your way on the lane,' says Mrs March. 'Don't slip on the mud and use that great ugly yew tree in the churchyard as your guide. Can't go wrong if you keep it in sight and head straight for it.'

I thank her again and with a promise to Alice that we'll meet again tomorrow, I head off back down the lane. There's a sharp nip in the air now and white clouds scud across the sky, the sun a failing orange disc. It's late, I know that. And I hope I have not missed dinner. I try to concoct an excuse, but everything I come up with feels more unbelievable than the last idea. My fast walk becomes a run.

I keep the yew tree in sight, its dark silhouette knotted against the sky, its angle changing with every twist in the lane. Wet mud splats against my skirt as I quicken my pace and I slip once or twice, nearly falling. A blackbird calls in the end of the day and, as I reach the bottom on the hill, the smell of the heath deepens with approaching evening. Here the lane widens, and I can make out cart tracks and footprints, hear sounds from the nearby cottages, smell the smoke weaving from their chimneys. A woman calls for her dog, a child cries. But as slip through the churchyard for the vicarage gate, I swear that it is the sound of pipes that I hear, coming in on the wind, the melody floating towards me with a story. A long-forgotten memory. A memory that, I am beginning to think, has nothing to do with me.

11

KATE

Dorset 2026

I place a tripod stool close to the yew tree. The day is a breath cooler than it's been recently, and I have a travel mug of coffee with me which I set down in the long grass. We've spent most of the week unpacking and the vicarage is starting to feel… not quite like home, exactly… but like somewhere I could live. For now, at least.

It's Saturday afternoon. We've spent the morning doing jobs – putting up shelves in Ben's study, pasting jungle wall stickers in Noah's room, and trying to deal with a shower that keeps blocking. *Let's take the afternoon off,* Ben had said, after pouring two bottles of unblocker down the shower drain. I'd looked at him, one eyebrow raised. Ben still has nearly a week's holiday before work officially begins, but it's not like that for me. I need to get started on another project. So, taking the hint, Ben's taken Noah out exploring on the heath, while I seize my chance. I let them go earlier, welly-clad and with a spare pair of trousers for Noah, trying not to sound too eager as they tramped off towards Coffin Lane, Noah's dinosaur rucksack joggling fiercely on his back. I waved and promised to sort something for tea.

So now, I have the afternoon to work and I'm looking forward to it. Mug in hand, I make a circuit of the trunk, trying to get a feel of the space, checking I've got the angle right. Gordon Moss's insistence that I shouldn't paint the tree flashes through my mind with a dash of annoyance. I get that in places like Hope-under-Barrow, people don't like newcomers. They think we're ignorant at best and, at worst, I'd probably rather not know. Though I suppose we are ignorant, in some ways. Ben and I can't be expected to know how things have worked in this village for the past century or more, nor understand the ins and outs of some strange tree ceremony. But Gordon Moss isn't the one who needs to keep a career going, who needs to bring in some money to supplement Ben's measly stipend. More than that though, I'm not letting some local man and his weird rituals dictate what I do. Painting this tree has become a necessary battle for me; a battle that I'm determined to win.

I think the tree will look best if I set it with the church in the background. It will give it a bit of local flavour which, in turn, might spark some interest later down the line. And, having completed my circle of the tree, I know I'm right. I will paint a sunset scene with the light warming the tower and casting a golden glow over the yew tree, which stands to the west of the church. Today though is all about sketching, getting a feel, making plans on paper.

I sit on my stool and take a sip of coffee. I splutter. I like my coffee strong but not even that or a double helping of sugar masks the taste of the vicarage water. I swallow and run my tongue around my teeth, as if I can scrape the residue away, then tip the remaining drink onto the grass. We need to buy a water filter if I'm not going to end up dehydrated. I sigh and open my pencil box, then freely sketch a few lines, trying to capture the essence of what I'm seeing. I rub out what I've done and start again. That's rubbish too. I scrub the rubber furiously across the page, close my eyes and count to ten, then begin drawing fresh lines.

For some reason, it's not working. I'm not getting the angles right and the gross taste of the coffee is lingering, stringent and off-putting. It reminds me of the vicarage and the new life I've been plunged into. Our dark bedroom where I can't seem to sleep at night, the cold linoleum floors downstairs which desperately need rugs, Noah's persistent dreams about the crow. Every night, since that very first one, he's woken up, crying about the bird. Back in Hillsby, he'd always been such a good sleeper. We'd prided ourselves on it.

An owl killed the crow, Noah says, whenever we speak to him about his nightmare. *A nasty owl killed the crow.* Time and time again he gulps these words, drowned in messy tears, while I fold him in my arms and try to coax him back to bed, then sit with him until he falls asleep. But he always wakes again. Always. With the same dream. *An owl killed the crow* and then, sometimes, *the girl knows too.*

I rub my eyes and tear the sheet of paper from my pad, screwing it up and chucking it to the ground. I'm exhausted by these night-time disturbances, and that's why I can't do this. Why I can't make my sketches work. I glare at the tree, then prop my hands on my hips and arch my back before standing and making another circle of the trunk. The coffee has given me a headache, which seems impossible, given I hardly drank any of it, but there's a dull thumping building across my forehead. I scuff at the dusty ground as I walk, thinking, planning, imagining colours, shapes, texture. Then, I try again. Branches, long sweeps across my sketch pad.

You have to do this.

The memory clicks into my mind out of nowhere.

You need do something to make things better. The memory crowds in on me, suffocating me.

And then I see her running. Julie Moon. Long pale legs, needle-like scratches from the brambles. Bright red bubbles of blood springing up over her skin. Rucksack bobbing. White shorts, streaked with mud and grass stains, the torn t-shirt, the wild, uncertain look in her eyes as she throws a glance over her shoulder.

Julie. Julie!

Her feet pound the earth, harder and harder. Faster and faster.

Julie!

She turns once more but this time, she looks different. Not Julie as I remember her. Her face is thinner, there's a mole under her left eye, her hair is lighter.

Who—

The memory is snatched away, and I'm left panting and dizzy. I reach out towards the trunk to steady myself. I'm cold, and not just because the day is a dull one. A creeping cold grips me from the inside. The cold that used to get to me at night right after it had happened. The cold that wouldn't let me sleep and which wrapped itself around me in the daytime like a shroud.

Why this memory? Why now? Leaving Hillsby should have been enough to loosen those last tendrils. But perhaps guilt isn't like that. Perhaps guilt just festers inside of us forever, eating away at everything until there's nothing left.

The scrunch of tyres on gravel makes me look across at the vicarage.

A red Fiesta has pulled up. A woman with dark cropped hair emerges from it. She's wearing a baggy checked shirt and a pair of green wellies. Checking her reflection in the car window, she heads for the front door. I watch as she presses the doorbell once, twice, and then, with a shake of her head, retreats to the car. There, she pauses, fingering the door handle, as if she's just remembered something. She looks back at the house and returns to our front door, car keys dangling from her hand. This time, she doesn't press the doorbell, but lingers, occupied with something in her pocket. She bends over. Then, she goes back to the car, glancing all about the drive, as if checking whether she's been seen. She gets in the car and drives away, spitting gravel and leaving only a cloud of dust behind her.

I head back to the house, pausing at the front door, trying to work out what the woman was doing. And then I see it. On the doorstep, right in the corner where the step meets the wall. So small, I would probably miss it if I hadn't been looking for something.

I freeze.

Bright yellow, tufty hair. An ugly, grinning face.

A troll. One of those collectible figures that kids used to go mad for. Not so popular these days, fortunately. Because they creep me out. Really creep me out.

A small shiver scuttles down my spine as I pick it up. Then, in a rush of energy, I hurl it into the nearest bush, before leaning with my back against the door, panting, waiting until I catch my breath again.

12

OCTAVIA

Dorsetshire 1866

I return from the farm to a dark and silent vicarage. It is also creeping with cold, and the smell of damp assails me as soon as I enter the passageway from the back door. As I am hanging my coat on one of the wooden pegs by the door, Nanny Butterworth emerges from the kitchen.

'Miss Octavia!' she exclaims as soon as she sees me. 'Will you look at the time!'

'Am I late?' I say, attempting to make my face a picture of innocence. My stomach squirms as I move away from the pegs and stand still in the gloom of the corridor. It smells of boiled meat and vinegar.

Nanny Butterworth huffs. 'I have had to tell your father that you are in your room with a headache and cannot be disturbed. Where on earth have you been, child?'

'Up on the heath,' I say. 'At the March farm.'

'The March farm?'

'I've made friends with Alice March. She took me to see the farm. There was a newborn lamb who can't suckle and her brother—'

'Your father will have no time for lambs and farms; you know that don't you?'

'I don't see why not,' I say, sulkily. I slink past Nanny Butterworth, peering into the kitchen as I pass her. There's a ham on the table, half a loaf of bread, a cheese.

'He doesn't like you to go far. As you well know.'

I stop at the end of the passageway. Here the wallpaper is hanging off, having been shed by the damp walls beneath. I finger the shreds. 'Where is Father now?'

'Over at the church. He's trying to draw up a plan to renovate the building and is inspecting the extent of the water damage so that he can see to the repairs.' Nanny Butterworth steps towards the kitchen. 'I will bring some cold meat and bread up to your room. You missed dinner.'

I shake my head. 'I'm not hungry,' I say. Which is quite untrue. But there is something important that I must do. Something I must do before Father returns.

I inch open the door to Father's study. Nanny Butterworth is safely in her room attending to some sewing, but still my heart hammers as the door whines open. I do not know how much time I have. Father might return at any moment and if he catches me…

The study is a particularly dark, sombre place. I have only been in it twice before, it usually being completely out of bounds. The first time was when we moved to Hope-under-Barrow and Father took me on a tour around the vicarage, forbidding me ever to go into the study. *It is a place of work and scholarship,* he had said, *of prayer and learning. It is no place for girls.* The second time was when Mother died and Father called me into the prohibited room to impart the news. He on one side of the desk, me on the other.

The shutters were drawn, the mirror above the fireplace covered. Mother had died during the night, he told me. Just like that. Stiff, his face unwavering, no trace of emotion. We had known that it was coming. Death had unlatched the door to her room many weeks before and we had watched how, mercilessly, it had snuck its way into every crevice, every shadow, every inch of the space. Its odour touched everything, it softened our voices in that place, it made us tread as if we should not be heard. But that did not lessen the shock or allow me to accept the reality any more easily. As the tears leaked down my face and my legs trembled, Father sat unmoved, his hands crossed and laid neatly on the surface of his desk. *You may go now, Octavia,* he had said, finally. *You should change your attire to something more suitable.* And I had run out into the hall where I was met by Nanny Butterworth's embrace and where my tears had met hers.

Now though, the shutters are open, allowing the dusky light to seep into the room. The mirror reflects back my image, and I see how frightful I look, how prominent my cheek bones have become, how long and lacklustre my hair is as it hangs about my face in a manner that does not suit me. I turn from the image and walk past the large mahogany desk and towards Father's bookcases. The reason I am here.

He has many books, all neatly shelved and sorted by subject, which makes my assignment easier. For Father has a particular interest in local antiquity and has, I believe, a number of books on the subject. I am sure that, amongst his collection, he must have some book here detailing the history of the barrow in the churchyard. Something that might connect my recent experiences with fact. I scan the great tomes on theology, commentary after commentary, the titles as dry as old bones. 'Where does he keep them?' I mutter. I run a finger along the titles, occasionally glancing at the window which affords me a view of the churchyard. 'Leviticus,

Isaiah, Proverbs…' my finger bumps along the spines, faster and faster. 'Luke, Romans, Galatians…' Darkness slides into the room, but I dare not turn a lamp on or light a candle. Father would spot the glow at once should he choose to walk home this way.

In the failing light, I crouch to make out the titles on the lowest shelves. To my surprise, they're not theology books but a collection of essays and poetry by authors unknown to me. Unlike me, I had never supposed that Father enjoyed poetry and, for a moment forgetting the urgency of my mission, I pull at one of the volumes, my interest getting the better of me. All six or seven titles fall to the ground together with a thump. The noise is too loud, and I look up, holding my breath, sure that Nanny Butterworth will coming running. But when she doesn't, I turn my attention back to the volumes on the floor. It is then that I see that they are not, in fact, books but some sort of false book box. My pulse races and I know that I should replace it at once. The box is probably locked anyway. Perhaps it contains money or important documents such as wills or church deeds. I lift the box from the floor, my hands lingering on it as I make to place it back on the shelf. I pause. Run a hand slowly over the cracked leather. Surely it would do no harm just to look. To satisfy my curiosity. To find out whether, as I suppose, it really is locked. I slide my fingers under the cover of the largest book and lift.

It is not locked. The lid lifts easily.

I hesitate, my thoughts fluttering.

But then I decide it will do me no detriment just to see. To look and then replace the box on the bottom shelf where it belongs. I sit in the dark corner where two bookshelves meet and hoist the box into my lap. There, I open it fully.

I am not prepared for what I find. Cold clutches my scalp and my fingers tremble as I sift through the things inside. Mother's lace collar, an ebony brooch, a Valentine's card, a pressed flower, a kid glove. I smell her scent. Not the stench of sickness and feverfew, but of *her*, before the illness. It's as if it's been sealed within the box: orange flower, thyme, and lavender. At once, I am transported to the past, and almost feel Mother's gentle breath on my neck, the softness of her skin as she holds me in an embrace, and I realise I would do anything for those things to be a reality once more. My eyes glaze with tears as I realise that this is what Father wants too. This is why he has kept these things. This is his box of private memories because, though he hides it, he too loves Mother and needs, sometimes, to return. To wish. To dream. To hope.

I slam the box shut. There *is* no hope. Mother can never return, and I feel a spike of angry grief coupled with the guilt of trespassing on Father's private memories. I should not have opened this box. It was not mine to open. I cram it back on the shelf and stand, breathing deeply and slowly. I return my gaze to the theology books, willing myself to concentrate on my original task. I rub my eyes, scrubbing those guilty, grief-laden tears away and force myself to look at the titles once more. Except I cannot because I am aware that the atmosphere in the room is different somehow. Darker, fuller.

My skin prickles as I turn, slowly.

Father.

He is standing in the middle of the room, arms folded, face burning red. His lip is curled. And I have no idea how long he has been there.

13

KATE

Dorset 2026

'Did you get much work done?' asks Ben, shovelling pasta into his mouth. His lips are stained orange with the tomato sauce I've made.

'Absolutely nothing.' I push mushrooms around my plate. Outside, rain smacks against the windowpane and the clouds loom low and dark, making it feel much later than it actually is.

Ben lays down his fork and looks at me, concerned. 'That's not like you.'

And he's right. It's not. Once I have an idea for a project, I'm not one to sit around waiting for the creative muse to hit.

'So, what got in the way?' Ben spears a piece of fusilli. 'Was there—'

'We walked for miles and miles and miles,' interjects Noah. 'At least a hundred.' I smile, glad of the change of topic, though normally I'd tell him off for interrupting. I don't want to talk about the tree and the less-than-ideal afternoon I've had. The memory. Julie running. The horrible troll on the doorstep.

'What did you see?' I say, leaning across to Noah. 'Anything interesting with those binoculars of yours?'

Ben looks at me sharply. Stupid of me. On walks, Noah likes to carry a pair of bright yellow binoculars in his dinosaur rucksack. He uses them to spot birds. But, obviously, right now, birds are the last subject we need to be bringing up with him.

'We found a ruin, didn't we, bud?' says Ben, before Noah can answer.

'It was a house that was all crumbled down,' confirms Noah. He crashes both hands onto the table as if to demonstrate the demise of the building.

'An old farm, by the looks of things,' explains Ben. 'There were outhouses and a small yard, old troughs, and rusty machinery. It's been derelict for a while, I'd say.' He eyes me carefully. 'I think you'd like it there.'

I know what he's getting at. He thinks it may be inspiration for me. If painting the yew tree doesn't work out. I mask my discomfort with a smile and quickly turn to encouraging Noah to eat his pasta.

'It tastes funny,' he says, refusing to eat any more with a vigorous shake of his head.

'That's rather rude, Noah,' says Ben. 'Mummy cooked it for you.'

'But it's weird,' protests Noah. 'When Mummy makes it at home, it tastes normal.'

Ben pushes his plate away. He's eaten every last scrap. 'This *is* home, bud.' He places his fork down with a neat clink. 'Tasted perfectly fine to me.'

I abandon my own cutlery. 'Noah's right,' I say, sitting back. 'I think it's the water I cooked the pasta in. We need to get a filter.'

Ben shrugs. 'Can't see the problem myself.'

Ever the discerning palate.

He sighs. 'But, yes, let's get a water filter, if it makes you happy.'

'It's not about making me happy,' I begin. And then stop and smile instead. 'Sorry, love.' I reach out and rub the back of Ben's hand. 'I'm being grouchy. You know how I get when my art doesn't work out.'

'Don't worry,' says Ben. He doesn't look at me as he helps Noah down from the table and steers him towards the room we've made into a play space. 'How about some TV while Mummy and I wash up, eh?'

'So, fancy taking a walk up to the old farm tomorrow?' Ben whisks a tea towel around Noah's Thomas the Tank Engine plate.

'Could do,' I say. 'Although I want to have another go at that yew tree in the morning.' I eye my sketchbook where I dumped it on the worksurface earlier. It's open and even from across the room, I can see how bad the angles of the branches are. 'Perhaps we could go in the afternoon?'

Ben says nothing and I can tell there's something on his mind. He lays the Thomas plate down carefully, picks it up again and carries on drying.

'What is it?' I say.

'I've been thinking,' says Ben. 'Maybe you shouldn't paint that old tree, after all?'

'What? Why?' I recall the uncomfortable memory that gripped me this afternoon but shake the thought off as quickly as it came. I'm not giving in to local superstition, and I certainly can't explain any of those memories to Ben. I've never told him about Julie Moon. There are some things you can't tell anyone. Not even your partner. Some things you have to bury deep until they rot away, like dead leaves in the earth.

'It's just that…' Ben finally puts down the Thomas plate, evidently satisfied that it's dry enough. 'Well, you saw how Gordon Moss was about it the other day.'

I think of his warnings, about keeping away, about keeping Noah away. 'And?' I say.

Ben sighs. 'I mean, obviously, *I* don't believe the tree's dangerous or anything like that, but in a village like this...' He closes his eyes, opens them, as if summoning the effort to explain himself. He sighs again, deeper this time. 'This is my new job, Kate. I haven't even started it yet and I don't want to... well... you know, get off on the wrong foot.'

I plunge my hands into the hot washing-up water and watch as the bubbles sparkle and pop. 'Painting's *my* job,' I counter.

'I know that, but—'

'But what?' I bring my hands out of the sink to grab a handful of cutlery. My skin is bright red, and I can smell the water, even over the lemon washing up liquid. Mould and forgotten things.

'Kate, it's like this... I can see I need to be blunt with you.' He reaches over and grabs a fistful of knives, dries them, then drops them into the drawer with a clatter. Then he lays his tea towel down and looks at me, arms folded. 'I've decided I don't want you to paint the yew tree, okay? It's really not going to help my position here.' He frowns but won't meet my eye directly. 'I think that's enough of a reason, don't you?'

'What? Ben!' I shake my head, unable to believe what I'm hearing. 'Be reasonable. How can you—'

'Kate, this is important. My job. This place. I won't have you messing it up because of some selfish notion—'

'Selfish! *Me*? You're the one who—'

'There's a whole bloody heath out there to paint and a million other trees. Find a different one, *any* other one. Just not that tree. *Please.*'

'I want to paint the yew,' I say, my voice low, quavering. I glance over at my sketchbook. 'And you're not going to stop me. You've no right to stop me. Your job is nothing to do with mine. You...'

Ben suddenly lunges at the worksurface and grabs my open pad. Without a breath, he tears the pages from the book and drops them in the kitchen bin, his face scored with determination. 'There,' he says, closing the bin lid and dusting his hands as if he's just finished a particularly nasty chore. 'Paint something else, Kate. I mean it.'

My head swims and tears press my eyelids. I'm shaking and want to storm off and hit out at Ben all at the same time. I want to shout, but no words come. Instead, I stand, water dripping from my hands, bubbles popping across my fingers. *How could he do this?* I need to get away, find some space to think before I lose it.

But, before I have chance to move, Ben sidles up to me and plants a soft kiss in the crook of my neck. 'I'm sorry,' he says, his hot breath tickling my skin. 'But I know I'm right about this one. And it's for the best, darling. You'll see. I just want us to be happy here.'

I'm still trembling, and I let the tears slide down my cheeks without brushing them away. We finish the washing and drying in silence, the only sound Noah's TV show babbling on from the room next door.

'I guess we should get little man ready for bed,' says Ben, hanging up the tea towel, as if nothing has happened. 'He's going to need a bath, I'm afraid. It was a bit muddy out there on the heath.'

I sniff loudly, then wipe my hands across my face. Noah can't see that I've been crying. He can't know that we were arguing. He can't know any of this.

I make for the stairs to run the bath, pretending that everything's normal, while Ben heads for the playroom to scoop up Noah. I'm about halfway up the stairs when I hear Ben call out. The TV snaps off and there's just Ben calling Noah's name.

'What's up?' I ask, as Ben hurtles past me up the stairs and towards Noah's room. There's a strange look on his face. 'He's not here,' he calls back down to me. He raises his voice. 'Noah!'

'He's probably hiding,' I say. 'Heard the dreaded "B" word.' *Or maybe he heard us arguing,* I think but don't say.

We search every room in the vicarage, pulling open cupboards, peering beneath beds, behind curtains. But Noah is nowhere to be found.

14

OCTAVIA

Dorsetshire 1866

'May I ask what you are doing in here, Octavia?'

Father's voice is as I have never heard it before. It is low and steady, pulled tight with anger. Although when he speaks again, it trembles at the edges and bubbles of saliva form at the corners of his mouth.

'As you know, you are forbidden to enter this room without permission.'

'I'm sorry, Father,' I rush. *Did he see me with the box? Did he watch me root through Mother's possessions? Did he see me inhale her scent?*

'I repeat: what are you doing in here?'

I twist sweaty fingers, my mind scrambling for an answer. The box burns behind me, and I feel sure that it will give me away. *Have I put it back correctly on the shelf?*

'Well?' he enquires. 'I am waiting, Octavia.'

I look at the ground, study the knots and flecks in the old wooden floorboards, note where the moth-eaten rug curls at the edges.

'Were you looking for a book, perhaps?'

I look up. 'Yes, indeed.' It is not a lie.

'Then why not just ask?' Father takes a step towards me, and the presence of the box in the room is everything. But then he surveys the shelves, perhaps trying to guess which book it is I require. I follow his gaze to the dusty old theology volumes.

He does not know, I reassure myself. *He does not know about the box. He does not know that I touched his precious relicts.*

'I did not want to trouble you,' I say, looking straight at him with what I hope is conviction. My answer is partly true, although the real reason for my covertness is much more complicated. To explain the reason for my wanting to know about the barrow in the churchyard is not something I can easily voice. Even, really, to myself.

'Well, trouble me now,' says Father, his gaze roaming my face, trying to extract the truth. His voice is stern, and I know that I dare not refuse him an answer.

I twist my fingers once more, this time harder. 'I was interested in the history of the area, that is all. I was in search of a book on local antiquities.'

Father frowns, but I feel his anger ease, the unpleasant atmosphere shift a little. 'And why does this interest you? I would hardly have thought it held much appeal for someone such as yourself.'

His words sting and I fight the desire to protest.

He lifts his shoulders, pushes them back. 'Your time, I'm sure, would be better spent on other pursuits.'

'Please, Father,' I burst. 'Just one book. I will not neglect my duties.' Although what these are, I am not altogether sure. Perhaps reading my Bible; helping Nanny Butterworth with the mending or the cleaning.

He hesitates, then lights a number of candles on his desk to do battle with the encroaching evening. When he has finished, he turns to look at me. 'What in particular interests you?'

'The barrows,' I say. I do not specify which barrow.

'I see,' says Father. 'Dorsetshire is renowned for its barrows, and we have many fine examples hereabouts.'

'I wondered at their meaning,' I say. 'And the people who made them.'

Father looks at me in a strange manner. 'Peculiar,' he mutters. 'They are burial chambers. I suppose you know that much.'

'Yes, Father.'

'Many were subsequently reused. Barrow diggers have found a number of skeletons, and goods too – brooches, necklaces, beads. That sort of thing. Spanning the centuries.'

I chew my lip, thinking. 'What about the barrow in the churchyard? Have barrow diggers ever excavated that one?'

Father frowns. 'How could they?'

'Because of it being in the church grounds, do you mean?' Is there a church law forbidding it?'

Father tuts. 'You know nothing, Octavia,' he says with a sigh. He closes his eyes, then opens them, as if the extent of my stupidity is burdensome. 'The religious landscape of Dorsetshire is quite complex,' he says. 'No doubt there was once a site here of great significance and the importance of the place has lingered on, passing down through the generations. Hence the church was built.'

I stare at Father blankly. Not quite understanding.

He sees my expression and waves a hand. 'No matter. I cannot expect you to understand, only to say that the land on which St Hilda's is built will always have been of great importance to the people who lived round about it.' He pauses. 'The point of interest for you is that diggers could not touch our barrow because of the tree.'

I fling a look at the window, searching out the monstrous yew tree. But outside, it is dark now. An endless black. All I can make out are the yellow flickering flames from the candles reflected in the glass.

'Within our barrow,' continues Father, 'lies a network of roots. Diggers could not excavate it, even if they wanted to. Any man buried there is deep under the ground and, given there are no headstones close by, I doubt anyone has been buried there since ancient times.'

I imagine thick roots twisting under the ground, wrapping themselves around a skeleton, fixing it firmly in the earth forever. I shudder.

Father walks to the bookcase. 'You may borrow this.' He hands me a great tome – *The Antiquities of Dorsetshire: A Scientific and Cultural Study* by Doctor Jeremy Bartlett. It is heavier than it looks and the weight of it makes my arms sag.

'Thank you, Father,' I say. I open one page. The print is tiny, the words pressed close together and the sentences are long, with terms that I do not understand. I try to dismiss the thought that Father has intentionally given me a difficult text.

He nods and motions that I should leave him.

As I reach the study door, the book pressed close to my chest, he calls my name sharply.

I turn.

Father is standing at the window, his back to me, a reflected halo of candlelight dancing about him. 'Octavia, if I ever catch you in my study again, the consequences will be most severe. Do you understand me?'

'Yes, Father.'

'Such is your disobedience and deceit, I can hardly look upon you. You are of great disappointment to me. Tonight, when you kneel to say your prayers, you must ask God for forgiveness, and for the strength to do better.'

'Yes, Father.'

I promise never to trespass in the study again.

But as I turn once more to leave, I catch sight of the box of treasures on the lower shelf and know that I have uttered a promise that I am not entirely sure I will keep.

15

KATE

Dorset 2026

Noah is not in the house. We've searched frantically, calling his name, our voices becoming more ragged and urgent with the passing seconds. Croccy has been abandoned on the playroom floor, but Noah's own bedroom seems untouched. Just as it was after my tidying session earlier in the day.

'He must be outside then,' says Ben, shoving his feet into his trainers. 'Come on.'

I pull my own trainers on, clumsily tying the laces and stumbling out of the back door.

The garden is still and cool, the sky a mottled purple. The rain has stopped and everything sparkles in the last light. Birds chatter noisily from the trees, but nothing moves. Ben breathes heavily, his chest heaving and shuddering as he tries to maintain his calm. He shouts. I shout. But there's no response when we call out here either, when we look behind the trees, prise our way into the fallen-down shed, peer into a cold, empty outhouse, and push through the tangle of overgrown bushes.

'What do we do?' I rake a hand through my hair, real panic

beginning to set in. Because up until now, I wasn't really expecting him to be properly missing. I expected Ben to call, *he's here*, at any moment and be filled with a flood of relief. 'Do we call the police?'

Ben shakes his head. 'Not yet. He's not been gone long.'

'But...' My jaw quivers. *He's my baby.* I can't help thinking about all the missing child stories I know. The headlines. Those media images of distraught parents. The pleas, the ominous updates. The dead ends.

Ben places a firm hand on my arm, all tension between us dissolving, the awful scene in the kitchen no longer important. 'We'll find him,' he says, his voice convincing, even if the expression on his face is wavering. 'We haven't looked everywhere yet.'

'Haven't we?' I glance at the house. At the blank, expressionless windows, then at the garden – the nettles, the overgrown grass, the shed door, now open, hanging desperately on one rusty hinge, the scraggy daffodils, already at the end of their lives.

Ben removes his hand from my arm. 'I have an idea.'

'And what's that?'

He doesn't answer but heads off towards the iron gate that leads to the graveyard.

An icicle shiver scutters down my spine as follow him, picking my way along the overgrown path. Tall nettles brush my hands. But I don't care.

We just need to find our son.

The graveyard is shrouded in shadow and the last of the purple has leached from the sky. I feel uneasy and press close to Ben as he unlatches the gate. It squeaks loudly and a flutter of pigeons rise from a nearby tree.

'What's that?' I say.

'Just birds. We scared them off. The gate needs oiling.'

'No, not the pigeons...' I press my ear to the growing gloom. '*That*.'

Ben holds the gate to stop it from swinging back on itself and we both listen.

There's an odd scratching, scrabbling noise.

'Noah?' I call, softly.

Ben motions me to hush, placing a finger on his lips. Then, he points in the direction of the yew tree. 'Over there.'

'What is it?' I whisper. I peer beneath the dark green branches and, at once, I'm torn by the desire to run and scoop my child up and the need to understand exactly what he's doing.

I take a step towards Noah and stop. A switch flicks inside my head and it's as if there's something bellying through the earth towards me, rooting me to the spot as a memory rushes at me. I rub my temples, trying to massage the deep, throbbing pain that's forming. Then, I feel the coarse material of a dress, a thick, heavy coat, rough woven stockings. There's a smell – rich, dank, animal-like. Sickness rolls in my stomach, and a sense of helplessness engulfs me. I panic, not knowing what to do. It's dark and I need to think quickly.

Screams fill my head, there's shouting and everything is a confusion of noise and horror. Then there's a face. Thin, angular, pale. A dark mole under her eyes. A girl. Calling, pleading. *Please leave,* she shouts. *Please.* I shouldn't be here, I think. I should have stayed away... but I couldn't... I... The face morphs into another. Twisting and melting and becoming.

Julie Moon.

'Kate?' The voice is somewhere outside of me. 'Kate, are you alright?'

The memory dies and I'm standing in the churchyard once again, staring at Noah as he rummages in the soil.

'Kate, you look as if you're about to faint.' Ben has his arm around me. 'Noah's okay. Look! He's fine.' He jiggles my shoulder. 'Kate?'

I shake my head, scattering the remains of the memory. 'Sorry,' I mutter. 'I felt a bit odd for a moment.' I smile, weakly. 'I was worried, that's all, and it got to me, just then. Noah, he...'

Ben tightens his grip, pulling me into his side. 'It's okay now,' he whispers. I smell the familiar scent of him and breathe it in, letting it fill me and root me to the present. 'It's okay, Kate.' He rubs my arm and chuckles. 'We just need to find out what on earth that little monkey's doing over there.'

Noah is crouched beneath the yew tree, raking at the earth. There's soil flying over his shoulder, peppered with bits of grass and moss. In the dimming light, I see the withered dandelion heads that had decorated the crow's grave spin through the air, some already crushed beneath Noah's shifting weight.

And then, I come to the terrible realisation. I put a hand to my throat. 'Ben, he's digging up the crow's grave.'

16

OCTAVIA

Dorsetshire 1866

The book that Father has lent me is hard to understand. Every day, I try to read a little of it but my attention wavers when I look at the dense text and try to untangle the long, dusty sentences. Further, it has not yet told me what I need to know – whether there is any particular story attached to the barrows in this area of Dorsetshire, and in particular, tales connected to the barrow in the grounds of St Hilda's. Why should I see a man on the mound beneath the yew tree who vanishes as abruptly as he appears? And what of the music that sounds so close by? I have considered that the man might be a vagrant, but I have not seen him at any other time, or in any other place. I have spoken to Nanny Butterworth about him, but she does not know of anyone hereabouts matching his description. I conclude that he must be something to do with the barrow itself. An apparition, I dare to suppose. Although such a notion seems fanciful, I cannot dismiss it and with each passing day, it seems the most satisfactory conclusion. But there is nothing on that theme in Father's book.

Abandoning the tome, I decide, instead, to make my own investigations.

I rise early, before dawn breaks, when the outside world is silent. At this time of day, I know that I will be alone. No one will be making demands of me or insisting that I stay indoors. Since the day I was caught in the study, Father has been keeping a close eye on me, and I am sure that he has instructed Nanny Butterworth to make sure that my time is amply occupied. Always there is mending to do, chores to attend to, or piano practice to engage me. It seems, these days, that I barely have time to myself, and I have not seen Alice in over a week.

Carefully, I slip out of bed and dress hurriedly. I wince at the cold floorboards beneath my feet and wrap a shawl around my shoulders to shut out some of the mildewed atmosphere of the vicarage. Opening the door to my chamber, I pause and listen.

Nothing.

The air heaves with a sense of unease and I know that it is because I am doing something that Father would certainly disapprove of. But I must try to understand this thing. I *must*.

I creep down the stairs, pressing myself against the banister to avoid the creaks and moans and feel my way along the passageway towards the back door, where I jam my feet into my boots. I unlock the door, my heart hammering as the bolt slides back. Outside, the air is cool. Streaks of red are already sketched across the sky and as I hurry down the path towards the graveyard, the first blackbird takes up its trill. By breakfast time, I tell myself, I will be back indoors, as if nothing is amiss.

I open the iron gate and slip into the graveyard. A moment of doubt seizes me. I wonder whether the man will be there or whether I might uncover anything more about him by the tree. The church bell tolls the quarter hour as I shut the gate quietly behind me. There is so much about this I do not understand and, as I make my way towards the tree, I realise that it was probably something that no book could ever tell me.

'Mother, help me,' I whisper into the dawn. 'Show me what to do.'

The tree looms, a dark shadow against the emerging morning, proud atop the rounded hump of the barrow. There is no sign of the man but, as I draw close, amongst the rising cacophony of birdsong, I hear the familiar pipes threading through the jumble of melodies. I stop and listen. My head grows dense, as if I am puzzling over a hard conundrum.

And then something shifts.

I remember the man once more, old and bent, telling stories from his life by the light of a fierce fire. There are many seated around him listening, knowing that it will be the last time. Faces are lit in the flickering orange light, shadow and fire, fear and passion. They drink something warm and spicy and eat strips of charcoaled meat and spoonful after spoonful of barley. They laugh, and cry, and, while the food fills their bellies, their spirits become heavy with an overwhelming nostalgia. They know that this night is the last. The old man is weary of his storytelling – I feel the heavy weight of the tiredness he is carrying like a millstone – and, at last, he even lays down his pipes, the final notes of his song lingering, like the smell of smoke, long after the fire has gone out.

Around me, the birdsong grows and fills the air as the memory dies, and I am left shivering under the great yew tree. I draw my shawl firmly around my shoulders and breathe in the sharp air of a new day. Shadowy graves take form as the sky turns a vivid, deep blue and I pick out Mother's headstone in the beginnings of light.

I strain, trying to pick out the melody of the pipes again, but it has gone, leaving me with a feeling of sadness and a sense that someone has touched me from some other space in time. The memory belongs to the man. Suddenly, I am sure of it. Somehow, I am remembering a life, long buried. Buried beneath this yew tree.

It seems impossible but I can think of no other explanation and, even then, I cannot begin to understand it.

I back away. The clock strikes once more. Half past the hour. If I am quick, I can run to the March farm and be back in time for breakfast. For I must speak to Alice. I must tell her all about this. Her way of life is different to mine. She works with the seasons, with the constellations in the sky, with cinders left in the fire and with signs from the natural world.

Perhaps she will know what this means.

17

KATE

Dorset 2026

We're on Noah at once, pulling him back, asking him what on earth he's doing.

Noah's small face creases in confusion as we pull him to his feet, as I dust his joggers and bring him close. 'Why?' I manage. A half-voiced question breathed hoarsely between gulps of air.

'What are you doing, bud?' Ben attempts to move in to hug Noah too, but the circle I have made around my son is too tight. Noah tries to struggle out of my grasp, and I release him, look down at his grubby face, his messy hair with lumps of soil in it and a scattering of yew needles.

'I need to move the crow,' he says. He speaks calmly, with unusual precision. 'I want to bury her somewhere else.'

Ben and I glance at each other.

'What do you mean, sweetheart?' I look from Noah to the patch of disturbed earth under the tree, then stare in horror at the large black bird lying by the heap of soil, feathers limp, body in the first stages of decay, wings now a network of fine bones. I curse. Too loudly, not guarded as I usually would be around Noah. Something moves and I jump, realising that there's also a mass of woodlice, or some other insect, scuttling over the corpse. Fat worms writhe over the soil which is strewn with hard yellow bone-like lumps. I tell myself they're stones.

Ben pulls Noah by the arm. Roughly. Completely unlike the Ben I know. The kitchen incident flashes through my mind once more and I swallow the sense of rising unease. I lay a warning hand on his shoulder, but he shakes me off. 'What did you do this for, son?' he demands. His voice is stern and echoes around the dead space.

Above us the yew tree rustles.

'I need it to stop,' says Noah.

'What do you mean?' I say softly, knowing we need to keep this under control. The tone of Ben's voice is all wrong.

'I don't want you playing around here,' snaps Ben, before Noah can answer. 'Do you hear me, son? You mustn't come here.'

Noah looks at me with his huge blue eyes and then he begins to cry, until it becomes an unbreakable sob where his words won't form properly and all we can do is to take him back to the vicarage. Between the sobs, I tell Ben to take things easy. He relents with a shake of his head, then trails behind us as we make our way across the garden to the back door. We'll deal with the crow tomorrow.

Back at home, we wash Noah down, liberally rubbing strawberry hand gel between each finger, then put him in his pyjamas, and take him to the lounge. Ben sits on one sofa, and I sit with Noah on the other, wrapping him in the old, yellow blanket he used to have in his cot when he was a baby and which I can't bear to part with. I swear it still retains that sweet baby smell and it's as soft as anything. I pull it snugly over Noah, wanting to make him feel secure, and plonk Croccy beside him. I've also made him warm milk with rainbow sprinkles scattered on top – his favourite – and watch as he takes small sips, his face slackening as he watches the colours from the sprinkles bleed into the white froth. His breathing calms.

Ben and I exchange looks and he nods at me to take the lead. I sense he doesn't trust himself.

'So, do you want to tell us what you were doing?' I say, gently.

Trying to prise something – anything – out of a five-year-old is a skilled operation. Push them too hard, too early, and they'll come up with some elaborate story, invented on the spot. And if that happens, you'll never learn the truth.

There's silence.

'Was there something worrying you?' I try. 'Something we can help you with?'

'It's the crow,' says Noah, licking his lips. He has a blue sprinkle stuck to one cheek but, instead of dusting it away, I leave it there, afraid that any movement may distract him from opening up.

'What about it, bud?' Ben says.

'Her,' says Noah. 'She's a girl crow.'

'O-kay,' says Ben slowly.

I take the empty beaker from Noah and place it safely on the carpet. 'What were you doing with her?' I say. 'Why were you digging her up?'

Ben glares at me.

Okay, too blatant. I shrug.

'I don't want to turn into her,' Noah says. He doesn't look at either of us and pokes his toes through the patterned holes in the blanket. I want to tell him to stop.

'What do you mean, *turn into her*?' I ask.

'She was hurt by an owl, and she had six eggs to look after and now she can't do that, so the birds-who-would-have-been-birds are all dead too. It's sad, Mummy.'

'Noah…' I begin but then catch Ben's eye and stop.

'I'm really scared of the owl,' continues Noah. 'He chases me and he's fierce and he's going to catch me over and over again unless I make it stop. The girl's there too, like the crow is.'

'Which girl? Where?' says Ben. 'Is this a new friend of yours? Someone from the village?'

Noah shrugs. 'The girl at the tree,' he says. 'But she's not scary, like the owl is.'

I think of the night-wakings. Noah crying, distressed by his dreams about an owl. 'It's not real,' I say. 'It's just a dream. A bad dream. That's all, sweetheart. There's no girl, no owl.'

Noah pouts. 'It *is* real,' he says. 'That's why I needed to move the crow. So that she can be properly dead like the fox we saw on the motorway.'

I shake my head. This is not making any sense. Perhaps in the head of a five-year-old it does, but to me it sounds like a kid finding it hard to adjust to his new surroundings. I press a hand to his forehead. He does feel rather warm. Perhaps he's ill. A slight fever or something. 'Tell you what,' I say, ruffling his curls. 'How about we get you up to bed and have a story? Then tomorrow, we'll do something really fun.'

'Like what?'

'Like… I don't know. Like go on a picnic, or we could make a den from some of the packing boxes.'

His face lights up. 'Could we have ice cream?'

I smile. 'Definitely ice cream.'

Ben grins at me, silently praising me for deflecting the situation. I pull Noah close with a sigh and the room falls silent once more. While the current crisis may have been averted by the promise of a sugary treat, I have a feeling that we are far from over.

I glance at the window. Dark has snuck in, and the surrounding trees press in on us, as if rounding for a fight. Trying to intimidate the newcomers, I think. Trying to test us. See what we're made of. And this evening has proved that we're not as strong as I would have liked to think. Cracks that I would never have imagined are beginning to show.

I get up and yank the curtains shut.

No, I realise. This is just the beginning.

18

OCTAVIA

Dorsetshire 1866

'Octavia, what are you doing here?' Alice stops in the yard and lowers the wooden pail she's carrying. In the first hints of light, she looks fresh, as if she has been awake for hours.

'You have to come with me,' I hurry. I'm hot and breathless from my swift walk, half run up the hill to the farm.

She looks at me in surprise. 'Come with you? Where?'

'The graveyard.'

Alice frowns. She tucks some stray strands of hair beneath her cap. 'The graveyard?'

'Please. It's important.'

'But why? And what's so important that it's sent you racing up the hill before it's even light?'

I heave, trying to slow my breathing. Sweat trickles from my brow. 'I can't really explain without showing you. But you have to come. I promise you it's worth it.'

She considers and looks around. I hear sheep in the distance, cows in the byre, the snuffle and snort of pigs from the nearby pen. 'I don't know, Octavia...' and then she sees something in my face and falters. Her shoulders sag, but she smiles. 'Well, maybe…' She picks up the pail. 'I'll just feed the pigs their slops. But I can't be long. I have things to do here.'

We hurtle down the hill, scree tumbling on ahead of us, the sky etched with red, splintering the remains of darkness. The air is sharp, and it causes us to run faster, the nip of it biting at our cheeks, pinching our fingers.

'What's all this about?' Alice says time and again as we run, and once more as we scramble over the low wall into the graveyard. 'Pa will kill me if he finds out I've been running around the village when I've work to do.'

I don't answer but lead the way around the back of the church. I stop by the yew tree. It's black and monstrous in the approaching morning. And from close by, I hear the pipes, just distant notes mixed with birdsong.

'There! Can you hear that?' I say.

'Robin, siskin, pied wagtail.'

'No, no, not the birds.' I shake my head, my pulse racing. 'The music. Can you hear it?'

Alice cups her hands around her ears, trying to listen beyond the birdsong. 'Music?' she says, after a moment. 'No.'

The pipes get louder, spiralling around the tree, weaving on the air, the melody threading itself through the birdsong. I clutch Alice's arm. 'Can't you hear it? You must be able to hear it.'

Alice remains very still and for a while does not speak. She is so close to me that I can see her breath escape in tiny wisps, smell the sweet scent of the farm on her skin and on her clothes.

'Yes,' she says, at last. 'Yes, I think I can hear something.' She turns to me. 'But what is it, and where's it coming from?'

We circle the tree, keeping close to the edges of the barrow, at first. I'm looking for the man but there is no one there. Then I run right up to the trunk and look between the complicated web of branches until my head sways. From here, the melody is more distinct and it's so familiar that I can predict its coiling rise, twisting through the needles. 'Alice, come and listen from here.'

My friend joins me at the base of the tree and together we press our ears to the sound.

'I know that tune,' says Alice and she tries to sing to it, her voice sweet, light. 'But I don't know where from. It's not one Ma's taught me.'

We look at each other. 'It's the most curious thing,' I say. 'And it must mean something. It must come from somewhere.'

'The song of the tree,' breathes Alice, her face alight with the magic of it. She grabs my hand and squeezes it. 'A secret song, just for us.'

But then the music stops abruptly, and we are left in the soft morning light, the sun breaking above the hills, and easing away the chill of dawn. There is nothing else.

We sit on the graveyard wall. The sky is a now a pale blue. I attempt to explain to Alice about the memories I have of the man. 'They come sometimes when I'm near the tree. Sometimes it's just the music, like today, but at other times, like earlier, I… I remember things. It's like I'm watching an old man but *am* him at the same time. Sometimes, I even think I see him.' I pause, praying that Alice will believe me. After all, she did hear the music. 'Does that make any sense?' I venture. Then, I frown. 'I don't know why this tree, though. What makes it different to any of the other trees?' I look over at the elm tree near Mother's headstone, its leaves brushing the fragile morning air. If only I could remember things about Mother under *that* tree and feel the closeness I feel to the unknown man.

Alice rubs her chin.

'I will admit that it sounds incredible,' I say, looking away from the elm. 'I've asked Father, and he says I've never known such a man, so the memories I have of him can't be mine.'

Alice pulls at some moss embedded between the stones on the wall. 'So, what you're saying is that the music and the memories somehow come from the tree?'

I sigh. 'I don't really know what I'm saying. I suppose I think they're coming from someone buried beneath the tree and the tree is somehow a channel for the spirit. It's the best theory I have. It's either that or I'm a lunatic.'

Alice glances at the yew. 'Memories from the person buried there in ancient times,' she muses. She's silent for a moment. 'Octavia, it's making me think...' She throws moss onto the track on the other side of the wall. Then her face lights.

'What is it?' I say.

'Supposing you're right...' She looks at me. 'If these strange memories and the music are somehow connected to the tree and whoever's buried in the barrow beneath it, then it must mean that there really is life after death. I know your Pa teaches that from the pulpit an' all, and there's people who say they've seen ghosts... but no one has ever really proved it, have they?'

I bite my lip. *Whosoever liveth and believeth in me shall never die. Believest thou this?* 'I suppose not,' I concede.

'Well, what if *we* can... What if *we* can prove it?'

My stomach flutters with excitement. 'How?'

Alice kicks at the wall with the heels of her boots. I watch as a cart trundles along the lane, the beginnings of the new day stirring. She jumps from the wall, suddenly. 'I have to go now but I have an idea.' She stares at me, seemingly reading everything about me before she speaks, her solitary mole like that third eye.

'The lamb my brother Edgar was feeding...'

'What about it?'

Alice's face clouds. 'She died early this morning. She stopped feeding.'

I swallow a rush of sudden emotion for the small animal. I open my mouth to offer some sort of platitude, but Alice calls over her shoulder as she hurries towards the coffin lane.

'I have a plan. Meet me here at dawn tomorrow. And bring a garden spade.'

19

KATE

Dorset 2026

There's a harsh jangle as I open the door to the small grocery shop in the village. Inside, it's dark and cramped. Newspapers are stacked by the door and to the other side are a few battered crates of fruit and vegetables. The smell of overripe bananas fights with the stink of shrunken cauliflowers, shrivelled peppers, and tomatoes. Tiny flies hover above the measly selection. I will definitely be getting an online shop in.

'Can I help you?'

I peer into the dark recesses of the shop where a lady sits behind the counter. She smiles. 'Not seen you here before.'

'I've not been here before,' I say. I take a basket and absent-mindedly grab two tins of baked beans and a box of cornflakes. 'I've just moved in.'

'New vicar's wife.' It's a statement, not a question, and I wonder exactly how sprawling the grapevine is in Hope-under-Barrow.

'My name's Kate,' I say. Being defined by what Ben does for a job has always been a source of irritation for me. People don't refer to Ben as *the artist's husband* and I don't see why I should be any different. 'Kate *Greenwood*,' I stress.

'I'm Janice,' says the lady. 'How are you finding the village?'

I consider, trying to work out how to answer. 'Good, thanks,' I mutter. Non-committal. Neutral. I grin. 'Still getting to grips with country life, I suppose.'

Janice watches as I reach for a bag of pasta. 'Well, if you need anything, just ask.' She unpacks a box of confectionary and begins stacking sweets on the counter stand. 'Oh, we have an offer on cereal bars at the moment. Middle aisle. If you're interested.'

I'm not interested. But I dump the pasta in my basket and thank her anyway. The reason I'm here is to buy Calpol. Because I'm convinced that Noah must be ill. Combined with the unsettling nature of moving house, it seems likely that he's running a fever which is giving him these strange dreams.

I find the personal hygiene and medicine section tucked away at the end of the middle aisle, past the cereal bars. There's a woman with short, curly hair and multiple ear piercings there already, puzzling over boxes of plasters. She has a pack of Peppa Pig ones in her hand and as I approach, she exchanges them for a set of unicorn ones.

'Can't decide,' she says, looking at me with a smile. Her nose is pierced too, and it suits her.

'Unicorn,' I say. 'Cheaper too.'

The lady assents and shoves the plasters into an overloaded basket. It's then it clicks. There's something familiar about her, and I realise that she was the person who came to the vicarage. The one who left the horrible troll on the doorstep.

'You came by, yesterday,' I say, the words tumbling out. 'The vicarage. I was in the churchyard and saw you drop by.'

The woman frowns. 'Not me,' she says. 'You've got me mixed up with someone else.'

'But I'm pretty sure...' I eye the checked shirt the woman's wearing, the same green wellies. 'Well, at least I thought—'

'You were mistaken,' says the woman, puzzlement etched across her brow. She grabs another box of plasters. 'You can't have too many,' she says, with a forced smile.

I smile back my agreement, inwardly cursing myself for being pushy and getting off on a less-than-ideal footing with one of the locals. And maybe I was mistaken and have just made a fool of myself. She certainly looks as if she's telling the truth. *Think of something else to say, Kate,* I tell myself. *Something normal.*

The aisle is narrow, and I can see the Calpol on the other side of the lady, but the space is too tight to squeeze around her. 'Could you reach a bottle for me, please?' I say, pointing.

She passes it over with a grin. 'You have a son, I hear.'

'Wow, news does travel fast in this place,' I say, glad of the change of topic. 'Yes, Noah. He's five.'

'My Daisy's the same age,' says the lady. She pats her basket. 'Running out of plasters is not an option.'

'Same with the Calpol,' I say, backing out of the aisle so that we can both pay. I motion for the lady to go first. Janice chatters on as she runs the groceries through the till: the shortage of books in the phone box library; the tabby missing from across the way; the potholes on Coffin Lane.

'See you around, I'm sure,' the lady calls to me as she leaves the shop, the same jangle resounding through the small space. The door shuts with a clank.

'That's Lisa Hall,' says Janice as she struggles with my cornflakes. The cereal box has somehow wedged itself tight in my small shopping basket.

Lisa Hall. I know that name. I rack my brain, trying to think where I've heard it before. And then, just as I'm swiping my bank card on the machine, it comes to me. Gordon. In our kitchen the other day. Barrow Man Day. The reception in the village hall. Lisa Hall is organising it with her husband. Iain, I think his name was. I bag up my shopping and thank Janice before heading for the exit.

As I reach the door, it opens with another loud jingle and an old lady with a terrier, straining on its lead, shuffles into the shop. Her face is worn with a thousand crinkles, but her eyes are bright and clear. She looks me up and down. 'Who are you?' she says, briskly.

Behind me, Janice laughs. 'Don't mind Hilary, Kate. She likes to know what's going on.' Then louder, 'This is Kate, Hilary. Kate, Hilary Bates.'

'Pleased to meet you,' I venture.

Hilary peers at me. 'I saw you the other day. In the churchyard. With a man and a small boy.'

'That would be my husband and son,' I say. 'We've just moved to the village.' I smile and try to skirt past, but Hilary blocks the way.

'He came back then.'

'Excuse me?' I look to Janice for help, but she simply shrugs.

'The man,' continues Hilary. 'I remember him from when he was a child. It's the gait, you see. Very distinctive. I taught him in the village school for a while and... well... it's nice to see him back.'

I shake my head. 'That can't be true, I'm afraid. My husband's not from Hope-under-Barrow.'

Hilary pulls at her dog who is sniffing at the dubious vegetable display. 'How strange,' she says. 'I never forget a face, you know. In all my years as a schoolmistress, I've never—'

'It was someone else,' I say, as politely as I can manage. The shop suddenly seems too small. I'm not used to people interrogating me like this and the need to get out is desperate. 'If you'll excuse me...' I take a step towards Hilary, and she moves with some reluctance as I reach for the door handle. The bell sounds again as I open it and I step out into the fresh spring air, just catching Hilary's final musing.

'I can't remember his name, though. Must be getting old. But I'd swear blind that it was him.'

I breathe with relief.

The village centre is quiet. The day is just opening up, the sun now full, the sky forget-me-not blue. I walk past the snug cottages with their low-browed thatched roofs and tiny windows criss-crossed with lead, and head up the slight incline towards the church and the vicarage. I think about my day ahead, the washing I need to peg out, more unpacking, then work in the afternoon.

'Kate!'

A voice from behind makes me turn. Lisa Hall is hurrying after me, shopping bags swaying in each hand.

'I was just on my way home,' she pants. 'But then I was wondering whether you'd like to get the kids together for a playdate. I'm Lisa, by the way.'

'I know.' I smile. 'Janice told me.'

Lisa readjusts her shopping bags. 'Everyone knows everyone in this place,' she says, with a sigh. 'I've heard all about you, you'll be pleased to know. And I presume Noah will be joining the reception class at the village school.'

'That's right. We're just waiting for his place to become available.' Another thing to do. I add uniform buying to my mental to-do list. I clear my throat. 'So... er... would you like to come up for coffee? The house is a bit of a mess – we're still unpacking and sorting things out – but we have a good-sized garden for the children to play in.' *She probably already knows this*, I think. *She's probably already been in my garden. And my house.* Hope-under-Barrow is that sort of place.

I catch a flicker of uncertainty pass over Lisa's face, but then it's gone and is replaced by a smile. 'Come over to mine,' she says. 'I have ice pops in the freezer for the kids and I'm not in the middle of unpacking. It's number three, Coffin Lane. Just on the bend. There's a red Fiesta parked outside. You can't miss it.' She heaves her shopping and turns to go. 'See you in half an hour.'

'See you.' I watch her go, neat, dark hair shining in the morning sun. *So, it was you,* I think as I turn and head for the vicarage. *The red Fiesta. It was you came by. It was you who left the troll.*

But why lie?

20

OCTAVIA

Dorsetshire 1866

Mr Jefferies, the sexton, is also our gardener. Father cannot afford to pay for a proper gardener so Mr Jefferies does what he can, as a part of keeping church property tidy. He barely manages. We have many weeds and overhanging branches and, aside from the roses in summer and the spring daffodils, we do not have many flowers.

As there is no space at his cottage, he keeps the tools, both for our garden and for the churchyard, in a dark outhouse to one side of the vicarage. I do not like it in there; it is full of spiders, and it smells strange, of earth and moisture, turpentine and rotting damp.

I have agreed to meet Alice just before daybreak. I have barely slept and when I hear the church bell strike five, I get out of bed and, taking an old paraffin lamp with me, slip out of the back door towards the outhouse. I'm shaky, worried that any noise will have Father rising, looking out of the window, and seeing a wavering light making streaks through the dark. I hurry. The sooner I get out of the vicarage grounds, the better.

The outhouse is kept unlocked, for which I am thankful, but

the door whines loudly as I open it. I freeze. But the only response is a screech owl somewhere in the black, a rustle deep in the undergrowth. I step inside the small room and shine the lamp around. A spade, Alice had said. The orange glow highlights a multitude of tools propped at all angles around the small room. Mr Jefferies does not keep the place in order, and I'm forced to place the lamp on the floor and sort through the items until I find what I want. A trowel or a squat shovel would be fairly easy to transport and are some of the first tools I locate but, at last, I find the large spade with a pointed end, pushed against the far wall. Aside from turning over our garden, I've seen Mr Jefferies use this spade to dig grave plots and I don't really like the thought of us using it. It is also heavier than I expected, and I struggle to free it from the prongs of a rake. The rake falls to the stone floor with a crash, taking a small ladder with it. I right them with haste, then carry the spade, together with the lamp, outside. It knocks against my leg and the paraffin lamp sways as I pick my way across the garden towards the graveyard.

There's another crash from the direction of the outhouse. I halt. The rake or the ladder again, I presume. I can't have secured them well. I consider going back but then decide that Mr Jefferies is not going to notice anything out of place amidst the rest of the jumble. Instead, I go on, pushing my way through the iron gate, my stomach twitching with nerves as I head towards the yew tree. What is Alice's idea? What does she mean by this?

I reach the tree and shine the lamp around. The first birds are breaking the silence and there is a glimmer of light scored above the heath. But there is no sign of Alice. I lean the spade against the trunk and wait.

Soon after the clock has struck the quarter hour, I catch a dark figure enter the graveyard from the far side. It's Alice. But she does not clamber over the wall as she usually does. I find this strange at first but then I realise that she's carrying something. Something that makes her passage across the graveyard slow and lumbering.

She reaches me, breathing heavily, and when she speaks, the effort of her journey has snatched away her voice. 'Here she is,' she says, hoarsely. Clumsily, she places what she has been carrying on the ground.

I shine the lamp at my feet and gasp. Lying there in the dirt, amongst the fallen yew needles, is a scraggy lamb. Its body is rigid, its fleece dirty and matted and its golden-yellow eyes are open, empty, staring into nothing. Blisters form clusters around its mouth which has bled with a crusty discharge.

Edgar's lamb.

21

KATE

Dorset 2026

Ben is getting ready to go out when I get home from the village shop. Although his new job hasn't started yet, apparently this Barrow Man Day is serious business, and he has a planning meeting with some of the committee. 'Got to show willing,' he says, giving me a peck on the cheek.

I tell him about Lisa and Daisy, pushing all thoughts about the troll to the back of my mind. It doesn't mean anything. Just a bit weird. But making friends is something concrete. It's what we need to do. 'It'll be good for Noah to meet one of his classmates before he starts school,' I say.

I pull my hair back, securing it with a vintage-style clip, and put on a bit of lip gloss. It feels important to make some sort of effort. Ben watches as I get ready and, suddenly, I remember the lady in the shop. 'Oh… before you go…' I pull a couple of strands down from the clip, softening the look. 'Did you ever come here when you were a boy?' I survey my image in the hall mirror.

'What? No. Never set foot in the place until recently. Why?'

I pull a cord jacket from the coat-hook. 'It's just something an old lady I met in the village shop said. Hilary something-or-other. She said it was nice to see you back here. That she remembers you from when you were little. I said you'd never been here before, but she swore she'd met you before. That she'd taught you in the local school.'

Ben laughs. 'Poor old dear's got me muddled up with someone else, I suspect.' He pushes his fringe back and stares at me like he's trying to make a connection that I'm not quite feeling. 'Now, you and little man go and enjoy yourselves,' he says, quickly. 'I'll sort lunch when I get back.'

I pull myself away from Ben's gaze, and moments later he's left the house with a slam of the door. I take Noah's temperature, which is fine, and check he doesn't feel ill, which he doesn't. Then I bundle him into a coat, explaining that we're going to go and play with someone from his new school.

'But I have friends at my normal school, Mummy,' he says, as I pull up the zip on his coat. 'Charlie and Evie.'

I swallow, not really wanting to go into this now. 'You're going to a different school soon,' I say, not for the first time. 'And one of the little girls who goes there really wants to make friends with you. That's nice, isn't it?'

'I don't know,' says Noah. He pushes his feet into his trainers, and I do up the Velcro. Then I pause and give him a hug. 'Everything's going to be fine, love,' I say. 'Pinky promise.'

Noah doesn't say anything but lets himself be led out of the house, down through the village and off the main street onto Coffin Lane. 'We're looking for number three,' I say. But I've already spotted the red Fiesta parked outside a small modern house with a tiny square of lawn in front. My stomach rolls.

The front door opens before we've even reached it and Lisa is standing on the threshold, her smile broad and welcoming. Peering out from behind her is a skinny girl with the same dark hair, large eyes, and a face spattered with freckles.

'Come on in,' says Lisa. 'You'll have to excuse the mess. Hey, is this Noah?' She bends, trying to match his height. 'Daisy's so looking forward to playing with you and showing you all her toys.'

The two children stare at each other and I kind of feel sorry for them. Just because they're the same age does not mean they will get on and forcing them together like this is a bit presumptuous. But we adults do this to our kids all the time, and I figure Noah needs to make a friend here. As do I.

'Thanks for having us over,' I say, pulling Noah along behind me. 'It's really kind of you.'

Lisa shuffles backwards so that we can enter, and we step into a narrow hallway. The walls are magnolia, the carpet cream and there's a pink toy pushchair abandoned in the centre of the passageway, a lone doll with long, matted hair half hanging out of it.

We all skirt past the pushchair, Daisy grabbing the doll as Lisa leads us into a kitchen at the back of a house. It's small, characterless, and smells of cat litter and washing powder. A mountain of breakfast dishes linger by the sink and there's an open box of Coco Pops on the worksurface. Lisa puts on the kettle. 'Tea, coffee?'

'A coffee would be great, thanks. One sugar.'

Opening a tiny freezer compartment above the fridge, Lisa takes out two ice pops and snips the ends with kitchen scissors. One is vivid lime, the other strawberry red. She offers them to Noah, and he takes the red one. Daisy scowls.

'Now, how about you two go and play in the garden?' Lisa says.

I look out at the small, neat lawn fringed with stone-effect paving slabs. There's a red and blue swing, and a sandpit housing an assortment of pink plastic toys.

'You love playing with sand, don't you, Noah?' I say.

He nods and silently follows Daisy to the back door.

'Posy likes sand too,' Daisy says, holding up her doll. She tugs at the door. 'She wants to go and play.'

Noah says nothing and the two step out into the garden.

Lisa smiles after them. 'Let's go through to the lounge,' she says, handing me a steaming mug. 'We can see the kids from there. Check they're not getting up to mischief.'

I follow her into another magnolia room and sink into a comfy armchair by the French doors. Daisy is already in the sandpit with her doll, while Noah looks down on her, sucking at his ice pop. I can tell, by the way he has a hand shoved in his pocket, that he's not sure yet.

'So,' says Lisa. 'What do you want to know?'

I shuffle in my seat. The cushions shift around me like an ocean swell.

'I mean, about the village.' Lisa takes a slurp of her coffee. 'Ask me anything. Not that there's much going on, really.'

'Well, I guess the school...'

'So, it serves the few children from the village and also all of the surrounding hamlets. It's small, friendly – the staff, that is – some of the mums are a bit standoffish.'

'How do you mean?'

'They drive around in massive four-by-fours, live in their posh, converted barns, and go on exotic holidays.' She presses a hand to her chest. 'Whereas *we* drive a Fiesta, live in a bog-standard new build, and take Daisy to the Isle of Wight in the summer. And even then, we just stay in a ramshackle cottage that Iain's grandparents left him.' She sighs. 'No, most of the mums couldn't really give two hoots about the village and what it stands for.'

I take a sip of coffee. It's good. Strong and creamy, and I realise as I swallow that it doesn't have that bitter, musty undertone of the vicarage water. 'And what *does* the village stand for?'

Lisa gazes out of the window. 'Hope-under-Barrow has a long and interesting history,' she says. 'Which is why Iain and I try to get involved in community events. We want Daisy to grow up feeling like she's a part of it. Like she belongs somewhere.'

I think of Noah, on his third home already and only five years old. 'Tell me about the history,' I say.

Lisa puts her mug on top of a neat nest of tables. She tucks her feet under her. 'The land around here is really ancient,' she says. 'Lots of stories. Some of them quite wild.'

I nod. Even though, surely, the whole country is equally ancient.

'Tribes, druids, murder. You name it, we have it.'

'I heard some weird folklore about the barrow in the churchyard,' I say, with a laugh. 'Gordon Moss – the churchwarden – told me all about it. And Barrow Man Day.'

Lisa's face changes and she leans forward. 'There are some things in Hope-under-Barrow that you shouldn't joke about,' she says, her tone quite altered. 'And that's one of them.'

I swallow. 'I'm sorry... I—'

Lisa shakes her head. 'Don't worry about it,' she says in a voice that implies the complete opposite. 'It's just that Barrow Man Day is more than a quaint folk tale to be told around the fire on a winter's evening.'

'So, you – I mean people – actually believe that something will happen if you don't hold your ritual every year. Just like Gordon Moss said?' I realise at once how that sounds. 'I mean, as an outsider, this is all new to me. I've never lived anywhere that—'

'Back in the Second World War – 1944 – when there were blackouts and people didn't go out at night, the villagers didn't perform the necessary ritual – or at least didn't do a proper one. The story goes that they started the ritual and then there was a bomb scare, and they abandoned it. That year, crops failed, animals became diseased, and a child died, falling from one of the crags on the heath, splitting his head open.'

'That's terrible.' I cradle my mug.

'In the sixties, they tried to liven it up a bit. You know, make it into more of a folk festival. Swinging sixties and all that. Big mistake, it turns out – two youths from the village went missing on the heath. They were never found.'

I pull my mug closer.

'Then back in 2002, it was watered down – people had got complacent I guess – and a girl died in another awful accident. The family no longer live here, but the girl's buried up in the churchyard. And in Covid, during lockdown in 2020, Barrow Man Day was cancelled, as everything was that year. We lost six villagers.'

I want to say that a lot of people died that year, but it doesn't seem the moment to point it out.

'I know how it sounds,' says Lisa, evidently reading something in my face. 'But once you've been here for a while, you'll understand.'

'How long have you lived here?' I ask, eager to move the conversation on.

Lisa picks up her coffee. 'All my life. I always swore I'd go as soon as I could. But Hope-under-Barrow isn't like that. Once it's caught you, it becomes very difficult to leave.' She gives an empty laugh. 'But sometimes in life, you just have to make the best of what you've got and be grateful for it. See the positives – a close community, a history, beautiful countryside. And I want to make this a good place for Daisy.'

I shiver, despite the sunlight flooding through the French doors. I take a welcome gulp of hot coffee.

Lisa untucks her legs. 'So, Gordon Moss told you all about the Barrow Man, did he?'

'Sort of. Well, he told me about the dancing and the reception, and Ben has to write some special prayers, apparently.'

Lisa brushes a hand through her dark crop. 'No one knows the exact identity of the actual Barrow Man. He's from the Bronze Age so, even if we did dig up his skeleton, it would be impossible to tell. But legend has it that something terrible happened to him and if the ritual isn't performed, his spirit will take revenge on the community.' She lowers her hand. 'And, like I said, we've seen first-hand what happens when the ritual is neglected. Some people have even seen the Barrow Man. His ghost, I mean.'

I'm really not getting this at all. It all seems far too fantastical. Like something from a horror film. I glance over at Lisa. She looks just like a normal mum. I can picture her standing at the school gates, chatting about lunch boxes, homework, and chicken pox. Nothing like this. I frown. Surely, she can't believe such nonsense. But I know better than to make the point. Her face is deadly serious and her eyes flick to the mantelpiece above the fake fire, where there's a picture of a much younger Daisy and a little boy not much older than her now.

'So, this ritual,' I say, slowly. 'Has it been going on since the Bronze Age? Seems like a long time for a tradition to survive.'

Lisa shakes her head. 'It began in Victorian times. There were some horrible tragedies back then, one after another, and people began to make the link.' She sighs. 'A figure was seen in the churchyard just before something bad happened. A man with hollowed-out eyes. The Bronze Age man. It's like he's an omen, I guess.' She gives a mock laugh. 'Sounds crazy, right?'

I shrug. Though, *crazy* seems not half as descriptive enough. 'The vicar back then, Reverend Kibble, decided that something needed to be done to protect the village, and he came up with the ritual. A way of pacifying whoever's buried there. He was some sort of mystic, they say – very spiritual, you know. In touch with the *other side*.'

Kibble. *Kibble*? 'He's buried in the graveyard,' I burst. 'I've seen his headstone. Next to his wife.'

'That's right,' says Lisa. 'There's stuff about him in the church guidebook too. He's pretty important to the village's history.'

'Didn't he have a daughter too?' I remember the other Kibble headstone, underneath the yew tree. I was sketching it earlier in the week.

'Yes, but we don't know much about her,' says Lisa. 'She's not made it to the guidebook.'

I open my mouth to ask whether people have any idea why she's not buried near her parents, when the lounge door flies open, and Daisy comes running in. She's crying, hard. She dives at Lisa, who hurriedly puts her coffee down. 'Poppet!' exclaims Lisa. 'What's happened? Have you got sand in your eyes?'

Daisy mutters something into her mother's chest.

'I didn't catch that,' says Lisa.

'The nasty boy,' wails Daisy.

My heart plummets.

'Look what he did.' I see now that Daisy is clutching Posy, her doll. 'See!' She brandishes Posy in the air. Her hair, once long, has been shorn. Jagged clumps now sprout from her scalp like tufts of wild grass and form a point on the top of the head. There are bald patches too, pitted with holes that once held her curls. The doll looks like... I swallow... looks like a troll. 'The horrid boy got the ice pop scissors from the kitchen, and he made her ugly.'

I get to my feet. I feel wobbly, sick, brimming with shame and embarrassment. 'Noah... Noah did this?' I stumble.

'He's a bad, bad boy,' cries Daisy. 'I don't want him to come to my school.'

I mutter a jumbled apology at Lisa and excuse myself before heading out into the garden to find my son.

22

OCTAVIA

Dorsetshire 1866

The earth beneath the yew tree is hard. There are roots, too hard to break, and we are obliged to try several places before we can dig with any success.

Alice and I take it in turns with the pointed spade, sending soil spraying into the air, small stones flying. Alice is stronger than I am, on account of her work up at the farm and, after a while, she takes the spade from me.

'Let me do this,' she says. She glances at the sky. 'It will be light soon and we can't be seen doing this.'

She is right. We barely need the light from the lamp now. The sky is a murky grey and the shapes of the graves, of the church, are becoming more and more distinct with every passing moment. I step aside and let her continue with the work. Digging a hole big and deep enough to bury Edgar's lamb.

I cannot look at the lamb while Alice prepares the ground. The vacant, yellow stare is too much for me. Thankfully, Mother's eyes had been closed when Nanny Butterworth had taken me to see her. Mother had lain on the bed, hair brushed, covers drawn. She had been a shell, incomplete. Her soul – what made her Mother – had already fled to the realm whose existence Alice and I are now seeking to prove. Because Alice's plan is this: we bury Edgar's lamb and then we watch, and we wait to see whether she returns. Whether her spirit comes back to us beneath the branches of the yew tree.

'It's ready,' says Alice, finally. 'Lift her, quickly now.'

I do not really want to touch the lamb but find myself shuffling towards the small, shrunken body. I bend and lift her from the ground. The fleece is cold and springy, the legs stiff and unmovable but, as I stand straight, the head lolls over my arm, exposing a scrag of neck. I fight the rising sickness and step towards the hole, trying to appear bold, though my legs are trembling.

'Place her inside,' says Alice. She looks once more at the hazy sky. 'We must be quick, Octavia. We're running out of time.' I lower the tiny body inside the hole and Alice grabs the spade once more. She looks around, expression fearful. 'I'll cover her over. You keep watch.'

But instead, I stare at the little lamb hastily laid in a shallow grave, wondering at the incredulity of what we are doing. I wrap my arms around my chest. The spring morning is still cold and a thin mist shivers on the edges of the graveyard. It is surely madness, I think, watching as Alice sprinkles the first dirt on top of the lamb, then heaped spadefuls. Heap upon heap upon heap.

I cannot draw my gaze away as gradually the animal is swallowed by earth.

And this is why I do not see him.

I do not see the figure until it is too late.

23

KATE

Dorset 2026

I find Noah sitting in the sandpit in Lisa's garden. He's shovelling great spadefuls of sand and dumping it on the grass.

'Noah, don't do that!' I say, wrenching the spade from his hand. 'You'll spoil the lawn.' I pull harder than I intended, and he cries out.

'You hurt my hand, Mummy.'

I push my fingers through my hair, close my eyes, open them. 'I'm sorry, Noah,' I say. I take a long breath during which I decide not to accuse him straightaway. After all, I only have Daisy's side of the story. 'What happened to the doll?' I ask. 'How did she end up looking like a…' I shake my head, as if I can shock all thoughts of trolls away. 'Never mind that,' I continue. 'Just tell me what happened.'

'I cut its hair off,' he says. *Its*, not *her* hair. And his voice is bright, like he's telling me what a great time he's had at the park.

I feel my anger rise. Not just because he's destroyed something that belongs to someone else but because he's jeopardised our first attempts at friendship here. It's also completely out of character. 'You know that was naughty, don't you?' I say. I try to keep my voice controlled, self-conscious in case Lisa is watching from the window. 'Very, very naughty. Mummy's cross with you.'

'Daisy was naughty first.' Noah scoops a handful of sand and lets it trickle through his small fingers onto his lap.

I cross my arms. 'And what did Daisy do, exactly?'

He rubs his grainy hand on his joggers. 'She chased him out of the garden.'

I wrinkle my brow. 'Chased who?'

Noah looks up at me, his blue eyes wide. 'A crow. But he was only watching us play. He wasn't going to hurt us or nothing.'

My stomach flips. Not another crow. This new corvid obsession baffles and worries me in equal measure.

'Daisy ran at him, and he flew away over the fence.'

'Okay,' I say. I breathe, slowly. In and out. In and out. Kids do that kind of thing, I reason. They're basically human scarecrows. And the crow probably would have flown away anyway with the two of them crashing about the garden. 'But that didn't give you any cause to spoil Daisy's doll, did it? Imagine if someone destroyed Croccy. We'll have to replace her, Noah. And, more importantly, you need to go and say sorry.'

'But I'm not sorry,' says Noah. 'Daisy was mean, and she deserved to have her stupid doll spoiled. Anyway, all I did was give it a new haircut.'

My stomach lurches.

'It looks okay, really, Mummy. Daisy's just a big cry-baby.'

'The doll does not look okay.' A warning note creeps into my voice as I wonder how best to deal with this. Not having Noah tip over into hysterics is a key consideration. Goodness knows what Lisa already thinks of us. Tears and tantrums would be less than helpful at this point.

'Daisy also said that our house is not very nice, and she's not allowed to go to it.'

I glance at the French windows where I can just make out Lisa, still sitting in her chair, arms wrapped around Daisy. Was that the real reason she invited us here? Because she didn't want to bring her daughter to ours, for some reason. I think of the vicarage – its cold, dark interior, the horrible linoleum, the dated kitchen, and ancient bathroom suite. I mean, it's not great but it could be worse. A lot worse.

I lift Noah from the sandpit and dust him down. And I'm angry all over again. I grab his hand and march him towards the back door. 'We're going to go inside and apologise, young man. Right now.' He screws his face, sticks his chin out, and tugs at my arm to try and slow our progress. 'Then after that I'm going to take you home and we'll see what Daddy has to say about all of this.'

Lisa is reasonable. More than reasonable really. She tells me not to worry, tries to give Noah a hug – which he wriggles out of – and asks to swap numbers. It's awkward and I can't help thinking I'd feel better if she'd screamed at Noah and refused to have anything more to do with us.

Noah and I trudge back up the main street after that, me reminding him what a bad start we've made, while Noah says next to nothing. And when we get back home, and I spill out the story in a torrent of fury and regret, Ben does nothing to back me up. He's made a mountain of cheese sandwiches and cut up apples and grapes, carrot sticks for Noah.

'It's just kids, Kate,' he says, helping himself to a handful of sandwiches. 'Seriously, you're getting too worked up.'

'It's not just kids,' I retort. 'Noah practically shaved the doll bald. Made her look like a... well, never mind that. The point is, we'll have to find Daisy a new one. The poor girl was distraught.'

Noah takes a huge bite of his cheese sandwich and watches us carefully. Ben and I so rarely disagree, he doesn't know where to place his attention.

'But Lisa was fine, wasn't she?' says Ben. He piles carrot sticks onto Noah's plate. Noah pushes them to one side.

'Well, yes, but—'

'So, it's fine.'

'It was embarrassing.'

Ben sighs. 'You worry way too much what other people think of you.'

'I don't. I—'

'You do. You've blown this whole thing out of proportion. Noah didn't mean anything by it. It was just a thing that happened in the moment. They had some kind of argument over something probably neither of them can even remember now and Noah got a bit worked up.' He looks at Noah who's chewing away on his sandwich. 'Isn't that right, bud?'

Noah doesn't say anything and looks at me for help. He's conflicted, I can tell. Doesn't know which parent to side with, even if one of them is defending his corner. I lay a hand on his, take in his endearing curls, his blue eyes. If only I could believe it was nothing, brush it off just as Ben's doing. But I know there's something more to it than that. I can feel it; something slithering beneath the surface of our lives.

I think of telling Ben about Lisa and the troll. But then, I reason, what's there to tell? If it *was* Lisa who left it – which I'm pretty convinced about – what's to say she didn't find it on the road outside the vicarage and simply presumed it was Noah's? Then, when we didn't answer the door, she left it there, just in case. People do that sort of thing all the time: a single glove on a fence, a bobble hat on a wall. I sigh. But if that was all it was, denying it later doesn't add up… unless she forgot all about it. I rub my head, trying to get it all to make sense. But it doesn't.

Ben gets up and dumps his plate in the sink. 'I need to review the notes from my meeting this morning,' he says, and he heads off to his study without waiting for us to finish our meal. It's the first time he's ever done this, and I stare after him as the thing that writhes beneath us triumphs, pushing to come up to the surface and break through into our reality.

24

OCTAVIA

Dorsetshire 1866

The dawn light is steely and flat. Birds chatter, the pipes begin again; a sad, haunting melody singing on the air, hanging on the strained atmosphere. It is beautiful but, inside, fear has me gripped. I cannot breathe properly, and I dare not move even though everything in me wants to run.

Father stands over us, wrapped in his thick clerical cape, buckled at the front with a silver clasp. It looks as if he has giant corvid wings to match the guttural cawing in the branches above us. He fixes his gaze on the hole we have dug, then on Edgar's poor lamb, stiff and small, in the dark, black earth, only the legs and shrunken head now showing.

'What is this?' he says, his voice breaking the morning. The pipes waver and the lightest notes spin into the air. The cawing takes on more urgency and there's a flap of wings as a large black bird takes into the sky. Father looks at me enquiringly, brow furrowed, eyes sparking. His knuckles crack, a snapping sound that makes me think of the many skeletons laid about us in this place. 'Octavia, I repeat my question, what is this?'

I look from Father to Alice, back again to Father.

'A lamb,' I say. 'From the March farm.'

'Don't be facetious, child,' warns Father. 'That is quite self-evident.' Again, the bones in his hands crack. 'But what are you doing?' He spits each word like ammunition. Sharp wet flecks my cheek.

'We... we were burying her, Father,' I say. My own voice quivers. I ramble, my fear causing my narrative to run like the wild wind, desperate as I am to find an explanation that he will accept. 'She would not suckle. Alice's brother, Edgar, tried to save her, but in the end, it was useless and...' My story loses breath and dies.

'This is sacred ground, Octavia. You have no business digging it up, burying common farmyard animals here.'

'But Father—'

The pipe song swells in the topmost branches, then dives, coming back to earth again.

'I will go to the March farm myself this morning. Explain to Farmer March that his daughter has behaved in a disgraceful fashion, has encouraged my own daughter to follow in most abominable ways.' Foamy spit bubbles at the corners of his mouth. It is yellow, like the scum that sometimes froths on the heath streams. 'It is quite a scandal. If anyone from the parish had seen you... I do not like to think. My reputation! My standing!' Father shifts and his cape rises and falls, thick and heavy. He glares at Alice, snatches the spade from her with a trembling hand. He spears it into the hole, narrowly missing the lamb's head. 'My own daughter,' he mutters to himself. 'Should she not have known better?'

'Reverend Kibble,' says Alice in a small voice. So small that it is almost hidden by the sounds of the morning. 'Octavia and I had to do this. We simply had to.'

I slide a glance at my friend. Try to warn her. Warn her not to involve Father in this. She does not understand him as I do, does not know what he is really like. He is more than the serious-minded academic that he likes to portray about the village.

But she pays me no heed. 'We think we have discovered something, Reverend. Something marvellous.' She takes a step towards him. 'Reverend, can you hear the music playing around us? Now, if you listen hard.'

Father cocks his head to one side, rubbing his temples, as if easing away a pain there. He opens his mouth to dismiss Alice but then stops. The melody rises and tumbles, rises again, making acrobatic turns through the branches of the tree. 'Why, I hear some sort of wind instrument,' he says, with a frown. He looks from us to the village, trying to locate the source. 'But where in the devil's name—'

'We think it is coming from elsewhere,' dares Alice. 'From the world beyond our own, Reverend.' She shuffles. 'From heaven, perhaps. What you hear is a memory of something that's gone before us, but which carries to this day.'

Father's face changes and, in it, I see a flicker of interest. I try to reach out and pinch Alice, to make her stop. But Father catches me, and, with that, I know that I have lost.

He frowns. 'What are you talking about, child? What trickery is this?'

'It's not a trick,' says Alice. She folds her arms.

The pipes flutter and then the melody becomes sonorous, ripping at something deep within me; a grief and longing for Mother that rises to the surface and spills out in a gulping cry.

Both Father and Alice look at me, and Alice lays a quiet hand upon my arm. 'Reverend,' she says, in a low voice. 'We think we can prove that there is life after death. In some strange form, at least.'

There is a moment of absolute stillness, despite the cacophony of birdsong and the beauty of the pipes. Alice's words balance as if on a taut tightrope. I watch Father, see him consider our incredulous claim, see something ripple beneath his severe expression.

Then, he lowers his face to match Alice's height, softens his voice. I cannot tell whether he believes her or not, but I see him glance at Mother's grave and I catch a momentary flash of sadness. 'Let it be true,' he whispers. 'Oh God, let it be true.'

The pipes fade and die. Father closes his eyes, as if in a trance, and words which I cannot comprehend scurry across his lips.

Suddenly, he straightens, the change in him so abrupt that I am greatly unnerved. 'Finish your burial, children,' he says, his tone short, serrated. Alice flinches at his sharpness, unused to it as I am. 'Then you must come to the vicarage, have breakfast, and explain all.'

25

KATE

Dorset 2026

I pull on walking boots and grab a rucksack, shoving my sketching stuff and a thermos of sweet coffee inside. The filter hasn't arrived yet but I'm hoping that plenty of sugar will mask the taste of the water. Ben is taking Noah swimming, insisting that a change of scenery will do him some good. *Go and find some inspiration*, he'd said. *Check out that derelict farm we told you about*. I'd wanted to remind him that we'd talked about going to the farm together but, actually, the prospect of an afternoon to myself, especially after what had happened at Lisa's, fills me with relief. I also can't dismiss the feeling that Ben doesn't want me around. I've irritated him over the doll incident, and he wants time out. Time away from me. Although maybe… I think over the past few days… maybe we both need a bit of space. We've not discussed me painting the tree since the awful argument, but my anger is still twisting inside, threatening, at times, to erupt and send things way out of control. I've been snappy, not myself.

I grab my keys and phone and head outdoors.

As I turn the lock, I think about what my mum always said.

Marriage is about compromise, Kate. You'll learn that. What she didn't say was that compromise could sometimes feel so hard, like a denial of self, of integrity.

Leaving the vicarage grounds, I breathe in a sudden rush of freedom.

Although the sky is a perfect blue, I've bundled myself into a waterproof, taking heed of the weather app on my phone telling me there's a chance of rain later. But it's warm, so hood down, zip open, I set off through the village towards Coffin Lane. I hurry past Lisa's house, scared that she'll look out of her window and see me, and follow the winding road to the heath. The tarmacked section soon comes to a dead end where the new-build houses run out. After that, there's a padlocked gate with a stile next to it and beyond that, the old road continues as a track, zigzagging up into the hills. A sign informs me that this is Barrow Hill. Also, that there's a herd of North Devon cattle grazing on the heath, a flock of Dorset Horn sheep, and ground birds nesting. Walkers need to stick to the main paths and dogs should be kept on leads.

I climb over the stile and begin my ascent, the spring breeze blowing in my face and feeling its way through my hair. It's fresh and cleansing and while I'm concentrating on walking, I can almost forget the niggling worries I've had since moving to Hope-under-Barrow and the decidedly rocky ground I've been treading with Ben. He's just naturally nervous and tetchy with a new job looming, I decide, and Noah's simply taking time to settle. I've always been a worrier, convinced that life is about to trip me up at any moment, and I tend to have trouble believing that things will turn out well.

I shift my rucksack higher up my back, determined not to let my well-honed negativity spoil my afternoon. And the reason for my outlook is definitely not something I want to untangle right now. I just need to enjoy being outdoors, maybe get some inspiration, perhaps find this old farm, like Ben suggested.

And after twenty minutes or so, I see a cluster of ruined buildings a little way off from the path I'm following. It must be the farm. The heath sprawls out for miles either side of the ruins and I think how lonely it must have been living up here with nothing to hem you in. To help you feel safe.

Despite the notice, I veer off the path towards it. There's no one here to see me and I tread carefully so as not to disturb birds, if there are any. There's no sign of the cattle or sheep. I stop when I reach the ruins. The place is awesome, but also creepy and I'm filled with a sudden sadness too. This was once someone's home, a place of work and family, of birth and death, of happiness and sorrow, and now...

Now.

The remains of a stone farmhouse stand at the centre, the windows empty holes, the roof long gone, a tree sprouting from where the timbers should be. A thick door tilts on a single hinge and one wall has crumbled so that the top is uneven, like ugly, stumpy teeth.

The outbuildings are worse. They have been at the mercy of the worst of the weather and have most likely been beaten back by years of storms and baked to cracking point in hot summers. There are several barn-type buildings, cobbles just visible in places, then what I think might have been a pigsty, and in the corner of the central yard, a dark outhouse with a huge iron ring hanging from the wall. Perhaps where they kept a bull or a heavy horse. Bits of rusty machinery lie abandoned in the yard and an old cart, suffocated by ivy, lurks broken by the entrance to one of the barns.

The place is forlorn and the atmosphere that hangs over it is heavy, as if the farm is stuck in time and that any sudden movement will disturb things. I creep around the site, torn between wanting to get my sketchbook out and wanting to leave, to hurry back down the hill to the safety of the vicarage.

I get my sketchbook out.

There's a broken-down wall on one side of the yard and I perch on it and try to figure out my focus and angles. I make a few small sketches. They're not bad. I capture a section of the tree thrusting its branches into the sky where the farmhouse roof should be and scribble down the outlines of some of the old machinery so that I can look it up later. I'm pleased with the way my work is flowing and turn my attention to the outbuildings, trying to figure what I can pick out from the dilapidated jumble of stones.

It's cold, though.

I rub my hands together, blow on my fingers, grateful of the raincoat despite the thin material. When I left the village, it was pleasantly warm, but up here the wind is keen and sharp, and the blue sky has been torn away, leaving an ash grey. Dark clouds gather on the horizon. I unscrew the top of my thermos and swallow some coffee. Still disgusting, even with the sugar. But at least it's hot. Taking another sip, I grimace and decide I'm calling in at the village shop on the way back to get some bottled water in.

Abandoning the coffee, I walk about a bit to help retain some of the heat and consider having a bit of a poke around some of the outbuildings. Maybe not terribly safe, but I'm curious and my sense of creativity is on fire. I find the need to explore is almost overwhelming. Before the rain comes in.

I leave my rucksack on the wall and jump down into the yard before checking out the barn nearest to me. Half of the roof is missing, it's dark, and smells of something I can't place. A sweet, cloying stench. It's also empty. The pigsty – if that's what it was – is also empty, save a rusty trough in one corner of the pen, the skeleton shape of a bucket next to it, only the iron bands remaining to hold it together. The wood has long rotted away. The ground is churned up and young ferns spring from a low roof that is miraculously still attached to the squat building.

The next barn is small and houses several more pieces of rusty machinery and after that, there's the outhouse with the ring attached to it. At the top there's a window with bars and close up, I see the words, twisted in wrought iron: *bull house.*

I peer inside.

It's dark and unpleasant, the lower sections of the wall are black with mould, the setts dirty and slippery. The heavy feeling I sensed earlier becomes a dragging weight. I imagine a bull tied to the huge stake set against the wall and shiver. I need to get out of this place; there's something about it that makes my skin fleck with cold. I wrap my arms around my chest and swallow an irrational bubble of fear that rises in my throat.

I'm just about to go when I see something etched onto one of the crudely whitewashed walls. It's a name. *Alice.* Something makes me reach out and trace the letters. They've been carved into the stone – rough and uneven letters. *Alice.* Who was she? Some sort of farmhand maybe, a girl who helped with the milking, collecting eggs and other such chores. Maybe someone from the village. Maybe the farmer's wife or daughter. I remember the grave in the churchyard, the one beneath the yew tree. The girl Alice who died so young. Could it be the same person? I run a finger over the letters again with a sigh. Alice is a common enough name and there's no way of telling.

But seeing a name in this place makes it sadder somehow. Sadder and more uncomfortable; that time has passed and now there's only a shell to say that people once lived and worked here. I get my phone from my pocket, take a photo of the name, then quickly scan the torch across the wall to see if there's anything else. There's not, but as I go to turn the torch off, the light catches a flash of colour on the floor. I train the beam on it. It's a small object; plastic, with a shock of synthetic pink hair at one end.

A child's toy.

This is not a place for children. I head over to look at it – just to see what it is. I hope to God Ben didn't bring Noah in here. The dense atmosphere is enough to give anyone nightmares, not least a five-year-old already suffering from bad dreams.

I pick up the toy and that's when I really think I'm going to be sick. There's an acidic taste in my mouth as I turn the small chunky figure over in my hand. Lurid pink hair, ugly brown plastic, impossibly large eyes, a wide nose, and vast grin. Another troll.

The memories come rushing in.

Julie Moon.

She had hundreds of them. They graced every available surface of her topsy-turvy, mismatched bedroom – she'd been collecting them since she was small. She'd carry them around with her too, even when she got to high school. Julie and I would walk home together every day, through the woods. A shortcut that all the kids used to get from Hillsby High to the Victorian terraces where most of us lived. All except Julie, of course. She lived in the large redbrick vicarage, just off Patten Road, the neat church grounds dividing her life from ours.

We'd scuff through leaves, me with my navy unbranded rucksack, Julie with a bright red one, several troll keyrings dangling from the clasp. Trailing the well-trodden path, we were involved in the secrets of our own world, the world that had been ours since Julie had moved to Hillsby halfway through junior school. We ignored the abuse hurled at us from some of the older boys, pretended we didn't hear the snide comments from the bigger girls.

When we reached the vicarage – Julie's house – I'd leave her with a painful twist of relief. She was my friend, but in high school, I was changing, and she didn't want to follow. She didn't want to hang out with the other kids in our form, go to their parties or mooch around the shopping centre in town. She just wanted me. For herself.

But slowly, inevitably, things *did* change.

There was a shift, almost imperceptible at first: new friendships, dynamics changing. A new bag – Adidas – a different way of fixing hair, a change in language, swear words fizzing in the air like sparklers.

My stomach rolls with guilt.

I chuck the troll back on the floor and wipe my hands across my jeans. The memory – or perhaps the coffee – makes me sick. I glance at the stake, at the name on the wall, at the black mould and back away with a shudder.

Outside, fat splats of rain begin to fall, bringing with them the heady scent of petrichor. I step out of the bull house as the clouds churn overhead. Within seconds, it's pelting down. I run across the yard to the wall and shove my sketchbook and pencils back into the rucksack. My raincoat is no match for this and even as I hurry back towards the path, I find that water has already seeped through the flimsy material and my sweatshirt is sticking to me with the wet. A mournful moan tells me that the cattle are close by and then I see a group of them: copper-coloured beasts huddled shoulder to shoulder under a wiry tree.

I dash down the track, slipping on stones and mud, almost falling a couple of times as I make for the graveyard and the shortcut home. There, I jump over the low wall and skirt past the headstones. The great yew tree is thrashing in the wind as if it's alive and, as I run past, I have a sudden memory of a man in the bull house. A man who did a dark and terrible thing. A girl crying out, convulsing.

You promised, he says, his voice ragged with panic and intention.

I see his face; pale eyes, thin lips, chiselled features twisted with the force of some dreadful purpose.

You promised. And promises must always be kept.

I will. I will. But you're hurting me. You're hurting me.

I retch and the contents of my stomach spill, sour and liquid, into the long grass of the graveyard.

26

OCTAVIA

Dorsetshire 1866

Father herds us into the study. It is cool, dark, and silent. The morning sun does not creep around to this side of the vicarage until later, leaving it, in the meantime, in cold, miserable shadow. My own room is above the study, and, because of the way the house faces, I never like to be there until at least the middle of the day, favouring the other side of the building until that time. Standing in the shadowy study now, all I feel is a deep melancholy. In the dim light, everything looks so much drabber, so worn and tired.

I dare not look at the shelf where I know the box sits and tug my gaze in quite the opposite direction.

Father strides across to the window and yanks at the curtains, forcing them back as far as they will go. But it is useless. The room remains depressed, the atmosphere leaden and stale.

I think of the lamb, the tree, the hole we dug. None of it feels real and now, here in Father's study, it has taken on a weight that is almost intolerable. I shuffle from foot to foot, alarmed when I see clumps of mud falling from my boots. I subtly kick them under a scratched ottoman.

I catch Alice looking about her, taking in the rows of books, the spacious desk, the bay window with its battered shutters. And I think of the March farm; the chaos of pots, chopping knives and other utensils, the dancing fire, the smells of baking and happiness.

Here, in contrast, everything is austere, unfriendly, and sombre.

Alice clutches at her skirt and, for once, she is silent. A visitor in an environment quite unnatural to her.

'Sit, please.' Father gestures to the two armchairs placed either side of an unlit fire.

Never before have I been asked to sit in the study, and I hesitate before lowering myself gently onto one of the chairs. The leather is smooth and worn and the cushion sags under my weight. Next to me, Alice perches on her own seat, tucks her feet beneath the chair. She too deposits mud on the floor.

Father takes his place behind his desk and nets his fingers together, resting them firmly on the polished mahogany surface. His knuckles are white, and I detect a faint tremble in his hands, as if he is trying to contain some great anger or excitement. He surveys us in turn, allowing a long silence to build between us in the dusty gloom. 'I request that you give me a full explanation,' he says, when the silence has settled under a blanket of heavy unease.

Alice and I peek at one another. I realise that she is expecting me to provide the narrative. After all, this is *my* father and Alice should be elsewhere, back at the farm, attending to her daily chores. *Some of the cattle have died these last days and others are sick,* she has told me, and they must sell the newborns before the strange sickness spreads and it's too late. *There's more work than ever. Pa needs us all.* If she finds herself in trouble, any scolding will be on account of a member of *my* household. Rightly, this is an explanation for me to undertake.

'It is a difficult thing to explain, Father,' I say, my words falling like droplets into a vast, deep lake. A trickle of cold sweat weaves down my neck and I tug at my shawl. 'You see, we have come to understand something quite peculiar about the yew tree in the graveyard. You heard the music…' I fight with my instinct. I do not want to tell Father any of this and yet…

I snatch a look at the shelf where the box containing Mother's precious items sits and something stirs within my gut. Perhaps this peculiarity can help bring us comfort at the very least. The secure knowledge that Mother is safe in another realm. In heaven.

'Go on, Octavia.' Father's voice is austere and persuasive, and I realise then that there is no escaping the truth of what we have discovered. Because any story that I make up will not sound half as fantastical.

I fill my lungs with air, pull my shoulders high. 'It is as Alice said in the churchyard, Father…' And I do my best to explain what little I know about the man and the music, the odd, vivid memories. 'It is all so very curious,' I conclude. 'And Alice and I only thought that by burying the poor weakling lamb, we might investigate further, prove our theory and moreover prove the existence of something after death. We wanted to see whether the lamb would come back to life, in our minds. Whether its memories were still living on and whether we could access them.'

Father leans back in his chair and laces his fingers beneath his chin. There is a long silence, during which time he taps his forefingers together.

He does not believe me, I think. *He assumes that we were committing some great misdeed, some foolery, and I am making up a story to cover the facts of it. Trickery, he called it earlier. But then he heard the music. He* heard *the music.*

The small carriage clock above the mantelpiece strikes the hour with a flat, dreary chime. Seven o'clock. Alice counts off the chimes on her fingers, then stares at me in alarm. She is thinking about the farm, I am sure. About the chores that she should be doing. About being missed and the scolding that will inevitably follow. She looks at Father, her chest rising and falling fast like the beat of a butterfly's wings, but he does not appear to notice. He is staring down at his arched fingers, the concentration on his face like strings pulled tight.

Alice opens her mouth to speak, and I feel her panic, but Father gets there first.

'Children,' he says in a breathless whisper. He brings his hands away from his mouth and I see an expression on his face that I have not witnessed before. Then he laughs, claps a hand on his thigh. 'Children, children, children.'

'What is it, Father?' I say at the same time as Alice exclaims, 'Reverend!'

Father shakes his head, wipes his brow with a handkerchief. 'Do you not see?' he says. He gets up from his chair and walks to the bay window. From there, the yew tree looms large, sending a sprawling shadow into the already gloomy, overgrown garden. He turns to face us. 'If what you say is true, and we can prove it, then we are deemed for greatness. True greatness!' He looks from me to Alice. 'Your experiment in burying the lamb – I presume it was your idea, was it not?'

Alice nods. 'Yes, Reverend.'

Father claps. 'Quite ingenious!'

Apart from the fact he believes what I have told him, to see him so buoyant is a revelation to me. In my mind, Father is always angry and wears his grief like sackcloth, never taking it off, becoming so accustomed to the weight of it that it has become a part of him. He never smiles out of joy or shows enthusiasm for much beyond his beloved church building. But now… the grief that has made him so has also made him desperate to establish the truth of the doctrines he preaches so fervently from the pulpit each Sunday. That and the thirst for recognition.

'This will be the greatest experiment of all time,' he breathes. 'Beyond the greatest scientific minds, beyond Mr Darwin, beyond religion, even. If we can prove this thing – that there is some form of life, or consciousness, after death – then we will live on forever in this world as well as in the next. People will remember us.'

I shift a little and try to look at Alice. But she is transfixed by my father.

'You approve of our experiment, Reverend?' she says.

Father stares at Alice, incredulously. 'Child, as I have said, proof of our immortality will make us great in the minds of men.' He gets up and walks to his desk, where he picks up a leather notebook and ink pen. 'I will make a record of any developments now that you have buried the lamb,' he says. 'It is important.'

Suddenly, there's a knock at the door and Nanny Butterworth appears, spewing her concern about my disappearance. She sees me and stops, mutters an apology. Looks at Alice with a frown.

'All is well,' says Father. 'Octavia is safe. Very safe.' He rises. 'Tell Cook we will breakfast now.' His spirits are great as he ushers us towards the door. 'You will eat with us, Alice?'

Alice shakes her head. 'I dare not. I'm late. I will have been missed, and Pa will be proper angry. It's my duty to see to the bull. Morning and evening, regular as anything.'

Father nods, curtly. 'Then you will come to the vicarage tomorrow at sundown. I will go to the farm and explain the urgency to your parents. For there is much to discuss.' He pauses as if struck by a sudden thought. 'Alice March, you will play a tremendous part in this experiment, a contribution of the greatest magnitude.'

We step out into the hallway as a shard of light suddenly cuts through the glass panes above the front door. A kaleidoscope of colour. Father rubs his hands together, sparking with excitement. I wonder what it is he has in mind for Alice, what part he would have her play. And, as I wonder this, a sudden worm of discomfort wriggles within my stomach. Because I realise then that whatever his scheme is, I do not want to be a part of the success and posterity that he is considering. I only want proof of a comfortable, secure destination for Mother who we laid cold in the ground this past year.

Of greatness, I am thinking nothing.

27

KATE

Dorset 2026

I lie in bed, restless, fragments of the day darting through my mind. Nothing remains long enough for me to grasp it. Lisa, the bull house, the bald doll, the troll, Alice. The yew tree. Julie Moon. Then, later, after supper, Ben went out for ages – he said he was going over to the church but he was gone for hours and came back quiet and distracted. Not himself. I stuff my face into my pillow, willing sleep to come. But it doesn't. I'm cold too. My pyjamas are wet with an icy sweat and sticking to me, my sheet has come untucked at the corner and my pillow is lumpy and misshapen.

Next to me, Ben sleeps calmly, oblivious to my night from hell. He begins to snore, just lightly, but it's more than I can bear. I turn my back on him and stare into the black. Seeing him sleeping so well makes me more irritated than it should. I also realise, with annoyance, that I'm thirsty. I run my tongue over my lips, swallow. But it's no good.

I get out of bed and tiptoe downstairs to the kitchen. When I open the fridge, the bottled water I bought isn't there and I spot the container by the back door, ready for recycling. Ben. There's a carton of orange juice, but when I lift it, I realise it's empty. Ben again. I curse and reluctantly traipse across to the sink. I run the tap, sticking a finger underneath the stream of water until it runs cold, watching as it splashes and gurgles into the plughole. When it's cold enough, I run myself a glass and take a sip. I gag, my head swims, I shiver. I hold my nose and take a gulp, just enough to quench my thirst, then pour the rest into the sink where it pools, not draining. I swear. The shower upstairs is still blocking too and we're spending a small fortune on Mr Muscle. And now it looks like there's a similar problem down here.

I bang my glass on the draining board. We'll have to sort it in the morning: it's more than I can cope with at this hour. My bad mood worsening, I head back upstairs and get into bed, but Ben's snoring is louder and, as I try and get comfortable, I know there's no way I'll be able to sleep. I count to ten, trying to calm myself, but the thoughts come back, this time twisting, running one into another as if they could make sense, if only I could unravel them. I shuffle, flip my pillow over, tug the duvet over my shoulders. I can taste the foulness of the water on my tongue and sense the edges of a headache.

In the end, I get out of bed again and make for the studio. I'll do some work, instead. Check out the sketches I made at the farm, maybe sketch out the yew tree again from memory. I'm still determined to paint it and will broach the subject again when I'm not feeling so angry about it. I sit at my desk and wrap the massive woollen blanket I keep on the old bed around my shoulders. The stark light in the studio makes the darkness beyond the window complete. Although the rain's stopped, there's no moon and it's impossible to make anything out. The farm is there somewhere, in that endless dark.

I pull out the sketches, wondering about Alice. Did she live in the village or up there in that remote, black place? Did she love it or… I remember the bull house… or not?

I work solidly, forgetting my inability to sleep as I sort my drawings and work on the tone, colour and medium for the yew tree. Acrylics, I think. I work on and on until a heaviness comes over me and my head dulls. I no longer hear Ben snoring from our bedroom and…

I wake suddenly, stiff, hunched over my desk, my neck pulled tight. I have no idea what the time is, but I'm exhausted. The harsh light scrapes at my eyeballs as I look about me, my head thumps, and the rancid taste of the water in my mouth is worse than before. I tug on the blanket and stumble across to the old bed. The need to go back to sleep is overwhelming and I don't want to risk being disturbed by Ben again tonight. I flick off the light and curl myself in a tight ball on the mattress. It's comfortable and I find my eyes closing once more, my mind thickening and the deep silence of the night wrapping me in its arms.

28

OCTAVIA

Dorsetshire 1866

Farmer March is proud that the Reverend wants Alice to help with an experiment, even if he does not know the nature of it.

'He says it could be the making of me,' says Alice as I admit her into the vicarage the evening after we buried the lamb. 'I don't know what Pa meant, mind. Making of me? It is a queer phrase, don't you think? But at least it takes me away from the farm. Things are bad up there.'

'What do you mean?' I say. 'Bad?'

'The cattle are still dying. They're rife with fever, their eyes and noses are leaking something nasty and their breathing is too fast. They smell something awful too. Cattle plague, it's called.' Alice bites her lip. 'Pa's really worried, even if he's trying not to show it. But we can't sell them at market for milk or meat. No one would buy them.'

'Can it not be prevented?' I ask.

Alice sighs. 'We're trying to keep the bad ones away from the healthy but it's not easy. The only thing left is to slaughter them.'

I say nothing as I cannot think of any word fit to soothe my friend. Instead, I take Alice's bonnet and shawl and hang them on the hatstand. They smell of woodsmoke and hay. My stomach is rolling with nerves, and I have barely slept, my thoughts occupied with imagining what Father's plan might be and how we might assist. I know that he worked in his study long into the night, for I stood at the window in my bedchamber for a time, unable to sleep, and could see the reflection of the light from down below, spilling onto the grass and tinting it with yellow. Then, later on, I heard the back door open and shut, and when I tiptoed once more to my window and peeked through the curtains, I saw a lamplight weaving its way across the lawn towards the graveyard, the glow from it highlighting Father's black coat and hat.

At that point, I had lit a candle and snuck down into the study. The desk there was covered in books and sheets of paper bearing Father's thin, spidery writing. I did not dare stay long to read it in full but saw that he was writing a tract, or maybe a sermon, on the topic of the raising of the widow's son. There were words scored through, great ink blots in the margins, the letters not fully formed in places, florid in others. I had drawn myself away and taken, once more, the secret box of Mother's things from the shelf. One by one, I had lifted them out – the collar, the brooch, the Valentine's card, the flower, the glove. I had pressed each to my lips with a soft kiss. *You are not lost to me, Mother,* I had whispered. And I had prayed that she was safe in the place that we all dreamed of. The place we sought to prove existed.

Now, Alice and I look at one another in the drab hallway. The light outside is already fading, Nanny Butterworth has been instructed by Father to remain upstairs, and as I lead Alice towards the study, I sense the covertness of our operation and feel the hairs lift on the back of my neck.

Father is waiting for us in the study and calls for us to enter after I had knocked only once. He seizes upon Alice at once. 'Sit, sit, sit,' he hurries, almost pushing her into the armchair. 'You too,' he adds, without looking at me.

We do as bidden.

'It is quite remarkable,' he says. 'Quite extraordinary.'

'What is, Reverend?' says Alice.

Father does not sit himself, but paces the study, from one end to the other in great, even strides. 'I went to the graveyard last night,' he says. 'There, I spent a considerable amount of time in the company of strange entities.' He pauses, his face alight. 'The farm, the farmhouse...' He nods at Alice, resumes his pacing. 'Your brother...'

'What of him, Reverend?'

'All of this, and more, seen through the eyes of a meek lamb.'

Alice and I exchange a glance.

'You saw the lamb's memories, Father?' I ask.

'They were brief and unclear, but yes. And then...' He swivels to pace in the other direction. 'Then, there was the most beautiful music, as before.'

'The man!' I exclaim. 'The pipe player.'

'He was a good man who loved his people.' Father stops striding, brings his hands together, as if in prayer. 'This is the greatest miracle of all time,' he says, softly. 'We have been blessed that such flowers from heaven have bloomed here. *Here* in Hope-under-Barrow.'

A flame of excitement sparks within me. 'So, what do we do, Father?'

'That, my child, is an exceedingly good question. If the knowledge of this thing is broadcast crassly, then we will surely become the subject of unwelcome attention. So, I propose, in the first instance, that we conduct further experiments. In order to be sure and to understand this miracle, as far as we are able.' He clears his throat. 'Experimentation is key to understanding.'

I frown. 'What do you—'

'Small mammals, birds, insects, if we must. I will write up our findings in a scientific manner and then, at a suitable time, convey them to the congregation so that all here may know how blessed we are.' He smooths his shirt and pulls himself tall. 'From there… well, that is the distant future… but it is likely that knowledge will spread far and wide. When we are ready.'

'And should we, for now, keep mum?' asks Alice. 'My ma and pa—'

'We must!' says Father, his voice suddenly loud and filled with urgency. 'Until the two of you stumbled upon its secrets, no one paid much attention to that old yew tree. It is in a dark, unpleasant part of the graveyard, overrun by nettles and brambles. And it will remain that way while we conduct our research. In the meantime, we must snare rabbits and use them for our experiments.'

I think of fur matted with blood, broken legs snapped and caught at abnormal angles, dull, lifeless eyes. When the game are strung up in the kitchen, I always have to scurry by, afraid of their cold, empty shells, and of the sadness hanging about them.

'On the heath, there are plenty of rabbits,' continues Father. 'Jefferies will show you how to set a trap.'

'I know already,' offers Alice.

Father nods. 'Of course, of course.'

Something uncomfortable shifts in my stomach and I feel my supper rise. I swallow, tasting a sourness on my tongue. 'And then?'

Father smiles, his eyes gleaming as he surveys us both. 'Then, we will move on to greater things.'

Extract from a sermon given
by the Reverend Phineas Kibble,
April 1866.

The text for today's homily is taken from the Gospel according to Saint Luke, chapter seven.

'And when the Lord saw her, he had compassion on her, and said unto her, weep not.

'And he came and touched the bier: and they that bare him stood still. And he said, young man, I say unto thee, arise. And he that was dead sat up, and began to speak...'

... The miracles of Jesus, such as the raising of the widow's son in Luke, simply demonstrate the existence of laws of nature that are yet undiscovered or understood.

No phenomena has been disrupted here.

By bringing the dead back to life, Jesus does not violate natural law or science, but illustrates a hidden truth that man is not yet privy to.

Yet it is a truth, my friends, that I am surely beginning to understand.

Here, in Hope-under-Barrow, laws of nature yet unknown to men are making themselves known to me.

29

KATE

Dorset 2026

Lying in the old bed in the studio, I dream.

The woods on the way home from school. Laughter. The laughter of summer and freedom. Of not caring.

But something changes and the laughter becomes hollow, insincere. Scornful.

Then I'm running. Something or someone is chasing me. The atmosphere darkens and I look up to see giant crows swooping down from the trees, their beaks open, their eyes glowing red, like sirens. One of them has Noah clasped in its claws. He screams for me and before I can do anything, his body slackens and drops, falling into oblivion.

I run to the place where he should be. But Julie is standing there, her arms outstretched, mouthing something that I can't make out.

Julie and me. Me and Julie. Breaking.

Her body in the woods.

At the foot of the giant oak tree.

Broken neck, limbs splayed at freakish angles.

I see it now and cannot turn away.

I grind my teeth, looking for a way out. There is nowhere to go.

She fell, a voice calls from behind me. *Such a tragedy*. The voice sneers and the laughter comes again. *No one's fault*.

I know the truth, and it twists in my belly, the pain sharp and unyielding.

There's blackness and shouting. The others at school, mocking, taunting. They don't want to know me anymore. They yell at me, faces pushed up close, spit hitting my cheeks.

Then Julie's face rushes at me in the dark, mouth open in a scream, lips pulled back, gums tight and pink, blood running from her nose. Eyes flaring with shock.

Then eyes not seeing. Blindness. The end.

I wake, the memories and sensations fresh, pulsing through my veins, pulling me back. Back in time.

I pant into the black, afraid, my face wet with tears.

Afraid because it is all so real again and there's no one I can tell.

30

OCTAVIA

Dorsetshire 1866

We use a steel-jaw trap, borrowed from the March farm, and set it at the mouth of one of the rabbit burrows on the heath. Then, in the cold, blue dawn, filled with anticipation and dread, Father and I make our way up the hill to unearth our prey. No one must see us, and we hurry, hats pulled low, early morning stinging our faces as we run to beat the blood-red sunbreak. Father's strides are long, and I am out of breath keeping up, wanting, but not daring to tell him to slow down. Alice is not with us, having her early morning duties up at the farm, saving things from getting any worse. *But she will play a part,* Father assures me. *She will play a part in this greatness.*

It is the most time Father and I have ever spent together alone. Father mutters as we journey, not to me – to God perhaps, to himself more likely, and sometimes he recites long passages of scripture. The miracles of Jesus. *Transgression. Resurrection. Truth.* I might almost be a party to one of his sermons in church, except that I am caught tight by a nervous, boiling excitement instead of tedium. A fascination and dread of what will come next.

When we reach the trap, Father makes me look first. As if it is an honour.

I dare not object, but I hate it. Afraid of what I might see. I draw close, my pulse thrashing in my ears.

There is a rabbit there, no more than a kit, a fuzz of grey.

My mouth fills with saliva and I swallow, feeling almost that I might choke. I pull my bonnet down low over my brow and turn to Father. He stares at me, eyes of steel, reading the meaning in my reticence.

'Step back, Octavia. Scan the coffin lane to make sure we are not seen.'

I look up and down the track, arms held about my chest, furtive glances everywhere. It gives me something to do while Father unlocks the trap.

Sorry, I whisper, when Father frees the rabbit because I cannot. He places the lifeless body on the ground and sets the trap again, then lifts the rabbit in his careful hands. And as he carries it down to the graveyard for its poor burial, I tell myself that this is all for Mother. To reach an understanding of what has happened to her since she departed this life could change everything.

We bury the small rabbit beneath the yew tree. Father has dug the lamb up and moved her – I am not sure where – and her hole becomes a vast tomb for its latest occupant. *One subject at a time,* he explains. *Too many animals buried beneath this tree could result in confusion.*

Then, when it is done and the day draws long, Alice joins me, and we watch and wait and listen. Sometimes we hear the pipes, sometimes I remember the heat of the open fire and the taste of sweet milk. At other times, there is nothing, not even a ghost of something long forgotten.

And then, a whisper of a memory comes to me: a nest, deep in the earth, moving, squirming, eyes seeing for the first time, the confusion of life and the beauty of existence.

Straightaway, I run shrieking to the vicarage to report to Father. I burst into his study, knocking only twice and not waiting for admittance, eager to share the results of our experiment. The evening sun streams through the window as I babble and tell my story with much embellishment. 'I remembered,' I shout. 'I remembered those first days. I did, Father, I did!'

Father greets me with less enthusiasm and says that he will chart my experience, dig up the kit and leave it for the foxes.

'We will then experiment once again, child.'

My hands flop. 'But is this not enough, Father?' I say. 'What with the pipes and the man, the lamb, and now the rabbit. Surely, we have proof enough?'

Father shakes his head. 'Not in the age we live in, Octavia. These days, everything must be proven to the very limit, everything must be tested, the truth sought out and rigorously challenged. What we have discovered so far would convince no one.'

I frown. 'But if we let people experience this for themselves...'

'And become the laughing stock of Dorsetshire. I should think not.' Father picks up his pen. 'Our theory must past the harshest of tests before we place it before the eyes of the world.'

My spirits fade as I realise then the nature of Father's project.

He writes down all that I say in his notebook and dismisses me.

After that, setting traps becomes a part of everyday life.

Sometimes, the animal has managed to escape, wringing itself free from the trap and leaving behind a bloodied paw, torn sinews, and gristle. But most of the time, we find a stiff, lifeless body, usually a rabbit, though sometimes a stoat or a weasel, and the experiment begins again.

I want to ask Father more about it, when it will stop, when

we will have experimented enough. 'Soon...' I say to Alice one afternoon as we sit beneath the yew tree, a fresh burial at our feet '... soon there will be no rabbits left up on the heath.' Alice laughs but I see something in her eyes that makes me uneasy. 'What is it?' I say.

Alice unties the knot on her bonnet and lays the hat at her side. Her hair flows, loose and golden. 'Have you thought what your father might do when he's finished killing all these animals?'

I frown. 'He will write up the experiment,' I say, decisively. 'It will be the greatest step that mankind has ever taken, he believes. And it will prove...' My eyes roam the churchyard, settling on Mother's grave. 'It will prove that something lives on after death. Why, already, he has begun to speak of the tree from the pulpit, hinting that our understanding of the laws of nature is limited. And once he has the truth...'

Alice plays with the fraying edge of her bonnet ribbon. 'If you say so.' She looks at me with a frown. 'These days, I'm not so sure.'

'But...' I gesture around me, at the shaded area under the yew tree. On the breeze, I hear pipe music. 'Every day – or nearly every day – we remember things. Things that have never even happened to us.'

'But that only tells us something about this place. This tree.' She stands, grabbing her bonnet, a strange look on her face. 'I don't think it really proves anything. And I want to know more. Because there *must* be more. I want to know where my brothers who have passed over are and whether I can talk with them. Maybe they can see more from the spirit world. Maybe they can show us what to do to recover the farm. Spirits must surely be able to see more than we can, they must know things, see the future and the like.' She settles the bonnet atop her head and stands. 'Octavia, your father needs to do something more.'

'Like what?' I call after her.

But Alice does not answer, and I watch as she runs, then leaps over the churchyard wall, boots scuffing the stone, bonnet strings flapping in the breeze.

31

KATE

Dorset 2026

Ben flings his phone on the sofa. Despite having had a better night's sleep than me, he looks tired. Bags hang beneath his eyes, and his skin has taken on a greyish hue.

'The drain guys will be round at eleven,' he says. 'Are you okay to see to them?'

'Sure.' I nibble on a piece of toast, spread thinly with Marmite, but I'm not really hungry. All I can think about is Julie Moon. The trolls hanging from her rucksack with their crazy tufty hair – one purple, one blue, one yellow. She lost the yellow one in the end. The day some of the boys in the year above chased us through the woods, hurling spit balls at our backs. Later, we went back to try and look for it, hunting through the dead leaves, beneath the trees, in the undergrowth. But we never found it.

Ben rolls his shirt sleeves down. He's wearing a clerical shirt today. First time since we've moved to Hope-under-Barrow.

'Where are you going?' I say.

Ben digs his hands into his pockets. He doesn't look at me. 'Lisa and Iain Hall. I'm going round to their place.'

My stomach rolls. 'Is this about yesterday? Are they really upset?' I think of the doll, Daisy crying, inconsolable.

Ben shakes his head. 'Nothing like that,' he says. 'It's about Barrow Man Day. They want to talk about the reception in the village hall.'

'What's that got to do with you?'

'I'm not entirely sure. Iain called this morning. I think everyone just wants to make sure I'm up to speed with it all. This day is really important to them.'

I recall the shrill ring of Ben's mobile breaking through my sleep. After my nightmare, I'd fallen into a deep dreamless state, and it had been long past daybreak when the ringing had punctured my rest. I'd woken groggy and disorientated and dragged myself down to the kitchen where a murky pool of water sat in the sink, and an unpleasant sulphurous smell made my stomach turn. Ben had been talking loudly on his phone – presumably to Iain – and I'd, out of necessity, made myself a strong coffee with tap water, since we were out of the bottled. It had immediately given me a headache and made me nauseous. Julie Moon had floated on the periphery of my thoughts, swimming in and out as I'd made toast for Noah, poured him a beaker of milk, emptied the kitchen bin.

'Do they realise you haven't properly started work yet?' I say, feeling slightly irritated on Ben's behalf.

'My job's not like that,' snaps Ben. 'You know that. People need me and those needs can't just be put on hold because we've not yet reached my start date.'

I bite my lip, forcing myself not to retort. I watch as Ben retrieves his phone from the sofa and jams it into his pocket. He looks weary, but worse than that, irritated. 'Look, I'll do something with Noah later,' he says with a sigh. 'So that you can paint or whatever.'

I fight with myself. *We should do something together,* I want to say, *be a family*. Like we always used to.

But Ben is already heading for the door, and I hear Noah's game of trucks crescendo in the hall. I need to be a mum right now. I need to bypass my tiredness, engage with Noah, and tidy up while I wait for the drain people.

I play trucks with Noah and stack the breakfast dishes neatly by the sink. Washing them is quite impossible and the smell in the kitchen is unbearable. Then we wait.

Eventually, a van, with *Drain Busters* blazoned across the side, arrives just after eleven. A guy called Mike gets straight to work while I make him a tea, apologising in advance that it might taste a bit odd.

'Nah, it's fine,' he says, taking a large slurp. But I catch him grimacing as he turns to his tool bag.

I leave Mike to it and spend some time playing more truck games with Noah in his playroom. The smell in the kitchen is bad: even from here, I smell sulphur and rotting matter. Perhaps Reverend Allen poured gallons of bacon fat down the sink or something. It certainly smells bad enough.

'Mummy, play properly,' interjects Noah, ramming a yellow truck into my leg before going to select another one from his overloaded play tub of vehicles.

I'm sitting on the floor pushing a blue lorry around idly and, at once, try to engage, making it circle on the horrible fake wood effect linoleum, then up and over my lap.

'What's wrong with the kitchen?' Noah asks, wheeling a red pickup truck along the windowsill. 'Is there a dead crow in the sink?'

I crash the lorry into my leg. 'A crow? No! Why?'

'I thought that's what was making the water bad and smelly.'

I shake my head. 'The drain's just blocked,' I explain. 'It's nothing to do with crows, okay?'

'Okay,' says Noah, lightly. 'But every time you make me drink the tap water, I feel poorly and have scary crow dreams. I like water out of bottles best.'

'Me too,' I say. 'But the tap water will be fine soon.'

'I hope so, Mummy.'

I watch as Noah drives the truck off the windowsill and down the wall. 'Mike, the man in the kitchen, is going to unblock the drain for us,' I explain. 'And sort out the taps.'

Noah halts, truck almost at the skirting board. 'I thought my crow had floated down the drainpipe into our sink.'

I frown. What a weird thing to think. But then kids think weird stuff. I rev the lorry. 'No, sweetheart. That's not possible. It—'

Just then Mike pops his head around the door. 'Roots,' he says.

'Excuse me?'

'You've got roots in your drainpipes, love. Plumbing's buggered. Drainage too.'

I bite back my annoyance at being called *love*. 'So...'

'I'll need to get them removed. Water will be off while I work out the extent of the problem. I think they run quite a way.' He rubs his stubbly chin. 'They're probably from one of the trees in your garden, or even the churchyard.'

I let go of the lorry. It clanks to the floor, spins, and rolls towards Noah.

'Mummy!'

I flash a look at Noah. *Sorry*, I mouth. I imagine roots twisting from the yew tree, thick as rope, infiltrating the water system, feeding poison into the pipes. Or remnants of the crow, somehow. 'Sorry,' I say, again, realising that Mike is talking to me. I ask him to repeat himself and then say yes, it's fine to go ahead. The diocese will foot the bill. They look after all church buildings, and we just need the job done.

'It's urgent,' I say.

And it's only as I voice this that I realise quite how urgent it is.

32

OCTAVIA

Dorsetshire 1866

It is breakfast time, and the dining room is flooded with stark sunlight. I am weary; exhausted by days of getting up before dawn to loosen the trap, to take the new catch down to the tree and bury it. To dispose of the last animal, flinging it into the bushes for the foxes. Sometimes we leave the wretched bodies in the grave for a few days if the memories do not come straight away. But, more often than not, they do. Perhaps because Alice and I have become so attuned to listening and seeing, to placing ourselves in such a mind that we can hear the murmurs of the past with ease.

This morning, the memories were sharper than ever: an old coney half-deaf and blind, nearing the end of its life anyway. I remembered it dragging itself across the heath, eyes weeping pus, bones leaden. I felt the weariness in its legs, the curse of its dimming vision, its desperate, vital need to rest. And then it seemed that I was up on the heath with it, the wind blowing through my hair, the smell of the wild gorse and the sheep all around me. I knelt beside the coney as it hauled itself across the scrub in the direction of the trap. 'I am sorry,' I said. I reached out to stroke its bristly fur and it stopped abruptly, having no strength to bolt. For a moment, I saw the clear-eyed, sweet creature it had been. New sunshine, fresh wind, and life's thrill. Then it dulled once more. 'I am sorry,' I said again and then I screwed my eyes so that I could not hear the sharp snap of steel.

Shaking myself from the memory, I felt my stomach turn with sickness. It had been more real than ever that time – I had lived the coney's last moments, but I had been alongside it too. I had touched it and spoken to it, as if in the real world.

The scourge of the memory shook me as I picked up the spade to begin the exhumation. I dug the poor creature up and a large dog ran away with the carcass before I had the chance to dispose of it, shaking the scraggy body in its jaws, tufts of fur floating in the morning air. I have become hardened to this near-everyday task. Because I have had to. But today felt different. It *was* different. I had been with that coney in its last moments, and the pain of that afflicted me greatly.

After that, I walked slowly back to the vicarage, the breeze raking my hair, the early sun on my back. I thought hard about what we are doing and of what we are becoming. This new way of life where life and death blur and where we tread a tightrope between two worlds.

I let myself through the back door and walked along the gloomy passageway towards the dining room, and breakfast. Father no longer comes up to the heath with me in the morning, of which I am glad. It saves me the awkwardness of his presence, the weight of his indifference towards me. Instead, he works late into the night, charting our experiments and writing sermons – long, complicated tracts to read out to the villagers. I'm sure they have no hope of understanding his treatise, but I dare not tell him. His thoughts and theories are forever changing, he tells me, but *little by little the miracle is revealed and soon we will tell all of it. People in Hope-under-Barrow must know how blessed we are.*

This morning, at the breakfast table, Father looks tired. His skin is grey, his hair unbrushed and stringy, and even his clerical dress does little to make him appear more respectable. Earlier, when I arose to check the trap, I saw beneath the study door a slip of light; a candle burning. And although it had been extinguished, or had guttered, when I passed by the window later to collect the spade, Father cannot have had more than a couple of hours' sleep. He must have spent the chief of the night working. By the deep creases across his forehead and his crumpled appearance, I wonder whether he even made it to his bed and, instead, spent his short slumber slumped across his desk.

The sunlight is too bright, and it hurts my sleepy eyes. I angle my chair away from its glare and take a sip of tea, thinking. I try a crust of toast and scoop some buttered egg onto my fork. Tiredness yawns within me as I consider the best way to phrase the question pressing on my mind. 'Father,' I begin, at last.

'What is it, Octavia?' Father cuts into his bacon, the knife screeching across the plate.

The sound makes me shiver. I push my own bacon to one side, scrunch my nose at the smear of glistening fat it leaves on the plate. I cannot eat it. Not now that I know. Know what survives after death. 'I have been wondering about our experiments,' I say.

Father looks at me. A question mark.

I fiddle with my egg. 'You see, Father, I have been wondering about Mother.'

Something in the atmosphere snaps. Father's cutlery clatters to his plate.

'After what we have discovered...' I continue, '... I wonder whether it might be possible to...' I swallow, '... dig her grave, move her, so that we might once again—'

'Exhume the body?' he shoots.

I wriggle on my chair, thinking about what Alice said about the spirit world and all that we have found out about the creatures we've buried beneath the tree. If only I could have access to Mother, to her guidance and love. 'It's just that I miss her,' I manage. A lump wells in my throat. 'I miss her so much. And if we were to move her, then—'

'Enough!' Father brings both hands to rest hard upon the table, making me jump. The plates rattle, milk sloshes on the shiny surface from the tiny jug. 'Octavia, you cannot let such sentimentality overtake you. It will do you no good. Your mother is dead and risen once more in God's heavenly kingdom. She sits with the Father, in the company of angels. She is not here. It is too late!'

'But Father—'

'Do you dare to contradict me?' His face is ashen, his eyes bulge, red-veined, the whites yellowed by overwork. But I see something else too. A guard that he will not let down. A grief that he must keep under control. An appearance to be maintained.

I push my plate away. 'Alice says that more must be done. We cannot keep trapping and burying rabbits forever. Surely there must be a conclusion to all of this. A reason. An outcome.'

Father gets to his feet, fast. He upsets the milk jug completely this time and a river of white runs across the table, cascades to the floor, splashes and pools. 'And what the hell does Alice know of this?' he shouts, storming across to the dining room door. 'She cannot own the same thirst for knowledge that I do and see where this project must lead. A mere farmer's daughter! I do not care one iota for Alice's opinion.' He exits, slamming the door behind him.

It is the first time I have heard Father swear by hell, and I am shocked by it. My cheeks are hot, my pulse races.

But I know also, that beneath his anger, beneath his front and his denial, behind his *thirst for knowledge*, there is a deeper emotion. The emotion that causes him to keep a box of Mother's things hidden away on a shelf in his study. The emotion that he will not share because it causes him shame and makes him feel like a lesser man.

33

KATE

Dorset 2026

'The roots extend all the way to the churchyard, to the yew tree,' I say, when Ben finally returns for lunch. 'They're going to have to put chemicals down the drains to dissolve them and sort out the mains.' My shoulders sag. 'Apparently, it could take up to two weeks for it to work.'

'Well, that's good, then,' says Ben. He shoves a lump of cheese and bread into his mouth and chomps loudly.

I shake my head, push my own bread and cheese away. The plate rattles across the kitchen table. 'It explains a lot though, don't you think?'

Ben stops chewing, cocks his head to one side. 'What do you mean?'

'Noah. All these headaches I keep getting. The dreams.'

'What about them?'

I sigh, shove my hair out of my face. 'It's all because of the water. It's been polluting us. The roots have been poisoning it. Making all these things happen. The tree... it's, well, it's...' The words won't form. Not without me sounding crazy. To Ben. To myself.

Ben laughs. 'I don't really think—'

'That's the problem,' I snap, a sudden rage rising. 'You're not thinking. You're not seeing what this place has done to us since we've arrived. We're arguing. We never argue.' I look about me, as if I'm expecting to see someone or something closing in on us. Something to prove my point. The kitchen stares back blankly. 'This place is making us all act out of character. We're not even having lunch with Noah – he's stuck in front of the TV eating crisps and celery sticks by himself while we bicker. It's like we're a different family. Diseased.'

'Kate!' Ben flops back in his chair. He laces his fingers behind his head and laughs into the ceiling. The sound reverberates, bounces off the surfaces, loudly. He lets his hands drop and leans forward, angling himself towards me. 'Just listen to yourself, darling. You're making it sound as if we're extras in *The Day of the Triffids* or something. We have a blocked drain, that's all. You're letting the move get to you. You're tired. Everything's new and different. You need to relax, chill out. You need—'

'Don't tell me what I need!' I spring to my feet, head for the kitchen door.

'Where are you going?

I pause, clutching the handle. 'Out,' I say. I feel like a teenager again. Arguing with my parents, storming out because, in my eyes, they're being so unreasonable.

'What about Noah?' says Ben.

I open the door. 'There's yoghurts in the fridge. He likes the apricot one best.'

I feel Ben staring after me as I speed towards the front door. He calls but I ignore him as I spill out into the bright sunshine and run across the overgrown drive.

He won't follow me, I know that. He has to stay with Noah.

I find myself in the churchyard, staring up at the yew tree. What is it about this tree that keeps pulling me back? My artwork maybe – not that I'm making much progress there – but it's more than that. It has a strange hold over me. It wants something from me. It's trying to tell me something. Noah's crow is a part of it. Because by being buried there, the bird somehow…

I shake my head.

My thoughts are out of control, just like everything else in this place. And if I start getting more funny ideas about the tree, I'll end up buying into all this Barrow Man stuff.

I stare up into the dark, green needles and I'm climbing a tree. I'm strong and pull myself up branch by branch. I smell the dry-scented bark and ignore how it scratches my skin. I want to stop. To tell myself that I don't have to do this. That this is madness. That I will fall. But I do have to do it. I have to prove myself to the others. Not let my friend down.

Despite the cool night air, I'm hot. I'm thirsty and uncomfortable. The battle drum of feet on the woodland path sounds. The rhythm of power and supremacy. Closer and closer. I look up and see the moon; a thin, bright cut already shining in the blue.

'Julie.' A voice calls from below. 'Julie!'

There's a scuffling. 'Get away from me!' My voice is breathless, shuddering with resolve. 'I can do this.'

The memory snaps shut. I try to breathe it away, telling myself I was just thinking about the past. But as I try to convince myself, my gaze is drawn to something in the trunk. It's as if the bark is shifting, melting, and a face appears there. For a moment, it looks like Julie, her features distorted as if she's pushing her way out of the bark. Screaming to get out.

I rub my eyes. The image has gone: it's just a tree again. I clutch my chest, as if holding my heart in place, panting loudly. Everything is still, the spring sun warm, the wildflowers about the graveyard bright and waving in the light breeze. There's a faint mist curling around the tree. Pollen. A sign of spring. But my skin is crawling with the discomforting image, my head hurts and, despite all the rational thoughts I want to hold on to, I have the sense that something is terribly wrong.

34

OCTAVIA

Dorsetshire 1866

Instead of the season ripening into the haze of early summer, the weather unexpectedly turns cold and wet. No longer am I required to trap rabbits and bury them, for Father tells me that he is working on something much greater. I am relieved that these experiments have ceased. But now that I am forced to remain indoors on account of the worsening season, the vicarage is a most miserable place to be. Usually, at the tipping of the season, I would be out in the country lanes, gathering wildflowers, spotting birds, marvelling as the leaves turn to the brightest green. Mother and I would go about the village, arm in arm, pausing to soak up the last of the spring as it made its way softly into summer. And there would be a glorious sense of expectation at the languid days ahead.

Not so now. For one thing, Mother is dead. And for another, the weather is so deplorable that I should be whisked away if I dared venture out of the vicarage. The wind howls and rages down the chimneys, wet runs down the wallpaper so that it can be torn off in shreds, and the roof has sprung many leaks. Nanny Butterworth has laid cloths along the windowsills and Mr Jefferies has gone about the house placing pails to catch the numerous drips. And so, my daily activities are accompanied by a solemn metallic *drip, drip, drip.* Not that my day promotes much excitement. Each one is the same and sometimes I fear I will grow sick with the monotony of it all. Damp lingers in the air and a deep sense of melancholy hangs about the house. Rats scratch in the panelling and mice run about the kitchen. Strangely though, I am thankful for these rodents, for they are the only other living creatures, aside from those who make up our insular community. We have fewer visitors than ever. Parishioners do not come to our door and Father does not go out, other than to bawl from the pulpit and deliver long and ever-fiercer tracts about the afterlife. The village school remains unvisited and the sick and elderly live and die alone, without the comforting assurances of the vicar to console them.

Now, it has gone four in the afternoon. The sky is dark and heavy, the rain incessant. I have been sitting in the kitchen this past hour, watching Cook making pastry, nibbling at the cut-offs, and helping to stew unripe plums. It is so dismal that Cook has lit a candle to help her review the neat lattice work that strings the surface of her tart. The shadows cast by the solitary flame leap and dance across the dark walls like mythical forest folk, and the light catches on the silverware, the jelly moulds, a large ladle hanging near the unlit fire. I breathe in the syrupy smell of the fruit and sigh. The room is warm with sugar and steam, and, for a time, I have been able to forget my anxious thoughts about where Father's plans might lead next. My tongue is sweetened with the mixture I have tried, my fingers are sticky with fruit juice, and it is just as I am washing them over the cracked sink that Nanny Butterworth appears at the kitchen door.

'Octavia, miss.'

I turn, wiping my wet hands on my skirts. 'What is it, Nanny Butterworth?'

She looks from Cook to me. 'Your father requires your presence in the study.'

'Did he say for what reason?' I ask.

Nanny Butterworth shakes her head. 'Only that you must go immediately. He has company.' Again, she looks at Cook and something passes between them. I sense that the two of them have been talking about the matter at some hidden moment. Perhaps the uncommon occurrence of visitors is worthy of gossip.

Untying my apron, I step quickly across the flagstones and down the hallway, avoiding the huge pail that Mr Jefferies has set in the centre of the passageway to catch the drips. Its twin stands on the gallery landing above, and I have spent much time listening to the rhythm they produce. Almost in synchronicity, but irritatingly not quite so.

I rap on the study door.

'Enter.' Father's voice is firm.

I push at the door and admit myself.

On one of the chairs by the fire I am surprised to see Alice. Sitting on the other, an even greater surprise, is Mr Jefferies. Alice's hands are folded in her lap, and she looks thin and tired, her dress swamps her diminished frame, and the sole of one of her boots is curled and broken. Her eyes, however, are bright, like those of a greenfinch, darting about the room, searching but seemingly not finding. For her gaze does not rest and skips over me, refusing to linger and connect. Mr Jefferies does not acknowledge me either. He stares straight ahead, leaving only his lumpy profile available for examination.

Father himself sits at his desk, hands clasped, and, before him, is the false book box. For one terrible moment, I fear that he has somehow found out that I have discovered his secret. But he makes no allusion to it and rather bids me to sit on a footstool next to Alice.

I do so, with a little hesitation, wondering what this interview concerns and what part Mr Jefferies has to play in it all.

Father clears his throat. 'Octavia,' he begins.

Mr Jefferies coughs, wheezing and rasping as he draws air into his lungs. He regards me now with a red, bullish face. He has always disliked me, though I am not sure why. And today, he looks at me as if I were a particularly nasty insect that he would rather eliminate.

Father glares and begins again. 'Octavia, it only seems right that we should inform you of the latest development of the plan. Given that you were so involved in the earliest of stages.'

'Thank you, Father,' I say, looking at my feet, away from the critical scrutiny of Mr Jefferies. I try to appear meek but, in reality, anger is boiling in the pit of my stomach. That I should be brought in last, when the plan has evidently already been formed and when it was I who had first discovered the miraculous nature of the tree.

'Octavia, you may wonder why Mr Jefferies is here.'

I say nothing but look up to see Father smiling broadly. Not at me, but at his companions. 'Mr Jefferies is a man of great skill, as you will no doubt agree. He can undertake many a project with deftness and integrity. You cannot fail to notice all that he has done about the vicarage and the church.'

I think of the pails scattered about the house, the mess of tools in the outhouse, the roughly turned over beds with barely a flower to their name. 'Yes, Father,' I mutter, careful not to meet his eye. Instead, I glance at Mr Jefferies, who scowls back, then sets about in a fit of coughing.

'The experiment with the animals was a great success,' says Father, once Mr Jefferies has quietened. 'And, of course, we have picked up other things too. Memories from long ago. I have come to look fondly upon those ancient stories and have christened their owner the Barrow Man.'

'The Barrow Man?' The name sticks in my throat. It seems too distant for the strands of memory I have recalled; the beauty of the pipes, the tales he told, the people he loved and who, evidently, loved him. Once again, I look at Mr Jefferies to see how he is receiving Father's words. The man is smiling beneath the bushiness of his moustaches, and his eyes are alight with understanding. So, he knows about this too, I think. Has remembered things, even. *Why*? Why did Father tell such a despicable person?

'It is time to realise the magnitude of our scheme,' continues Father. 'And, after that time, we will reveal the extent of our findings at large. Already our lives have been changed by the certainty that there is consciousness beyond this world, just as our good Lord revealed in his most holy book. And soon, this knowledge will change things for all men, not least for Alice and the future of the March farm.'

'The farm?' I frown, uncertain how it might be connected to all we have discovered.

'For our lives will change beyond measure once this thing is known,' explains Father. 'We will surely be revered. We will attract both fame and fortune. And soon we will have a true living witness to that which is beyond.' He smiles at Alice, who twists her hands in her lap with vigour. Then turning to me: 'You recall the coney, Octavia? The memories you experienced. How you felt that you were alongside the animal in its final wretchedness.'

I nod, remembering how I had stroked the coarse fur as if I really had been there and whispered last words of pardon to the animal.

Father clears his throat. 'It is clear from this, that we can enter deeper into the memories than we ever supposed possible at first. We can communicate with those who have passed over into the other realm. And so now, it is time for us to press this matter further. For us to fully discover what is beyond our mortal state.'

I eye the box of Mother's things, thinking how so much has altered. Nothing has been the same since that dark and terrible morning when I was ushered into the study and the unhappy news was imparted. I swallow the memory away. 'What do you propose to do next?' I ask, feeling a ripple of nervousness.

Outside, it seems to grow darker. The poor light in the room worsens. I shuffle nearer to the fire, hoping to benefit from its meek glow. In the process, I startle Alice. She too is nervous, I realise.

Father looks to Mr Jefferies and takes a long breath. 'Mr Jefferies, perhaps you would explain the scheme to my daughter. I feel that you would do the explanation far more justice than I would.' He looks to me as an aside. 'The technicalities...'

Mr Jefferies heaves himself in his seat and gives a phlegm-filled cough. 'I am building a contraption,' he says. Still, he does not look at me. 'It has taken me many hours of labour thus far and much strife to get it exactly as it needs to be. Currently, it is occupying a space in the outhouse.'

Whatever this contraption is, I cannot think where it might be placed, such is the jumble and chaos of the outbuilding. 'I see,' I say. Although I do not.

Mr Jefferies pulls at his jacket. It is speckled with dirt, and I notice too that his calloused hands are ingrained with the evidence of arduous work. 'I have used the very best wood, strong screws and cord, and I have nearly completed something that would, I believe, rival other such contraptions.' For the first time, he turns to me, using his hands to demonstrate some workings of which I have not the slightest reference point nor understanding. 'There are a series of pulleys,' he explains. 'Like this... and like that...' He moves his hands to demonstrate. I notice Alice looking on keenly. 'And right at the bottom, there is a bell. It is small, but shrill, and the occupant should have no trouble in sounding it when the time is right.' Mr Jefferies glances at Father, who nods his encouragement. 'Alice would only have to tug on the pulley once or twice and the operation would be set in motion.' Again, he moves his hands this way and that, mysterious maps drawn in the air.

I frown. The words and the notions jumble and I cannot make any sense of what I am being told. Behind Mr Jefferies, the fire spits and cracks as a tremendous gust of wind courses down the chimney. He smacks his lips together, coming to the end of his discourse and placing his hands across his stomach, as if satisfied after a good meal.

'The whole invention is quite ingenious,' continues Father, before I can ask for clarification. 'And, of course, necessary if we are to present an irrefutable case. To have a witness who can recount and bear testimony will give our revelation the greatest credence. Just a small draft is all that will be needed.'

'Draft?' Cold clutches my core. 'Father, what is it that you propose, exactly?'

Father clears his throat, then waves a hand as if what he is about to say is a trifling matter. 'Just a small drink made from the needles of the yew tree. But it will make Alice… it will make her sick. Not sick enough that she will come to any lasting harm, of course. Just enough for her to touch the edges of the realm beyond. You see, the proportions will be quite exact, yet the result astonishing – enough to convince people that she has truly gone hence from this world, and enough to bring her to the line that divides our world from the next, enough for her to get a glimpse…'

I stare at Alice.

I want to know where my deceased brothers are and whether I can communicate with them. Maybe they can see more from the spirit world. Maybe they can show us what to do to recover the farm.

But this cannot be…

Spirits must surely be able to see more than we can, they must know things, see the future and give us guidance.

My head swims. The idea is quite preposterous, if I understand it at all. But Alice does not seem troubled. Indeed, she looks to Father, enrapt by the prospect. She trusts him, I realise. Trusts him with her own life.

'And that is where the contraption comes in,' explains Father.

I shift on the footstool. It is worn and uncomfortable. 'Forgive me, Mr Jefferies,' I say, my voice small and wavering. Sickness writhes in the depths of my stomach. 'But I'm afraid I do not understand. What is this contraption? I am not sure I have followed your meaning.'

Mr Jefferies stares at me, incredulity spanning his spider-veined face. 'Why, Miss Kibble. Miss Kibble! I have just explained the workings of a coffin.' He leans forwards, lowering his voice. 'A very fine safety coffin. Alice will be given a good Christian burial, but secure within my coffin, she will rise again, like the fortunate Lazarus...'

'To tell all,' concludes Father. 'To tell all what lies beyond. We will have her memories *and* her testimony. Oh, what a glorious day that will be! There will be such a show, such a performance for village! A day when grief and mourning will turn into joyful dancing.'

35

KATE

Dorset 2026

I sneeze repeatedly, the pollen from the yew tree misting around me in clouds. Backing away, I consider what to do. I circle the church, inspecting some of the graves, trying to distract myself by thinking about work. I don't really want to go back to the vicarage, not after this latest argument with Ben, and consider a walk on the heath. But as I try to skirt past the house unnoticed, the front door swings open and there's Ben peering across the drive.

He sees me and raises his arm. 'Don't you have Noah with you?' he calls.

'What?' I cross the drive towards the house. 'What are you on about?'

'Noah. I was washing up and went through to the playroom to get his plate and beaker, give him a yoghurt, and he wasn't there. I thought he was still with you.'

'*Still*?' I drag a hand through my hair. I seriously don't believe this. Not again. 'He was never with me. You saw me leave. Have you actually checked the house properly?'

'Of course I've checked.' Ben doesn't bother to disguise his irritation. 'I went all through the house and when I got to my study, I saw him through the window, heading towards the churchyard. I could see you – your pink top – and, well… I presumed he'd find you.'

I try to stop myself from screaming and concentrate on keeping my voice level. 'Ben, he's five years old. You can't *presume* anything about him.'

I head back off down the drive.

'Where are you going?' calls Ben.

I let my hands flop. 'Do you even have to ask? I'm going to find him.'

Noah is at the yew tree. We must have missed each other somehow, probably when I was looking around the churchyard. The clouds of pollen are already dispersing, blown away by the breeze, allowing me to see the cool, green branches bowing low, almost touching Noah's head. He's sitting by the mound of disturbed earth that used to house the crow's body. It had been Ben's job to sort the carcass after Noah dug it up and I don't really know what became of it. Moreover, I didn't want to know. I just wanted a complete end to the whole business.

As I draw closer to Noah, I see that he's holding his orange beaker from lunchtime. His favourite one with a cutesy, fat tiger on the side. He's just lifting it to his lips to take a sip when he sees me.

'Mummy!' He scrambles to his feet. 'I made a yummy drink. Do you want to try some?'

I'm really not in the mood for playing tea parties right now, but nod enthusiastically as I head over to join him. Really, I should be chastising him for running off again, but the prospect of more conflict is more than I can deal with. 'What is it?' I say, waiting for one of Noah's imaginative names. One of the magical made-up words he usually comes up with when we play food and drink-related games. 'What's it called?'

'Tree drink,' he says, simply. He lifts the beaker again.

And then it clicks. I sprint across to him. 'What did you say?'

'Tree drink.' Noah holds out the beaker for me to see. 'I collected together some spiky leaves that had fallen from the tree and added them to the orange juice Daddy gave me.'

I snatch the beaker from my son's small hand. 'You mustn't drink that,' I cry. I peer into the bright orange liquid to see several floating yew needles. *Taxine*. The name of the poison springs to mind, suddenly and violently remembered from a teenage passion for Agatha Christie. 'Yew trees are very poisonous, Noah.' I tip the drink onto the soil, watching as the dirt absorbs it. 'You would be really, really poorly if you drank that. You could have been sick.' *You could have died*, whisper my innermost thoughts.

Noah stares at me in puzzlement, his lower lip trembling. 'It's only for pretend, Mummy,' he says, his voice wavering. Two spots of red blossom across his cheeks. 'Like when we make mud pies in the garden for the birds. I wouldn't die or nothing. Anyway, the man said it would be okay even if I did drink some. As long as it wasn't too much.'

'Man? What man?' I stare down at Noah, his little face crumpled in confusion. And *die*? I said nothing about dying. It's almost as if he's read my thoughts. I kneel beside him and draw him close. 'What man, Noah? Was it someone from the church? Mr Moss, perhaps?'

Noah shakes his head. 'I don't know.'

'What did he look like?' I press. 'Have you seen him before?'

'I can't remember, Mummy. But he had a big black cape, like a vampire.' He tries to push me away, his voice rising in agitation.

'A vampire?' I mutter, my mind turning over the description and drawing a blank. I pull Noah close again and, this time, he lets me.

It's then that I remember my own weird thoughts about a man here, when I came back from the farm in the rain. Perhaps the image was in Noah's mind, just as it was for me. I clamp him to my chest. 'Look, you weren't doing anything wrong but promise me you won't play with yew needles again. They're very bad for little boys. In fact, stay from this tree. Daddy's already told you not to come here, hasn't he?'

'Yes,' says Noah, his voice muffled in my soft cotton top. 'But I needed to check my crow's properly dead now we've moved her. She is, cos she's not in my head no more. The nasty owl who killed her has gone too.' He sounds as if he's about to cry.

I pull him to his feet. 'How about we walk down to the village and get ice cream?' I suggest.

His face brightens a little, before dulling. 'If you want to,' he says, in a flat voice. I stare after him as he makes his way to the iron gate leading to the vicarage garden. Not running but walking slowly, head down. It's as if we left the spirited little boy we knew so well back in Cheshire.

I clutch the tiger beaker and follow him, my stomach churning with anxiety. *He's just adjusting,* I tell myself. *This is all new. For him. For me. For all of us.* But as I reach the fringe of the yew tree's shadow, an image fills my head. A memory, tapping on the sides of my skull; a beating headache. There are flashes. Disconnected images. The bull house. A girl. A vial of dark green liquid. Dribbling. Stained white flesh. Enlarged, bulbous eyes. Lips turned to a greyish blue. A forceful hand and a desperate, choking plea.

36

OCTAVIA

Dorsetshire 1866

I lie in my bedchamber, unable to sleep. The rain has turned to mizzle, and the atmosphere is thick and muggy. My window is open to allow the air to circulate and there is a hint of a near-full moon behind streaks of turbulent cloud. I almost want to fasten the window however, for now all I hear is the steady *knock, knock, knock*ing of Mr Jefferies at work in the outbuilding. He has been occupied with finishing his deadly contraption for several days now, returning to his cottage only at dusk. Frequently, Father has been called to the outbuilding to give opinion, or to be shown what progress has been made and, after each visit, he has called me to the study to expand upon the apparent ingenuity of Mr Jefferies.

'Should you not like to see it?' Father had asked me after luncheon today. 'It is quite something.' When I replied that I should not, Father gave me a curious look, as though I was bypassing a rare opportunity.

But there is a coil of nervousness set deep within me, and whenever I think of the scheme, I am overcome with panic. Nanny Butterworth worries that my appetite has waned and that I have become pale and distracted. But I cannot tell her what is troubling me for she is not to know. Father forbids it. He says she will learn of it when the experiment is complete, and all is revealed. Though I wonder whether he too worries that the scheme may fail and that, if it does, we will be guilty of nothing less than murder.

I twist and turn within my bed, seeing Alice's face before my eyes, imagining what is to come. And I am only able to fall into a troubled sleep once the banging from the outbuilding ceases.

I wake before dawn. The light outside is grey and dusky. Everything is still. I steal out of bed and dress quickly. For my mind is made up. I must go up to the March farm and speak with Alice.

Outside, the air carries a bite despite the claggy atmosphere, and I hurry towards the heath, hardly wanting to look at the yew tree as I run past the churchyard. The track is sludgy with mud after the rains, and I slip and slide as my worn boots fail to make purchase. Soon, I am splattered with dirt, but I do not bother to give it much attention as I stumble up the hill towards the farm. I will fabricate my excuses to Nanny Butterworth later.

I reach my destination and, at once, see how things have changed. The cattle plague is making its mark. There is not the usual activity and bustle that I remember from my previous visit, nor the sound of animals snuffling and grunting about the place. I scan the yard, looking for Alice. I peer into the bull house where the great brute is snorting and eating his feed. But she is not to be found.

The farmhouse then.

I cross the yard once more and approach the house. Smoke rises from one of the chimneys, a thin grey stream that tells me that there is, at least, someone at home. I knock on the solid door and, when there is no answer, I push at it gently and look through the crack before admitting myself into the kitchen.

The difference in Mrs March is shocking. The woman I met before was round and red-faced, smiling with the joys of home. This woman, hunched in the old rocking chair, is old-looking and worn. Her shoulders curve inwards and she is muttering to herself. Words that have neither sense nor direction. She sits close to a fire which does not seem to warm the room and, this time, there is no smell of cooking or laundry soap. A grey film of dust hangs about the place and dirty crockery mounts in the large sink. A skillet, thick with grease, emits a rancid odour and a jug of milk on the table is evidently on the turn.

'Mrs March?' I venture.

She stops rocking and turns abruptly. 'Who is it?' she says, as if she were an old woman, confused by age and time.

'Octavia Kibble,' I say.

'Kibble. Kibble?' She tries the word several times upon her lips.

'I came to see Alice,' I say, slowly and deliberately. 'I need to speak with her.'

'Ah.' Mrs March resumes her rocking. 'Alice is in her bedchamber. I sent her there after she'd fed the bull. I fear she's unwell. First Edgar, and now my poor Alice.'

I look towards a small wooden door set in the panelling and guess that it must lead to a staircase. 'May I go and see her?' I twist my hands in front of me. 'It really is of some importance.'

Mrs March sighs. 'Take care on the steps,' she says. 'It's steep. Alice's chamber is at the top, opposite the staircase.'

I unlatch the small door and find a narrow set of steps leading upwards. There is no rail, and I press a hand against the wall as I climb, wondering what state and what humour I will find my friend in.

The door to her chamber is open and, for a moment, I stand at the threshold regarding Alice as she looks out of a tiny window over the heath. She must sense me, for she turns, her face at once crumpling in confusion.

'Octavia! What are you doing here?' She pulls herself away from the window and sits on the neatly made bed.

'Your ma said you were unwell. I hope it is not too bad. She said that Edgar is also suffering.'

'He has a fever,' says Alice. She picks at a thread on her coverlet. 'He should be well enough in a few days. But Ma does worry. She worries about most things nowadays.'

'And you?'

'I do not have a fever.' Alice brushes her brow, as if testing for unusual hotness. 'I am fit to go with Pa onto the heath to look for dead and dying cattle. But Ma has detected something about me and will not let me go.'

'What has she detected?' I ask.

Alice sighs. 'She presumes that I am suffering with the same affliction as my brother but really, it is an attack of nerves, I suppose.'

'Nerves?' I lower my voice. 'About Father's plan?'

Alice does not move for a moment but then nods and glances over at the window. She is imagining, I suppose, the church below the heath and, within its grounds, the yew tree. She draws her gaze away. 'But you must see why I have to go ahead. Now that you're here, you can see what this place has become. We're losing animals daily. Ma is... not herself.' She thumps a fist on her mattress. 'I must do something. I cannot sit by and watch everything die, watch Ma lose her mind.' I bite my lower lip as Alice matches my tone. 'If your father's plan works,' she whispers, 'I will speak with my brothers in the spirit world, and they will show me what to do. With their help, I will save the farm. I will save my family. And with all the money and fame that it will surely bring in, the outcome can only be a good one.'

I shuffle uncomfortably, the floorboards creaking beneath my feet. 'But... Oh Alice, I am so afraid that it will fail and that I will lose you.' I lift my shoulders, trying to swallow the stone that is blocking my throat. My voice cracks. 'I cannot lose you.'

Alice rises. 'You don't understand. You can't understand. This farm is everything to me. To us. I must take the risk, and I trust your father. He has spoken about the afterlife with conviction time after time in the pulpit. Anyway, it is well that Ma presumes a fever, for then I will not have to lie when the time comes.'

'Lie?'

'Just as your father explained. There must be a show. The carrying of my body in procession down the coffin lane. The funeral, the burial. And then...'

I press my hands to my ears, hardly wanting to hear this.

Alice steps towards me, her face hard with resolve. 'When the draft has worn off... when I have seen over into the other side, spoken to the spirits, to my brothers, and come to understand the mysterious workings of the yew tree, I will ring the bell to be let out.' Her face lights then. 'And that is when the telling of our story will truly begin. That is when I will save everything, Octavia.'

I shake my head. Alice surely cannot believe that this will come to any good and I cannot risk losing my friend. 'I will not allow it,' I say. 'I must stop Father. It is dangerous and wrong and... why, surely, we have all the evidence we need.'

Alice sighs. 'Your father has already explained this to you, Octavia. I have explained it to you. We must go further. Your father – the Reverend – is a very clever man. He has taught me a great many things. I have learned about all that Mr Darwin has argued and how he explained his theories in such great detail, after conducting many experiments. He could not have hoped to be persuasive without proof.'

'We have proof,' I say, dully.

Alice folds her arms. 'We must go further,' she says, again. 'We cannot stop now. And I… I must save the farm. I must speak to my brothers and gain from their knowledge. Can you not at least try to understand that?'

Our eyes meet. I see a dark determination written there and I realise that my journey here has been futile. I should never have come. Alice March means to go through with Father's terrible plan, whatever the state of her nerves.

I break my gaze and back away towards the door.

Alice does not move. I look at her one more time, at the gold of her hair, the tilt of her jaw, her dark eyes and the tiny mole. Everything that I love so much. *Please,* I beg, silently. *Please. Do not do this.*

But the air trembles with the strength of her resolve and I see that she has a belief in Father that I do not.

It is still early when I leave the March farm and make my way back along the coffin lane to the village. I run, slipping on the mud, stumbling on the scree, my mind rambling. I cannot let this thing happen. The feeling of dread and wrong is within my bones and I know that I must find some way of stopping Father before it is too late.

As I draw near to the church, I see him: a dark shadow moving slowly in the moist atmosphere. He is near the yew tree and is bending at intervals, plucking something from the ground and letting it fall into a small enamel bowl which I recognise from the vicarage kitchen.

I then see that what he holds in his fingers is green. The darkest of greens, and I realise at once what he is doing. He is collecting yew needles from the ground beneath the tree.

'Father!' I shout, racing towards him, not caring that my demeanour is erratic and would potentially draw attention to the scene from the village. 'Father!'

He pauses, glaring at me through the mist. He looks about him, panicked, and presses a finger to his lips. But I stumble through the long grass, calling and calling, the dew soaking my stockings, the leather tips of my boots drenched and admitting a cold sting. 'You must stop,' I say, arriving at the yew tree hot and breathless.

'Are you out of your mind, Octavia?' Father places the bowl at his feet and grabs me by my wrists. 'What do you mean by this? Why are you screaming like a madman?'

I stare down at the dark, deadly needles. 'Please, Father. *Please.* Can we stop now?'

'Stop what?' Father brings his face close to mine as I look up. The whites of his eyes are yellow and pink-veined, his are lids heavy, his skin grey. *This* is what these experiments have done to him.

'If we go any further, Alice might… she might… *die.*' The word escapes my mouth in a whisper that dissipates into the mist.

Father releases me. 'Do you not trust that I know what I am doing?' he says. 'Do you not trust me, Octavia?'

'It is not a matter of trust, Father,' I dare.

He picks up the bowl and clutches it close to his chest. 'It has everything to do with trust,' he says, and he bends to snap another handful of needles.

On the air there is music.

The pipes.

Tears fill my eyes as I remember the old man – the Barrow Man – looking on at his community, sadness filling his heart with the knowledge that soon he will leave them.

37

KATE

Dorset 2026

A couple of days later, Ben officially starts work, and suddenly everything is hectic. While he encourages Noah to finish his dinner, I offer to set out chairs for the church meeting. Ben's running late and Noah really isn't helping matters.

'I don't like it,' Noah says stubbornly, pushing the plate away. 'I hate broccoli.'

'No pudding then,' I retort. I slam the kitchen cupboard door shut with a sigh. I'm trying to find mugs without chips, so that at least Ben can offer everyone a drink. And we can now – the drain chemicals seem to have done the trick, working far quicker than I'd hoped for. So far, I have four mugs, and I need five.

'I want pudding,' says Noah.

'Then eat your broccoli.'

The argument is circular, and eventually, Ben offers to be bad cop. He's actually really good at this – firm and convincing. Whereas I get irrational and threatening – removing the promise of pudding and scraping uneaten food into the waste with unnecessary force.

‘There’s a stack of prayers on my desk,’ Ben says to me between Noah’s protests. ‘Could you just make sure they’re handy?’

I withdraw and head for the study where the meeting will be held. It’s the final Barrow Man Day committee meeting, this one to, apparently, check that everything’s in place. I do find his job strange. Having to care – or pretend to care – about something like this seems like far too much effort. Especially when there are, presumably, sick people and bereaved people and other worthy causes to attend to.

I look on Ben’s desk for the prayers but there’s nothing immediately obvious. I move a couple of things and eventually find them under a newspaper. And that’s when I see it. A blue envelope, shoved between a lectionary and an old prayer book. I go cold. The writing on the envelope is so familiar that, in that moment, the years are stripped away. Fat bubble writing, the type we both loved and spent hours practising. Julie Moon’s writing. Clear as anything, almost as familiar as my own hand. The envelope is addressed to Tommy Moon – Julie’s brother – a weird kid I never took to and who was away at school most of the year anyway. But what the hell is it doing here in Ben’s study?

From the hallway I hear Noah yelling, then Ben’s footsteps and a lecture on eating vegetables.

Hurriedly, I shove the envelope into the back pocket of my jeans and begin setting up five orange plastic chairs in a circle near the fireplace. They’re from the stack of matching chairs that were here when we arrived – *always used for meetings*, Mrs Butterworth informed us fondly. My mind is full and empty at the same time. Julie. *Julie Moon*. Ben. How? Then, as I dump the last chair down, it wobbles. There is actually proper wooden flooring in this room – about the only one that hasn’t had the original boards covered by linoleum or cheap carpet. I frown. The floorboard is loose, I realise.

I stand on it and make it see-saw, then shift the chair a little. Maybe the flooring needs looking at. Yet another thing to add to the endless list.

I'm just moving a small coffee table to the centre of the circle for people to put their drinks on when the doorbell rings. Ben doesn't get it. It rings again. I peer around the study door to hear the broccoli saga still ongoing and sigh. I'd been hoping to scuttle away and hide somewhere before the meeting started, especially now that I want to investigate the contents of the envelope... but I tug at the door, forcing it to submit...

'Lisa, hi.' I stand, awkwardly, not wanting to meet her eye.

A tall, red-haired man next to her holds out his hand. 'Iain,' he offers.

We shake hands, his grip firm and confident, while Lisa glances over her shoulder, as if she's afraid someone might see her. Briefly, I recall what Noah said about Daisy not being allowed here. Immediately, I shut the thought out and wonder whether to mention the doll incident. Check that things really are smoothed over.

But Lisa speaks first. 'Let's see what you've done to the place, then,' she says. 'Starting to feel like home yet?'

'I... er...' I step back to let them in, conscious that Lisa is looking about her. Our stack of welly boots, the scratched hall table with a landline that's not yet connected, a pack of twelve loo rolls by the stairs destined for the bathroom above. I'm sure she must be expecting more, but if she is, she doesn't say so.

'Meeting in the usual place?' asks Iain. Then seeing my face. 'Sorry, you show us.'

I head towards the study. At that moment, Noah comes tearing into the hall, broccoli debacle clearly concluded. He stops short when he sees Lisa, turns, and runs for the playroom.

'You should have brought Daisy,' I say, before I can stop myself.

I want to scoop the words back straightaway. 'I mean, I could have watched her while you were in the meeting. Noah—'

'We got a sitter in,' says Lisa. And I want to imagine it, but she sounds abrupt.

I say no more, and push open the study door, ushering them inside, just as the doorbell goes again. 'Excuse me,' I mutter, grateful for the interruption. 'I'll just get that.'

This time, it's Mrs Butterworth. She bustles in as if she owns the place and without asking where the meeting's being held, marches straight for the study. 'I trust you'll be joining us, Ms Greenwood.'

'Well, no, actually… I—'

Mrs Butterworth pauses. 'And why ever not? Surely you want to know what's going on. As the vicar's wife, you need to—'

'I have to look after Noah.'

Mrs Butterworth's face breaks into a wide smile. 'Ah, I see. Well, bring the little fellow into the meeting.'

'I don't think—'

'Nonsense! Reverend Allen always used to bring his godson into meetings when he came to stay. Never did the boy any harm. That's not to say he couldn't have done with being a little quieter on occasion, but still, I'm sure your son will be just fine. Now run along and fetch him, and you'd better bring a book or two to occupy him. It's going to be a long evening.'

I show Mrs Butterworth into the study. Lisa and Iain are standing in the centre of the room, unsure whether or not to sit. I motion to the horrible plastic chairs.

'Ms Greenwood's just going to fetch Noah,' Mrs Butterworth says. 'I told her that Reverend Allen always used to bring his godson to meetings.' She glances at me. 'Character building. Sitting calmly and quietly for an hour or so. Children these days have such poor attention spans.'

I somehow find myself retreating to the playroom to find Noah. 'That woman!' I exclaim as I pass through the kitchen where Ben is spooning coffee into the cafetiere.

He laughs. 'Mrs Butterworth, by any chance?'

'She wants me to bring Noah into the meeting. She thinks I should be there…' I make air quotes, 'as "vicar's wife".'

Ben shrugs. 'You never know, you may find it interesting.'

'Are you actually serious?' I head into the playroom and extract Noah, along with a couple of trucks, Croccy, and his favourite Julia Donaldson. 'I'm only doing this for you,' I say playfully as I walk back through the kitchen.

I expect Ben to laugh, even to wrap an arm around me. But he simply stares at the cafetiere, preoccupied by something completely other.

'So,' says Ben.

I can tell he's nervous. He's sitting with his legs wide, elbows propped on his knees, trying to appear confident. But I know it's all a front. He stumbles over his words as he asks whether everyone has the agenda on their phones and sloshes coffee on the floor when he reaches for his. Is it because I'm here? Is he worried that I'm judging? Inwardly criticising? I sit back in my chair and the envelope crackles.

'Reverend Allen always used to print out the agenda,' says Mrs Butterworth. She fiddles with an old Nokia. 'I don't know how to—'

'Share mine,' says Gordon Moss, shoving a surprisingly sleek iPhone under her nose. 'We've done *Welcome* and *Apologies*, really.' He jabs at his screen. 'We're onto *Order of the Ritual*.' He looks up. 'I'll take this one, Vicar.'

Mrs Butterworth pulls herself straight. This is evidently what she came here for.

Gordon Moss takes a slurp of coffee. 'Firstly, the order of procession to the tree... at the front there will be you, Vicar.'

Ben nods.

'You will offer the rite of asperges as you walk towards the tree – sprinkling holy water over the assembled crowds. For purification. Reverend Allen always used a sprig of rosemary as a means to spray the water. You may wish to do the same. There's a large bush at the back of your garden.'

Again, Ben nods, his mouth twitching at one corner.

'Following behind the Reverend will come the children in their masks.' Gordon Moss looks over at Noah, who's wheeling his yellow truck between the legs of my chair. 'The children have all made masks at school. Crows...'

Ben and I shoot a look at each other.

Gordon Moss frowns. 'They make the most grotesque, frightening masks they possibly can – lots of papier mâché, black paint, and giant cardboard beaks. It's fun for the children but, of course, the meaning is a serious one – to frighten the Barrow Man back underground for another year and to guide lost spirits to the afterlife. Young Noah here will have missed the mask-making this year but I'm sure, Ms Greenwood, you might be able to cobble something together later so that he doesn't feel left out.'

I cough. 'I'm not sure I'm getting this,' I begin. 'Are you saying that...'

'Masks,' says Ben, cutting across me. 'Made at the local primary school.' He glares at me. I'm interfering with his job again, I'm guessing. But surely, he must be able to see that—

'Then, fire,' continues Gordon Moss, completely ignoring my interjection. 'Rush torches. At the back of the procession. A symbol of judgement and cleansing evil. Which, of course, is what this ritual's all about.'

Ben mutters agreement as Gordon Moss drones on and on, and Noah makes a screeching noise with his trucks. Mrs Butterworth glares. Flowers at the tree. The party afterwards. Morris dancers. Maypole. Someone to set up the trestle tables in the hall, first thing.

I sit with my arms folded, only half listening to the rest of it. The whole Barrow Man thing sounds okay in a kind of quaint, folky way, but the fact that these people are taking it so seriously is strange. They pass around copies of Ben's prayers, which he's printed out, much to the approval of Mrs Butterworth, and they all nod and agree that they are fitting for the occasion.

'Except,' says Mrs Butterworth, flapping her copy of the prayers in Ben's direction. 'There's no mention of the Reverend Phineas Kibble.'

Ben clears his throat. 'Reverend Kibble… er… should there be?'

'Of course!' Mrs Butterworth thrusts a hand in the air and sits back in her chair dramatically. The chair stutters backwards slightly and wobbles on the loose floorboard. She makes an exaggerated tutting noise.

'Most certainly,' says Gordon Moss, looking up from his iPhone. 'It is customary to include him in our prayers. Giving thanks for his wisdom and foresight, without which we, as a community, would never have survived.'

I smother a laugh which I quickly make out has something to do with Noah's truck game. Fortunately, Noah chooses that moment to run a toy car over my foot.

'I see,' says Ben, shooting me a glare, before scribbling on his bit of paper. 'Reverend Phineas Kibble,' he says slowly as he writes the name down.

'Very important,' stresses Mrs Butterworth. 'He's quite the hero in Hope-under-Barrow. And while we're ensuring protection for the present age, we must not forget and honour the past.'

A look passes between Lisa and Iain which I can't quite place, and I detect a shift in mood.

Outside, dusk creeps in. I stand and shut the curtains, the noise as they drag across the rails making everyone stare.

'Sorry,' I murmur, resuming my place on the plastic seat. Noah makes a vrooming sound and wheels his truck over my legs. He turns the Julia Donaldson book into a ramp.

Everyone looks at him, but no one says a thing. It feels just like it does before a storm. A thick stillness, waiting to break.

And then it does.

'I don't like to mention this,' says Lisa. She looks briefly at Iain, then reaches out and squeezes his hand. 'But *we* feel that now there's a child living so close to the churchyard, that extra precautions should be taken.'

I stare in disbelief. 'Do you mean Noah?'

Noah looks up, then resumes his game.

Lisa takes a sharp breath. 'I don't want to scare you, Kate – or you, Ben – but many of the tragedies that have occurred in the village have involved children. Not all, but many, and I think it would only be sensible to—'

'You can't actually be serious?' I cry, wishing that my son was anywhere but in the room, hearing this. 'What on earth's going to happen to Noah?'

Ben crosses his legs and shuffles his prayer papers feverishly. 'Kate,' he mutters under his breath.

But something has broken in me. I remember Lisa saying that I shouldn't joke about Barrow Man Day, I remember that I need to be accepting and play the part of the good vicar's wife and not make a fuss. But this. *This.* 'Nothing is going to happen to Noah,' I say, firmly. 'I've told him to keep away from the tree, but that's only because… because…' I find I don't want to mention the *tree drink* incident and risk us looking like negligent parents, '... because he might try climbing it and fall,' I conclude.

Gordon Moss clears his throat. 'I did warn Ms Greenwood,' he says. 'Not the finer details,' he throws a look at Lisa, '... but...' He trails off and takes a sip of his coffee, which must surely be cold by now. 'Ms Greenwood had a fanciful notion of painting the tree.'

'I *am* painting the tree,' I mumble.

Out of the corner of my eye, I catch Ben clenching and unclenching his fists.

'And I told her to keep the boy away,' finishes Gordon Moss, ignoring my interjection.

Noah stops playing with his truck and surveys the adults, realising that they're talking about him. 'Mummy?' he says, in a small voice.

'Well, I think that winds up...' begins Ben.

'No!' says Lisa, suddenly getting to her feet. Iain joins her, not looking at anyone, hands deep in the pockets of his baggy chinos. 'Tell her what happened,' she says to her husband. 'Tell them.'

Iain, who has barely spoken a word the entire meeting, clears his throat. 'Our son – Alfie – well, he... he died. Four years ago. On Barrow Man Day. Before the ritual was performed to keep us safe for another year. He was climbing the yew tree. Slipped. Hit his head on one of the gravestones. He was taken into hospital but... but he didn't make it.'

The room is silent.

I remember the photo on Lisa's mantelpiece. A good-looking little boy with copper curls, clutching his little sister tight.

Gordon Moss and Mrs Butterworth evidently know all of this already and I see Mrs Butterworth giving Lisa a sympathetic look. Iain pulls his wife close, as tears weave down her cheeks.

So, what is Iain saying? That the folk magic, protective

prayers, or whatever, ran out before midnight? Like in a fairy tale. Devastating, obviously. But preposterous.

I say nothing.

Then, somewhere, outside of myself, I hear Ben fracture the silence, urging the Halls to sit again, that he will say some prayers and consider any further suggestions they have to make. Noah clings to my leg, game forgotten. But I move into a different space. My head whirs and whirs, the room spins, and I see Julie, running, running, running, while I call after her, my voice caught in the branches, in the air, in that vital, tragic slip of time.

38

OCTAVIA

Dorsetshire 1866

There is a great storm on the way. I gaze out of the dining room window, after a solitary meal of pie and carrots. Father did not appear at the table, and I hated to think how he might be occupied with his bowl of yew needles. Weighty clouds hang low, the sky is darkening, and daylight is slipping fast. Rain splats the glass and it rattles as the wind hurls itself at the house. I think of the March farm and the cattle out there on the heath. The sick animals. The dying animals. The dead.

My imaginings are interrupted by the slam of the front door.

I rise and head for the window, peering out to see Father in his clerical cape hurrying in the direction of the church.

He rushes through the graveyard and disappears. At once, I know where he is bound and push back my chair. Some inner sense tells me that he is heading for the March farm to perform his ludicrous plan. I run out into the passageway and rummage on the coat stand until I find Mother's old woollen coat, which will stand some chance in a storm. I pull it on. It is stiff and still smells of her and a thousand storms before now. For a moment, I am motionless, inhaling and remembering.

Then there's a clatter of pans from the kitchen. I am rushed back to the present and do up the buttons, fingers fast and fumbling. Mother was a small lady, but even so, the coat is large on me, the material heavy and cumbersome. But there is no time to worry. It will have to do, and I cannot waste any more time and risk discovery. Nanny Butterworth, I know, would prevent me from going outdoors in this weather.

I fiddle with the latch and let myself out into the rain. The driveway is like a mire and, at once, my boots are soaked as I hurry across it and into the graveyard. I cannot see Father, but I can guess where he's gone and, as I round the huddle of thatched cottages and approach the coffin lane, I see him making his approach to the heath. I shrink back for a moment, afraid that he will turn and see me. But he presses on, head down against the rain and blustering wind. I quicken my step, making my own way towards the heath. Here, the weather worsens. Thick mud bubbles down the hill like lava and my boots sink into it with every step. I almost consider turning back. Back to the warm kitchen fire, to a certain reprimand from Nanny Butterworth, but to shelter and a shield from the elements.

I look over my shoulder, to the lights in the cottages, to the church and the vicarage. My gaze rests on the yew tree and, instantly, I turn back to the heath. I must press on. Up ahead, Father is making good progress, despite the weather. I swat away the wet hair plastered to my face and follow, my one driving motivation making me place one foot in front of the other as I clamber and slip and use every bit of my strength to make my way up to the March farm. I pass scraggly cattle, no more than bones and sodden coats. I pass gorse, bending and bowing in the wind. Then, I think I hear a lament, a sorrowful calling in the voice of the wind. Maybe it is simply in my mind, an auditory hallucination brought on by the cold and my distress. But that voice pulls me on and begs me to go faster.

Alice, it howls. *Alice.*

39

KATE

Dorset 2026

Everyone has left the meeting. Noah has been sent to pack away his trucks and book, and Ben and I stare at each other in the study.

'I can't believe you were so insensitive,' says Ben. 'That poor couple. What they must have been through. What they *are* going through. They—'

'How was I supposed to know they'd lost a kid?' I throw my hands in the air. But even as I do, I know I'm in the wrong and that this is worse, way worse than the doll incident. My response to their warning must have cut deep.

'Kate, you're too reactionary,' continues Ben. 'Too quick to judge. Too sure of yourself.'

'And you're not?'

Ben shakes his head, looks away from me. He shuffles some papers on his desk, slamming them about, muttering about something he's mislaid. I know what it is and can feel the stiffness of the envelope in my back pocket. He gives up and strides across the room, stopping as he gets to the door. He rounds on me. 'And I can't believe you're still intent on painting that bloody tree. We've discussed this.'

'No, we haven't. You told me not to paint it. That's not the same thing.'

Ben glares at me, his eyes like flint. 'Why can't you see that insisting on this is a bad idea? You've seen how they all are about that tree.'

'But it's all superstitious nonsense,' I counter, mentally dismissing some of the odd things I've felt there. 'I can't let them – or you – dictate to me like this.'

Ben sighs. 'I just need your support, Kate. But that's obviously too much to ask.'

'I—'

'Forget it. I'm going to run Noah's bath,' he says, reaching underneath one of the plastic chairs for Croccy. 'It's late. He should be in bed.'

I glance about me. The half-drunk cups of coffee, the plate with a litter of crumbs and a solitary custard cream, Ben's prayers dumped on the floor by the side of his chair.

'I'll just tidy up in here,' I say, quietly. Because I can't bear the thought of launching straight into the bedtime routine, pretending that everything's normal, putting on the act I know we need to perform for Noah. I need to clear my head, maybe admit to myself that I'm sorry. 'I'll be up in a bit,' I add.

'As you like,' says Ben, turning. And I feel a pang of sadness as I watch him retreat. Trace the back of the head I know so well, the curve of his neck, the broadness of his shoulders. A lump settles in my throat. *Oh God, what's happening to us in this place?* I hold my breath, let it out as Ben shuts the door behind him. I swallow the lump. *And where will it end?*

Quickly, I gather the mugs together, sweep crumbs from the

table onto the plate and dump the lot in the kitchen to deal with in the morning. Then I head back to the study and begin stacking the chairs.

The floorboard under Mrs Butterworth's chair creaks as I stand on it. I jiggle it with my feet, testing the extent of the problem, and notice, for the first time, it's not screwed in properly. It's missing a nail at one end. Maybe explains it. And then, as I look, I see that there's something protruding from one side. I'm pretty sure it wasn't there a second ago, so I'm guessing I must have disturbed things.

I look closely.

It's a tiny corner of yellow paper.

My chest dances with excitement as a rush of mystery stories from my childhood bubble in my mind. Loose floorboards, hidden treasure, secret maps, keys to mysterious places…

With a clatter, I shove Mrs Butterworth's chair into the stack with the others.

We could be sitting on an absolute fortune.

Don't be ridiculous, I tell myself but, all the same, I find I'm calling upstairs to Ben, telling him I'm just doing something and will be up shortly to say goodnight to Noah.

Then, I'm sorting through the toolbox, still dumped in the corner of the study from when we put the shelves up, searching for the nail puller and utility bar.

It won't take a minute, I'm sure.

The wood is old, and soon I have several splinters, but the board comes up easily enough, releasing puffs of dust and the smell of damp. I peer below. More dust and rubble but also… I reach into the gap and brush my hand over a bundle of yellowing paper. Just as I thought. It's old and brittle to the touch and I ease it out carefully.

There are other things too, beneath the paper. My mouth is dry and my hands tremble as I lift each one out in turn and lay them on the wooden floor.

There's a brooch, black like a lump of coal, and decorated with flowers and pinecones. There's a fine lace collar, yellow with age; a single glove, soft and made to fit the smallest of hands; some sort of greetings card with fat cherubs on the front and the single initial *A* written inside in dull ink, and a dried, shrivelled flower that crumbles when I lift it. Finally, there's an old leather notebook. I open it and flick through. It appears to be filled with strange diary entries but what they mean, I can't say.

Monday April 2. Fine day. Rabbit. Burrow 6–7am.
Tuesday April 3. Wind NW. Kit. Nothing until midday. Burrow.
Wednesday April 4. Dull day. Weasel. 8pm or thereabouts. Heath.

'What is this?' I whisper to myself. Then, 'Ben, come here!' I yell in the direction of the ceiling, my argument with him temporarily forgotten. 'Ben! You have to see this.'

I turn my attention back to the papers. There are many of them, bundled together and tied with string. I unpick the knot, my fingers shaking, sure that I must have stumbled across something of great importance. Something important enough for someone to hide away. The string gives and the papers fall, curled like thin layers of peeling bark.

I pick one up. There is writing all over it, scribbles in the margins, spots of ink, great blots in places. And the script is small, hard to read. I bring it close to my face to make out the words. *April 1866*. And then I see the word *homily*.

My heart sinks.

At that moment, Ben crashes into the room, annoyance written all over his face. 'What is it now?' he asks. He snatches a look over his shoulder and I know he's also thinking about Noah and the unfinished bedtime routine.

My hands flop onto my lap. The paper slips to the floor. 'Sermons,' I say, my chest deflating. Suddenly, all I want to do is go to bed. I wipe my mucky fingers on my jeans. 'I just found a bunch of old sermons. More your thing than mine, right? But...' I gesture to the collection of other items. 'I also found some pretty cool things. Really old stuff. Take a look.'

Extract from a sermon given by the Reverend Phineas Kibble, May 1866.

The text for today's homily is taken from the Gospel according to Saint Mark, chapter ten.

'And Jesus said unto him, Go thy way; thy faith hath made thee whole. And immediately he received his sight, and followed Jesus in the way...'

... Dear friends, the healing miracles of Jesus encourage us to see the truth of our created order.

Many may argue that they are instances of the mind's ability to triumph over the body. But I say to you that, rather, they demonstrate greater, miraculous power outside of us.

It is a power that I now witness every day.

40

KATE

Dorset 2026

Ben pours two large glasses of wine, and we take them into the lounge. The collection of items I found under the study floorboards lie on the coffee table like police exhibits, filling the room with questions. And, in my back pocket, I feel the burn of the envelope and the curiosity that threatens to overwhelm me.

'I'm sorry,' Ben says, as soon as we sit down, crunched on the too-small Ikea sofa.

'Me too,' I offer. Though to be honest, I don't really know what I'm feeling about any of this. At St Martin's things were straightforward. Back there, Ben ran Bible studies and visited sick people. The older members of the congregation were sweet and doting, if a little overbearing, and the younger members were mostly from socially deprived areas, looking for a different way out. All stuff I could just about understand and try to relate to. This, however, is completely out of my comfort zone. All these strange superstitions and ancient beliefs, spoken about as if they're real, as if there's something out there that will get us all if we don't quite get the magic formula right. And the things under the study floorboards. There's something there that I can't quite grasp. Something nudging at the corner of my mind, just out of reach. Irrationally, it feels connected, though I couldn't say how. 'I just don't get any of this,' I say, a poor summary of my wandering thoughts.

Ben takes a gulp of his wine.

I do the same. It's sharp-tasting, cheap, with a slightly petrol-like overtone that makes my head swim.

'Places like this are unique,' he says. 'You're used to other problems – crime, poverty, dysfunctional families, failing schools.'

'You mean real life,' I say.

Ben takes another sip of wine. 'A different life. This is real life, too, you know.'

I shake my head. 'But it's not. I mean, do you really believe something's going to happen to Noah if we don't say some crappy made-up nonsense or offer gifts to the tree gods, or whatever?'

Ben is silent.

'You don't believe in the ritual, do you?' I say. 'Surely…'

'Kate, sometimes it doesn't matter whether things are *true* or not.' He makes air quotes around the word. 'What matters is the meaning people give to their words and actions.'

'You mean like a placebo effect.'

'Sort of.' He shifts slightly on the sofa so that our legs are no longer touching. The small gap between us feels like an ocean. 'I guess what I really mean is that if something brings comfort, or a feeling of safety, or a sense of belonging then it's worth doing. Even if it seems irrational or nonsensical to outsiders.' He pauses and looks at me. 'Lisa and Iain need all of this because of their loss, and the rest of the village need it to feel safe and secure. It also brings people together. Gives us a sense of community.' He twirls the stem of his wine glass between finger and thumb. 'And it's my job to make sure that these things are upheld and that they give people the comfort and reassurance they feel they need.'

What he says all makes sense, even if I'm not ready to admit it.

Silence grows and spins around us.

I think of the tree and the weird things I've remembered when I'm near it; the face I thought I saw in the trunk. Despite my scoffing, if I'm completely honest, it almost seems as if the area has a power, some sort of strange energy, just as the villagers say. The very energy they want protection against. Not that I'd admit any of this out loud. I'm having enough of a problem trying to make sense of it to myself and still desperately want to believe that I'm just getting carried away in this place.

I take a mouthful of wine and splutter as the harshness hits my throat. My head reels.

It's likely that I'm highly stressed and things from my past are surfacing and mutating into new monsters. I'm simply reinventing the old demons that have been haunting me since childhood.

We drink our wine. I top up the glasses. The silence pounds.

'Anyway, what about all this stuff you found?' says Ben, after a while. His tone is different, brighter, the effort of trying to change the mood jarring.

I shrug. 'It's pretty weird. As in, why would someone hide all of this away? It's not exactly treasure, is it?'

'I don't know,' says Ben. He lays his wine glass down and picks up the black brooch. 'It's like I was saying, these things must have had meaning to someone at some point. Only that meaning is completely lost.' He turns the brooch over, rubs it softly. 'I'm guessing all of these things belonged to the same person.' He puts the brooch down and picks up the card. '*A* – whoever that was. She obviously wrote the card – a Valentine's card, maybe. Certainly looks tacky enough.' He runs a finger over one of the fat cherubs on the front, then fingers the notebook. 'This looks like some kind of nature diary or something. It's pretty boring, whatever it is. The other stuff is probably hers too.'

'Except the sermons,' I say.

Ben looks at me quizzically.

'Women didn't really write great long theological papers in those days, did they? The other things obviously belonged to a woman, but whoever she was, she almost certainly didn't write those sermons. Maybe not the card either – *A* could be a man, for all we know.'

'I guess.'

I reach over to the coffee table and pick up the bundle of sermons. 'Why would you bother saving all these? Hiding them away?' I'm speaking more to myself than Ben, but he leans over and tries to read as I unfold the papers.

'Book of Job,' he says. He tries to take the paper from me, but I hold onto it, suddenly, unreasonably, protective. This was *my* find. He mutters, reading out a word here and there. 'Well, this guy certainly knew how to keep an audience rapt,' he says with a laugh, sarcasm brimming. 'His congregations must have been hanging on every word.'

'They were long too,' I say, flicking through the sheets. The paper is brittle and smells strongly of damp. It gives me an odd feeling too, a sort of weird connection with the past and the people who once lived here. I make out a sentence or two with growing interest.

For one day you will surely die, and if you are cold, then that coldness will follow you into the earth and be with you there, forever.

I shiver. Morbid, or what? I look at Ben, who's still trying to read over my shoulder. 'I suppose, at the time, it was the clergy's main form of communication,' I say. 'I mean, most of the village would have attended church in those days and the priest had the chance to have a big influence. The pulpit was his soapbox.'

'Yeah, not like today.' Ben falls back on the sofa. The springs whine. He downs the rest of his wine. 'I'm going to turn in,' he says. 'It's been a long and trying evening.'

And immediately, he's driven the wedge between us again, reminding us both of earlier.

'You go up,' I say, quickly. I flap the papers. 'I'm just going to...'

Ben stands, heads for the door. 'I'll leave you with your dusty old priest,' he says. He tries a smile. 'Don't wake me when you come up. I'm done for.'

He leaves and I listen as he makes his way up the stairs, the creaks and groans a heralding of my solitude.

I breathe out, the room emptying and sighing.

I will read the sermons. For reasons I can't even begin to explain. But first... I dig the blue envelope out from my back pocket. I smooth it over and then open it, edging out a letter from inside. Carefully, with a shaking hand, I unfold the single sheet of paper and begin to read.

The Hole,
Cheshire,
24th June 2002

Dear Tommy,
I hope you are feeling a bit better after your cold.

I have exciting news! Tonight, Kate Greenwood is letting me come with her to the Shadow Woods to hang out with Frankie, Ryan and the others! I am so happy. As you know,

Kate has been mean to me lately – going off without me, hanging around with them and pretending I don't even exist. But, at last, I have a real chance!

I have to do a test though. To prove I'm worthy. Kate's sorted it all out for me – it was her idea. You know the Death Tree in the woods? I have to climb right to the top of it, even to the places where the branches get really thin and spindly. I'm a bit scared but I think it's going to be worth it. Kate says I have to do it and that if I don't, she's ditching me because it will prove I'm boring. She can be a bit like that sometimes.

Have you ever wanted something so much that you'd do anything to get it? Well, that's how I feel about this thing. I want to be accepted and not get bullied anymore. Frankie, Ryan and co. make my life hell. Since you left, I have to make my own way. Anyway, I trust Kate, even if I'm a bit worried about it all. It's this evening. Think about me (even though by the time you get this letter, I will already have done it and will be one of them).

I can't wait until you come home. This place really is a hole without you.

Love, Julie.

P.S. I've included a photo of me and Kate in the park. Mum took it.

41

OCTAVIA

Dorsetshire 1866

The farmhouse is in darkness. It is possible that Mrs March is sitting within, rocking backwards and forwards in that old chair of hers. But no smoke rises from the chimney, and the only sound is that of the wind whipping at gorse or wailing around the stone farmhouse in agony. The storm has truly taken hold now, and I find myself buffeted in all directions, Mother's coat flapping at the bottom, the fabric damp and heavy, making it difficult to move with any speed.

Through the rain, I squint into the dark evening, looking for Father. For anyone. But I have already seen two of Alice's brothers out on the heath, on my way up here. Out by the sheep pens, fighting with wooden fencing in the gale, herding the beasts into their fold. They lost their dog but a fortnight ago and now it is just the men, doing what they can to save the farm. The sheep and a few pigs are all they have now.

With frantic fervour, I look around the farmyard, careful to stick to the deepest shadows lest Father spots me, but there is no one to be seen. It is almost as if the place has been deserted, left to the elements.

But then, the farmhouse door opens, creaking on its hinges in the wind, and a figure emerges, holding a lantern high. The light sways in the wind, the flame within darts, and catches the figure's face in its meek amber glow.

Alice.

I duck by the wall as she hurries across the yard, right to the corner where the bull house is. I remember now:

It's my duty to see to the bull.

I suppress my instinct to call out a warning and wonder how best to attract her attention without Father knowing. For he must be in the vicinity. Watching, waiting for his moment.

Alice hovers on the threshold of the bull house.

Morning and evening, regular as anything.

Father knows this too and I see now that he has timed his visit to perfection.

In the wind, Alice struggles with the lantern and the pen gate and, at last, places the lantern on the ground while she slides the bolt back. I think she must sense something for, just before entering the bull house, she pauses and scans the yard. I catch the gleam of her pupils caught for a moment in the light reflected from the ground and read the uncertainty in her face. But she dismisses whatever has concerned her and turns her attention back to the task. She pulls her shawl tighter around her frame and retrieves the lantern from the ground.

No sooner has she entered the bull house than I watch Father's form reveal itself from the shadows. He follows Alice into the small building.

A cry of shock carries on the wind, and at that moment, the moon emerges from behind the rampaging clouds. I take the opportunity of the light and run across the farmyard, calling to Father, calling to Alice, my voice shouting to the heavens. From the bull house, there's the sound of something falling, crashing to the stone floor, and when I reach the building it is in darkness. The light from the lantern has been snuffed out and, somewhere, the lamp is rolling on the stone. A *clatter, clatter, clatter* that slows and eventually stops.

'Father!' I shout. In the moonlight, I catch his hands around Alice's neck and see that he's pushing her against the wall. The bull is thrashing and tugging at his chain. There is fury in the animal's eyes, his nose is wet, his breath billowing.

Father has a vial, and he has it pressed up to Alice's mouth. 'Drink this, Alice,' he says, his voice rough and urgent. 'A few careful sips. Just enough for you to see to the other side. And remember what to do when the sickness has passed. The bell, remember, the bell.' He tells her to trust in the Lord and in Mr Jefferies, who has made the despicable coffin with its evil workings.

Alice will not drink. She refuses and struggles and tries to push her assailant away. She, who had once been so keen to conduct the experiment, is taken by shock now, her natural instincts fuelling her as she kicks out and throws her arms about.

I call out once more and rush at Father.

'No!' I cry. 'Do not do this. Stop it, Father! Stop it.'

Father rounds on me, for a moment, relieving Alice. She splutters and gasps. But he still has her held and she cannot move. Cannot raise an alarm or run to the farmhouse for safety, as he must suppose she will.

'Get away from here, Octavia,' yells Father. The warning in his voice is fearsome, a rage to match the storm. 'I know what I'm doing.'

'Oh, but you don't,' I scream. 'You cannot do this to Alice. I cannot lose her. I love her too much.'

I reach out, trying to stop him, but miss as he pushes me back with his elbow. He catches me sharply in the ribs. There's a spike of pain and I give a winded cry.

'Leave me be.' Father turns back to Alice and calls to me over his shoulder. 'Go home, Octavia! This is too great an involvement for you.'

I smell the yew tree then or, at least, my mind tricks me into thinking so. The rich bitterness of it, the dank earthiness. The memories swim through my head in a haze – the man with the pipes, the lamb, the heathland animals.

Father gives a throaty cry as he tips the vial once more. He calls over his shoulder again, his voice coloured by hatred and irritation. 'It is a thing that a foolish child such as yourself cannot begin to understand.'

I see a glint of glass, hear Alice splutter. 'Reverend, release me. Please. I will do your bidding, if only you will release me. In my own time, sir. And by my own hand. Not like this, I beg of you.'

'No!' I shout. 'Alice, Father, no!'

In the darkness, the bull huffs.

'You will defy me, Octavia?' Father's voice rises to match my tone. 'I can see I will have to deal with you later.' He punches each word out, the threat mounting. 'Now go!'

I laugh. He means to discipline me. Put me back in a place I will not go. 'I refuse,' I cry with all my strength. And I launch myself at Father's back. At this, the bull pants and cries. It is a terrifying sound that rips through the small confines of the building and makes the hairs on my neck bristle.

Father broadens his shoulders and pushes Alice against the wall with new vigour. She screams, splutters and spits. 'Octavia, please leave,' she manages. 'Please.'

But I batter my fists on Father's back, pummelling him hard. He tries to shake me off at the same time as he attempts to administer his concoction, working quickly, before the noise of the bull summons others to the enclosure. My pleas make no difference so, with both fists, I beat him, slamming at the space between the shoulder blades. He cries and flies around. 'You stupid, stupid, girl.' His voice is a-tremble. Soft and stuttering, now. 'What have you... what have you done?'

My hands drop at the sudden change in his tone. It scares me. He is no longer shouting, no longer full of vigour. 'Father?'

'The proportion,' he says, shaking. 'She was not meant to take it all.' He releases Alice and grips my wrist so tightly that I gasp. Behind him, Alice slumps against the wall, crying and wheezing. 'You caused my hand to slip,' he says. 'With your infernal beating and rough handling.' He brings his face close to mine, his breath rank with meat and stale port. 'If Alice should die, her death will rest upon your shoulders, Octavia. You will be damned for the whole of eternity. You will burn in hell with sinners.'

'Father?' This time it is my voice that trembles. In the weak moonlight, I pick out Alice, slumped, sliding down the wall to meet the hard floor. She is gasping, clutching at her throat where Father had her held tight. My friend. I want to run to her, but Father still has me by the wrist and bars my way.

'Octavia!' she breathes. 'Help me. Please, help me. I... I swallowed it all.'

But Father tightens his grip. 'You are coming home with me,' he says. 'I cannot think what the outcome of this will be. If the girl dies, we cannot be found here.'

There's a sudden splitting sound, the clunk of a chain, a terrible metallic dragging. The hideous, mad snorting that has been our background turns into a rage that fills the night.

'The bull!' I cry.

Somehow, the great beast has wrenched its chain from the wall. Hooves stamp on the stone, while the chain and its fixture clank and rattle. The bull moans, a hell-filled sound of outrage.

And from outside, there is shouting on the wind. Men's voices, coming up from the heath. Alice's brothers, her pa. Have they heard the commotion from the bull house? Do they suspect intruders?

Father pulls at my wrist and yanks me into the cold, into the wind and the beating rain and we run into the night, leaving Alice alone to her fate.

42

KATE

Dorset 2026

I lower the letter, a panicked sickness churning in my stomach. How has Ben ended up with a letter from Julie Moon to her brother? What must he make of it? It certainly doesn't paint me in a good light, and for valid reasons. I drag my nails down my face. I need to think this through. Calmly, rationally. I let my hands fall to my lap, my panic mounting. *Think, Kate, think.* He won't understand any of it, I assure myself. He won't know how it all spiralled into disaster after she wrote that letter. He won't know my part in it.

I eye the fat bubble writing again, the letters merging one into another.

Why hasn't Ben asked me about it? Why has he kept it to himself?

I make a quick decision and, after gulping the dregs of my wine, hurry outside to where we keep the wheelie bins. The night wraps itself around me and I shiver as I lift the lid of the recycling bin. Then, in fast, jerky movements, I rip the letter into a million pieces, before rearranging the existing rubbish so that the bits float to the bottom like snowflakes. A pale moon shines down on me, illuminating my covert activity. I shut the lid quickly, scanning the driveway as if afraid someone might have seen what I was doing. The black yawns back at me and a cold breeze stings my face. There's no one there.

I slip back into the house, and collapse on the sofa in the lounge. I wish there was more wine. Something to deaden my anxiety. But the letter has gone, I tell myself firmly, straightening up with attempted determination. It's the end of it. I will never have to bring it up with Ben. I can forget about it. The anxiety tightens my stomach, and I know I'm lying to myself.

I try turning my attention to something else and lean forwards, reaching for the sermons and the notebook. On closer inspection, they were clearly written by the same person. The curves, loops and formation of the letters is the same. Also, the way that the author has paused at the end of some words so that a blot of ink has formed on the paper is a feature throughout both.

I begin with the sermons. My eyes are soon stinging as I try to decipher the old-fashioned writing and pull apart the antiquated rhetoric. I skim some parts, especially those bits which read like long commentaries on complicated Biblical texts. But slowly, bit by bit, I start to build up a picture.

I flash a look at my phone.

Nearly midnight, and next time I look, it's gone two.

The house is deathly silent, and I lean back on the sofa, trying to digest what I've read. I haven't gone through all of the sermons; the writing is small and hard to read and, frankly, a lot of it is boring. But I've read enough to tell me two things. Firstly, that they were written by Phineas Kibble because I found his name scrawled at the head of one of the pages. And secondly, that he was crazy. He had a dramatic and sudden change of opinion about the yew tree in the churchyard, going from wonder to fear, seemingly overnight. He preached, in some of the earlier sermons, that the tree was sacred; and then later, he tells his congregation to stay away from it, for fear of the Barrow Man. A belief that still holds. It's clear that his mind deteriorated, that he twisted theology for some unknown purpose. That he was not the upright man the villagers today believe he was.

I turn to the notebook, easing open the leather cover with a soft cracking noise. Page after page is filled with strange entries that I don't understand.

> Thursday April 5. Light rain. Rabbit. Noon precisely. Heath.
> Friday April 6. Wind S. Very warm and close. 9am. Burrow. Very clear and strong.

I skip through the pages.

> Tuesday May 29. Dry. Coney. Heath. Magnificent experience alongside creature. Best progress yet.

It goes on and on, telling me nothing and confusing me more. I flick through the book trying to locate something that will make sense.

And then I find it.

A different entry, right at the end of the book.

I go cold.

I read the words again, wanting them to reform into something else. But the meaning is quite clear. I trail my finger under the sentence and whisper the words into the night. *'For the death of Alice March, I am guilty, and for that sin, I will burn in hell.'*

I snap the notebook shut, the sound sharp in the quiet of the house. Phineas Kibble was more than simply deluded, more than a man who had lost his mind. He was a *killer.* He caused the death of a girl called Alice. The confession is quite plain.

I rub at my arms, my gaze darting to the dark corners of the lounge as if someone or something is there. Silence thumps until I can no longer stand it. I bundle the sermons up and shove them, together with the notebook, on a bookshelf.

I think of the small headstone beneath the yew tree. Was that the Alice he was referring to? And then there was the name *Alice* carved into the wall of the bull house up at the old farm. Could it be the same person? Did Reverend Kibble kill a fifteen-year-old girl who lived or worked on the top of Barrow Hill?

I swallow the rising nausea as I contemplate the dreadful thought that tomorrow – Barrow Man Day – the whole village will perform a ritual and celebrate in honour of their hero and saviour, Reverend Phineas Kibble. The man who was a killer.

Extract from a sermon given
by the Reverend Phineas Kibble,
June 1866.

The text for today's homily is taken from the Gospel according to Saint Matthew, chapter twenty-four.

'And because iniquity shall abound, the love of many shall wax cold...'

... Beloved, there are many distractions in this world, many evils and evildoers who are intent on drawing us away from the true path of faith.

I urge you today to hold fast to your faith in Jesus Christ, so that you will not grow cold. For one day you will surely die, and if you are cold, then that coldness will follow you into the earth and be with you there, forever. Others will know of it, even in death, and your torment will be great.

Friends, I have now heard the dead speak of their ills.

I have heard them with my own ears.

Be that not so for you and be sure to live good and holy lives.

43

KATE

Dorset 2026

Barrow Man Day dawns bright and warm. By the time I wake, the sun is already high in a sky of perfect blue. Despite everything, I've slept longer and deeper than I have in a long while, a dreamless sleep which has left me spaced out and disorientated.

Ben is already up, the covers on his side of the bed pushed back, the sheets cold. I glance at my alarm clock. Noah must be up by now too and I feel a rush of gratitude that Ben didn't wake me, that he must have fixed breakfast for the two of them and let me sleep. It almost feels like the old times.

I get out of bed and shove back the curtains. The yew tree scowls at me, and I feel a moment of heaviness, thinking again about the previous evening; the meeting, the letter, the sermons I've read, the notebook. The awfulness of it all.

I slide my slippers on and head for the door. My mouth feels rank after the awful wine, but my mind is sharp, my pulse singing with everything that I discovered the previous evening. Although… I pause… I still can't help feeling as if there's something I'm missing. Something hiding that I can't find.

I throw on a dressing gown and shuffle downstairs, stopping near the bottom when I hear voices from the kitchen. My shoulders sag and my gratitude dissolves into irritation. That's the thing about living in a vicarage. It's never really a proper home. People feel they have a claim on it. For Ben it's also his office, for me it's a place I can never quite call my own. And there are people in the kitchen when all I want to do is have breakfast.

I turn, ready to creep back up the stairs when Ben appears in the hallway clutching a mug. 'I made you coffee,' he says. 'With sugar *and* cream.' He hands me the drink.

I make myself smile as I take the mug. 'I'll have it upstairs,' I say, nodding in the direction of the kitchen. 'Is Noah—'

'We went for a walk on the heath while you were sleeping. And now he's just eating his Shreddies. He wants toast and peanut butter as well. Don't disappear. Could you—'

'Ben!' I gesture to my dressing gown with my free hand.

'It's only Gordon Moss and Mrs Butterworth. They won't mind.'

But I do, I think. I'm just opening my mouth to tell him so when Mrs Butterworth pokes her head around our kitchen door. She gives me a thin smile. 'I'm sorry,' she says, bypassing Ben and looking straight at me. 'But your little boy has just upset his cereal. It's all over the place, I'm afraid.'

'I'll sort it,' says Ben at once, darting a look at my dressing gown, feeding off my reaction. Knowing what I was about to say and how much I mean it.

But Mrs Butterworth shakes her head. 'I don't like to interfere, Vicar. But we need to get on with the arrangements for tonight. I've put the flowers in the sink, Mr Moss is folding the leaflets for the ritual. Lisa and Iain are down at the hall already and I think we need to go and give them a hand as soon as we're done here.'

Ben and I exchange glances, and I can tell he's wavering.

'It's okay,' I say, with a sigh. I slip past Ben and into the kitchen where Noah is trying to spoon up soggy Shreddies from the kitchen table into his mouth. He's also covered in mud – evidence of his early morning walk, I presume. Gordon Moss is ignoring the mess and is pressing neat creases into a stack of leaflets: *Barrow Man Day, 2026.*

'Noah, stop eating those,' I say, trying to keep the irritation out of my voice, the sense of intrusion biting at me as I yank the box of Shreddies from the cupboard and find a clean bowl.

'Busy day,' says Gordon Moss, looking pointedly at the leaflets. 'Lots to do. We need all the help we can get.'

I clamp my lips shut, not trusting myself to speak. I empty fresh Shreddies into the bowl, thinking. 'Could I ask you something?' I say, pulling milk from the fridge.

'Go on,' says Gordon, shortly. He thumps a pile of leaflets to one side.

'What's known about the Reverend Phineas Kibble?' I place the new bowl of cereal in front of Noah and grab a cleaning cloth. 'I mean, about his life here in Hope-under-Barrow.'

'He was a great man,' says Gordon. 'As I think I've mentioned before, he realised that protection was needed from the Barrow Man and created the ritual we use today.' He shakes his head, his face marvelling at something beyond my comprehension. 'The power of prayer never ceases to amaze me.'

I don't comment and hand Noah a spoon. 'But what else did he do?' I ask.

Gordon frowns. 'I'm not sure I understand.'

'Well, do you know anything more about his life here?'

'He tended to his flock, cared for the poor and sick as well as any other incumbent of this parish has over time. He was beloved by all who knew him.'

'So, no other details?'

Gordon presses a sharp fold into one of the leaflets. 'He was a good and holy gentleman, Ms Greenwood. A true shepherd of the flock. And his legacy speaks for itself.'

Ben brandishes a reel of tape to set up around the yew tree. Yellow, like it's a crime scene or something. I watch as Mrs Butterworth collects the made-up posies from our kitchen sink. She's taking them over to the church where they will sit in the cool building until the evening. Despite my annoyance, I find myself getting Noah into his coat to head down with Ben to the village hall. He's still covered in mud and there are lumps of crusty Shreddies on his top but, apparently, there's no time to change him. Gordon Moss is going to follow on when he's finished with the leaflets, and we leave him sitting in our kitchen amidst the dirty breakfast dishes and the snipped ends from the flowers that seem to litter every available space on the worksurface.

'Come on,' says Ben, tucking the tape into his jacket pocket, while I look in dismay at the mess in the kitchen. I've barely had time to get myself ready for the day. I've not even showered and am dressed in a scruffy hoodie and jeans that need washing. 'We can sort all this later, Kate. We just need to get going. Lisa and Iain need our help.'

You *need to get going*, I think as I pull on trainers. *This is* your *job, not mine.* I do up the Velcro on Noah's shoes. Everything in me is screaming against going to help. I don't want to be a part of this day, especially now that I know what I do. I don't want to comply and get dragged into something that repels me. Lisa and Iain hate me, I'm pretty sure but, moreover, no one really understands. No one understands the truth about the tree and who Phineas Kibble really was.

I want to destroy their illusion but can only imagine the hysteria if people really knew that Phineas Kibble was completely off his head; that his sermons are rambling evidence of someone losing their mind and that he killed a girl. Several times, I've thought about pulling Ben aside and telling him what I'd read deep into the night. But somehow, I can't do it to him, not when he wants this job to work so badly, not when things are so rocky between us, and definitely not while Gordon Moss is sitting in our kitchen. But as we head into the village, I feel a dragging sensation in my stomach, a feeling that I should be anywhere else apart from in this place, at this time.

'Mummy, what are we doing here?' asks Noah when we arrive at the hall. Bunting is strung all around the railings in red, white and blue, and coloured lanterns are tied to the gate. Beyond the wide open doors to the building, Lisa struggles with a trestle table while Iain sets up chairs around the outside of the hall space.

'We're here to help Daddy,' I say to Noah. 'We need to put some chairs and things out.'

Ben leads us all into the building, greeting Iain and Lisa enthusiastically. At the front of the hall, near an old, battered stage, I spot Daisy playing with her ruined doll, with its one twist of hair. My stomach lurches. Because Noah hasn't started at the school yet, I'd forgotten it was an INSET day, but now I recall Lisa mentioning it. I catch her looking from her daughter to Noah, her mouth tight as if she's tasted something sour.

'Noah, are you going to play with Daisy while I help Daddy with some setting up?' I say. Noah clutches the sleeve of my hoodie. 'Please,' I try. 'We won't be here long.'

'How long?' he says. 'I don't like it here.'

I scan the hall: the poky windows with threadbare curtains, the walls badly in need of a paint, the scratched wooden floor. 'We won't be more than half an hour,' I promise. 'We're going to make it all nice, ready for a party later on.'

'Party?' His face lights up. Noah loves parties and I can tell he's already thinking about pass-the-parcel and chocolate cake.

'Kate!' Lisa strides across to me, short curls bouncing. She's smiling, despite everything. 'How about you get plates and glasses from the kitchen?' We've set up tables for the food and I was going to hang balloons.' She gestures to a couple of bulging bin bags.

'Sure,' I say with a shrug, looking over at a serving hatch on one side of the room. The kitchen, I presume. I head over, glad that I don't have to stay in the main hall and make conversation. Noah tries to follow me, but Iain helpfully opens one of the bin bags and tosses a silver balloon into the air. Immediately, both children run to catch it. I smile and push at the kitchen door, letting myself into the small, dark room. I hunt around a bit until I find the plates, then carry them in batches to the buffet tables.

I'm thinking hard about Phineas Kibble's sermons. How he preached about what the tree was and insisted that the villagers must be protected from the Barrow Man. His teachings range from being practically ecstatic that the tree exists to the sudden creation of a culture of fear which still has a hold on people today. I grab another stack of ancient plates. Fear today of what will happen if the villagers don't perform some mad ritual and pick at a buffet in the village hall afterwards. My rational brain is telling me that all these so-called misfortunes and evils would have happened anyway. I look over to where Lisa is smoothing a paper tablecloth over one of the trestles. She's laughing at something Ben's said. Ben, always the charmer. Yes, even Lisa and Iain's son falling from the yew tree on Barrow Man Day, before the ritual. Even *that* was just a coincidence. A sad, tragic coincidence. And coincidences like that were ones that Reverend Phineas Kibble used to convince people to stay away. And stay away they did, a grip of fear binding them to this day.

I cross the hall towards the buffet table, the pile of plates clattering in my hands.

But why? Why did Phineas Kibble want to scare people away? He said he had come to learn about the Barrow Man and his terrible life. How the Barrow Man was intent on avenging the villagers for some wrongdoing he had suffered. The details are hazy, but they have had a hold. For years and years.

I remember the Bible verse from the last of the sermons in the stack I found. The words spin through my mind. *For in much wisdom is much grief: and he that increaseth knowledge increaseth sorrow.*

And then it comes to me. Like a flash of sudden light.

Things hidden. Secrets. The need to conceal for fear of what knowledge might bring.

I shift the plates a little, the tower slanting against my arm.

I think of Julie Moon and all that I have needed to bury. The layers upon layers of narrative I have had to build to suppress, to forget, to get on with my life. The lies I have told myself and others. And suddenly, I understand a part of this. Not clearly, but like an image caught in a fly-blown mirror.

What I am certain about is that nothing is as it seems. Because in life, it never is.

I remember the strange things I've thought about near the yew tree – the bull house, the green liquid, the man, the girl pleading with someone to leave, then the crying, the convulsions. And Noah too, haunted by similar things. The very thought makes me sick, that my son should have experienced such disturbances. I think about the drink he made with the yew needles, the man he talked about with the black cape like a vampire, and it all comes together in a rush. Those things were real. They weren't just my stresses acting out in weird thoughts. Those were Alice's last memories.

Her memories before Phineas Kibble killed her. Memories that he needed to keep hidden. Crazy as it sounds, I suddenly know that the Alice buried beneath the tree is the girl Reverend Kibble killed. It's almost as if the tree's a conduit or something and Phineas Kibble knew it. He couldn't have anyone finding out what he did, for that knowledge would be catastrophic and so…

My hands are clammy, I feel dizzy, the voices in the hall waver and merge.

'Kate?' Ben's voice, loud, concerned.

There's a sudden crash, pain as shards of crockery spit at my bare legs.

The plates bounce and spin and break into a thousand pieces. Lisa is pulling Daisy and Noah out of the way. Ben is running towards me, and I am shaking and spinning words that are forming from nowhere.

'This is all lies,' I cry, gathering momentum. 'All lies. None of you really understand.'

Ben grabs me by the shoulders, tells me to calm down. Tears of frustration leak down my face. I see Julie. Alice. Hear her scream. Hear them scream. I scream back. And then everything goes black.

Extract from a sermon given
by the Reverend Phineas Kibble,
July 1866.

The text for today's homily is taken from Proverbs, chapter thirteen.

'Hope deferred maketh the heart sick: but when the desire cometh, it is a tree of life...'

... Brethren, for many months, my heart was sick as I mourned the death of my dear wife, so recently departed. But now I know and can prove for certain that she lives on. That certainty is, for me, made known through the tree of life.

... My friends, it is my belief, that a root from this most blessed tree of life has been planted here in Hope-under-Barrow. Oh, how blessed are we to be the guardians of such a sacred plant! A plant which imparts knowledge.

Friends, soon I shall share with you soon the cause of my conviction.

44

KATE

Dorset 2026

'Drink this.'

I feel a dribble of water weave down my chin, the coldness of it shocking. My head is woolly, and my elbow and leg hurt like crazy. I squint into artificial light and see Ben's face up close. 'What happened?' I say, my voice cracking.

'You slipped and fell,' says Ben, softly. 'I think you might have fainted for a moment. With the shock of falling.'

I swallow and look about me. I'm lying in the middle of the hall floor with Ben's sweater shoved beneath my head. Balloons dance overhead, the stark hall lighting dashes my face, and a trail of bunting dangles from the ceiling, the task of hanging it unfinished. There are other people too, crowded around me, looking down with concern. Gordon Moss, clutching a dustpan and brush, Lisa and Iain, a lady I don't recognise brandishing a Henry vacuum cleaner. Noah and Daisy are sitting on plastic chairs at the edge of the hall, nibbling biscuits and clutching beakers of squash.

I'm washed by a wave of embarrassment. 'I'm so sorry,' I manage.

'Could have happened to anyone,' retorts Mrs Butterworth,

scanning the area. 'The cleaner polishes this floor so hard you could see your face in it.' She sniffs. 'It's an accident waiting to happen. As you've just proved.'

I nod, slowly. It hurts. Everything hurts and I feel bruises forming in all sorts of places. There's something nagging at me too. Something on the edge of my mind, clamouring for attention.

'Can you stand?' Lisa leans over. Her dark curls bob, her piercings flash in the light.

I blink. 'Yes, I think so,' I say, as Ben urges me to be careful.

'Let me make you some tea. And I think there are some biscuits somewhere – if the kids haven't eaten them all.'

Lisa helps me to my feet. I take her arm gratefully as she leads me towards the kitchen. 'Let them get on with the preparations for a bit.' She nods over at Iain. 'Keep an eye on the kids, won't you? I think Kate needs a bit of peace and quiet for a few minutes.'

Iain shoots a look at Noah and Daisy who are still drinking their squash and not talking to each other. 'Sure thing,' he mumbles, as Lisa guides me across the room.

In the kitchen, Lisa makes me sit down on a wobbly stool and turns the kettle on. She slings a cheap teabag into a flowery mug. 'Do you want to tell me what all that was about?' she says.

I hesitate. Why is Lisa being so nice to me? Why, when last time I saw her, I basically shouted her down, and the time before that, my son destroyed her daughter's toy. I sigh. 'It's just all this,' I say, looking over at the kitchen serving hatch, gesturing to what's going on back in the hall. 'The reason we're all here.'

'You mean the party?'

'Sort of, yes. But, I guess, the whole Barrow Man Day thing.' I look down. My hands are sticky with sweat and suddenly, I feel more out of place than ever. I want to just grab Noah and go. Moving here was—

'You don't believe any of it, do you?' says Lisa. She hands me a mug of strong tea and I sip it, grateful for having something to do.

'I believe it has a function,' I say, carefully.

Lisa scrunches her brow. 'What do you mean?'

I clasp the mug, thinking about my conversation with Ben the night before. 'I mean, it makes people in the village feel safe. It brings the community together.' I nod towards the hatch. 'And I guess it's an excuse for a good party.' I pause, remembering Lisa's son. 'Look, I'm sorry about what happened to you and Iain. And I'm sorry too about my outburst last night. It's just… it's just that nothing seems to have made sense since we moved here. It's all so different to where we lived before.'

Lisa shakes her head. 'Forget it,' she says. But there's a sudden coolness that falls over the small kitchen. She busies herself: putting away the teabags, placing the teaspoon carefully in the sink, brushing away crystals of spilt sugar. 'Kate,' she says, at last, turning back into the room.

I put my tea down on the steel worktop. 'What is it?'

'A word of warning.' Lisa pushes dark coils out of her eyes.

I look up. The atmosphere is tight and the hum of the electric strip-light above our head suddenly seems intrusive. 'Warning?' I breathe.

Lisa takes a deep breath. 'The customs of Hope-under-Barrow may seem odd to you. Quaint, outmoded rituals that you're too sophisticated to take seriously. Lies, as you called it all back in the hall just now.'

I flinch. How superior and condescending I must seem. 'It's not that…' I begin.

But Lisa holds up a hand. 'You need to tread very carefully. Just let today happen and forget about it for another year, okay? Don't go probing or unearthing things that are best left buried.'

I open my mouth to speak.

'And drawing the yew tree...' She flicks a glance out of the kitchen window. It looks out in the direction of the church. 'I suggest you stop. It's dangerous. It's not built on a lie, as you seem to think. And with all due respect, you've only just moved here. You don't understand. Not really.'

I pick my tea up. Put it down again. 'Honestly. I—'

'Just stop interfering with our traditions,' says Lisa. Her voice is soft, not matching her words. It's almost as if she pities me. 'Keep away from the tree. It's safer that way.'

I rearrange myself on the stool, and it wobbles again. I wonder whether to let on what I've figured out about the tree, what I've learned about Phineas Kibble. Explain that the memories the community keep alive really *are* lies. That they conceal something else, something just out of sight. 'It's simply that the stories we tell are not always the truth,' I say, quietly. I remember Ben's words from the previous night. 'We tell stories because they help. Because they represent something. Because they mean something to us.' I pause and look out of the window, my gaze fixing on the distant shape of the yew tree. 'But what if those stories are masking something that shouldn't be hidden? Some dark, terrible truth that people should know about.'

Lisa follows my gaze. Her face is twisted, her eyes gleam. For a moment, she seems lost. But then she turns from the window and lays a hand gently upon my arm. Our eyes meet. 'Kate, just stay away. Please, stay away.'

45

OCTAVIA

Dorsetshire 1866

They slaughtered the beast. The bull that had trampled poor Alice March to death. No one thought to check her body for poison. Her pa and brothers found her lying in the bull house, legs broken and mashed, spine curved, eyes like cold, grey marbles, rolled back and unseeing. *It was a terrible tragedy,* people said, *another misfortune for the March family to bear.* Father sent me up to the farm with our condolences and a pot of Cook's plum jam. That was a frightful thing. Alice's body was in the back room in preparation for the funeral and all I could think about were her last gasping moments, her slumping body, the smell of earth and approaching death. The angry cries of the bull.

I could not look at Mrs March, nor at Edgar sobbing softly for his sister beside their unlit fire. They couldn't afford the fuel, Mrs March explained, but they would light one after the funeral, when they would gather together as a family and tell stories of the girl they'd loved and lost. *The greatest loss of all these past months,* she said. They had already lost so much. But this – *this* – was worse than anything else.

How I wept on my way back down the heath to the vicarage. I could not bear the unspeakable guilt that bubbled and spat inside me and Father would not even glance at me during the long days that followed. He prepared his homily for the funeral, and I remained in my chamber, not eating or sleeping, the wickedness of what I had done eating away at me from within.

Now, we line the coffin lane. Alice's broken body, dressed in Sunday best, is to be brought down from the farm to the churchyard. Many mourners have already been up to the farm to pay their respects, but I could not. I feigned illness. For to play a part in that ritual was more than I was able to bear. Nanny Butterworth went up and told me what a dreadful affair it was. How the coffin remained closed because Alice's body was so badly damaged, how Mrs March wailed but how Father had cut a twig from the yew tree to bury with her, to symbolise her resurrection in Christ. At this, I was sick to the stomach, lending credence to my tale of illness.

Before this, Father had ordered Mr Jefferies to burn his hideous contraption and Alice now has a coffin of her own, the cheapest. All that the Marchs could afford to spare from their funerary fund. *Who knows when they will need it again*, the villagers muttered, *for soon they will not be able to feed themselves*. She will have a stone though – it is not quite a pauper's funeral. A simple one, bearing her name and her dates. Father has paid for it. A gift of thanks for Alice's friendship to his daughter, he said. But I knew really, it was a twisted guilt that motivated him.

Farmer March has arranged to have Alice buried beneath the yew tree as he knew his daughter spent much of her time under its thick branches with her friend, Octavia Kibble. Father, I know, tried to dissuade him but could only protest to a degree without appearing unreasonable and, in the end, was obliged to instruct Mr Jefferies to dig a plot. The same plot that the lamb and heathland mammals had lain in so recently. The village supported the farmer as the family are well loved, and what with Father's declaration about the sacredness of the tree, it was regarded as fitting for such a *good, God-fearing girl* who met with such a terrible end. But as the arrangements were made, I could sense Father's growing unease, his dread of discovery, and I knew that he was trying to find a clever concealment. A way of ensuring that no one would ever know what had really happened. *The bull had atoned for what I had done and that was it,* Father said. We do not need visitors to the graveside stumbling upon the truth, if Alice's memories ever surfaced. As surely, they will.

There is a fine rain now. I stand by the row of thatched cottages with Nanny Butterworth, waiting for the coffin to appear, her dabbing at her eyes, me staring at nothing and as still as stone. Father is leading the procession and will be first at the graveside to greet the mourners. His service is prepared, his sympathy and assurances of everlasting life ready and waiting. *No one will ever know the truth,* he says. *No one must know. I will make sure of it.* What scheme he has constructed to conceal the misdoing I do not know, and dread lies heavy in my gut as I look up the mud-thick path and feel the cold spit of rain hitting my cheeks.

Nanny Butterworth puts a hand on my arm. 'Here it comes, Miss Octavia. Look to the brow of the hill, now.'

I lift my eyes to the horizon and see a small black huddle making its way down from the heath along the steep incline of the coffin lane. A sudden burst of sunlight flickers on the miserable party but it is quickly swallowed by the darkening clouds and the rain that continues to fall.

'I cannot bear it,' I say, and my words hold more truth than

I can ever express to my old nanny. The other mourners press closer to one another, and a deep hush falls over the assembly as we watch and wait.

The rain grows heavier.

The church bell tolls.

'I will walk with you to the church gate,' Nanny Butterworth whispers. She had done the same when Mother died, when I had no one to comfort me. Father, of course, was taking the service and we had no other family. So, Nanny Butterworth had stood with me, and we had wept together as we listened from afar to Father's monotone and watched the coffin being lowered into the ground. His apparent lack of emotion was deep and wounding as I nursed my own loss, and I remember thinking him heartless. Now, I know that he has hidden his feelings well. His grief is as deep as mine, and it is something that I think he will never surmount.

Time seems to expand. The bier draws closer, but it can only manage the gradient at the slowest speed, so it seems hours have passed before it reaches the village. The solemn tolling of the bell rings on and on and I imagine each as a blow hitting my stomach, cursing me for what I have done.

And, at last, it passes us, the old bier from the church, so dirty and worn. It spits loose, wet splats of muck at us as it goes by, but no one moves back. Now is not a time to worry about getting wet and muddy. Father is at the front of the party, the family behind. I hang onto Nanny Butterworth's arm as we follow on with the rest of the village, a snaking black procession making its way towards the churchyard. There, all women and children stand back, and the men proceed to the graveside.

I am numb and only hold onto Nanny Butterworth's arm, fearful that otherwise I will fall. 'Let's go back to the vicarage now, Miss Octavia,' she says.

I shake my head. Somehow, I cannot. Not yet.

'You'll catch a chill out here, for certain.' Nanny Butterworth moves to go, but I stand firm, rooted, watching. Around us, the crowd disperses, knowing that it is over. They head back to warm fires and tea and stories of the great bull. A cosy, shocking tale for a dismal afternoon.

'Brethren.' In the graveyard, Father calls the congregation of men together, his voice like the needles of rain that now fall upon us. I blink the mingling water and tears out of my eyes.

He mutters verses from the Bible, and the words thread their way over to me. *Resurrection. Life. Victory over sin and death.*

A sharp wind circles us, and I shiver in the wet.

There will be no memories yet, but they will come. I know they will. And what then? What will we do? Move the body, like grave robbers?

I imagine I hear a pipe on the wind and turn away.

Nanny Butterworth is right. We should go.

46

KATE

Dorset 2026

The sun is beginning to set, and the air is warm. Crowds stand at a distance from the yew tree, huddled in cliques, whispering to each other and throwing glances at Ben, their new vicar. For some of them, it's probably the first time they've seen him and they're curious. 'He's quite young,' I overhear one person say. 'Doesn't look a vicar,' says another. And I smile to myself. People have stereotypes and it's true: Ben just looks like an average guy; a dad, the kind of person you could imagine in the pub on a Friday night sipping a quiet pint or two. That's how I've always seen him too. Until recently, at least.

The procession halts by the yew tree. The rush torches are flickering, and the masked children stand at a distance from the tree, kept in order by a couple of teachers from the village school. Noah is looking at the hideous crow masks and he moves closer to me as some of them make croaky cawing noises. At the tree itself, the yellow tape has been removed, and Mrs Butterworth's posies have been placed in a ring around the trunk. No one is allowed past the floral barrier, only Ben, and only while he performs the ritual. Noah and I stand alone, separated from the rest of the village by an ancient tomb with an inscription so faded, it's impossible to read. Mrs Butterworth has checked we're okay of course, before easing herself away and going to stand with the rest of the grey-haired St Hilda's community.

Ben clears his throat and announces himself as the new vicar. Everyone stares. All I can think about is Phineas Kibble and what he did. What would happen if I stopped the ritual and told everyone? I want to, so badly. But my throat is blocked and as I stare at the crowds, I feel more alone than ever. Would anyone even believe me? Me, the outsider.

'What's Daddy going to do?' says Noah. Then louder, 'And when are we going to the party?'

Mrs Butterworth glares. I squat down. Ben is just beginning a prayer. Something about life, and death, and journeys. I hear snatches about protection, banishing evil, God's love. 'This won't last long,' I whisper. 'Daddy just has to bless the tree and say prayers for the village, then we can go to the party, okay?'

'But why?' Noah puts a hand on my thigh, upsetting my balance a little. I grab at the tomb to steady myself, scraping my knuckles as I do.

'Why what?'

'Why does he have to say prayers for a tree? Usually, he says prayers in church.'

'Because...' I watch as Ben reaches out and touches one of the branches. 'Because it's a tradition here. And traditions are important. Like opening stockings at Christmas and searching for chocolate eggs in the garden at Easter.'

Noah frowns.

'Not long, now,' I assure him. I hold up a hand, fingers splayed, indicating five minutes. I'm just getting to my feet again when Noah tugs at my top. 'What is it?' I mouth.

'I've got a headache, Mummy.' He rubs the side of his head. 'Right here.'

Inwardly, I sigh, but fumble around in my bag for Noah's Thomas the Tank Engine water bottle. It's not there. Damn. I must have left it on the kitchen worktop. I glance at the gate to the vicarage garden. Perhaps we could just slip away and join the others at the party when they're done here. Or I could just stop this whole ritual and tell everyone the truth. I could—

'The child! Ms Greenwood, the child. Stop him!'

I'm shocked out of my thoughts by Mrs Butterworth shouting and realise, with horror, that Noah is no longer by my side. Instead, he's racing towards the tree. He calls for Ben.

'Noah!' I cry. I lurch forwards, embarrassment swamping me as I push past a couple of young mums with children, younger than my son, behaving as they should.

I catch up with him but not before he's dashed through the ring of flowers, trampling several posies, crushing them into the dirt. 'Noah, what's got into you?' I snap, in as quiet a voice as I can. 'Can't you see Daddy's busy?' I grip him by the wrist, then loosen my hold, realising that people out there are probably judging me, forming their first impressions of the vicar's wife.

Ben moves away slightly, trying to keep up his professional appearance. 'Go with Mummy, bud,' he says in a low voice. He brandishes his prayer sheet, like a shield. 'We'll be done here soon.'

'No!' Noah screams. 'There's a sad girl in the tree, Daddy, and she'll make you sad too. She'll hurt you like she hurt her friend. There's another girl too and she has something to tell Mummy. She tells me what to do. All the time. In my head.'

I want to be sick.

Ben steps backwards, looks at his prayers, trying to find his place.

'Noah,' I urge. 'Come on. Let Daddy do his job.'

'They're all like the crow we buried, only much worse.' Noah begins to sob. 'And there's a man. A bad man. He… he…'

Helplessly, I scan the assembled villagers. The young mums are looking one to the other, eyebrows raising, heads shaking. One of them stares right at me, a look of disgust on her face. Her own child is sleeping in a pushchair. The gang of crows push and start talking to each other while the teachers try to reassemble them and call them to order.

Noah shrieks before coming to an absolute halt in front of Ben.

No one speaks at first, but then Lisa steps forwards. She's shaking. 'Take Noah away, Kate. Ben needs to finish here. If it's not already too late. Please, Kate. Now. The Barrow Man ritual must be completed. It's vitally important.' She looks at the crowd, then fixes her gaze on me. 'For everyone.'

The air smells of burnt sugar and hot dogs. Practically the whole community is gathered outside the village hall watching the Morris dancers. There are sticks clashing and tatters of purple, silver and black flying across the tarmacked car park in front of us. It's a warm evening, the sky a perfect pale blue, the faintest hint of gold brushing the horizon. Everyone is relaxed and in a party mood, despite the earlier upset. Though no one is speaking to me – they move around me as if I'm invisible and none of the other children are letting Noah into their games. I try telling myself that all children have strange outbursts from time to time and Noah's probably just overwrought after the move. But I can't really let it all go. Not now. The memories have been controlling Noah, I'm sure of it. Making him do things and say things that are not a part of him. I need it to stop and, right now, I need to make sure that he stays close to me, that I don't let him out of my sight.

One of the melodion players in the band starts an improvisation on the Barrow Man folk melody that everyone seems to know. People sing. A fiddle joins in, then a drum, then a flute, until everyone is caught in it.

On the eve of May
To keep Barrow Man at bay,
We dance and we sing,
And to the yew tree we bring,
Garlands so bright and so gay.

People clap and stamp, half-singing, half-shouting the words they know so well. The tune weaves in and out of the crowd, louder and louder. My mind is full of the sound, and I try to let it take me. I try to forget. But I see her again. Julie Moon. Smiling. Screaming.

Go away, I tell the image. *Go away.*

I concentrate on the band, on the singing, and the party atmosphere. The dancers start again. A whirl of colour and movement. Noah is transfixed.

Go away.

Go away.

Go away.

The dance finishes with a clash of sticks on the tarmac and there are claps and whoops from the audience.

Noah pushes a sticky hand into mine. He's stuffed full of toasted marshmallows and asks whether he can have an ice cream. I relent and draw back to the hall, leading Noah to an ice chest packed full of Cornettos and Magnums. While he rummages inside, looking for strawberry flavour, I arch my back and sigh deeply, glad of the opportunity to be away from the crowd for a moment. I realise how tired I am. An overwhelming tiredness that weighs on me like a stone. All I want to do is to head back to the vicarage and crawl under my covers. The evening has been too full. Not just Noah's disruption of the ritual and his unsettling behaviour. But also watching Ben meeting new people, the effort he makes with small talk, then him calling me to his side and me having to make the pretence that I love everything about Hope-under-Barrow and that I'm sorry about what my son did earlier. It's feels like a betrayal, almost. A betrayal of Noah. A betrayal of myself.

Noah finds his ice cream, and we make our way to the outside door, back towards the whirl of the music and the shouts of the dancers.

Ben is on the threshold, surprisingly alone.

'Kate,' he says when he sees me. 'You looked whacked.'

I push the hair from my eyes. 'Thanks,' I say. And I try to smile.

'Mummy, can you open it for me?'

'Magic word?' I say automatically.

'Pleeeeease,' says Noah. He bounds over to me and hands me the ice cream. While I peel off the wrapping, he skips around me, sugar-filled and evidently not sharing my levels of tiredness. Something falls from the pocket of his joggers, and he leaps to pick it up just as I bend to hand him the ice cream.

My heart stops.

It's a small troll with bright pink hair.

'Where did you get that?' I say, a hot pulse thumping at my temples.

'Found it,' says Noah.

'Where? Where did you find it?'

'On our walk this morning. At the old fallen down farm. Daddy said I could keep it. He said *finders keepers*, didn't you Daddy?'

I round on Ben. 'Why did you let him keep it? I can't believe you let him bring that manky thing into our house. It's probably full of germs. You should have left it where it was.'

I remember the bull house, the thick, oppressive atmosphere. The sense of wrong. The memory at the tree.

Ben looks surprised. 'It's just an old toy,' he says with a shrug. 'It's no big deal.' He shoves his hands into his pockets. 'Come on bud,' he says, holding out an arm to Noah, 'let's go and see the rest of the dancing. You too, Kate.' He holds out his other arm. 'Coming?'

'Wait!' I fold my arms, root myself to the spot. 'We need to discuss this.'

Ben turns. 'Discuss what?'

I falter, my words and thoughts clattering to a halt. I'm hot and I'm tired, and I'm afraid. I see the pink hair sprouting from Noah's fist where he's still clutching the troll. His fingers are shiny with strawberry ice cream. I want to tell him to let go of the troll. I want to take him home. No, I want to take him away from this place. Far, far away.

'Kate, what's up? Are you—'

'Ben, I need to go home.' I shiver, the heat I felt only minutes ago flipping. 'I... I don't feel well. I—'

'I'll come with you. This little man should probably get going about now anyway. It's getting late. I'll come back later, if I feel like it.'

'But Daddy...' Noah holds up the ice cream he's barely started.

'It's past your bedtime,' says Ben. He looks over at me, rolling up his sleeves as if ready for action. I see the pale birthmark on his forearm, remember tracing it with my finger when we first got together, feeling the uniqueness of Ben, the gratitude for what I had found in him. Suddenly, I feel a pang of sadness for what has been lost in this place, for all the things that have changed. I reach out, wanting to touch it now, but then lower my hand. Everything is different now.

'Come on, Noah.' Ben's voice is sharp, impatient, and I'm jerked back to the present reality.

I shake my head. I need to be on my own. 'Let Noah stay. For a bit. Come home when you're ready.' I force a smile and glance around the hall, at the scraps of buffet food, glasses abandoned in all sorts of places, fallen balloons bobbing lightly across the stage. 'Besides, Noah could prove a useful excuse later on.' I gesture to the mess.

'Well...' Ben looks out towards the car park where another dance is starting. 'If you're sure.'

Noah's face lights up and he looks from Ben to me, the balance of his evening hanging on my response.

'I'm sure,' I say.

Noah hugs me, a blob of ice cream landing on my sleeve. I breathe in the scent of his hair, that sweet, homely smell. I close my eyes and when I open them, I see Lisa standing a little way off from us. She doesn't look at me because her attention is elsewhere. She's staring straight at Ben, her mouth open.

I don't go home. Without even processing my decision, I find myself in the graveyard. It's shady and cool, the warmth of the evening dying. Up here, away from the crowds and the noise, I feel I can finally breathe. The posies are all over the place now; partly Noah, partly the evening breeze that has scattered them.

I find myself walking towards the tree and looking at the two graves there. There is more to discover, I'm sure of it.

My legs quiver and, for a moment, I think I'm going to faint. I reach out towards the trunk to steady myself, feeling the cool, rough bark beneath my hands. I try to concentrate on the real things of this world, the music drifting from the party, the heady floral scents that come with evening. I think of Noah and of Ben. All real, tangible things. I think about what we're going to do next. Whether we're trapped here in Hope-under-Barrow or whether we can just up and leave.

Above me the branches of the yew tree rustle and I shiver.

The church bell marks the hour. It reminds me of that very first evening here when Noah found the dead crow.

Nothing has been right since.

I realise then that I'm standing in just the place where Noah crawled into the hollow. I put a hand inside. Into the beating heart of the yew tree. And then, because of a strange compulsion, almost as if I am in a dream, I slip right inside the tree.

I am half-afraid, half-convinced that there I might unearth the ending of Alice's story.

47

OCTAVIA

Dorsetshire 1866

In the days that follow Alice's funeral, the vicarage falls under a deep depression. Father locks himself away in his study which, while I am spared all communication with him, I find unsettling because I am certain that he is working on a plan. Some plan to try to right things.

But it cannot be righted.

The thing we have done – that *I* have done – is too terrible for that.

If only I had not tried to stop Alice. If only I had remained at the vicarage that night, all may be well now. I could have been celebrating the greatest insight in history instead of carrying around this monstrous guilt and grief. This hatred of myself.

At night, I dream of hellfire and eternal punishment, and during the day, I am seized by a melancholy so great I fear that I will die from it. Nanny Butterworth does her best to comfort me, thinking only that I am mourning the loss of my closest friend, if that were not enough. She has no thought of the guilt I am suffering or of the hellish visions that haunt me. The wickedness I have committed suffocates me and dominates every moment, and no amount of hot broth or cocoa, warming stews or fresh cakes will soothe me. I cannot help but think of Alice's body under the ground, slowly breaking down and becoming one with the earth, feeding the roots of the yew, her memories being sucked deep into the soul of the tree. The very thought sends me into a wild panic. Already, I have seen the shrunken, stooped figure of Mrs March laying a sprig of heathland heather on the mound. I watched from our garden as she lingered, as if in prayer, as I hastily shot my own petition to the heavens that she should feel nothing of Alice, that no memory should spring unbidden to her mind.

That night, I barely slept and counted the church bell at every hour.

Three days after the funeral, I make up my mind. I have to know. I wake early and wrapping myself in Mother's coat, I hurry to the graveyard. A strong wind sweeps down from the heath and dried leaves whisk across the path ahead of me as I unlatch the little gate that leads from our garden. The yew tree looks black and grotesque and, as I approach it, my stomach rolls and I chew at my lip until I taste blood. The mound is small and still fresh. Mrs March's bundle of heather from the other day has been blown away and my throat thickens at the sight of the solitary lump of earth. I swallow and brush tears from the corners of my eyes. I do not deserve to mourn, I know that. I should not be permitted to feel for one moment what Alice's family are experiencing. With a deep breath, I step under the low branches of the yew tree and stare at the simple stone with dry eyes.

ALICE

Born July 1851

Died October 1866

That is all, I think. All there is to tell people in years to come who she was and what she stood for. Unless her memories live on. And what then? My shoulders quake but I struggle to still myself, for a memory – the first – weaves unprompted into my mind. Then it falls, like a sudden and heavy shower.

Running on the heath with Edgar. Laughter and singing, good-natured teasing and a sense of freedom. In the distance healthy cattle graze on the scrub and sheep bleat, the warbling sound hearty and full, the ruddle marking their fleeces bright, like poppies.

'Come on, Alice,' calls Edgar. 'Do hurry!'

I pick up my skirts and jump over ferns, my ankle unsettling me for a moment as it turns on a small rut, but it is nothing and I race to catch up with him. This day could last forever, I think. It is a Sunday. Church is over and we have a bundle of food from Ma and are not expected back at the farm until supper time.

'Let's hunt for snakes,' says Edgar. 'Not boring grass snakes. I want to find an adder.'

I am not too keen, but it is Edgar's birthday, and I do not want to make him crousty, so I follow him as he bounds up ahead, arms splayed outwards for balance, the breeze working his blonde curdles backwards.

We reach the lower heath, near to the village, and Edgar scours the ferns, then looks to the dry pathways where bright sunlight bakes the mud. 'We're sure to find one,' he says. 'This is just the day for snakes.'

The sun burns hot and bright in the sky, and I want to suggest that we find a flat stone to sit on and eat our food. We have apples from the store, ginger cake, cheese and hunks of new bread. But Edgar is poking about in the ferns with a stick, and I know that any suggestion I make with regards to a meal will fall upon deaf ears.

I hear the church clock strike and look over at the graveyard.

Two crows spin into the air from the elm tree, cawing, perhaps startled by something, and land on the top of the giant yew tree, the one Ma says is at least a thousand years old. Then there's silence, and other than the thrashing of Edgar's stick through the ferns, a perfect stillness. I watch him for a while but I'm hungry and wonder whether I can start on my apple while I'm waiting.

I draw it from the bundle and take a small bite, tasting autumn and sweetness. It's perfect. I gaze into the blue sky and watch the clouds until I feel dizzy. My thoughts are nowhere and everywhere, until suddenly I'm jolted into the present reality by a loud scream coming from the graveyard.

Edgar drops his stick. 'What's that?'

'I can't say,' I call, but already I'm running in the direction of the church, dropping my uneaten apple in the dirt. 'Come on,' I shout.

'No fear!' Edgar yells. 'Gives me the crims.' He hates the graveyard, scared as he by the tales of ghosts and spirits that Pa tells us on cold winter nights.

'Someone might be hurt,' I call. 'We ought to go and see.'

But my brother does not follow me. I scramble over the wall, pulling a thread in my skirt as I do so. I land in the long grass, breathless and panting. Hands on my hips, I look around.

The place is silent now. Nothing moves.

But then, I spot a girl. She's sprawled on the grass and lying perfectly still.

My breath hitches. At once, I fear she is dead.

Here, the memory fades, drawn from my mind into the cold air like threads of mist. It was me, that girl in the grass. The first time I met Alice, that blissful day back in the spring, when I first accessed the so-called Barrow Man's mind.

The wind blows cold, the branches above me rush.

I am left with nothing and realise I am crying now.

Tears run freely down my face as I finally allow myself to mourn the friend I have lost.

I run into the vicarage, my eyes raw, my limbs shaking.

'Miss Octavia.' Nanny Butterworth stops me as I almost collide with her in the kitchen passageway. 'Whatever is it?'

I shake my head.

She eyes me, reading everything about my expression. 'You visited the grave, did you not? *Her* grave?'

I incline my head, slightly.

'Oh, Miss Octavia.' Nanny Butterworth enfolds me in her arms, and, for a moment, I let myself be taken by her, let myself fall into her soft bosom and breathe in the smell of the soap we use to do the laundry. It hangs about her clothes and briefly I feel comforted, as if all of this is just some terrible dream.

But then the memory assaults me once more and I pull away. 'I must speak with Father.'

'Your father is in his study, not to be disturbed.'

This is the way of things these days. He cannot face anyone or deal with any matter. He eats alone and moves only between his chamber and the study. 'I must see him,' I say, shuffling past Nanny Butterworth. 'It is of vital importance.'

Once again, I find myself knocking on the study door and admitting myself immediately. The room is gloomy. One shutter is drawn, the other half-open, allowing only a slice of light from outside. The air smells stale and dust motes flicker in the lit space.

Father is seated at his desk and looks up at me without a word. His face is drained of colour, his eyelids heavy. 'What is it you have come to say, Octavia?' He gives a laboured sigh, as if he knows already.

'Yes, Father, it is true,' I say, quietly. 'The memories have already come.'

He stares at me: a dead, unseeing stare.

'Nothing that would incriminate us,' I add, with haste. 'But…'

'But that might well happen in time,' Father says. He draws a hand over his thinning hair. 'Leave me, Octavia. I must be alone…' He lets his hand fall heavily on the desk. 'I must determine how best to execute my scheme.'

48

KATE

Dorset 2026

It is dark inside the tree. The air is tight with the scent of bark, of earth, and of ancient things. As if in a trance, I run a hand, then both hands, up and down the inside of the trunk, moving around inside the hollow, trying, almost hoping to find my way back into the memory. However awful it is, I need to know.

Nothing comes. Growing more desperate with each passing minute, I silently beg for something to happen. I plead with everything that I have. I want to remember now. I need to. Because if I can find an end to the memory then maybe, somehow, I can right things. I can tell the villagers what really happened here all those years ago. Persuade them that Phineas Kibble is not the man they all revere. They are living in fear because of him, a fear that has taken away who they are, who they could be, a fear that is shaping the way things will be in the future unless they break free. I need to find where Alice's story ends. I need—

I cry out. A cacophony of swear words. I've stubbed my foot on something solid. I bend to clutch it, to hold the pain as my eyes smart and toes throb. When, at last, the pain fades, I look down to see what caused the injury. I'm guessing a protruding tree root. There's nothing obvious. It's getting dark and I'm anxious not to hurt myself again, so I fish out my phone and find the torch, shining it on the ground.

Something gleams. Like a shiny pebble... or... I bend and brush at the dust and fallen yew needles, shuddering as I scatter several black feathers, a reminder once more of the crow. My hand glides over something smooth. A tablet of some sort. I shine the light over it. It's a memorial plaque. Quite a modern one – the sort you see in newer cemeteries when people bury ashes. I frown. It seems an odd place for someone to bury ashes, and I wonder what the story is behind it. I let my torch light hover over it, trying to find the date.

2002.

And then my heart freezes. I drop the phone and, somewhere, there's screaming. I inhale, choking on the sound which I now realise is coming from me. I put my hands over my face, my body trembling as I try to draw myself together, try to stop the terrible noise I'm making. For a moment, several moments, my thoughts are ransacked as I try to make sense of what I have seen. It seems to grow darker inside the hollow and I feel trapped in a black void. As I have been, ever since it happened.

I see youthful limbs running, climbing. Shouts, laughter, cries. Then those same limbs splayed, cartwheeling through the spaces between the green.

The sickening cracking.

The deadening thud.

The silence.

Somewhere, high above, in the fringes of the tree, wings beat the air, birds cry, the sound circling into the sky. With those sounds, I snap into the now, my entire body pulsing.

This can't be. And yet...

I peer through stretched fingers, then prise my shaking hands from my face and look again, the letters jumbling at first, then becoming just legible in the faint glow of my phone. From where I dropped it, the beam grazes the stone.

I read once more, the clarity of it stark and unforgiving.

Julie Marie Moon
1989 – 2002
Always in our hearts

Extract from a sermon given
by the Reverend Phineas Kibble,
August 1866.

The text for today's homily is taken from Ecclesiastes, chapter nine.

'Whatsoever thy hand findeth to do, do it with thy might; for there is no work, nor device, nor knowledge, nor wisdom, in the grave, whither thou goest…'

… Friends, the grave is a certainty. Death will eventually find us all. Therefore, I urge you to commit to living good and faithful lives, lest you die without a story to sustain those who still live.

For while death is the end of our mortal existence, the truth about each one of us lives on into eternity.

This I know, for sure.

49

KATE

Dorset 2026

I think, my brain pulsing. Julie Moon. Here. *Here?* In Hope-under-Barrow. It seems impossible. I swing my torch light over the slab again. Same dates. Same middle name. How could it be anyone else? I rub my forehead, my thoughts murky, a labyrinth of monsters.

After it had happened, it was bad. Really bad. A heavy cloud fell over the whole community, people talked of nothing else. Low, dark whispers slithered from one group to another. *Did you hear about the vicar's daughter?* Coffee cups chinking in the rundown café on the corner. *Always a strange one, she was.* The queue in the chippy. *Close family funeral. Burial at the last parish.* The congregation at the back of church on a Sunday morning. *The boy's coming back from that school they sent him to.* Eyebrows raised. *As if they haven't got problems enough.* But then, like so often in life, eventually, the comments and the judgements and the theories died and something else took its place. There was another drama, another trauma, and gradually, people forgot. Or at least ceased to remember. Julie's family moved away. To Derbyshire, I think. I made other friends, bulldozered my way through the rest of high school, finding distraction wherever I could. Boys, drinking, dubious parties by the million. Because I needed to somehow fill the hole inside, find some way of numbing out the terrible, aching grief. The guilt. The truth about what happened.

Meeting Ben in some ways saved me.

Saved me from the downward spiral I was intent on taking.

Reminded me that there were other things in life. My art, love, and eventually Noah.

My head thumps and I shiver, realising I need to get away from the tree. When the headaches come, I know something is about to happen. Moments earlier, I'd wanted the memories, but now... now... I stumble for the entrance of the hollow. I should get home. Before Ben and Noah. Get into bed and pretend to be asleep before I find myself talking about any of this. Because if Ben knew...

I think of the letter I destroyed.

What does Ben know?

I take the path leading from the graveyard to our house. Could it really be Julie? Or could it just be one massive coincidence? Strange things do happen; perhaps this is just one of those things.

Then I think of something.

I turn and hurry back towards the church. The building had been left unlocked in case anyone wanted to go in to pray after the ritual. They didn't. But Ben left it open all the same.

I slip into the church. It's dark and cool, the smell of old hymn-books and polish familiar and momentarily comforting. I don't want to turn the lights on and draw unnecessary attention, so I use my phone to negotiate the rows of pews, the font, the stack of old-fashioned chairs and the poor excuse of a children's corner. I step into the tower area. The bell ropes are hooked on their spider, the red, white and blue of the sallies picked out in the gloom. For some reason, they make me think of hangings. I shiver. My mind is running all over the place, taking dark turns. I'm not thinking straight.

I shine the torch over the stone walls until I find what I'm looking for.

It's there, hanging on one side, below a row of bell boards.

The list of previous incumbents, that no one ever really looks at, apart from, I guess, the odd rambler or amateur historian.

Quickly, I scan the neat calligraphy. Reverend Phineas Kibble is there, of course. Followed by a Reverend Montgomery Sage… I train the light on the more recent names: Reverend Albert Stoning, Reverend Canon Rex Habersham, Reverend Vicky Reynolds, Reverend John Allen. Ben's name is still in pencil, I notice, ready to be inked over after his official induction service: *Reverend Benjamin Thomas 2026 –*.

I look up the list again and sandwiched between Rex and Vicky, he's there.

Reverend Richard Moon.

He served between 1989 and 1996.

I go cold.

This proves it. Even I know, coincidences don't stretch that far. Julie Moon lived here. Here, in Hope-under-Barrow. And they brought her back here to be buried under the yew tree. I knew she'd lived in the countryside before she turned up at my primary school, but she didn't say where. Kids don't. I flick the torch away from the board as if that will magically make the information go away and pick my way back across the silent church towards the south door. There, I step into the night, shaking, my thoughts darting. Just in that short time, the light has faded completely and the countryside is impossibly dark. The graves are now shadowy lumps, the yew tree a dark mass, a giant. I jog down the path towards the vicarage, relieved to see the house unlit, the drive black and empty. No Ben. No Noah. No questions.

At the front door, I jam the key into the keyhole and fall into the house.

I flick on the lights and head upstairs where I climb straight into bed, shedding my clothes in a heap on the floor and not even bothering to use the bathroom.

I lie there in the dark, willing sleep to come, covers pulled tight. I'm cold, so cold, and I can't stop shaking. I just want to forget: this awful evening, this place, *her.*

But it's impossible.

All I can see is Julie Moon.

You promised, Kate, she mouths. *You promised.*

I twist under the covers, thinking and thinking. There's something I'm missing. Something hiding I can't reach. Like a summit that moves every time I get close.

Extract from a sermon given
by the Reverend Phineas Kibble,
September 1866.

The text for today's homily is taken from Genesis, chapter two.

'And out of the ground made the Lord God to grow every tree that is pleasant to the sight, and good for food; the tree of life also in the midst of the garden, and the tree of knowledge of good and evil...'

I urge you, for now, to look upon the great tree from afar. Gaze upon it and watch and wait for me, your earthly shepherd, to reveal its blessings to you.

Soon that time will come.

50

KATE

Dorset 2026

I lie in bed for what seems like hours, trying to expel the memories of Julie and my discovery at the yew tree. Ben and Noah don't return and, somewhere outside of my thoughts, I make out the faint trickle of music still playing from the direction of the village. Late night for Noah. I try to hold onto that thought; to focus on my son, on normal, mundane things. His bedtime and the probability that all the other kids from the village school are also still out. The fact that he needs new shoes. The everyday inevitability that his room needs tidying.

It doesn't work.

I twist, burying my face in the pillow, trying to push out those other things clamouring for my attention. The more unwelcome thoughts knocking – no, hammering – to be let in.

Downstairs the front door opens and clicks shut.

I freeze. Snap straight into consciousness. I need to pretend I'm asleep. I'm way beyond capable of dealing with others at the moment.

There are footsteps in the hallway. I strain. Just one set, not the frantic scurrying I associate with Noah. There are no voices either. But then, I reason, Noah may have fallen asleep. Ben may be carrying him, hoping to sneak him into bed without a fuss, as we used to do when Noah was really small. I smile to myself. The thought of Noah in Ben's arms has a softness to it that I suddenly crave so violently. Because it's so normal and familiar. It's an image from before.

I want to be a part of it. I don't want to pretend I'm asleep anymore. I feel a pang of guilt at my selfishness. This is my family, for God's sake.

'Ben?' I call from the bed, still lying beneath the duvet, awaiting a response, or a desperate hushing because of Noah's sleeping state.

There's no answer.

Footsteps on the stairs.

I prop myself to a half-sitting position. 'Ben?'

The footsteps pause and there's a tense silence before they begin again. *Fourteen, fifteen, sixteen.* Then across the landing. Any minute now, Ben's going to pop his head around the door, cradling our sleeping son. Or Noah will wake, struggle out of Ben's arms, and come rushing in, bleary-eyed but still bright with marshmallows and ice cream.

The footsteps head towards our bedroom.

A swirl of unease turns in my stomach, and I'm caught by a slight chill as the footsteps halt outside the room.

Something's wrong.

I push the duvet down and sit properly, wondering what to do. Thoughts of intruders and maniacs, plotlines from my favourite crime novels and TV dramas all compete for my attention.

There's a sharp knock on the bedroom door.

Vaguely, I wonder whether a murderer would actually knock. But before I have time to debate, the door swings open and I'm bathed in a sudden and unwelcome light as someone flicks the switch.

I screw my eyes shut.

When I open them again, I cry out, confusion and surprise making me leap out of bed. 'What are you doing here?' I gasp. 'How did you get in? How—'

'Reverend Allen gave me a key once. When he went to Cannes, and I agreed to feed his cat. He never asked for it back, and I figured it might be useful one day.' There's a pause. I tug at my pyjama top. 'Turns out I was right. Kate, I need to speak to you. Urgently.'

'But you can't just walk into someone's house like this—' I begin. But even as I say it, I know that people do. It's how vicarages work. Especially in a community like Hope-under-Barrow.

That said, right now, I'm in my bedroom and there have to be limits. 'I was asleep,' I say, sinking back to the mattress. 'Or at least *trying* to sleep.'

'I've come to tell you that you need to leave.'

I rub my forehead, then let my hand fall to the sheet with a dull thud. '*What*?'

'Leave. Stay here and everything will be destroyed.'

I shake my head, tugging the duvet over my lap. Trying to make myself feel less vulnerable. 'I don't know what you're talking about,' I say.

'I think you do.' Lisa holds out her hand and unfurls her palm. 'Because of this.'

Extract from a sermon given
by the Reverend Phineas Kibble,
October 1866.

The text for today's homily is taken from Proverbs, chapter ten.

'The memory of the just is blessed: but the name of the wicked shall rot...'

... So says the writer of Proverbs. But, my friends, this is not the truth of things. The names of the evil ones do not fade. They do not rot or decay but remain forever.

Evil abides unto the end.

51

KATE

Dorset 2026

I look at the small troll in Lisa's hand. Its bright pink hair is matted and its snubby nose dirty.

'Where did you get that?' I say.

'Noah dropped it outside the hall. I didn't think you'd want him to have it back.'

My mind whirs. 'I… I don't know what you mean.' Lisa's words are like a slap. How does she know? *What* does she know? For a moment there's silence, a terrible pounding silence, so thick I can almost grab it.

'You need to get away from here,' says Lisa. She lets the troll fall onto the mattress beside me, but I can't look at its ugly, squashed-up face. Though I feel its energy, burning into my consciousness, reminding me that I can never forget.

'What do you mean?' is all I say. I think of Noah, the haunting memories. Julie. Getting away from Hope-under-Barrow is what I want most in the world. But impractical.

'Do you have a bag?'

I look up at her.

'A holdall. You need to pack whatever you need. Quickly, before—'

'Wait.' I hold up a hand, shake my head in disbelief. 'Pack? What are you on about?'

'Ben knows,' Lisa says. 'I think he's always known. And I've only just realised.'

My stomach hardens. Lisa sits next to me, the troll between us, sullying my bed clothes. 'Look, this is going to be hard for you, Kate. But I'd never forgive myself if—'

'What do you mean?' I'm dizzy with panic. 'Lisa, tell me. What are you talking about?'

Lisa rams a hand through her cropped hair. I turn and see the darkness in her face, the shadow fixed there.

'What's going on?' I say, when she doesn't answer my question. I bite down on my lip.

'I saw him.'

'Saw who?'

'The man with the hollow eyes. The Barrow Man. Just after Noah disrupted the ritual.'

I slump, disappointed by Lisa's change of tack. *The Barrow Man is all lies,* I want to say. So is the ritual. But as I open my mouth to protest, Lisa speaks. 'Which means... which means that something bad is going to happen. Remember what happened to Alfie – our son?'

I can't say anything. Not when everything Lisa is saying is bound up with a grief so deep and a part of who she is. I nod.

Tears glisten in Lisa's eyes. 'Before he fell from that yew tree, I saw him. I saw the Barrow Man.'

'So? What are you saying?' I hold my breath.

'You're in danger here. You need to get far away. Just drive and drive. Make up a plan once you're on the road.' She puts a hand in her pocket and draws out a key. 'This is my car key. Take it and go.'

I shake my head. Outside, all is silent, and I realise the folk music has stopped. Ben and Noah will be back any minute. Lisa needs to get home. 'But why?' I push the troll away from me and it falls to the floor with a smack. Neither of us pick it up. 'Look, Lisa, I'm tired and it's late and Noah will be home soon. I should help Ben get him to bed. Now that I'm wide awake,' I add, pointedly.

Lisa presses the key into my hand and when she speaks, her voice is low, urgent. 'I realised tonight who Ben is – Ben Thomas. That birthmark on his arm. It's so distinctive. And before I came here, I ran home and dug this out. Just to check I wasn't going mad. Seems I wasn't. See.' She reaches into her coat pocket and pulls out a small Polaroid photo. She drops it into my lap. It's crumpled and faded but I can make out three small children sitting in the vicarage garden by the cedar tree. The hammock is hanging from the branches, intact, bowing in a soft curve. 'That's me,' Lisa says pointing to a girl in a yellow dress, with a mess of dark curls. She looks like Daisy. Lisa bites her lip and eyes me strangely. 'Do the other two look familiar?'

I pull the photo closer to my face and peer at the two children, either side of the young Lisa. My blood freezes. A boy of about seven or eight, a girl a few years younger. He is holding a polystyrene glider and she's clutching a Care Bear to her chest. Both are looking straight at the camera.

The boy is lifting his glider in the air as if he can't wait to fly it across the lawn. He's wearing a blue checked shirt and brown shorts, and he's half-smiling. A forced smile that speaks of impatience.

He is also, unmistakably, my husband. His birthmark is clear, on his forearm, just a little darker than it is now.

And the girl holding the pale pink Care Bear and wearing a floral sundress is Julie Moon.

52

OCTAVIA

Dorsetshire 1866

I file into the familiar box pew with Nanny Butterworth, and she turns the lock. The church is full, as usual, though our box seems cavernous with just the two of us in it. It has always been this way, a sense of separateness from the rest of the village. Father has created this barrier; keeping us apart, ensuring that he maintains his superiority. Although now, I wonder, as I sit on the hard wood, is it just grief that motivates him? Is he afraid of spirit and generosity, of the good nature and community of other people? Does he live with Mother constantly in his mind, afraid to let anything else in?

I let my head rest against the back of the pew, anxious thoughts swamping me. But I cannot sit still and find myself upright again, peering at the sanctuary, waiting for Father to emerge from the small vestry. Fear of discovery and agitation snatch at my insides and my stomach growls noisily. I could not face my morning porridge.

The small organ wheezes from the front and gradually, as Father appears in his vestments, the chatter from the congregation trails away.

He reads the liturgy in a monotone and, when the time comes, ascends the pulpit for his sermon. His text is from Ecclesiastes, and he speaks his chosen passage slowly and deliberately. 'For in much wisdom is much grief…'

I fiddle with my cuffs. Wisdom. I think of the tree, of all we have learned. Has it really made life easier? Does knowing that our memories survive give us comfort? Or does that knowing only magnify our grief?

'… and he that increaseth knowledge increaseth sorrow…'

I consider Alice and think of my misery, my guilt, the sorrow that knowing has brought. The horror and dread. That her end may be exposed soon, that it may linger in this world is almost more than I can bare.

'Miss Octavia?' Nanny Butterworth leans across to me with a whisper. 'Are you unwell?'

I shake my head. Although fleetingly, I wonder whether I can leave the church on this pretext. To stop the thoughts, to stop all of this.

I look to the pulpit and, in that moment, catch Father's eye. It is as if a world of communication is caught there in that instant before he looks away.

He clears his throat. 'My friends, since I last spoke, I have had further revelations. God, in his majesty, has spoken to me. I have had dreams! Visions! And I know now that a great evil lurks in our midst, beneath our very own yew. It is my bidding to you all that you do not trespass near our great tree.' He clutches the rim of the pulpit as if to steady himself. 'An iron railing will soon be erected for the safety of all.' He pauses and rounds his gaze upon the congregation. Someone coughs and I hear whispering behind me.

'*Safety?*'

'*Why is it unsafe?*'

'*We put Alice March to rest there not days ago.*'

'I thought he said it was a holy place. A root from the tree of life.'

Father draws himself to his full height before leaning forward. He waits until the whispering has ceased, and everyone is rapt once more. 'Dear Alice March is buried beneath the tree, but you must pay your respects from afar. For, I have come to learn, through the miraculous nature of the tree, and through visions bestowed upon me by the grace of God,' he stops, fishes a handkerchief from his pocket and wipes it across his brow, '...that there is a man buried beneath it – the Barrow Man – who, though innocent, suffered a most wicked and murderous fate at the hands of others. He will avenge all living creatures and, for that reason, we must stay away and offer only our prayers and tokens of appeasement. I have seen him with my own eyes. Many of you have also seen him.' He pauses and points a long thin finger at a bony woman sitting not two boxes in front of us.

'Why, Mrs Bastable. Did you not see a most foul man in the churchyard this St Stephen's Day past? And shortly afterwards, did not your horse break both its front legs on the icy track?'

The said Mrs Bastable mutters something to her husband. 'I'm... I'm not sure...' she says louder, for all to hear. 'I...' She trails off, sinking into her husband's side.

Father's finger roams the congregation, and I almost feel everyone holding onto their breath for all that it is worth. His digit halts, trembling there in suspension.

'And Mrs Legg, did you not deliver three stillborn infants amongst our community after witnessing an unsavoury character beneath the bows of our yew tree?'

People twist to view Mrs Legg, who shrinks within her box, her pallor quite shocking. Her husband offers an arm around her shoulder.

'Why even my own daughter, Miss Kibble, has seen this visual abomination, and did she not lose her mother, my own sweet wife?

I press myself close to Nanny Butterworth and look upwards so that the tears do not fall. That Father should bring Mother into this performance of his is so distasteful that, if I had the courage, I would run from the church.

Father clears his throat. 'These sightings are more than phantasmagoria, my friends. For the man who appears to you near and about the great yew tree is a terrible being who will destroy us if we do not take proper precautions. And so, the railing that I speak of will be erected this very week. You must not – I beseech you – trespass within its bounds. Though the tree be a miracle, that which feeds its roots has ungodly intents.'

I go cold, the magnitude of Father's lie snatching all warmth from me.

Elsewhere, there are gasps echoing around the building and I sense a shift in the atmosphere. All at once, Father's plan is unravelling before me. He wants to generate fear; he wants to ensure that no one will dare trespass by the tree. He wants people to live by the story he is creating.

He holds up a hand, silencing the ripple of conversation springing up around the church. 'Be assured of the next world, my friends,' he says, his voice loud now. Persuasive. Overruling the collective sense of unease growing within the church, like a restless and uncertain sea. He finds authority in his rhetoric. 'Be assured of the next world and seek only to know what is necessary in this realm.'

We stream into the churchyard after the service. The air is brittle, the ground carpeted with red and gold leaves, tossed there to rest by the recent autumn winds. Many of the trees stand almost bare now, picked clean and waiting for winter to arrive. But the yew remains green, its bark peeling like shedding scales, its thick canopy covering the new headstone. Alice. The congregation moves almost as a caravan dressed in the dark, muted colours of the season's dress, down the path, lingering as it comes parallel with the tree.

I want to rush past or take the alternative path around the tree towards the vicarage garden, but I find myself amidst the throng with Nanny Butterworth at my side, as if pinned there to live out my guilt as I should.

'What did he call the spirit?' says one man. He is the blacksmith. A good-looking man with a soft smile and pleasant manner.

'The Barrow Man,' says another. The butcher, whose temper is uncertain. A man I try to avoid. 'An evil, dangerous spirit, he said. It was the spirit that caused Alice March's death.'

'Is that what the Reverend said?' asks a woman close to me. She lives in one of the cottages, surrounded by hundreds of cats, or so it seems.

Father did not say anything about the spirit causing Alice's death but the butcher attests that it is so. 'Were you not listening?' he chides. 'We must stay away unless we want to bring more misfortune upon this village. Alice March was trampled to death by a terrible beast, for she was always seated beneath this tree. It was the Barrow Man seeking his revenge.'

'But why upon such a good, sweet-natured girl?' says the cat lady.

The butcher snorts. 'Spirits wreak revenge on any poor Tom, Dick or Harry, don't you know that?'

Mrs Legg shuffles forwards. Many a time she has helped women in their hour of need. 'It's true what the Reverend says.' She pulls her shawl tight around her shoulder. 'Never have I had such difficult deliveries after seeing that Barrow Man. I thought it was a vagrant or convict I saw, but after what the Reverend Kibble said, I now know different. We need to listen to what he tells us and stay away. He's a man of God, after all, and knows good from evil.'

Others murmur their assent.

'It's why we have had nothing but rain this past summer.'

'The cattle plague up at the March farm.'

'Even the dearth of the apple crop this year. And the fruit that we do have is rotten and bruised.'

The collective tale grows, and I feel helpless to stop it.

'And can this Barrow Man escape the boundaries of the tree?' asks one man, looking about his person and fidgeting with his collar.

'Didn't you hear the Reverend?' chides another. 'That's why we need the railing. To keep the Barrow Man in and us out. There needs to be no more argument on this matter. Plain as day, it is. We want no more disaster in this village.'

The congregation mutter amongst themselves and the fear becomes a palpable thing, growing and swelling and taking with it every soul in Hope-under-Barrow. Many of the villagers soon break away from the group and hurry home, keen to move away from the tree and its evil inhabitant. Others linger and look on with fascinated dread, maintaining their distance of course, and spinning tales that trespass along darker and darker corridors. Already, the foundations of a terrible myth are being laid. A myth that will protect Father and me but will, I am sure, change this small community forever.

'Octavia?'

Someone is at my side, and I turn to find poor Mrs March clothed in a black dress that strains across her middle. Her shawl is worn and patched, and I am sure that the unruly tendrils of hair that have escaped her bonnet are more flecked with grey than ever they were.

'Mrs March,' I say, and then I do not know how to continue. What comment to make when there is a group of villagers gawping and pointing at the tree, beneath which her daughter is laid?

Her husband, I notice, is striding away from the graveyard and towards the coffin lane, leaving his wife to make her own way home.

'A word with you please, Octavia.' Mrs March moves, stepping away from the last stragglers and motioning for me to do the same. I tell Nanny Butterworth that I will return to the vicarage presently and join Mrs March by the side of an old-fashioned tomb from the last century.

'What is it, Mrs March?' I ask when we are no longer in danger of being overheard. Billy Briers, the baker's son, is testing a booted foot in the direction of the tree, earning a cuff around the head from his father.

'You will think me peculiar, perhaps,' Mrs March continues. She twists the end of her shawl between forefinger and thumb. She opens her mouth several times to speak, and when she eventually does, asks, 'You are an educated person, are you not? And you were Alice's dearest and closest friend?'

I consider. 'I can read and write well enough,' I reply. 'And I am interested in a good many things. Moreover, I loved Alice as if she were a sister.'

'Just as I thought,' says Mrs March. 'And Alice told me about your reading and the like. And because of that, I wondered whether you had ever read anything about evil spirits, like the one your father, the good Reverend, told us about in his sermon just now.'

'I am not sure that Father said that he was an evil...' I trail off, realising just in time that it is for the best if the villagers fabricate his lies. It is what we need to protect ourselves.

'It's just that I am concerned for Alice's soul.'

'Her soul?'

'If she is buried near such an evildoer, will her soul not become tarnished?'

I rub my forehead, choosing my words with care. 'I do not think that Alice could ever turn into anything that was not good and light, sweet and true,' I say. 'She will, I'm sure, be quite safe.'

'My Albert was wondering, just now, whether we ought to get her body exhumed. Get her buried somewhere else.'

I laugh, in such a way as not to cause offence, but rather to dismiss the idea. 'Farmer March should not worry,' I say. 'I cannot think that exhumation would be necessary.' Inwardly, I am struck with horror, horror at what they might unwittingly discover if they insisted on such an operation. 'I'm sure that Alice is safely at rest. Her soul is in heaven, not doing combat with some restless spirit.'

Mrs March tugs at her bonnet and feeds her stray hair under the rim. 'I am so anxious for her,' she confides. 'She was always such a good child in life.'

'And so, in death,' I assure her, clutching at her hands and drawing them close. 'Perhaps speak to my father on the subject if your worries persist,' I say. 'But he will tell you, as I have, that Alice is safe and has been granted eternal rest.'

The days that follow that terrible Sunday are long and uncertain. The untruths, the deceptions that Father and I now hold close to our bosoms disturb my every waking hour and trespass into my slumber with increasing frequency.

I spend more and more time up at the March farm. It is the only possible passage for me. I have to do something to help, something that will at least soothe my troubled spirit, if not cure it. Each day, I rise before dawn and make the mile-long journey up the coffin lane to the farm. The mornings are colder now, and I must take a lantern to see the way. I trudge through frozen mud, the wind snapping at my face and pulling at my hair, the season biting at my fingers, and the cold in my heart hardening with each passing day. And when

I arrive at the farm, I am shrouded in the dying soul of the place. With most of the cattle lost and no money coming in, the farm has fallen deeper and deeper into demise. The wind has already ripped the roof from one of the barns; weeds have sprouted in the yard, and no one has removed them; the old bull house stands empty, haunted by its terrible tale.

Often, I wonder whether I should turn Father in. But his mind is failing, I see that daily, spiralling to other worlds and places that I know nothing of. His imagination holds no boundaries, and he lives between reality and another realm where his fictitious world holds sway.

Besides, if I exposed him, who knows what it would mean for me? Too often, the gallows on Barrow Hill come to mind.

I watch Father as he goes about his daily routines, muttering to himself some verses of scripture, tangled with proclamations about the Barrow Man, a myth that day by day he is growing to believe, plucked from that other world of his.

And I know that I will keep my silence forever.

Towards the end of the week, I watch as labourers from a nearby hamlet erect a guard of iron railings around the yew tree. Our own blacksmith has made them, with his apprentice's help. The sound of their making has been ringing through the village these past days and, with each burst of mournful hammering, I have felt the increasing sense of relief that soon our secret will be safe. A time, I knew, that could not come soon enough.

The railings stand now like slender black sentries, the tops pointed like arrow heads, sealing Alice within their bounds. Many of the villagers stop and stare, some gaping fearful and soundless, others muttering in dark, uneasy tones as they go about their business. And when the work is finally done and Father comes across to the church to pay the labourers, they take their money and leave quickly. I know by the looks on their faces that they have experienced something of the memories, and I pray that they will not speak of them, that they have not learned anything which will give away our secret. I watch, tense and fretful, as they climb into their wooden cart and take the road up the winding hill that leads out of Hope-under-Barrow.

I know they will not return this way if they can help it. Unless, of course, they have learned something that their consciences compel them to expose.

53

KATE

Dorset 2026

I let the photograph fall from my fingers. It floats to the floor where it lies face up, an accusation. Ben. Julie. It doesn't seem possible. And it doesn't make sense. Any of it.

Lisa slides a hand across, and I let it rest on my knee. 'I'm sorry, Kate,' she says. 'This must be a terrible shock. It—'

'I don't get it,' I say. My voice trembles. 'What is Ben – my husband – doing in the garden here with my old friend, Julie?' I think of the memorial stone, cold and stark beneath the yew tree. A dribble of sweat runs down my back, and I wipe a clammy palm on the duvet. I turn to Lisa. 'What's going on?'

Lisa moves her hand from my knee with a sigh. 'Kate... Ben was... is... Julie's brother.'

'*What*?' The room swims, colours merge and I think I'm going to pass out. I clutch at the duvet, balling it in my fist.

'I thought when you moved that there was something familiar about Ben, but I couldn't place it. And then tonight, that birthmark...' We both gaze at the picture, still on the floor, next to the troll. 'I doubt anyone else would recognise him.' She bends and picks up the photo, placing it between us. But I think of Hilary Bates, her insistence that she'd taught Ben at school.

'Ben went by the name Thomas, in those days,' continues Lisa. 'Julie used to call him Tommy, which he pretended to hate. Thomas Moon.'

My thoughts slam one into the other. *Thomas. Ben. Tommy.*

Lisa pauses, apparently lost in remembering. 'The Moon family weren't here long, by Hope-under-Barrow standards, and Julie and Tommy, or Ben, didn't really play with other kids.'

'They obviously played with you,' I say.

'Dad was a churchwarden. He used to bring me round here sometimes when Mum was working shifts at the hospital, and he had a meeting with Reverend Moon. They had no choice, I guess.'

I shuffle. I'm not sure I want Lisa to continue. The fear of exposure burns my face, my fingers stiffen around the duvet. But, at the same time, I have to know. 'So?' I venture.

Lisa looks down. '*I* think it was all just an accident, what happened to Julie, but Ben's been waiting for his moment,' she says. 'He wants his revenge for what you did. I'm pretty sure that everything he's ever done has been towards bringing you here to Hope-under-Barrow, to the place where they buried his sister. You see, Julie used to write to me after she moved... at least for a while...'

I picture the blue envelope I found in Ben's study.

'She told me she'd made a friend. A friend called Kate.'

I look up. 'Me?' I whisper.

Lisa nods. 'And tonight, I put two and two together. Up until this evening, I thought it was a weird coincidence that you'd moved from Hillsby, that you were called Kate, but now...'

'Go on,' I say, quietly.

Lisa sighs. 'After Julie died, I'd heard that her brother had gone off the rails, that they'd had to send him away to a new special school where they could handle him. Then one night, I heard Mum talking on the phone to Mrs Moon, Julie's mum. She sounded really worried and from what I picked up, Tommy – Ben – had become obsessed. He desperately wanted to pin the blame on someone for his sister's death and had become violent and neurotic. He once wrote to me asking whether Julie had mentioned someone called Kate. Of course, I wrote back saying yes, but I never heard anything else from him.'

I think of the letter I stole from the study. How it incriminates me. Ben must have kept it all these years.

'Then tonight, when I realised who Ben was and who he was obviously married to…'

'Lisa, I… this is—'

'And then I saw the Barrow Man.' She looks at me, her dark eyes intent and fearful. 'Whatever you say about it, something bad is going to happen, I know it. It's happened many times before and it will happen again, especially as the ritual didn't go exactly to plan. After the disruption tonight, I'm not sure anyone in the village is protected.'

At that moment, there's a sound from downstairs, a key in the lock.

Lisa and I look at one another. 'We need to go,' she breathes, snatching the photo from the floor. 'Out the back. Put some shoes on, quickly. Those jeans over there. Grab a sweater and your phone. A bag with some basics.'

'But—'

'You have to trust me,' Lisa says. She stands, pulling me up with her. I grab a holdall out from under the bed, not really thinking about what I'm doing. 'Trust me, Kate.' She seizes my arm. 'Now, come on.'

54

OCTAVIA

Dorsetshire 1866

I work at the farm until noon each day, although spending time with Mrs March is a great part of what I do. For hours she talks about Alice, and I must listen and let her stories grow and fill the farmhouse kitchen with love and loss. And after that, I head back down the coffin lane to the vicarage to have luncheon with Father.

'Where have you been?' he says every time, as I rush into the dining room on the last strike of the church bell, dishevelled, the season flushing my face, the muck from the farm staining my clothing.

'The March farm,' I say always, not daring to meet his eye.

But in his face, I read it all. His own guilt mixed with his growing fantasies. He mumbles scripture at me, or at some imagined being in the room with us. More and more, he mentions Mother, saying that soon we will meet her again, that the time is coming, that the yew tree has given us a great blessing in its assurances. I do not know what he means by all of this, only that the chief of his afternoon he spends in the graveyard, near the yew tree, or looking silently at Mother's grave, eyes fixed on the inscription on the headstone. He no longer spends hours working and studying and preparing sermons. His tracts from the pulpit are becoming even more difficult to follow, the congregation is waning, and people are making the journey to the non-conformist chapel in the next hamlet. They mutter to one another and, when I go about the village, I notice that people avoid me more than ever; doors and windows are shut, there are nudges and sly glances, rumours that it is not safe to enter the grounds of St Hilda's. Father does not notice, though, nor does he complain; he only bellows from the pulpit at the remaining villagers who dutifully assemble in the pews, telling them that the spirit of the Barrow Man is growing stronger, that Alice's death and the other tragedies were just the beginning and that soon, there will be another terrible calamity. A threat that makes me shrink with shame and embarrassment, mixed with the knowledge that this will lower our standing even further in Hope-under-Barrow and stir the pot of fear to a whirlpool.

The days drag on, the gloom thickens and there is no light, no way out. Then, one day, I arrive home after my morning at the farm to find that Father is not at his accustomed place in the dining room, ready to ask the same questions to which I will give the same answers.

Cook brings in a tureen of soup and when I enquire, she draws a blank.

'His study, Miss Octavia?' she suggests.

I rise and head for his room but after knocking several times, and admitting myself, I find it vacant. There is an odd silence to the space and when I look around, I see the box of Mother's possessions lying open on the desk. Quietly, I tread across the room and survey the contents. The lace collar lies atop the leather desk mat next to the ebony brooch, and next to that, the glove. I finger it, feeling its softness, remembering the hand it once covered. These relics hold Father's grief about them, and for a moment, I am choked by it. I blink back tears and when I lift my eyes, my gaze is drawn to the study window, to the swirling mist gathering outside, streaked through with light rain. And I know. I know where Father is.

Wearing Mother's thick coat, I cross from the vicarage to the churchyard. The dull smell of winter damp hangs in the air, heavy and mournful, and I bury my chin in the coat collar, bring my shoulders high. Mist and rain brush my cheeks with an almost soothing softness as a white sun momentarily breaks through the clouds. But then it is gone, and the dense greyness returns. I open the iron gate and head along the path past the railings surrounding the yew tree and towards the church. It is then that I see him. Father. Kneeling in front of Mother's grave, his clothing soaked in the long grass, his cape fanning out behind him. He emits a low moan that floats across the graveyard and catches in my throat. I swallow the rising sob and quicken my pace towards him. He clutches the headstone, as if to embrace it, and howls.

'Father!' I break into a run. 'What are you doing? It is me, Octavia.'

He does not appear to hear me, for he does not turn or relax his grip around the wretched stone. But then he speaks, his voice broken by grief. 'It is too late, my child.'

I stop. 'Too late?'

'We cannot move her.' Father spits a yellow globule into the wiry grass. 'If only I had known sooner, we could have buried your mother – my wife – in a place where we could have had access to her forever. Think on that, Octavia. Forever, we could have remembered her sweet life, her kind actions, her beautiful intentions.' He sobs wildly, a mournful cry that echoes around the graveyard. 'Think on that, child. She would have become more than a failing, dying, imperfect human memory. She would have remained alive to us!'

The clock strikes, and I shiver. The mist curls around us and the damp seeps beneath my coat and chills my skin. 'We did not know then, Father. We should hardly blame ourselves. We—'

'Have you ever heard of Robert Turner?'

I shake my head, sure that Father's mind is disintegrating.

He gestures towards the yew. 'I have a book... in the study...' he shakes his head, '... but no matter. It was the scholar Robert Turner, writing back in the seventeenth century, who suggested that the yew could absorb the gases released when a body decays.'

I shuffle, the wet soaking through my boots and stinging my feet.

Father laughs. 'Our yew tree – our *memory tree* – absorbs much more than that. If only we had known.' He clutches the stone once more. 'But now she is but bones, returned to the dust.'

His faith in the dogmas he has so readily preached is waning, I see that, and perhaps he no longer knows what to believe. For truth and lies have merged and it is now hard to tell them apart.

'She is gone, Octavia. Gone!' He moans and pulls on the stone.

I bite the insides of my cheeks, tasting iron as a flicker of my own memory of Mother catches me. To have such clarity of one I have loved. To have lived the rest of my days with access to her... the thought is attractive, I see that. She could have been mine for the rest of my earthly life. And yet...

Father staggers to his feet, looking upon me with curiosity, as if my affliction is foreign to him. The change in him is sudden, unnerving. He fixes a stern expression upon his face, regarding me as if I am a small child and have erred in some minor regard. 'We must not dwell upon it, however. It is not healthy. Come, child.' He wraps an arm around my shoulder, an uncharacteristic and awkward gesture. 'Let us return home and leave this place of death. Everything is nearly at an end now.' He looks back at the grave, his gaze scanning the lonely inscription. 'The tale is almost told.'

55

KATE

Dorset 2026

We hurry out, down the passageway by the kitchen and out of the back door into the cool night. It all feels so crazy.

'What about Noah?' I ask, my voice trembling.

'I'll make sure he's safe,' says Lisa.

'But—'

'For now, you just need to leave Hope-under-Barrow. Drive as far away as you can. Ben won't harm Noah. And if you take him with you, Ben might do something – call the police, or whatever.' She rummages in her pocket. 'Look, here's some cash.' She hands me a sizeable wodge of notes. I look at her, my eyes wide with disbelief, but she nods. 'Best not to use your card if you can help it,' she explains.

'But—'

'Do you have somewhere you could go?'

I think of my parents' house in Hillsby. What they'd say if I turned up out of the blue? My parents are sensible, retired people who live in a cul-de-sac with a neat garden, tacky ornaments, and ordered lives. We communicate, but not much. Mum never really talked about Julie Moon when it all happened, while Dad would always shake his head and repeat, *such a waste, such a lovely girl.* Nothing more. However, they never did quite understand me marrying Ben, so perhaps I could explain. A little.

'I've got somewhere,' I say. 'But are you sure this is necessary?' My head is reeling in confusion and I'm still not one hundred per cent certain I believe what Lisa is telling me.

'Go then,' she says. 'My car's on the drive. If you go through the churchyard, and over the wall on the other side, you can get to Coffin Lane without being seen.'

And suddenly, I see something in Lisa's face. Something that tells me she's deadly serious. I feel the key through my denim pocket. 'Thank you,' I say. I look into the black, picking out the little path that runs from the vicarage garden towards the graveyard.

'I'll call you,' she says. She places a hand on my arm. 'It was an accident, Kate. I believe that.' And with that, she lets herself back into the house and I hear her talking in bright tones to Noah. Then Ben's voice, low, questioning. I hear him asking where I am, why Lisa's here. Is there something wrong, he wonders.

Without giving myself the time to think any further, I run across the cold grass towards the iron gate, the breeze raking through my hair, the air ringing with jasmine and honeysuckle. My bag bangs against my hip as I hurry, jammed with a coat, some wash things and, weirdly, the book I'm reading. The village is silent now and there are only a few lights dotted about from the cottages. A pale moon blotches the horizon and the stars are few.

I slip through the iron gate. The graveyard is now pitch black and, though I desperately want to turn on my phone torch, I daren't. I walk fast, the leaves crackling beneath my feet, every rustle from the undergrowth making me glance over my shoulder, my heart quickening, my breath tight in my throat. I try not to think about Noah, what I'm doing leaving him here but, I figure, when I get to

Hillsby, I'll call Lisa. I'll make a plan. Everything will turn out okay, I tell myself. I have to believe that.

A rivet of pain shoots through my head as I pass by the yew tree, and I want to run. I stumble, feeling the long grass whip at my legs and, before I can get away, a memory snaps into place.

A sultry evening, where every breath leaves me exhausted, and my skin is damp with sweat. The smell of chips wafts down the street mixed with the dry, sweet stench of stale beer from The Rose and Crown.

'Are you sure about this?' says Julie. She pulls at my arm, bringing me to a halt on the litter-strewn pavement. A passing car honks its horn, and I lift my middle finger.

'It's fine,' I say to Julie. I adjust the cherry-red belt cinching my blouse to my neat waist. 'Though maybe...'

'Maybe what?'

I shrug. 'Maybe... I dunno... maybe dial back on some of those trolls.' I look pointedly at Julie's heavy rucksack. What she's got in there, I'm not sure. I myself have a small shoulder bag to match my belt, just enough to keep my purse in, a packet of Wrigley's, and a couple of cigarettes stolen from Dad, which I don't know how to smoke. But it's not really the rucksack that's the problem, it's the trolls. About a dozen of them dangling on chains from the rucksack. It's taken a bit of persuasion for them to even agree to Julie coming along and now we're going to turn up looking like a couple of primary school kids.

'What's wrong?' says Julie, hurt shadowing her face. She looks down at her worn trainers. And then she gets it. She lifts her head and stares straight at me. 'I embarrass you, don't I?'

'No, no, it's not that.' But my protestation sounds the weak, fake assurance that it is.

'It's just for tonight, see. We have to make out like we're one of them.' I sigh. 'Look, I've worked really hard on this, Jules. Can't you just… can't you just…'

'Pretend?' My friend looks at me with a cold, dead expression.

I begin walking again, kicking at a discarded chip wrapper, kicking until it spins into the gutter. 'Just be grateful,' I snap. 'And hurry up. We don't want to be late.'

The memory cuts out, leaving me with a heavy, heaving sensation in my stomach. I feel unclean, tainted with the reality of who I was back then, a smear, dark and heavy, drawn through my mind. I sprint away from the yew tree before it can catch me again. The cold of the evening curls around me and I make for the churchyard wall, intending to climb over it and run for Coffin Lane.

A heavy hand on my shoulder shocks me to a standstill and I stumble backwards, losing my footing on the wall. I scream, my heart in my throat. The holdall, I drop into the black. Someone is behind me, breathing loudly.

'Let me go,' I manage, my words coming in gasps. My legs almost buckle beneath me.

'Where are you going, Kate?'

It's Ben.

With his hand still on my shoulder, he turns me to face him. In the dark, I can just make out his features, shadows from the surrounding trees flicking across his face, his hair blowing in the nighttime air.

'What are you doing? Ben, what is this?' I think about all Lisa has told me.

He doesn't speak, but slowly releases me, as if I'm a scared animal he's afraid will bolt. I do think of making a run for it but then realise how stupid it would be. I wouldn't know where to go. Besides, Ben has always been faster than me and would catch up with me in no time.

The silence between us burgeons and all I hear is the rustling of the trees, the scampering of small animals or birds in the dark.

Suddenly, I can stand it no longer. 'What's going on, Ben?' I demand, sounding more confident than I feel. Then, in a breath of a voice, 'Tommy?'

He doesn't answer at first and only steps closer to me, his face blanched. When he speaks, his voice is low, deadly. 'It's because of *you* that my sister died.'

I twist my hands. 'I never meant—'

'But it happened,' says Ben. Spittle glistens at the corners of his mouth, his eyes bulge. 'Whether you meant it or not. She died because of you. Because of your stupid dare. She never would have climbed that tree if it wasn't for you. She never would have fallen. And I swore when she died, I swore I would find Kate Greenwood. I would find her, and I would kill her.'

My blood runs cold, and I imagine Ben suddenly dragging me onto the heath, strangling me and dumping my body. But after all these years, what is his game? 'Then...' I begin.

'I did find her,' says Ben. 'I found *you*. And I followed you, got to know you, I even changed my name so that you'd never suspect a thing. It was just a case of dropping Moon and using my first name as a surname instead. I was christened Thomas Benjamin, you see. All so easy. Too easy. But then... but then something happened...'

Silence falls between us again, filling the space suddenly and desperately.

'What happened?' I ask in a small voice.

Ben lets out a cry and clutches my arm, squeezing it so hard that I feel bone. He fights through harsh tears. 'I fell in love. I bloody fell in love.' He thumps his other hand against his chest. 'I was furious at the time and then...' He gulps back tears of frustration.

'Then?'

'I realised just how broken and hurt you were. How you were dying inside because of all that guilt eating away at you. You had no one to share it with and I didn't know how to tell you who I really was. But I wanted to help you. And I will help you, Kate. That's why we're going to do something very special now. I've saved this for Barrow Man Day. Especially for today. Which is why I couldn't have you painting the tree. I didn't want you to get too close to the truth until now.' He tightens his grip. 'I still love you, Kate, and I want to do this for you. The veil is at its thinnest now, you see, just like Gordon Moss said. It has to be done today.'

Despite everything, I reach out and wipe the spit from his lips, thinking of the years we've spent together; the holidays we've shared, Noah, the laughter, the good times. The lies. 'This is crazy,' I mutter. 'Absolutely bloody crazy.'

'Julie and I were so close,' continues Ben, ignoring me. 'So very close. And we could always feel things that other people couldn't. I've known about the yew tree since I was small; when Julie died, I asked my parents to bury her ashes there. Mum and Dad were only too happy because they didn't want her buried in Hillsby. They just associated that place with the tragedy. And one day, I knew I could come back here and live Julie's memories again.'

I close my eyes, hardly daring to believe what I'm hearing.

'The job coming up was perfect,' says Ben. 'And right from the start, I was able to access Julie's memories. I can even enter them now and speak to her.'

'What?' My head springs forward. 'Enter the memories?'

Ben sighs heavily, then winces. He looks as if he's in pain and in the pale moonlight, I catch jewels of sweat dripping from his hair. 'I thought if you did the same, you could make peace with her. Tell her how sorry you are, then get on with your life. Be the artist you should be. Be the mum, the friend – whatever, without feeling like something's weighing you down.'

'And how would I do that, exactly?'

'There are two ways,' says Ben. He shoots a glance over his shoulder. 'We go to the tree. Then we either bring you to a state where you've almost passed over to the other side and the tree is starting to suck up your memories. And we hope that you can meet Julie somewhere there—'

'You mean almost kill me?' I say, starkly. 'For God's sake, Ben.'

'Or...' he says. He wipes the sweat from his brow. 'Like I said, I've managed to enter Julie's memories myself and I think... I think I may be able to take you with me.'

56

OCTAVIA

Dorsetshire 1866

It is night. I wake suddenly, unsure of what has disrupted my sleep. I am cold and breathing heavily. It is as if whatever has disturbed me is close by and closing in. The darkness in my chamber is complete, and I stare into it for a moment, listening to the leaden silence that has fallen upon the vicarage. My heart thrashes in my ears as I try to calm my breathing and bury myself further under my quilt. But still, I cannot shake off the peculiar sense that something is amiss. No, that something is wrong. Rest will not come, and I find myself slipping out of bed, shivering as the quilt falls from my shoulders. The cold floor is shocking, and I fumble for my dressing gown which I keep folded over the bottom post of my bed. Tying the cord tight, I tiptoe across the room, feeling my way along the wall, and out onto the landing. The rain from earlier has stopped, leaving a clear night, and a shaft of moonlight pours over the stairs as I make my way down to the hall. Nothing moves. The grandfather clock in the hallway ticks loudly and solemnly. I note the time, just past midnight.

For a moment, I stand silently in the hall, the chill of the night holding me there as I consider what to do. But, deep down, some inner sense tells me. There is a *knowledge* that draws me to the study door, that compels me to turn the icy handle without hesitating, without knocking.

I step inside.

The shutters are open, and the study is lit by a silvery glow which bounces off the wooden floor and paints a section of the wall. Everything is still and cold, and the room is filled with it: the sense. The dark sense of ending, the shudder of silence in the air. The ending of my father's story. A tale told.

He sits, slumped over his desk. Mother's possessions are scattered about him; the ebony brooch, I notice, has fallen to the floor and glints in the moonlight like a dark eye. There lies before him a glass, upturned, the remains of some foul liquid spilled across the desk. A stack of papers – his sermons – are positioned before him.

I move forwards, the cold turning to a chilling dread as I approach him, the knowledge of what he has done suddenly so stark. There is a stench of vomit, and I see the contents of his stomach thrown across the floor to one side of the desk.

Then I see them. Needles from the yew tree dotted throughout the liquid. He made the deadly draft that killed him, I know that, and, in my mind's eye, I see his last heart-stopping moments, his staggering, his breathlessness as he throws himself on his chair with the final cry that woke me.

My gaze spins to the papers on his desk. His sermons preached so convincingly from the pulpit of St Hilda's. I riffle through them, remembering the terrible lies he spun and the hearts and souls of the community he deceived. And then, there's the notebook, charting our experiments. I leaf through, remembering the trap, the poor animals we snared, then waiting for the memories to surface. I reach the end of the book and see that Father has added a terrible addendum. Simple but stark, in his scratchy handwriting is a final sentence.

For the death of Alice March, I am guilty, and for that sin, I will burn in hell.

I lower the notebook. A confession and, in some ways, his poor pardon for my part in it. A pardon that I will never be able to accept. With a trembling hand, I touch Father's cheek. It is still warm, and I realise at once that I must think fast. I must continue to spin the tale that he told. I will not leave this confession to be found and aired, for his memory to be sullied, for my part in it to be exposed. I will place the notebook and these sermons together with my mother's possessions in a secret place. I cannot destroy them as perhaps I should, for they are a part of his tale, a part of his life – and his death. They will remain in this world even though he is no longer a part of it. And they will remain even when I am gone. They are hope, and grief, and love. It is not for me to destroy such fierce sentiments. I will simply draw a veil over them and, for now, continue to tell his stories.

I run to the kitchen and find cleaning things, fill a pail with water. Then I fetch a wrench from the outhouse.

Although I have come to despise Father, I cannot bear to have others know that the great Phineas Kibble put an end to his own life out of fear and guilt and an ill mind. For all that he was, his vanity and his disillusions, and despite the great evil that he did, I will not let my father be buried in sin and disgrace. And I wonder whether, in some ways, I do not dislike him as much as I think I do. Perhaps somewhere, deep inside me, just whispering, there is still some love left. Or perhaps I am simply fearful of what might happen to me if people really knew and accessed Alice's final memories.

I return to the study and place the pail on the floor, dip a cloth into the ice-cold water and scrub and scrub until my hands are raw and all evidence of how his life ended is removed.

Then, with quivering hands, I pull at the nails in the floorboard with the wrench. But I am not used to this kind of work, and my fear and panic make me clumsy. My fingers slip, my breath comes too fast, my hair falls in long, untidy straggles, obscuring my vision. I tug hard, littering my fingers with splinters before, at last, I manage to lever the wood free, revealing the dark cavity beneath. Then, in the dim light of an oil lamp, I scrabble through Father's desk, making sure that I have all his papers and, when I am sure, I tie them with a length of string and, together with the notebook, carry them across the room, laying them on the floor beside the hole. With courage, I gather Mother's possessions, scattered about the desk, and carefully place them deep in my place of hiding; her brooch, her glove, her collar, and the flower which I slip inside the card, written back in a time when love was fresh and unmarred by loss and shattered dreams. Tears sting my eyes as I fold Father's work, and cover his treasures, sealing the tomb of secrets, for an age.

I say a prayer, a mumble of half-remembered liturgy, then fit the board over the hole, forcing the nails back into place and using the fire shovel to knock them in as securely as I can manage. I wince at the noise it makes in the silent house, but no one comes, and soon it is done. I am sure it is a poor job, but a necessary one to ensure that lies and truth will not meet and that memories of my father remain pure in the minds of others. No one must know of the blot that now stains the foundations of this building. That must certainly be hushed in my lifetime.

I stand.

The mess on the desk I have already cleaned and there is just Father, lying there, heart still, body slumped. Ready to be found in the morning by Nanny Butterworth.

Silence beats as I extinguish the lamp and pick up the wrench to return it to the outhouse. 'Goodbye, Father,' I say, and I turn to go. White moonlight bathes the scene and sighs on my slight figure as I leave the study as quietly as I came. I run to the outhouse, then back up to my chamber, where I wrap myself in my covers and shake until sleep snatches at me in cruel, unsettling bursts. It is not a night for rest.

Tomorrow will be one of pain and earthquake-like shock, through which I will add my own surprise in muted tones as we all make the effort to adjust to what has happened. To a life that can never be the same again.

Father lived and loved, just like any other man. And now he must rest beside my mother, the woman whom he loved and for whom he did everything.

57

KATE

Dorset 2026

We sit in the hollow of the yew tree, our backs resting against the rough bark. Julie's memorial plaque lies in front of us, cold and hard.

Lisa has Noah, apparently. She wouldn't let him go after Ben ran off, and I only hope she doesn't call for help, because this would look…

'Absolutely crazy,' I say, my voice shivering with cold and fear. My jeans clamp my legs, my jacket feels too tight, and I undo the zip a little, shaking my head. 'We must be absolutely crazy.'

'But we also want to put things right, don't we?' says Ben. His voice is dead, cut into short, breathy syllables by the closeness of the space.

'I guess,' I say. I feel for his hand. It's warm and clammy, as if he's running a fever. The space around us is dank and there's a smell of earth and rot. 'And are you sure this is going to work?' I add. 'Because—'

'No, I'm not sure,' says Ben, abruptly. 'But we have to try and it's better than…' He trails off but I know what he was going to say. It's what we're both thinking. It's better than bringing me right to the brink of death. Playing with life, risking losing it, risking leaving Noah without a mother. The thought snatches a breath out of me. I open my mouth to speak again, but Ben lays a firm hand on my thigh. The strength of it makes me feel that we really can begin again. We can still be *us* in some way because I realise how much I still love him. After everything, there is still the inextricable love we have for each other. He clears his throat. 'I need to concentrate. *We* need to concentrate. We need to be open to anything that wants to get in. And I need to find Julie. It's time to release and forgive.'

We fall silent. I hear the rushing of the branches above me, the church clock striking the hour, the quiver of an owl close by. Ben is breathing nosily and complains of stomach pain. Nothing comes.

Minutes pass and still nothing. *Why is nothing happening?* I try to relax, to empty my mind.

Then, bit by bit, I feel the edge of a headache sneak up on me, building at my temples until there's something there. A mist clearing. I remember a girl and make out her outline in my mind. It's familiar. I've seen her before. The girl with the mole under her eye. 'Ben,' I whisper.

He holds my hand tighter in his.

'It's the girl. Not Julie. It's—'

'Sshh!'

I go back into my mind, concentrating on the image forming there. The girl is mouthing something. But I can't make it out. Shapeless words float across my consciousness, not quite forming, not quite making sense.

'What do you want?' hisses Ben. Then to me, 'Ask her what she wants?'

I do. But there is no answer. Instead, I remember an old, old lady. She's hunched in a scratched rocking chair, sucking her toothless gums, moving backwards and forwards, backwards and forwards over an uneven stone floor in a dark kitchen. She's weeping, her head in her hands, and when she parts her fingers, I see her eyes, sunken and hollow. Her lips are thin and blue, her skin papery and grey. She does not speak, and I feel my own tears fall hot against my face as I remember the weight of sadness that held this woman to the end. Her words are clear. 'Alice,' she moans. 'Alice. I am sorry. So very, very sorry.'

Octavia. It must be Octavia. But her words make no sense to me and I sigh.

Ben moves his hand from my thigh and curls his arm around my shoulder. It's uncomfortable like this and I have to crane forwards to make it work. But I don't pull away. I need him. I need to feel him near me.

The old lady in the rocking chair fades in my mind. I become aware of my body, its aches, its strain to keep the position, the cold. Nothing else comes. I look at Ben. He seems distant. So far away. He's muttering to himself. *Julie. Julie. Julie.* An incantation, a wish, a command. It's like he's in a trance and, suddenly, I want to pull him out of it. Because I want us to go home, to find Noah and Lisa. To start acting like a normal family, to tuck my son up in bed and read him stories, then maybe chill out and watch some TV. Reconnect. Rebuild.

'Ben…' I begin.

But then I see her. The memory comes clearly and suddenly.

Julie.

She's falling. The *thwack, crack,* tumble and rush of leaves, of breaking twigs, the *thud*s and screams, the breaking of bones. I call out her name, digging my nails into the soft flesh of Ben's palms. I feel wet. A thick wet. Blood. 'Julie!' I yell.

Ben moans and, suddenly, I remember standing there on the woodland floor, shoots of summer green clustered about the base of a tall tree, the air sweet with peeling bark and falling evening. This time, Julie does not lie at an unnatural angle before me, her body torn and broken. She stands at the foot of the tree, rucksack dangling from her shoulder, trolls swinging. Her hair shines in the last of the daylight that pushes its way through green and golden leaves, her skin is flawless, her posture tall and graceful.

I can't think what to say and can only stare at the girl before me, the memory of her growing stronger and stronger so that I can almost hear the soft whistle of her breath. I'm sure I could reach out and touch her.

Ben is beside me, warm and real, his hand still in mine. He holds out his free arm. 'Julie,' he says. 'We're here. We came here to meet you. Both of us, like I said…' He falters, looks quickly at me, then back to his sister. 'Is that okay? Julie?'

Julie looks from her brother to me. Her face is still, unreadable, and her eyes are glassy with something I can't understand. I meet them with my own and try to convey all my sorrow and regret as inwardly I ask for forgiveness. I want to say that I'm sorry a million times over, but my voice has turned to dust, and I can only think hard, and hope that she can hear me.

Julie says nothing but gives me the faintest of smiles before it is gone. Though in that, she has conveyed a river of forgiveness, and I begin to cry. I cry and cry until I think I might drown. Ben holds me tighter, as Julie reaches out for her brother and calls to him. *Tommy.* She calls his name, over and over again. Then the words change and the whole barrow is alive with the echoes of it. *Kate never meant for it to happen. It was all a game, Tommy, a game.* Her voice resounds through the surrounding trees, birds flutter from the branches at the sound, there is a scuttling from the undergrowth nearby. And Ben – my Ben – lets go of my hand. 'I'm sorry, Kate,' he says. 'I love you. And I always will. But I belong here. Here with Julie. I always have. I've spent so much of my life feeling so angry and I need to let that go now. I need to let you go. There's a time for everything, and this is my time.' He swallows hard, then coughs. 'It has to end this way for me. I made a drink earlier.' He smiles. 'A tree drink, as Noah called it. It will be enough.' He fixes his gaze on me. 'Goodbye, Kate.'

I try to scream my protest as he steps away from me and links his little finger with his sister's. But my voice is noiseless and when I try to move – to run after him – the memory fragments and breaks up. It's like a radio losing signal before it dies. In a sudden rush, I have a jumble of memories – a man telling ancient stories in a forgotten tongue, two girls running through the heathland, a large, black crow circling the sky, drawing closer and closer, wings outspread, touching the periphery of my vision. There's a loud squawking, blotting out all other sounds, and when I manage to see through the purple-blue tipped feathers, I catch Ben walking away from me into the lush green of the wood. Panic engulfs me and I try to reach out, to pull him back. But I am not strong enough. I do not have the same gift that he has.

In my mind, I cry after him one last time but the image snaps away, like a slammed door. I am aware only of the hollow yew tree, my erratic breathing and the dead weight of Ben's head lolling against my shoulder.

58

OCTAVIA

Dorsetshire 1866

The vicarage stands empty now. A shell, housing memories and secrets. There will be a new incumbent, when they find one, and I cannot stay here. Certainly, I would not wish to remain in a place where shadows creep and lies lurk in the brickwork, in the dark corners, in the forgotten crannies of the vacant house. Nanny Butterworth is going to retire to live with her brother and his large family in one of the cottages in the village. I cannot help feeling that she is pleased to be finally released. I suspect she has held this secret hope to her bosom for some time; that one day she will be free from the strange undercurrent that has run through the family since the death of Ann Kibble. Black, like bad blood. She will, I'm sure, tell her brother that we never got over Mrs Kibble's death, that we held onto her, tethered her to ourselves and never let her go free. And, I suppose, in some ways we never did. That's where the memory tree was really given life. In the hope – in the proof – that death is not the end.

Still, Nanny Butterworth holds me tight before she winds her way up the road towards the cottage, clutching her small box of personal items. She says she will miss living at the vicarage with me, and perhaps that is true. But as she reaches the cottage, she does not look back or call to say that she will see me about the village. I wrap my arms around my chest, blinking back water – tears or the cold I cannot say. A sharp wind pesters my bonnet and ruffles my skirts as the cottage door opens and admits Nanny Butterworth. It slams shut and she is gone. Then I turn my attention to my own box of possessions that I will take with me to my new dwelling. The only place I can dare call home. The only place that would take me.

The March farm.

One of Alice's brothers will fetch me at noon and take me up the coffin lane to the place of rot and decay, of failure and death. The place I know I will live out my days. Because I have to. Because it is a fate and punishment of my own making.

59

KATE

Dorset 2026

'Ben!' I shift, hoping that the movement will wake him, but he falls heavy against my shoulder. 'For God's sake, Ben!' A fresh surge of panic grips me and I shake him hard, check his pulse. 'Ben, Ben, Ben,' I plead. I hold his head to my chest, breathing him in, never wanting to let him go. 'Ben,' I whisper. 'Please.' There's nothing. I mutter both prayers and curses as I find myself scrambling out of the hollow, hardly knowing what I'm doing. My mind is racing, and I can't think straight. I need help. I need to call an ambulance.

I turn and look at the tree, wondering whether I can leave him in there. He might still be alive; they might still be able to save him. So, I can't move him; I shouldn't move him. I bite my lip, locking my gaze on the dark hole leading into the hollow. I may do more damage. I pull out my phone, fingers shaking.

A sudden burst of moonlight shines over the tree so that, for a moment, the dark green needles seem almost silver. It makes me look away from the hollow and it's then that I see it. In the trunk. Made from the swirls, knots, and the contours of the bark. A face.

Ben's face, calmly looking down on me. It distorts and becomes Julie's, like the face I thought I saw before.

The moon is swallowed by a cloud, and the face vanishes. I wonder whether I imagined it, whether it was some kind of pareidolia brought on by shock. I look again, but there's nothing to make out there now. Just a tree. Deep down, though, I know Ben's there, somewhere in there, with Julie. Tears rise and I brush them away, gulp back the sorrow swelling in my throat. I need to think. I need to act.

There's a sharp wind rising and when I look at the sky, the clouds are in shreds, skittering across the dark sky. I dial the emergency number and tell them that there's been an incident at St Hilda's church. I tell them that someone has died.

60

OCTAVIA

Dorsetshire 1871

It is not easy to attract a new incumbent to Hope-under-Barrow. It has been five years since Father's death, and no one seems fit for the post. Or perhaps it is more accurate to say that, apparently, the post is not fit for those who have considered it. And so, the vicarage remains uninhabited. Services at the church are taken irregularly by a neighbouring and elderly clergyman who is obliged to cycle the six or so miles from his own parish on the other side of Barrow Hill to perform the duty. Few attend, I am told.

I, myself, cannot bear to go to the church services, but as I pass the vicarage on my way into the village, which I must do from time to time, I often pause and look. Remembering, forgetting. Remembering. I wonder what ghosts roam its hallways; what memories rove the empty spaces. I imagine the inside; long dusty corridors scattered with mouse droppings, rotten floorboards with no pails laid out to catch the leaks, strips of wallpaper completely peeled back with the damp. And outside, slates have fallen from the roof; the windows are spotted with dirt and smeared green with algae; the paint on the front door is cracked and peeling.

It is a dismal sight, and I always hurry on, continuing with whatever errand I am tasked with, the truth sealed firmly inside me, yet haunting my every moment.

At night, I often cry out from my chamber, screaming with cold, dead dreams which rouse Mrs March to come to my aid. She soothes me, tries to placate me, imagining that we are suffering the same grief. But her grief is innocent and just. Mine is tainted, mocking, and so weighty that it might almost drag me to hell before my time. In some ways, it could be said that what I feel is as just. Just and punishing.

'When there is a new clergyman at St Hilda's, things will surely improve,' Mrs March says, time and time again, her voice, once so full and rounded, now trembling and filled with worry. 'Hope-under-Barrow is a flock without a shepherd, Octavia. We need someone to take care of us, to set us all on track, as your good father did, God rest his soul.'

I am led to understand that several young men have been sent to look at the parish, but all are reluctant to take up the position, even the fearless ones. For the dark and mysterious tales that ripple through the village have poisoned it, leaving any potential newcomer bewildered and uneasy. They shy away, like frightened cattle, when the offer of employment is presented, believing the terrible mirage that shivers about the place, the uncomfortable feeling that is threaded through the very veins of Hope-under-Barrow.

The congregation at St Hilda's dwindles further, the elderly clergyman takes fewer and fewer services – his developing gout readily excuses him – until, at last, he says he can no longer ride a bicycle. And so, all that is left are sad whispers in the aisles, stories which scamper through the graveyard like autumn leaves, carrying with them a great and terrible fear, driving the stragglers away with bitter warnings. Soon, people do not even visit their dead, and when Mr Jefferies becomes too infirm to work and no new sexton takes his place, the churchyard grows into a monstrous tangle of weeds which crawl and spread and claw their way over the graves and across the pathways. Ivy clings to the red stones of the church and no one pulls it down, lichen spots the graves, and the memory tree spreads its shadow, keeping all at bay.

It is well known that the Barrow Man is an entity to be feared: a terrible notion that has gripped the minds of the villagers and has become more real to them as time has passed. Stories blossom, rumours bloom. People make connections which become belief. They stir up disquiet which gives birth to wild terror.

Their words hiss and coil and wrap themselves around the village, binding it tight, suffocating all reason. And so, the incessant rain which, one spring, damaged the crops, was said to be the curse of the Barrow Man, the heat the following summer that caused several fainting fits was his fierce revenge on mankind. The severe frosts in autumn and the sudden, blasting winds were a warning before the harshest of winters which killed both man and beast.

All were blamed on the evil that haunts the graveyard.

The Barrow Man.

Then, one night, several men, after a hearty drink in the Red Lion, resolved to cut the tree down and destroy the thing that carries the Barrow Man's intentions. But that same night, a storm blew up and a large section from the tree fell, crushing one of the men as he wound his way home, killing him outright.

A curse. A punishment. An omen of worse to come.

They buried the man in an unmarked grave in a far corner of the churchyard, and the fallen timber they carved into a bed which nobody wanted, and which they abandoned in the one of the empty rooms of the vicarage for the new clergyman, if ever he should come. Beds made from yew deter bed bugs, people say, but I would never sleep in a bed made with wood from *that* tree.

After the incident, people talked ceaselessly about what my father had told them from the pulpit, and so they instigated Barrow Man Day in his memory. Having no priest of our own, a new religion and superstition was invented and kept. And still it grows. Now people say that my father, the Reverend Kibble, created Barrow Man Day himself. To keep us safe. To keep our crops from failing and our animals and our innocent folk from dying. Reverend Kibble was a holy and wise man, they say, and we dare not relax our rituals for fear of what might happen.

Father's lies have become the villagers' truth.

61

KATE

Dorset 2026

Weeks later, I sit at the table in the vicarage kitchen, a mug of coffee in front of me. Lisa sits opposite. I persuaded her to come over, assuring her that it was okay to bring Daisy with her, that nothing bad was going to happen. And it's true – Daisy's happily playing with Noah, wheeling trucks around on a homemade ramp in the playroom. Later, I'll see whether they want to stay for lunch.

I look over at Lisa, silently admiring the way her hair looks in the early summer sun that's flooding through the kitchen window. I wonder whether I can share the thing that's on my mind. The thing that's been bothering me since the paramedics confirmed what I already knew. So far, we've just been chatting about normal things: the new teaching assistant at the school, a party both Noah and Daisy have been invited to, the current offer on frozen food at the village store.

I stir a spoon around my coffee. 'Lisa,' I say, tentatively.

Lisa stops looking towards the playroom where there's a loud vrooming sound, followed by a cascade of giggles. She evidently senses this is serious. 'What's up?'

'I just wanted to ask...' I push a hand through my hair '... are people saying stuff about Ben? And about what happened with Noah on Barrow Man Day?'

Lisa takes a sip of her coffee, buying time, I realise. She shifts slightly, as the sun moves and shines straight across her face. She puts up a hand, shielding her eyes from the light.

'Well?' I press. 'I mean, if you don't want to say, don't feel you have to—'

'People *have* been talking,' says Lisa. She looks at the swirly pattern on her mug, then up at me. 'You have to understand, Kate, we take the Barrow Man ritual very seriously and, in the past, when things haven't been done properly, a tragedy has always followed.' She's quiet for a moment and I know she's thinking about Alfie.

'I get it,' I say, in a quiet voice.

Lisa dabs away the smallest of tears from the corner of each eye. 'I thought something was going to happen to you, but I was wrong. But if what happened to Ben wasn't because of the Barrow Man, then... well, it's strange, don't you think? A weird coincidence. Not that I'm blaming anything on Noah – he's just a child. It might as well have been Daisy – or any of the other village kids.'

I shuffle, then get up from the table and find the copies I made on the church photocopier of Phineas Kibble's sermons. I slide them across the table. 'I want you to read these,' I say. 'When you have time. There's also this notebook.' I pass over the old leather notebook with its cracked cover.

Lisa frowns. 'What's all this?'

'The papers are sermons. Written by Reverend Phineas Kibble. They're kind of odd and very old-fashioned, but I think they prove he wasn't quite the man people think he is.' I draw a breath. 'I also think they may help exonerate your barrow man. Read the notebook. It doesn't make a lot of sense but don't stop until you get to the end.'

Lisa looks up at me, her face marked with confusion. 'Really?' she says. She fingers the yellow paper before carefully placing the bundle in her shoulder bag, together with the notebook. 'Where did you find all this?'

'Hidden in the study,' I say. 'With some other old bits and pieces. I don't know why they were there. Someone wanted to keep them safe, I suppose. Maybe Reverend Kibble himself.'

Lisa glances at her bag. 'I'll take a look,' she says.

'And let me know what you think,' I say, returning to my coffee.

There's silence for a while, before Lisa speaks again. 'What are you and Noah going to do?' she asks.

I sigh, watching from the window as the sun creeps across the east wing of the vicarage, making the brickwork glow. The lupins are out and bright spears of purple, yellow and red warm the garden, making me want to sit out there all summer. There are roses too, waiting to open. 'I'm not sure yet,' I say, my thoughts pulling in all directions. In the past few weeks, I've got to appreciate Hope-under-Barrow – the way people rallied round to help me after Ben's death – meals, babysitting, help with organising the funeral and helping to feed all the people who came down from Hillsby. Most of all, for not asking the questions that I couldn't answer, about the circumstances surrounding his death. And all the while, I cried and cried, unable to contain a confusion of grief so great that it poured out of me in torrents.

'Noah and I have this house for six months,' I explain, now. 'And then I think we might go back up north. Maybe back to Hillsby, where my parents are.'

Lisa's shoulders sink. 'Couldn't you stay here?'

I smile at the bud of friendship emerging between us. For the first time in a long while, I feel I might be on the cusp of making a friend. I look out at the garden again, at the hammock that we never got around to fixing. Staying here would be tempting. Noah's settled at the school now and the countryside is definitely better for his asthma. But then I think about the tree, the memories, the past that lingers there. I turn back to Lisa. 'It wouldn't be fair on Noah,' I say, dismissing the thought of staying with a shake of my head. 'Not if people always thought, deep down, that he was responsible for what happened to Ben. I don't want him growing up with that suspicion hanging over him. Imagine what it could do to him.'

'I suppose,' says Lisa, dully. 'But make sure you visit, okay? Daisy and Noah have become firm friends recently.'

I listen to the shrieks of laughter coming from the playroom and promise that we'll come down for a holiday.

But, as I collect the empty coffee cups, the thread of an idea comes to me, and I wonder whether there might be a way of putting all of this right, after all.

Right for Noah, right for the village, right for me.

A way forward and a way to put the past to rest.

62

OCTAVIA

Dorsetshire 1893

My life is a singular one. Still, I have my home at the March Farm with the March brothers. Farmer March died within a decade of me arriving at the farm. The cattle plague and all that it took from him weakened his disposition and his health suffered. These days, I spend the chief proportion of my time at the farm; up on the crest of Barrow Hill, where winds wrap themselves around us and howl and curse, and where, at some times of the year, we cannot access the village because of snowfall and where my memories of the past are fixed in strange contortions, like the gorse bushes, blown distorted and stiff by angry storms.

There is not much to do here. There is no farm to speak of – just a few sheep, a solitary pig – and the buildings are crumbling around us. Most of the outhouses we leave, and let nature erase what it will. I do a little mending for people in the village: sometimes I wash stockings and drawers. But, between us, we do not really earn enough to live on, and the place has become one of bitterness and misery, of hardness and regret. Although, sometimes, a sweet nostalgia breaks through when the nights are long, and we sit by a rare fire and reminisce. Those times are the happiest. A spark of gladness, a smile etching the deep grooves of weary, weathered faces. Although, for all its short respite, beneath it, I still feel the tug of guilt as the brothers talk of Alice. I look into their eyes and am obliged to dismiss the truth, to push that terrible, wild guilt down deep inside me. The brothers think me quiet and solemn: perhaps a little dull. But I do not trust myself to speak much. I do not like to think about what would happen if I let anything slip. Occasionally, I catch Edgar looking at me for a moment too long, his face a question, his gaze searching. Then his eyes will flick away from mine when I acknowledge his curiosity, and he will shrink into a shadow self, a place where even his brothers cannot reach him.

I wonder whether he suspects. Suspects *what* exactly, I cannot say. But somehow, I feel that he *knows* I am hiding something. Once, I caught him rifling through my room and, when I confronted him, he told me that he had mislaid a penknife of his. Yet, although the lie burned his face, I did not dare ask him what he was really looking for. I doubt whether he even knew and, if he did, I am not sure I wanted to know.

Mrs March has also gone hence. After the violent death of her only daughter and the demise of her husband, she could not contain her woe. She lived in anguish until her last days: influenza stole her one wrathful winter night, when the coffin lane was running with mud and we could not send for the doctor. A calmer, less weary woman might have fared better. But Mrs March lived only a life of discomfort and unhappiness. She was tormented to the last by the fact that her beloved daughter and husband had been snatched from her so cruelly. And so, she passed, in a heat of fever and wet bedsheets, drunk on confused dreams and drowned in sweat and tears. She was buried alongside her husband at St Hilda's. Not near Alice. For that was not possible.

When I am not at the farm, I go about the village, propagating the rumours of the Barrow Man that Father instigated. People despise me. They hate me because of what I have to say: afraid, as they are, that even by listening, some dreadful ill will befall them. Less than a dozen villagers attend St Hilda's now, and services there are rare, for the fear I have spun has gripped them tight and with that, I feel that my fate is secure, and I can live and breathe easily.

I visit the tree every day, clamber through the space where the iron railings have buckled and are bound with young ivy. There, I stand and wait for Alice, for her memories. They always come, as certain as daybreak. In many of them, she is happy. She runs through hills full of radiant sunshine or red-blush sunsets. She is friends with the animals she cares for, at one with the nature around her. She laughs with her brothers and her parents, and her life is complete. She carves her name on the wall of the bull house because she loves the animal it houses, and her work there makes her happy.

At other times though, there is a darkness. The outhouse, the bull on that terrible night, Alice's fear as she swallowed the deadly drink, my father's hand as it slipped. Because of me. I remember the liquid she tasted: foul, and bitter, and dark. In my mind, I taste a dribble upon my lips, and I become her. I push at the Reverend in my panic, wanting to perform this experiment in my own time. But, in a sudden movement, he grabs my throat and presses. My head bangs against the wall and pain shoots through my skull. Then, with a hard grip, the Reverend pinches my nose so that I must breathe. Breathe or be extinguished, like the lantern. I gasp, feeling for air, trying to pull it into my lungs through my throat. I think I see a ghostly figure, simultaneously familiar and yet alien, if such a thing is possible. There is shouting and screaming, a conflict that I cannot follow or grasp. Then I realise it is Octavia. I bid her go.

Still, the Reverend grips my nostrils in his impatience, although the pressure around my throat has eased. I taste the sourness once more. There's a jolt from behind. Octavia. And this time, the liquid fills my mouth. Wet trickles from the corners of my lips, leaks down my neck. I try to spit but instead swallow. I panic, shout at Octavia. Close my mouth once more and cannot breathe. Nausea grips my stomach. My mind wavers.

Behind me, the great bull heaves and snorts like a man struggling for breath.

It is all so vivid.

I remember Alice's last moments of pain and agony alone, her chest clenching tighter and tighter and tighter until she could no longer fight.

That memory, when I am forced to face my sin and myself, is monstrous. It paints my daily pain anew. At those times, I remember her fear as if it was my own and I go back to the March Farm afterwards, shaking and incomprehensible as I utter strange stories and try to convince myself that the memories cannot hurt me away from the tree.

But they do. Those memories – although not mine – have become a part of me. I have lived them so often; it is like they are mine.

63

KATE

Dorset 2026

It's become a distraction from the grief and anxiety I've felt since Ben's death and, today, I've asked Lisa to look after Noah for me. She's taken him and Daisy to Swanage beach for the day, promising that they won't be back until teatime. So now, I sit in the study with Phineas Kibble's original sermons spread all over Ben's desk.

The villagers need to know about this. I know now that it's the only way they will be able to make a future and understand the lies that have been holding them captive for so long. It's the only way this community will ever be free. If they accept my evidence.

Out of the window, I can just about see the yew tree. I believe that once the truth is shared, the bad memories that keep replaying from the tree will no longer haunt the area and those buried beneath it will finally be at peace, dwelling instead on happier times. Alice will rest once the truth about Phineas Kibble has been exposed and Octavia… I never really got to the bottom of her part in it all, but she was bound up in it, I'm pretty certain.

I think about her as I sift through the sermons, making sure I keep them all in order.

Noah talked about a sad girl who hurt her friend, and perhaps *that* was Octavia. Perhaps she played a small part in what happened to Alice, despite Phineas Kibble's confession.

I turn my gaze to the window once more. Bright sunlight slices across the tree, sending golden bursts through the branches. I watch a crow take flight from somewhere near the top and I sigh. I guess I'll never know the full truth about Octavia, unless I sit under the tree waiting for memories that may never come. She was certainly sorry about something though. I've remembered the sad, old lady she became, begging Alice for forgiveness, and I've remembered the young girl she was before that, eaten by grief.

I lower the papers, lost in thought.

I don't want those memories to be all that is left of her, and maybe telling the truth about her father will help.

Julie's haunting has stopped. I've noticed the change when I've gone to visit the tree. She no longer needs to get my attention – any memories I've had from her life these past days have been happy, peaceful ones. But I think of how she haunted Noah and Lisa, coercing them to do things to make me realise she was there. Daisy's doll, the troll on the doorstep, Noah's erratic behaviour. It was all part of her attempt to communicate, and I didn't see it until it was too late. Ben's ashes will be placed next to hers in time, and I'm curious to see what that will bring.

I brush away soft tears and pull the sermons close once more. Squinting at the old-fashioned writing, I wonder how exactly I can bring this alive for the villagers. How I can best show just how Phineas Kibble's mental state deteriorated and how this led to him killing Alice. If I can do this, then so much could change – the Barrow Man will be exonerated, there will be no need for pointless rituals, and maybe, just maybe, Noah and I will be free to stay in Hope-under-Barrow.

Of course, revealing Reverend Kibble's final confession is vital. I jotted it down from the notebook before I handed it over to Lisa.

For the death of Alice March, I am guilty, and for that sin, I will burn in hell.

From the snatches of memory I've had at the tree, it's almost certain he poisoned her, but I won't include that – it's far too complicated and the confession is enough. It will come at the end of the leaflet I'm going to put together for the village and before that, I will pick fragments from the sermons he wrote. Fragments that show the descent of a great man who loved and lived and lied and who was ultimately deluded.

I head for the window and open it, letting in fresh, sweet air. It comforts me in this room of memories, and I breathe it deeply as I think about what I must do.

I will not let myself cry today. I will not delve into my own past. There is plenty of time for grief and remembering when this thing is done. I've started the process already by working on my painting of the tree. It's nearly finished and I'm pleased with it – the deep greens and russet red, the light, the sense of Ben's essence that I feel when I look at it. In many ways, this piece of art is my last gift to him and a final way of saying sorry. I know now why he didn't want me to paint the tree. He needed to get the timing right to be reunited with Julie, to put everything in place for forgiveness and the righting of wrongs. *There's a time for everything,* as he was always reminding me. A truth that I will always hold close.

And the time right now is the one to work through Kibble's legacy. *A time to speak.*

So, I head back to the desk and begin by selecting which sermons I want to include in my leaflet. Then, when I am sure, I fire up Ben's laptop and begin to type.

64

OCTAVIA

Dorsetshire 1941

So many have died. The evil in the world is so great and has taken so many good souls from us. I am alone now at the March farm. Even Edgar, the youngest, has not survived me and I have been left the farm – what is left of it. Now there are no animals at all. Most of the outbuildings have caved in, the yard is thick with weeds, and the machinery is red with rust. Indoors is not much better. I live in the cold, stone kitchen; a table, two benches and a chair are my only furniture. The upstairs I have left as it was when Edgar died of influenza at the end of the Great War. Besides, these days, it is hard to climb the narrow staircase, and for what? Chambers where no one sleeps. Memories only of the room that was once Alice's.

Downstairs, I spend my days in Mrs March's old rocking chair, thinking about the past, reflecting on my storm-tossed life with regret and absolute clarity. For never will I forget that night in the bull house. It lies heavy on my soul. I cannot confess it in this lifetime. Not now. But I have arranged with the vicar – a gentle man by the name of Reverend Montgomery Sage – that, when my time comes, I should be buried under the yew tree next to my old friend,

Alice. He was a little bewildered by the strength of my request, but it must be so. For one day, someone may learn what the tree is and pull my misdeeds into the light. Perhaps then, I will pay for them, forced to share those terrible and most ashamed things with a stranger.

For now, though, I live my solitary life. Sometimes, I walk on the heath: a dark, frail figure in my mother's old-fashioned coat, my hair long and unbrushed. A figure the villagers are afraid of. I have heard some children call me a witch, and maybe they are right to be fearful after what I have done. Mostly, though, I sit in the kitchen, listening to the wind, or to the rats running across the floorboards overhead. I nibble on the coarse bread that keeps me alive, or tart blackberries and mushrooms when they are in season. There is no meat on my table. Even if I could afford it, I have not eaten flesh since Father's experiments with the heathland animals. For too much can survive after death, that much I know.

I rise now and hobble to the window to look out over the heath. Sometimes, I fancy I see two girls running down the coffin lane towards the village. I hear their cries and laughter on the wind, see their hair streaming behind them, catch echoes of their innocent hopes and dreams as they throw them at the world.

Today, however, the window is streaked with water, and the heath is dark and grey. A buzzard circles in the turbulent sky, its plaintive mewing ringing through the air. Rain falls, slanted and heavy, and the wind shakes the deformed gorse bushes so that they almost bend to touch the earth.

There is no one there.

I strain, pressing my face right against the glass, my heart hopeful as I look for movement. But deep down, I know that there is never a soul to be seen. Not really. Not this far up on the lonely heath. Always, there is just me and my memories.

Mostly, I sleep.

I am so tired, so incredibly worn. When I am awake, my eyes smart and I must close them again and dream away the pain that runs through every part of my body. These days, I hardly know when I am awake and when I am asleep. But always in my mind is the one thing that destroyed me.

I have not been down to the village for years – I do not think I could make the journey, but still, I see it. The memory tree. Its gnarled branches, its thick trunk that divides and sprawls across the red earth. I see its thick branches, those thin, forest-green needles. Deadly; a nightmare that I can never shake off.

I rock in my chair, an old knitted blanket of Mrs March's over my knees. As I move backwards and forwards, I talk to the voices I hear in my head. They are incessant and come to me often, plaguing my nights and cursing my days.

Drink this!

'Father, leave her. She wants no part in it.'

She must. She must. I will see to it.

'No, Father. Please, no!'

Hidden glories. They must be exposed. Did not our Lord and Saviour—

'No!'

Laughter rings in my head. I imagine eyes of ice, shadows, dark things slithering through unknown places, the bull, the blood.

'No!'

The righteous shall be in everlasting remembrance.

I clamp the sides of my head, my hands riddled with the pain of age. 'Stop it, stop it. Stop it!' Tears dampen my cheeks, and I swallow the foul-tasting saliva that fills my mouth.

The voice dulls, the echo dies away, and I listen only to the wind, howling around the farmhouse, making the timber creak and the very structure of the building moan. Somewhere, outside, there is a crash as another part of the farm submits to the elements.

A rat scampers overhead.

A fox yowls out on the heath.

I rest my head on the back of the rocking chair, exhausted. My hands needle with pain, my eyes are watering, and my feet are swollen and throbbing. I bid sleep to come.

And suddenly, I am there. At the memory tree, barefooted, the grass cold and wet beneath my feet, the red dust of the earth but a step away. I close my eyes and remember her. Alice, a young girl, her buttery hair shining with sunlight. She stares at me, her face still and serene. From my youth, I remember the old coney, how I had stroked its tough fur and spoken to it. And now, I reach out towards Alice. My hands are no longer tormented by pain and spotted with age; they are young and smooth; my nails are cut short and clean. They are like the hands that stroked the coney. 'Alice,' I say. 'It's me. Please, Alice, forgive me. I never meant… I loved you. I only wanted…'

Alice places a soft finger on her lips and smiles. 'Not now,' she says. 'We are both tired of it. Forgiveness does not need to be so hard. See…' She walks towards me, as if stepping on clouds, and places a gentle kiss on my cheek. I close my eyes once more and hear the sound of the wind in the branches, the rush of the stream on the heath, the songs of glory that Mother used to talk about.

Birdsong pierces the air, somewhere a sheep bleats. And I smile.

The memory fades and I am alone in the dark farmhouse kitchen, shivering with cold, the echoing silence weighing heavy on the room. Then the wind hurls itself once more at the house and blasts down the chimney, sending a shower of soot into the hearth.

Was that a dream? Simply a dream?

But when I look down, I see that my feet are bare and specked with red dust, the edges of my skirts are freckled with wet. A scattering of yew needles litter the stone floor, and the smile has not left my face.

If it was a dream, I am not rested. I can never rest and yet… now. A glorious calm seeps through my aching body and I close my eyes, finding Alice's sweet face in the long, dark passages of my thoughts.

Soon, very soon, I want to slip from this world and enter the world of memories, afraid though I am. For that is a world, or so Father taught, where pain and weeping are no more. Where there is no sorrow or crying. No more death.

'I am ready,' I say. And I bow my head and brush my feet through the yew needles, the cold flagstones stinging my soles as I let the memories take me.

65

KATE

Dorset 2026

It's one of the first proper days of summer. The sky is a pure blue, and the air is sweet and full of expectation. I don't need a sweater, and Noah is in shorts and a T-shirt for the first time this year. Yesterday, I posted leaflets through every door in Hope-under-Barrow, and now I wait by the yew tree, with a basket full of ribbons that I've cut up to make streamers.

There's a new plaque inside the hollow now. I know the memories will merge there, and that Ben and Julie will rest together. The villagers, once they've read my leaflet, will maybe decide if and how they want to reform their community, how they will go about destroying old beliefs and developing new ones. I know it won't be easy, and there are bound to be those who reject my findings, but with the invitations I attached to the leaflets, today could be the first step towards erasing a fear that has gripped the community for one hundred and sixty years.

I sigh now as I look around the churchyard, at the many lives that have come to rest in this place. Perhaps we are all afraid, I think. Afraid to see the truth in things. In other people. But mostly, in ourselves.

I peer down the street towards the village, hoping my small act today will help spark a change, a dilution of this fear. I'm just praying it will work.

The first to arrive is Lisa, with Iain and Daisy close behind. Lisa knows of my plan, of course, and had said they'd be there, to choose a ribbon for Alfie.

'Iain and I read your leaflet,' she says, when reaches me. 'Those sermons weren't easy to understand – so old-fashioned and strange. Iain still needs to get his head around it all, if I'm honest. He still can't quite believe that Reverend Kibble isn't the great man we've grown up believing him to be. It's all a bit of a shock, really. But it's clear to me. Kibble was off his head, wasn't he?'

I nod. 'He was a sick man and he did some really terrible things in his lifetime, then used his position as a religious leader to cover it up.'

Lisa snorts. 'Wouldn't be the first time.' And then she quickly apologises. I guess there are things that people feel they still can't say to me, even though I'm now technically an ex-vicar's wife.

I wave away the apology and, as Iain approaches with his daughter, I lower the basket so that Daisy can look at the silky, coloured ribbons curled up inside.

'Choose one for your brother,' says Iain, gently. 'What colour do you think he'd like?'

'Red!' says Daisy, immediately, digging her small hand into the basket and pulling out a red coil.

'I picked a yellow one for Daddy!' says Noah. He lifts it to show Daisy, and it streams out behind in him the light breeze, like a ray of sunshine.

'This was a great idea, Kate,' says Lisa. 'This village has lived in fear of the Barrow Man for far too long. And maybe, it's time to do something about it.'

Iain says nothing and scuffs at the dusty ground with the tip of his trainer, but then he lifts his head and watches as Daisy races for the tree, red ribbon flowing behind her.

Lisa rubs his back, then gives me a sideways glance. 'Kate, if things do change around here... *if* they do, maybe we can persuade you to stay.'

I smile as Lisa flaps her invitation at me, and I scan again the words it took me so long to write.

Come and make memories at the yew tree in
St Hilda's churchyard!

2 p.m. this Saturday.

Tie a ribbon to the tree to remember a loved
one, or a pet, or to mark a special occasion or
anniversary.

Let's make this a happy place where we can
remember love and joy.

We watch as our children carefully tie their ribbons to the lower branches of the yew tree, then they run off, skipping through the long grass, racing between the old headstones. At first, I think no one else is going to come. But then I look down towards the village and see a small group of people heading towards us, the mum who'd been so off with me on Barrow Man Day amongst them.

Lisa squeezes my arm. 'Perhaps this is it,' she says. 'The beginning of a change here. I think maybe we need to rethink Barrow Man Day for next year. Mrs Butterworth may take some persuading; but, surprisingly, Gordon Moss is quite outraged by what he read in your leaflet. Though right now...' She smiles, and we watch as more people appear in the high street and make their way towards the church. '...right now, let's just enjoy this.'

I smile back, then lower my basket to a young boy who's run on ahead of his parents. He wants to remember his birthday forever, he tells me. He got a pretend tortoise, and he shows me a ball of cuddly green. 'I need a green ribbon for him,' he says. 'I'm going to tie it to the tree, then I'll always remember being six.' He extracts a coil and fixes it next to Noah's and Daisy's ribbons.

I lift the basket and hold it ready for the group just entering the churchyard. A spark of excitement lights in my stomach. I turn to look at the tree, at the three ribbons waving in the breeze. This could work, I think. It really could work.

And then, to one side of the yew, I see him.

Only briefly.

A man with wild hair and a worn face of a thousand seasons. He is holding a set of pipes, and I hear a trickle of long-forgotten notes rise through the branches.

His deep-set eyes meet mine before he fades and, in that snatch of time, I know that all will be well.

The Beginning and the End

After they had buried the chief, the men left the mound and went back to the rest of the clan. There were stories to tell. The chief's stories. The stories that would last them for a lifetime. The sun was slipping fast, the evening was biting with winter's edge, the first stars were needling through the deep blue canvas. The men thought of food and warmth, they thought of their women and their children, they thought of this life and the next.

The last act of service they had given to their chief was complete and there was hope in that. Hope that by placing a great man on the path to the next world, the cycle of his earthly life was complete. Now they could live by his example and prove the worth of his existence. For their chief was a man of great virtue. He was fair and kind, strong and yet gentle. He was the sparrowhawk and the dove, the wolf and the lamb. These were the elements of his being that they would tether to the community and use to teach future generations.

The men called to the rest of the clan and together they made a great blaze which shot flames into the darkening sky, and which carried, in sparks of fire, their dreams and secrets, their hopes and fears. Everyone sang and laughed, they cried, and then they were silent as they looked to where the new barrow lay: a solitary hump a little way off, frost already twinkling across the surface of the newly dug earth.

That night, a heavy moon shone down upon them and gave them its blessing.

And when sleep came to the clan, it was deep and true.

Many years passed, the sun sank and rose again, ten thousand times or more. The druids knew the ancient barrow was a good place and bid their branch to heal and restore all shattered spirits that were drawn to it. Their conjuration was for good, but the yew that rooted there could only exist according to its nature. It was not free to act.

Then the church was built, and the centuries rolled. The yew lived on. Its power was uncovered but could never be taken or owned, and no one could fathom the great secret of the end. They could find only fragments, threads of consciousness which had left a weal on the lives of those who had gone before and on those who survived. Sometimes the fragments were raw and full of hurt; sometimes they were adorned and full of beauty.

But they were never the whole truth.

That remains, hidden.

A great wind now sifts through the branches of the yew tree as it whispers again and again all that it knows. To those who listen, it tells of the radiant memories it has absorbed and guarded for centuries, but it also tells of those memories that have been teased into different shapes after the vaults of pain have been sealed and wrongdoing purged. Those memories will remain long after all those who made them have turned to dust.

ACKNOWLEDGEMENTS

This book was written during an extremely difficult period of my life. The sudden and tragic loss of a wonderful friend made my writing space a place of escape and reflection, a place to work through my questions and grief as I tried to make sense of it all. In the process, I fed some of my thoughts and memories into this story. But without the support and input of a number of people, *The Memory Tree* wouldn't exist and so, I must duly offer my hearty thanks to you all.

Firstly, to my editor, Daniel Carpenter, for your enthusiasm and dedication to my work – thank you for helping me to explore every bit of potential in this story. To the rest of the team at Titan and all those behind the scenes, with special thanks to the wonderful Neve Hinton, Charlotte Kelly, Rachel Vincent, Rufus Purdy, Kevin Eddy, Dan Coxon, and Rich Mason. Thank you also to Andy Bodrenkova for such beautiful cover art. To my agent, Charlotte Seymour, whose efficiency and kindness means so much, and to Anna Dawson – thank you.

My thanks go to the priests who have helped me with details

of this story, especially Rev Claire Brocklesby and Rev Ruth Wells for explaining to me how curacies work. I promise that you are nothing like either of the priests in this story!

Thank you to Swanage Primary School who were able to explain the school admissions process to me. I am very grateful and was losing all hope of ever getting a straight answer when I contacted you! Thanks must also go to the staff and students at Bournemouth School for Girls, for your continued support and tireless interest in my writing journey.

Many thanks to those who have been there for me while I've been writing this story. Special thanks to Lou Harper, Heidi Perry, Rob Davies, Jake Hope, and Belinda Stephens who have given me so many words of encouragement. You are simply the best!

Thank you to my family – to Suey and Darrol for believing in me and for giving me the vicarage upbringing that has woven its way into this story. You may recognise many of the quirks of vicarage life here! Thank you to Carly Reagon who shared my childhood in those strange houses, roamed graveyards with me and is still happy to embrace all sorts of weirdness. Thanks to Colin, for reading early drafts, helping me with tricky plot points and for so lovingly sharing every minute detail of the writing process with me. And to my beautiful teenagers – thank you for sharing my dreams – I know you both have the confidence and integrity to follow your dreams too!

Finally, grateful thanks to Rev Canon Gary Philbrick who has given me some of the best memories over many, many years. Memories that I will never forget, memories that are threaded into my story here and which will, I know, go on to inform my writing in the years to come.

ABOUT THE AUTHOR

Heather Davey has always been fascinated by ghost stories. Her first novel, *The Ghosts of Merry Hall*, was the highest charting UK horror debut of 2025 and amongst the top fifty horror titles of that year. In 2025 and 2026, Heather was a judge for the Carnegie Medals, the UK's longest running children's book awards for writing and illustration. She is also on the publication committee for the Churches Society for Psychical and Spiritual Studies and was a contributor to the BBC2 series Uncanny. Heather has an MA in Writing from Bath Spa University and completed one of the Curtis Brown Creative courses. Follow Heather on Instagram at @heather_author